Secc

at the
Little Village Sanctuary

Second Chances at the Little Village Sanctuary

Broclington Book 3

ELLA COOK

Choc Lit

A JOFFE BOOKS COMPANY

Choc Lit
A Joffe Books company
www.choc-lit.com

First published in Great Britain in 2024

© Ella Cook

Cover art by Jarmila Takač

ISBN: 978-1781897966

To all the rescuers, and those who love, champion, and celebrate the perfectly imperfects in this world, this one's for you.

Whether it's animals, people, dreams or places — know the differences you make are everything to someone!

CHAPTER ONE

'You, Mr Finnegan, are a menace to society.' The judge peered down at him over the top of her glasses. 'You've endangered lives, destroyed property, and not for the first time. The only reason no one died was due to the fast action of local medical teams, and sheer good luck. With a record like yours, by rights I should refer you for custodial sentencing, with the recommendation that you are locked up and the key is lost!'

'But you won't, will you?' He shot her his most winning smile. The Smile that removed lines at nightclubs, women's underwear and inhibitions, and any other impediments to the things he wanted. It wasn't quite award-winning, but it had certainly won him plenty of endorsements over the years.

'No, I don't think I will.' She leaned forward and took off her reading glasses. He crowed inwardly. The Smile — and it deserved the capital letter even in his head — never failed.

'No,' the judge continued. 'I don't think sending you to an open jail, not dissimilar to the spas and country clubs you're probably used to, would be of much use. And why should your antics be allowed to cost the taxpayer any more money? I would have considered court-ordered rehab, but I see you've had a few stints in treatment before, and it obviously hasn't made too much of an impression.'

That much was true at least, he had to admit to himself. His parents, and agent, had sent him to rehab before — more for the positive publicity than anything else. His sister had begged him to try, so he'd gone along and played pretend. But it hadn't worked, because there wasn't anything for it to "work" on. He didn't really have a drink problem, he just liked to party. Hard and often. He'd just pay whatever fine the judge was about to hand down. His parents, and agent, might give him a hard time again, and his sister would try to kick his arse, but she was easily ignored. To make it look good, he'd just behave for a few weeks. Then back to normal. It would be fine.

'You, Mr Finnegan,' the judge continued, 'are what I think of as a selfish, immature brat. You've never had to grow up, and I don't think you've ever been made to take responsibility for your actions. You've got a long list of minor brushes with the law — and there are probably more you've paid off or flirted your way out of.'

He tried not to smirk to himself, thinking how little the judge really knew.

'You're an adult, for goodness' sake. I think it's about time you grew up, and started acting like one, and gave something back to society instead of taking, taking, taking and taking more. So, in the interests of helping you with what I hope will become a new life goal, I'm going to try something a little new.'

The endorsement-winning smile faded as he wondered what was happening. This wasn't how this was supposed to go. He shot a nervous look at his long-suffering friend and lawyer, who shrugged his shoulders. Clearly he was none the wiser either.

'I'm sentencing you to a driving ban, obviously. You were three times over the legal limit to be driving safely. That will last twelve months.'

2

That was annoying, but not terrible. He'd just pay someone to run him around when his friends got bored of providing favours.

'Additionally, I find you guilty on the charges of criminal damage by reason of reckless endangerment, and two counts of causing serious injury by dangerous driving. I am handing down a community sentence under payback rules at the sentence of two hundred hours per offence. To run concurrently and be served in the community where you have caused so much damage. I'll let the local council for Broclington decide how to use you best. Do you have any questions?'

'Where the hell is Broclington?' He ignored his friend's heel grinding down on his toes.

'Mr Finnegan, the very fact that you can't remember the name of the village where you drunkenly destroyed a community café, and injured numerous people — hospitalising three of them — evidences that this is the right course of action. After several hundred hours serving the community you have damaged so dramatically, you'll hopefully be able to remember its name.'

'Shit.'

'Yes, indeed, Mr Finnegan.' The judge leaned forward again. 'And I'd like to add a personal note at this point. You, Mr Finnegan, are not the first person I've seen in my court with a criminal history like yours. People with such histories tend to go one of two ways. They either spiral out of control and end up seriously hurting themselves, or others — or behind bars. Or they seize a lifeline and turn themselves around. This is your last warning, Mr Finnegan. *This* is your lifeline. I really hope you take it as the opportunity it is, and walk away from this a better person.'

As soon as the judge had left the room, he let his aching head hit the table. 'Shit, shit, shit. Six hundred hours. Yvette's going to go spare.'

'Yeah, probably.' Josh clapped him on the back, switching from lawyer to friend mode seamlessly as he dragged him upright. 'So, Rick, where is your delightful other half, anyway? Didn't she fancy the limelight today?'

'She decided it would be better if she wasn't here. That she needed to protect her mental health from the stress of it all.'

'*Riiiight.* Because that makes sense. Not like you might have needed some actual support.'

'Mate, just don't. Not today. My head hurts.' He blinked in the too-bright light of the corridor. 'I can't believe I've got to do six hundred freaking hours of do-goodering in some arse-end of nowhere village. You were supposed to get me a fine.'

'You're lucky to not get a custodial sentence. I did warn you about this.'

'It sounds almost like you're agreeing with her?' He lowered his shades enough to glare at his friend.

'Maybe I do, a bit.'

'Some fucking friend!'

'Don't forget, unlike most of your friends, I know the full list of your legal run-ins and misdemeanours. And I've read the police report. And I know about most of the stuff that never makes it into those reports. You do need to sort your shit out.'

'And this is what I pay you a small fortune for? Advice like that.'

'One, *you* don't pay me. Your agent and accountant handle that, so I doubt you even know what my rates are. Two, when you drag me away from my personal life and make me put on my best court suit to deal with your drunken arse — in the legal sense — then yes, too bloody right I'm taking mate's rates off the table. And three, yes. This is exactly the advice you pay me for. But if you want it all wrapped up in expensive legalese — your list of previous offences is getting too long to be ignored. You're becoming a repeat offender. I'm actually relieved you only got community service, and that I'm not still in the courtroom trying to talk time off a custodial sentence.'

4

'So I'm supposed to be happy with six hundred hours of enforced volunteering?'

'Yes — at least they're not locking you up. Now, smile nicely when we go outside, in case there are any cameras waiting.'

* * *

Angela hopped, stepped and struggled with her crutches to manoeuvre herself around the chairs and into the seat next to her friend in the village pub. She fumbled with the crutches, muttering under her breath as she nearly toppled over, already regretting agreeing to meet her friend there — but Evelyn had been insistent.

'Here . . .' Evelyn jumped up and pulled the chair out for her.

'Thanks.' She handed over the crutches and groaned as she lowered herself into her seat. 'You think I'd be used to them by now.'

'You had a serious, complex break. And major surgery to fix it. You have to expect to be a bit wobbly for a while. You and your mum both need to take time to focus on recovering. I hear she's doing better at that than you,' Evelyn chided gently.

'Yeah, she's having a great time with my aunt. Bit of seaside air and TLC was just what the doctor ordered.' Angela glossed over the fact that she wasn't getting anywhere near as much rest, and hoped her friend would let it slide.

Not a chance. 'Well, that's great for Cathy. But I'd bet good money on the fact you're not resting as much as you should.'

'Please don't nag me,' Angela complained. 'It's been over a month, and I rested properly for the first week or two. But I'm fed up of having to rely on other people to help me at the sanctuary. I think I've burned through every favour I've ever had these last few weeks.'

'That's not true.' Evelyn sat down next to her and gave her hand a quick squeeze. 'You know that's not how most people round here think, and the Girl Scouts have loved helping out with all the animals. My daughter's birthday list is pretty much made up of houses for hedgehogs, squirrels and birds. Between your influence and my fiancé's, I think she's planning on curating her own zoo before she's much older.'

'I probably should apologise for that, but encouraging your Summer is good fun.' Angela laughed. 'Besides, our wildlife needs all the help it can get.'

'Funny you should say that.' Evelyn pulled out a folder from her bag. 'This isn't exactly a social get together. I'm not really here as a friend, or even checking up on you as your community nurse—I'm more here in an official council member capacity.'

'Why does that suddenly make me feel uneasy?'

'It shouldn't. It's a good thing, really, or at least I think it could be.' She slid the paperwork across the table towards Angela.

'What's Community Payback?'

'What they used to call community service.'

'What, you mean kids on ASBOs and stuff?' Angela shook her head. The last thing she needed was to be babysitting some mini-vandals and grumpy teens.

'Yes, but also, as it turns out, drunk drivers who crash into cafés.' Her friend had the sense to avoid Angela's gaze.

'You're kidding.' Angela shoved the paperwork right back. 'There's no way in H-E-double-hockey-sticks that I'm letting the person who did this anywhere near me or my animals.'

'Do you really have a choice?' Evelyn gingerly slid the folder back. 'Ange, you said yourself you need more help. And the court decided that the best place for the perpetrator to carry out payback is in the community most deserving. Specifically, Broclington. The probation service contacted the village council, and we thought it could, well . . . not kill two birds with one stone, because you're a rescue centre, but you get the idea.'

'It's a terrible idea.' Angela shook her head firmly and crossed her arms across her chest.

'He'll be supervised with regular visits from a probation officer. And you know our local policing team will keep an eye on things too. You need the help.'

'And you think that's what he'll be, do you? Help? What qualifications does he have?'

'Honestly, I don't know much about him,' Evelyn admitted. 'He's some sort of social media star.'

'What does that even mean?'

'I don't really know.' Evelyn shrugged. 'But the good news is the courts haven't put any restrictions or warnings on him—apart from the driving ban. Besides, if Girl Scouts can help you with lifting and carrying and cleaning, I'm sure a fully grown man can find a way to be of use.'

Angela was far from convinced.

* * *

The lights seemed to pulse in time with the thumping beat of the music vibrating through him. He necked more Bolly, straight from the bottle. He snaked his spare arm around Yvette's tiny waist, and dragged her hard against his hips. She moaned and ground against him for a few beats before laughing and flipping her hair. As one song blended into the next, she whipped out her phone and pouted and posed, pulling his face against hers.

'We are the hottest people here, babe.' She flicked through half a dozen photos before settling on the one she liked best, then uploaded it to her feed — tagging him and the club — all without missing a beat or move.

'Of course we are.' He twisted her around in a showy spin, fully aware there were several phones pointing in their direction from people — mostly girls — who'd likely shivered in the line outside for over an hour for this exact chance: to be on a dance floor with a celeb. It didn't matter that his stardom shone from the handheld screens of phones or tablets rather than the old, big, silver screen — they still loved him.

Yvette drew him down for a sexy, showy snog before laughing and leading him from the dance floor, through the velvet ropes and into the VIP area, her flimsy, barely-there skirt swishing back and forth around her legs. He bloody loved it when she was like this.

'Gasping for a smoke, babe. Let's go outside.' He flung his arm around her shoulders and they sashayed to the roof garden. An area even more exclusive than the already exclusive, velvet-roped and attentively staffed VIP stage in this eye-wateringly expensive club — at least it was for other people.

'I'm so glad you're not in jail, babe.' She lit her cigarette off his. 'I don't think I could have stood it if you'd been locked up. Even just thinking about it made me so sad I had to spend a month in the Oasis Serenity spa just to recover. I had to have my Botox topped up early. It nearly gave me wrinkles!'

'But your friend Jean — the one you texted me about — cheered you up, right?'

'Of course.' She smiled brightly. 'Anyway, aren't you glad I came back?'

'Of course. I did miss you.' He squeezed her fondly. 'And you look stunning, as always.'

'Awww, thank you, baby. Some new designer. Can't pronounce the name, of course, but it's exposure, innit?' She pouted before grinding out her stub with a heel so high he didn't know how she walked in them. Still, it did put her boobs at a great height for his enjoyment. And it was pretty clear, from his vantage point, that she hadn't restricted them for the night.

'So, was it a nice lady judge? Did you give her one of your smiles to get off scot-free?'

'Erm. Not exactly, no.'

'Meaning what?' She pouted into the phone again.

'Meaning I didn't exactly get off scot-free. I've got to pay for the damage. And I lost my licence for a year . . .'

'Oh, you poor baby.' She stroked his arm. 'But never mind, I can drive your car for you. I do look good in your Lamborghini.'

'You do, baby.'

'And it's so photogenic for my followers. But I'll have to get my nails redone. This shade will never match.' She studied her fingers for a few seconds before tapping out a message on her phone, which pinged a few seconds later. 'Perf. Shanelle can fit me in tomorrow. As it's an emergency.'

'Right . . .' He couldn't really see anything wrong with her nails, but if it made her happy, he wasn't going to complain. It was easier not to.

'You'll see, a year will pass in no time, and you might like me driving you about. It will be really couple-y, and we'll get loads of crossover followers. We can drive to all the best photo spots for the Gram and totally spam social media to celebrate your good news.' She tittered. 'Or, I can drive and you can be my sexy sidekick.' She flicked through her phone again. 'How about next week?'

'Can't. Busy.'

'Week after?'

'Busy again?' He winced, knowing the rest of the conversation was about to go downhill.

'Too busy for me? What are you doing?' Her eyes widened, 'Ooh, have you signed another deal? Was it the fitness brand? You can tell me, you know I can be discreet . . .'

He tried not to snort with laughter at her last comment, and instead focussed on the next few words. 'I didn't get the fitness brand. I got community service.'

'What?!' Yvette finally looked up from her phone, her pretty lips open in a picture-perfect gasp. She was always picture-perfect. She should be. She worked hard enough and paid plenty for it. But it was what her fans liked to see — the ongoing quest for the perfect face, figure and lifestyle.

'Community service,' he repeated.

'You mean, like reading to the elderly, or cleaning graffiti, or other dreadful things like that?' Her eyes grew almost as round as her mouth. 'Please don't tell me they're going to make you pick litter? You'd look dreadful in an orange jumpsuit! It would just wash you out completely.'

He took another swig of the champagne, which was rapidly losing its fizz — much like his night. 'I think it's some sort of animal charity thing.'

'Animal charity? That could be cute for photos. Fluffy kittens and stuff. Could open up a whole new fanbase.'

'Hmm, maybe.' Rick necked the rest of the bottle and slipped his arms back round Yvette's waist. 'Come dance with me more.'

* * *

Angela hopped, shuffled and winced as she dragged the feed bag across the yard, grumbling under her breath, when her toes snagged on the flagstone that sat slightly higher than the rest. She fought to stay upright while trying not to curse out loud. She knew it was there, but still it caught her unawares sometimes. But, then again, she knew she wasn't supposed to be lugging around heavy sacks, or trying to manage with just one crutch, but she didn't think Ernie and his jennet posse would care about her still-healing femur, or the wasted muscles and damaged ligaments in her right thigh.

And they certainly wouldn't care that the help she was supposed to be getting was already late. All that mattered to them was their food, which was wanted right now.

As if agreeing with her thoughts, Ernie kicked the fence post a couple of times, braying loudly before starting to *hee* and *haw* in the rudest and most impatient possible donkey manner.

'All right, all right, your majesty. I'm coming. Give your poor serf a few extra moments to allow for my injury.' She sighed, as snorting whistles were added to the donkey complaints.

'I'm working on only one good leg here, it's not exactly easy. You know, in some countries, donkeys are used as pack animals to carry great weights across huge mountains, sometimes they even carry people. Maybe you could come and fetch your own snacks? No, I didn't think so.' She heaved herself and the bag the last few yards, once again cursing the idiot who smashed into the village café and broke her leg into more pieces than humpty dumpty after his great fall.

She tried to remind herself that she should be grateful — that things could have easily been much, much worse — after all, she'd been hit by a car and had half a building collapse on top of her. And she *was* grateful, to Dr Liv who had crawled into the wrecked building and stopped her going into shock or bleeding all over the floor before the paramedics and fire brigade could get her and her mum safely out. Along with the little girl her mum had been babysitting. But that didn't mean she wasn't still angry that it had happened, and irritable from the amount of pain she was in daily.

And as much as she agreed with Evelyn that she needed help — especially when it came to managing her bigger residents like Ernie and his girls, she really was *not* happy about having the drunken idiot who caused the accident anywhere near her, or her animals. The more she thought about it the more she seethed. The anger gave her the strength to drag the bag the rest of the way across the courtyard and heave it over the fence for the ungrateful four.

'Impressive.'

'Thanks.' She scratched Ernie's ears, who whuffled at her before sticking his face back into the pile of hay. 'What can I do for you, Sergeant Brown? I'm assuming this is an official visit as you're in uniform. I really hope it's just a rescue, and not another animal cruelty case. I can't bear those, and I'm fast reaching my limit for today.'

'No. No animals in trouble at all, so Harry is fine today. Though I am here on official business.'

'Oh?'

'Wanted to introduce myself to your new . . . volunteer. Along with his parole officer, I'll be supervising him while he's here.' He stopped and peered at his watch. 'If he ever turns up, that is.'

'Yeah, not exactly the best first impression. Or second.'

'No, not really.' Harry leaned in to rub one of the donkey's ears. He snatched his hand back with a scowl as a set of yellowing teeth snapped sharply closed. 'Hey, that's assaulting an officer of the law Mr Donkey!'

'Not a Mr.' Angela laughed. 'That's Poppy. And she doesn't mean any harm, she's just nervous. A bit like me.'

'Oh?'

'This community service payback thing. Having that person here, around the animals. Around me . . . I think I might hate him, Harry.'

'I don't blame you for that. But part of his court-ordered rehabilitation is to give back to the community he damaged. And the village council decided at least part of that should be given to you and your animals.' Harry gently took the bag from her and offered his arm. 'Lean on me. Should you even be without your crutches yet?'

'Probably not,' Angela admitted. 'But this place won't run itself, any more than Ernie will fetch his own food or clean his own shed.'

'Which is exactly why you're getting the enforced volunteer support.'

Enforced on who, Angela wondered. 'If he ever turns up.'

'Oh, he'll turn up.' Harry's smile darkened. 'Because if he doesn't, he'll be back in handcuffs.'

* * *

He peered into his selfie camera and tweaked one of the curls in his fringe to flop in a slightly different direction, before popping a couple of painkillers. Still watching himself in the shiny, expensive phone, he settled his shades back on his nose.

He hadn't made it to bed until nearly dawn, and when Yvette woke him by slipping beneath the covers — to do what

12

she did best — he couldn't have been so rude as to refuse her, so he was late arriving. But he wasn't worried. He already knew what this sanctuary manager would be like: some crusty, middle-aged, do-gooder who probably lived in handmade cardigans — and not the luxury, organic cotton and silk ones he imported specially for when he wasn't in sponsored gear. No, hers would doubtless be some shapeless beige bag with tissues stuck up the sleeves. And maybe a cat or two. Even her name, Miss Turner, made her sound like a dinner lady. In fact, he was sure one of his school dinner ladies *had* been called exactly that.

He'd flash her the Smile, impress her by lifting a few heavy things and maybe do a few reels for the socials to get her some more online exposure, and she'd be so grateful that she'd let him off early. It would be easy.

'We're here, mate.' The car rolled to a stop.

'Are you sure?' The pretty stone cottage, while totally Instagrammable, wasn't exactly what he thought an animal sanctuary would look like. If he'd ever bothered to think about what they should look like. But weren't they supposed to have long, winding driveways or be on farms or something? He was sure he'd seen that in a film.

'It's the address you gave me. You getting out, or you want to go somewhere else?'

He checked the address on his phone. 'Nope, I guess it's round here somewhere.' He tapped in a tip and waved his phone over the payment reader.

'Thanks.'

Rick walked up and down the pretty street a few times, stopping to pose for selfies outside a couple of the chocolate-box cottages. It would have made a brilliant film set for some cutesy series, the type where the women were all long dresses, boobs and bonnets. He was so busy making sure his followers had something to follow that it took him nearly another twenty minutes to spot a small sign on the gate of a cottage in the furthest corner of the street. He bent down to take a quick snap of the carved badger that read *Bill's Sanctuary*, before flicking the phone back into video mode.

'Well, good morning, Rickheads!' He made a point of flashing his Rolex as he checked the time. 'Oopsie, maybe that should be good afternoon. As I know a lot of you saw — thanks for the love and stars always—' he blew a quick kiss to his fans '—the gorgeous Yvette — that's hashtag VettyBaby to anyone lame enough to not be following her yet — and I were out club-hopping last night, and I might be just a little bit late getting up today.' He laughed and flashed the Smile around. 'Anyway, you all know about my little accident — thanks for all the love and support, BT dubs — as you can see, I'm totes back to norm, and today I'm trying something a bit new. Exciting, right? I'm going to be volunteering at an animal sanctuary and spreading some love, so you can all expect lots of content of adorbs fluffy critters. Come with me while we go check in.'

He sauntered through the little gate, up the side of the cottage and to the much heavier, larger gate at the back. 'Oh, would you look at this? A proper, actual brass bell with a rope. Oh, we've got to give this a good ring.' The clanging echoed satisfactorily, bouncing off the ancient stones. 'Oh, that was good. Shall we do it again?' He gave the rope another hard shake, sending the noise bouncing around. He winced inwardly, the noise making him regret the last few drinks Yvette had insisted they stay for, because apparently no one who was anyone went home before 3 a.m.

But, as much as the noise reverberated around his skull, he knew that wasn't the reality that his Rickhead followers wanted to see. So, instead, he flicked the Smile to full beam and turned the camera back to himself. 'A third time for luck?'

'No, thank you. Once is quite enough.' The prim voice was muffled by the wooden gate, the top half of which slowly creaked open to reveal a short brunette peering up at him through a mane of curls. Her frame was swamped by a rainbow tie-dye fleece (seriously, who wore tie-dye without irony nowadays?). Despite her dress sense she was surprisingly young — he'd expected some middle-aged old fuddy-duddy, but he guessed she was nearer thirty — nearer his age.

'Well, don't just stand there,' she commanded. 'Hand him over.'

'Him who?'

'You're not the man who rang about a moorhen he'd wrestled away from a cat?'

'Nope, I'm—'

'Are you filming me?' She spotted the camera. 'If you're from that flaming animal rights group, you can go find a short pier to take a long walk. I've told you before, the animals here are rescues. They're either being rehabilitated, or aren't suitable to be returned to the wild. And I won't apologise for giving them a home. And no amount of well-meaningness will change the fact that a blind hedgehog can't survive in the wild.' With that she slammed the heavy gate shut, leaving him gaping in shock.

'Well, that wasn't the welcome I'd been expecting.' He grinned into the camera. 'Maybe she's not a follower—yet. I'm sure she'll become a loyal Rickhead in time.' He rapped on the gate again.

'Just pop him in the cage, I'm just getting the kit — oh, it's you again.' The unironic rainbow did nothing to detract from the irritation in her smoky grey eyes. 'I don't have time for your silliness today. Please go away and take that blasted thing with you. I've got a rescue coming in who's probably going to need medical attention.'

'Right, sorry.' He flipped the camera back around to himself and flicked on the mega-watt smile. 'Well, that's us told, Rickheads. Catch ya on the flip!' He flipped his fingers from the birdie to the peace sign in his trademark sign off, then turned his smile on the walking, scowling rainbow. 'I'm actually here to help. I'm looking for Mrs Turner.'

* * *

15

Her mum? But she was staying with her sister while she recovered — everyone in the village knew that — not that the person staring at her expectantly was a local. Angela was momentarily perplexed, until understanding dawned in a moment of horror. Surely this couldn't be him? The person who had hurt her, her family and her community so badly was this smiling, flashy, phone-waving . . . character, dressed in skinny white jeans, and what looked a lot like suede boots. She was pretty sure that his shirt cost more than her whole outfit, and he was supposed to be helping her? It was a ridiculous notion, and she already knew that he'd be far more of a hindrance than anything else. Just what she didn't need, to be babysitting a fashionista while trying to keep her head above water — and the sanctuary running — until she was properly on her feet again.

She closed her eyes and counted quickly in her head — three things to be grateful for. One — she had a lot of good friends. Two — the weather was deliciously warm and sunny, despite it being closer to Samhain than it was midsummer. Three — she was . . .

'Did you hear me?' He interrupted her few moments of peace. 'I said I'm looking for Mrs Turner. She's the owner of this place.'

'Actually, no she isn't. Mrs Turner would be my mum. And she's semi-retired.'

'So who runs this place?'

'That would be me.'

'You?'

'Yes, me.' Angela shifted slowly, trying to ease the ache in her leg. She'd done too much already today, and still had a to-do list the length of her arm. Not to mention an injured bird on the way. She only hoped his injuries were ones she'd be able to deal with, and not require another trip to Badger's Hospital and Jake the vet. She didn't have the time, or the money, right now. And she could really do without any more stress. And she had the strongest feeling that the dark-eyed

16

man standing in front of her, peering at her through his dark, floppy hair, was going to be exactly that. Trouble and stress.

'Right, then.' He held out his hand proudly. 'I'm Maverick.'

'And . . . ?' Her leg was really starting to hurt now, and her shoulders were complaining against using the crutches to move around so much.

For a moment the smile slipped and he looked confused, but within a heartbeat or two the cockiness reappeared. 'And this is usually the part where you introduce yourself.'

'Angela Turner,' she replied automatically while her brain caught up. 'I'm sorry, are you meaning to say your name is actually Maverick?'

'That's right, babe.'

'Really? That's what your mum put on your birth certificate, was it?'

'Nope, but that's what you can call me, babe. Maverick by name, and maverick by nature.'

'*Riiiight*.' She let the word drag as she tried to figure out exactly what to do with him. 'This is not an eighties movie and you are not some hotshot pilot, so I'm not calling you that.'

'But it's my name, babe.'

'And you are not calling me that.' Unbidden, her finger shot into the air to wave in his face, scolding him.

'Call you what?'

'Babe. Or hunny, or sweetie, or sugar lips or anything else like that. My name is Angela.'

'Sure thing, Angel.'

'Nope. Just no.'

* * *

He winced as she glared at him, her smoky eyes flashing with something akin to irritation. For the second time in recent weeks his charm and the Smile were letting him down.

'Let's try this again.' Her voice was clipped and terse. 'I'm Angela, and I own and run this place. And you, I assume, are the person who has been court-ordered to come and "volunteer" here and try to be of some help. Yes?' She paused for his nod. 'And your name is? And don't say Maverick, because that is not happening.'

'Some people call me Rick. Is that OK?' He didn't know why he was suddenly asking for permission, but something about the way she held herself made it clear that she wasn't the type of person who put up with any nonsense. Which was apparently what she viewed him as.

'Rick? Yes, that's much more sensible. Hello, Rick. I suppose you had best come in.' The bottom half of the gate creaked open, and he struggled not to wince as the noise sent shards of pain dancing behind his eyes. 'So, you're supposed to be the one helping me out around here for a bit.'

'Six hundred hours.' The thought of it still made him feel ill. Even if he *volunteered* for thirty hours a week, that was going to take him through the rest of October, all of November, ruin his Christmas and probably run into February too. He hadn't planned on doing anywhere near the full amount, but suddenly he was questioning his ability to get out of the hours like he'd assumed he could. He swallowed hard and followed her across the courtyard.

'Well, I'm sure we'll find some way you can be helpful.' She didn't sound particularly convinced or pleased at the prospect. To be honest, he wasn't feeling very convinced himself. He'd expected some cute fluffy animals, but all he saw was mess and run-down looking sheds.

One of her sticks slipped on the cobbles — seriously, who actually had cobbles? — and he lunged forward to offer a hand, too slowly, and she righted herself and shook her head, tutting.

'You know, I'm quite surprised to see someone like you in a job like this.' He tried to engage with her.

'Someone like me?' She twisted to look at him. 'What exactly is that supposed to mean?'

'Well, I thought you'd probably be a lot older. You know, like a retired hippy and not . . .' He trailed off, not sure what the PC thing to say was, and just pointed to the crutches.

'I'm not usually on these.'

That made more sense. 'Bit of an accident then?'

'Yeah. You could say that.' She spat the words out at him.

He wasn't sure what she was so annoyed about, but he was good at engaging with people and making them feel better. That was what the Rickheads always told him, so he gave the Smile another try. 'Sounds awful, but at least you're OK. And now you've got me to help.'

The look she gave him was so vicious that he actually took a step back. 'You have no idea who I am, do you?'

'The manager of this place?' Manager sounded respectful, didn't it?

'Yes, owner, operator, manager and general donkey's-body. But that's not what I meant. I meant do you know who I am *in relation to you*?'

It felt like a trick question, but he was too tired and in too much pain to figure it out, so he just flashed the Smile again. 'My boss for the next few weeks?'

'Yeah, I guess you could say that. The village council seem to think that helping out here at Bill's is the least you can do after doing *this* to me.'

Afterwards, he would blame the late night and headache for the next stupid comment, but in the moment, under the glare of her accusation, he turned around and snapped, 'I've never met you. How am I responsible for anything?'

'I was in the café.'

'Shit.'

'Yeah. It really was. But I'll thank you to not use language like that around me. And if you don't mind getting out of my way, I'm expecting a patient. You can go find Harry.' She flicked her fingers towards the corner of the courtyard before hobbling off in the other direction, the crutches snapping angrily as she did so. He didn't dare ask who "Harry" was.

CHAPTER TWO

'I'm struggling to see how he's going to be any use,' Angela complained as Jake examined her latest patient.

'The council thought it was a good idea. Evelyn thought it was a good idea. Maybe you're being a little harsh?' Jake, ever the professional, kept his tone calm and soothing while he examined the injured bird. 'I can understand you not wanting him around, and struggling to trust him — but are you going to tell me you don't need help?'

'I'll manage, I always do.' She was starting to feel like her friends were ganging up on her.

'I know you do, but you're injured.'

'Mum says you have to look after yourself before you can look after others.' Summer — one of Angela's favourite little helpers — peeped over the edge of the table as Jake gently stretched out the bird's wings to examine them. 'And you do have a lot of hedgepigs.'

'Your mum is right,' Angela grumbled. When even a ten-year-old could see that, she had to pay attention. 'And it's normal at this time of year for there to be lots of hedgehogs needing help. I just like your help better.' She winked, making the little girl laugh. 'Plus, he turned up in white jeans and suede boots.'

'That's silly,' Summer agreed. 'Visits to Bill's means old clothes.'

'Especially when it's you.' Jake put the carry box on his scales, zero-ed them, and popped his latest patient back in. 'But not everyone insists on climbing in with the donkeys or sitting on the floor with the guinea pigs.'

'It's more fun that way.' She grinned up at him. 'So, what do you think, Dad?'

'I think this little hen got lucky. Minor laceration to her left wing, but she got to the right place quickly. Thanks to Ange. Her weight is good, as is her muscle tone and reflexes. So, what do you think we need to do?'

Angela bit her tongue while Summer fiddled with her hair, thinking. She couldn't help but notice the little girl pursed her lips in a very similar way to Jake — the village vet who she now called "Dad" — as she pondered the question. 'Cats have lots of bad germs in their mouths. They're not nice clean animals like dogs, are they Tilly?' The little Shibu Inu yapped her agreement from her spot under Jake's desk. 'So you need saline to wash out her owie, and antibiotics to make sure the cat germs don't make her sick.'

'Good girl.' Jake rested a proud hand on her shoulder before pulling the bottles he needed off the shelves.

'So your training is going well?' Angela was well aware of the little girl's dreams — most of the village were. 'Still planning to be the youngest vet ever?'

'Yeah! Do you know Dr James Herriot? He's the Yorkshire vet who used to be on TV and writes all the books. I found a website that said he was twenty-three when he got his vet award.'

'Wow, that's quite a target.'

'Yeah. And the same website said there was a lady called Elinor something who was probably maybe the first ever lady vet who got hers when she was twenty-two. But all her photos are black and white so that was like really, really long ago, and no one is really sure.'

'Black and white photos, huh?'

'Yeah, so like really old history.'

'Positively ancient times.' Jake grinned and rolled his eyes over Summer's head. 'So, I'll give the wound a quick clean and irrigation, inject the first round of antibiotics, and pack the rest up for you.'

'Brilliant, thanks.'

'Usual care and follow-up regime. Give her another dose of the antibiotics at the same time tomorrow — orally is fine — and the next few days. Keep her dry today and tomorrow. If there's no sign of infection and she's mobilising well she can have a paddle on Friday, and you can look to release on the fourth day.'

Jake carefully opened the box again, gently dropping the cloth over the bird so he could scoop her up. Working quickly, he irrigated the wound and injected the meds into the thick muscles over her chest. She was back in the box, fluffed up and complaining in under a minute. 'Well, she certainly seems lively.' He handed the box back to Angela. 'Couple of days' rest with you, and I'm sure she'll be fine.'

'Thanks. What do I owe you?'

'Cover the drug costs and we'll call it even.'

'Are you sure?' She hated the thought that she was doing Jake out of his usual fee — even if he did usually knock off a fair whack for the sanctuary — but it would be helpful.

'Yeah. You're doing all the work. And you can't be doing much fundraising right now.' His eyes flicked down to her crutches. 'How's the leg? You know Evelyn will want to know.'

'Yeah, if he doesn't ask, Mum will tell him off.' Summer laughed. 'We saw Mr Davis and his dog Toffee last week, and Dad forgot to ask how his poorly chest was — Mr Davis, not Toffee, who only has a poorly leg — so Mum told him off.'

'Summer, you're not supposed to talk about people's health concerns with other people,' Jake chided gently. 'Remember when your mum talked to you about patient confidentiality?'

'Oh yeah. Sorry.' She screwed up her nose. 'But everyone knows Mr Davis has a bad cough.'

'Not the point, Summer.'

'Oh.' She grinned up at Angela. 'This is why I want to be a vet. Animals don't care about people talking about them. I think they're a lot easier to work with than people.'

'I think you're probably right,' Angela agreed, her mood darkening as she thought about a certain person she really didn't want to be working with. Maybe if she was lucky he'd have given up and left by the time she got back to Bill's.

* * *

Rick was not in a good mood. Harry had turned out to be the local bobby, and was clearly not a Rickhead. Instead of being won over by his smile and charm, he'd proceeded to lecture him on the behaviour that he would consider acceptable — or not — and made it very clear the whole village was highly dubious about his presence, and were basically waiting for him to screw up.

Once he'd finished reading him the riot act, he'd all but dragged him back into the courtyard, locked up the small office and kitchen, placed the key above the door — which made absolutely no sense to Rick — and had given him another warning before he headed back to do whatever policemen do in backwards little villages like this.

It was a far cry from the usual adoration, and he really did not like it. He couldn't wait to get back to the devoted arms of his Rickheads, and the sculpted perfection of Yvette.

Needing to reassure himself, he logged on to check his latest reel. If he was super critical, he could see that he did look a little pale — but the Smile was still in full force as the digital mini-him strode up and knocked confidently on the sanctuary's gate. Angela's less-than-friendly face and painfully bright fleece were attracting a lot of comments, and he started to grin as he flicked through them. He winced at the viciousness of some of his fans' support, then shrugged. They were welcome to their opinion — and if they thought Angela was a "miserable old cow" and a "lemon-sucking outdated hippy" who was he to argue?

'Oh, you're still here.' Angela glared at him. She screeched the gate open — setting his teeth on edge again — and hobbled in, clutching the wire box she'd left with, which banged against her crutch, making the black bird inside jump.

Belatedly remembering his manners — and that he needed her to like him — he jumped up from the wall and ran to take the crate from her.

'I've got it, thanks.'

'Really? Because he doesn't seem to like being bounced around that much.' He peered into the box. 'Hello, little duck.'

'That "duck" is a moorhen. And "he" is a she.' Angela put the thing on the wall. Apparently she'd rather balance the animal precariously than trust him. He supposed he didn't blame her for that, but it stung a bit to think he couldn't be trusted to even hold a cage. 'And I need to set up a pen for her, and settle her in, before I can get on with the rest of my work.'

'How can I help?'

'You can stay out of my way.' She huffed and rearranged her crutches to try and pick up the box, but struggled, unable to grasp the handle with the stick in her hand. He watched as she wove her fingers through the mesh, only to get a painful-looking peck from the ungrateful specimen within.

'Way to show me gratitude for trying to save your feathery behind.' Angela tutted at the bird. 'I know this isn't what you're used to, and you probably have a handsome mate missing you tonight, but you really do have to stay here until you're better — and hopefully until you learn not to play with cats!'

She stomped into one of the sheds and the door slammed shut behind her, making it very clear she didn't want to be bothered.

Not knowing what else to do, Rick pulled out his phone to check through the reactions, stars, hearts and follows his latest reel was attracting. He threw out a few likes and replied to a few comments, but he wasn't really feeling it, so tucked his phone away. He wasn't really feeling very "maverick", or like the cheery, teasing self that his Rickheads expected — and that brands paid so much for.

If he was honest with himself, he hadn't felt much like his online persona since the accident. It had shaken him more than he'd admitted to anyone. He'd tried, briefly, to talk to Yvette about it, but she'd brushed his concerns aside. It wasn't like anyone had died, and the negative feedback in the papers had disappeared pretty fast under the weight of his followers jumping to his defence online, who called for help on mental health issues and awareness raising.

He'd tried mentioning it to his agent, who had also brushed his concerns aside, reassuring Rick that the "volunteer" angle had gone down well with the test panel, and he was getting positive responses from everyone. Well, everyone apart from the person who he really wanted to get on side. He stared at the shed she'd hobbled into.

And hobbled was the right word. Yvette was right — he hadn't killed anyone, but he had hurt Angela badly. Maybe the judge did have a point.

* * *

Angela huffed and heaved the bird onto the work bench, trying not to disturb her newest visitor. The poor hen had already been through enough stress without needing Angela's bad mood to make things worse. And she really was in a foul mood — although, dealing with a moorhen, maybe that should have been fowl.

She shook her head at her own silliness before looking around for her waterfowl food. Of course, because it was typical of the way her day had been going, it was on the highest shelf — the one she usually needed a stool to reach. But with her still-healing leg she knew there was no chance that she'd be able to climb up, so instead she swiped at it hopefully with her crutch, succeeding only in pushing it further back. She sighed and tried again, flipping the crutch around to try and use the handle as a hook. Of course the blasted thing caught on something she couldn't see or reach and, when she wriggled it to try and loosen it, it snagged then suddenly gave — dragging the bird food and a couple of heavy tins crashing down with it. She did her best to cover her head, but one of the tins clunked heavily against her temple, making the shed spin and toppling her to the floor. Rubbing the sore spot, she gingerly and awkwardly stretched to start clearing up. She forced herself to try and be positive, to think of what she was grateful for.

One — she could be grateful that nothing had hit the moorhen. Two — even though a wastefully indecent percentage of the bag now littered the floor, at least there was still food in the packet for the moorhen. Three — she could be very grateful that Jake . . .

'Hey, I heard a crash and wanted to check . . . oh.'

She could imagine what she looked like, legs akimbo on the floor, sitting amongst the cascade of tins and explosion of stinky fish-meal-based pellets. Duck and waterfowl food was hardly the worst-smelling thing she dealt with on a daily basis, but the exploding packet had sent a cloud of fishy, algae-scented dust into the air.

To his credit, he didn't laugh at her, and barely wrinkled his nose as he surveyed the chaos, then reached out his hand. 'Look, I know you're not particularly thrilled to have me here, but I am supposed to be helping out — especially while you're on those things.' He gestured to the crutches that she loved and loathed in equal measure. 'Maybe we could start over, beginning with me offering you a hand up. I know you think I'm pretty useless, and not to be trusted, and you're probably right, but I can at least give you a hand up off the floor. And, useless or not, I'm pretty sure even I can figure out how to use a broom. Or one of those little scoop things.'

'Do you mean a dustpan?' She gaped at him.

'Sure, one of them.' He tried out the Smile, but it fell flat — again. She really did seem to be immune to one of his greatest weapons. 'Come on, Angela. I know you probably hate me — and with good reason. But are you really telling me that sitting on the floor surrounded by . . . whatever the hell this is . . . is better than accepting a hand?'

She stared at him for a long moment, before slowly reaching out. While he had apparently won, it seemed that it had been a close call. Her hand was firm and strong in his as he carefully helped her back to her feet. She snatched her hand back as soon as she was upright, and he tried not to be offended at the thought he was less appealing than a smelly, biting bird. Which reminded him . . .

'How is she? The bird?'

Angela stared at him for another long moment, apparently surprised by the question. Did she really think he was such a terrible person that he wouldn't even ask about an injured animal? Then again, he supposed that might be fair, given that he didn't even know what it was. She had told him its name, but it had gone out of his head. But at least he knew it wasn't a duck now. Or a boy.

'She's going to be fine. I've got to give her some antibiotics tomorrow, and for a few days.'

'Is she sick?' He wondered if he should worry about that. Bird flu was still a thing, according to the reels he saw online.

'No. But she was attacked by a cat.'

'Oh, so the cat was sick.' Now he understood.

'No.' She rubbed her head. 'Cats have some really nasty germs. If it's not treated quickly, even a small scratch can be fatal to birds, or a lot of smaller animals.'

He'd always thought that anything that cleaned itself with its own spit was pretty gross. 'It's the licking, right?'

'What?'

'When they clean themselves, they lick their arses. That's why they have so many germs, right?'

'Lots of animals clean like that.' She sighed. 'And are still a lot cleaner than cats. Dogs, rodents, rabbits . . .'

'Rabbits aren't rodents?' He'd always thought they were.

'No, they're Leporidae. Rabbits have four incisors. Rodents like mice, rats and squirrels have two.'

'Right.' He couldn't really see that it made any difference. She rubbed her forehead again, and he noticed it looked a bit pink. 'Did you bang your head?'

'One of the tins did.' She gestured to the mess on the floor. 'I couldn't reach the duck food. And yes, I know we've got a moorhen, but their diets are similar enough to have the same food.'

'Why did you put it so high?' It seemed silly to him.

'Because when I put it up there, I could still climb a stool.'

She didn't say it with any malice, but he felt the hit anyway. It was his fault. That she'd been hurt originally — and that she'd been hurt again now.

'Angela . . .' He started to apologise, and then realised he had no idea what he could possibly say that wouldn't sound trite or stupid or not even close to enough. So, instead, he went with the age-old fix-all of parents everywhere. 'Why don't you go make yourself a cuppa, and I'll clear up in here?' There, that sounded . . . nice. Maybe even helpful? He could do helpful.

'I'd love to, but I need to sort her out.'

'Can't we just lob some food in with her?'

'In the travel cage?'

'No?' It sounded like that was the answer she was expecting, but he didn't see anything wrong with the box cage she was in. The not-a-duck looked quite comfy to him, snuggled into a blanket.

'No.' Angela nodded. 'She needs to go into a pen. Which I need to set up.'

'Is that something I can help with?'

* * *

He *seemed* to be trying to be helpful, and her head was already starting to throb, setting up an unpleasant staccato with her leg. *Head, leg, head, leg, head, leg . . .* the pain reverberated through her. That, plus recent conversations — with even a child telling her she needed help — pushed the decision for her. It was that or have him watch as she ungainly dragged around the cage and everything else she'd need.

'You know what, actually you can.'

His eyes widened at her reply, as if surprised by her response, like he'd expected her to say no again. But that was tough. He'd offered, and he was supposed to be there to help.

He recovered quickly, sliding that too-bright-to-trust smile back into place. 'You got it, babe. Just tell me what you want.'

'Again, my name is Angela.' The headache was getting worse, and she couldn't wait until she was done, and could drag her aching body to the comfort of the sofa. 'Follow me, please.' She led him through to another shed where she stored equipment, including spare cages and enclosures. Lifting up an old blanket she pointed to one of the large runs. 'Could you grab that please?'

He did as she asked, heaving the bulky cage up and holding it awkwardly. It took her a few moments to realise he was trying to hold it away from his clothes, and had to hide a smile. He was going to have to learn — fast — that dirt had a tendency to happen around animals. But he followed her without complaint as she gathered up bedding and the shallow, solid dishes she needed for food and water.

'Right.' She opened up the small barn, dumping the blankets onto the floor. 'Put that over the top please, and make sure it's level. Then those—' she pointed to bricks in the corner '—go on top. One in each corner where the frame meets.'

'Like this?'

'Perfect. Now we go get her ladyship and settle her in.'

Ernie brayed loudly, and Angela had to hide another grin as Rick almost levitated. 'What the hell was that?'

'That is a donkey. And I really would appreciate it if you knocked the swearing on the head.'

He gave her a confused look. 'Hell's not a swear word.'

'I say it is, and it's my barn, so my rules.'

'Are you fucking serious?'

'Yes. I. Am.' She glared at him.

'Why?'

'Because I don't like swearing. And there are kids around here often enough that it's a bad habit to get into.'

'For fuc . . .' He trailed off under her glare. 'You're not joking, are you?'

'Nope. I really, really don't like it. And animals can be very sensitive. No animal comes to Bill's without some sort of trauma. I like to keep things as calm around here as possible for them.'

'You do know they can't understand English, right?'

'They understand a lot more than you think, and even if they don't understand the words they understand the tone. So we don't swear here, thank you.'

'Right.' He nodded slowly, clearly thinking. 'So, if you like . . . dropped one of these bricks on your foot, what would you say?'

'Ouch.'

'And if an animal bit or scratched you? That happens, right?' He waited for her nod. 'You'd just say "ouch" then, would you?'

'I might ask them to let go.'

'Right.' He shook his head, and she was convinced his lips were twitching like he wanted to laugh at her.

'Look, I know, in the grand scheme of things, swearing might seem like nothing to you. But I firmly believe in things like karma, and that you attract the same energy you put out into the world. Swearing is almost always negative, and there's enough bad in the world without adding to it, don't you think?'

Put like that, it didn't *not* make sense, she thought. He seemed unsure what to say, so instead wandered over to take

30

a look at the donkey. 'I think the last time I saw one of these, it was at the seaside, and I got to ride it.'

'Yeah, we don't really do that here.'

'Right, sorry. I guess they don't like that.'

'Sometimes they do. But not my little drove.'

'Your drove?'

'My little herd. There's four of them. This here is Ernie — the jack. And there's three jennets — Petunia, Poppy and Jolie.'

'So who are Jack and Jennet?'

'Jack's the term for a male donkey. The girls are called jennets. They'll be out in the paddock — there's a door so they can come and go as they please.' She pointed to the little hatch cut into the side of the barn. 'But Ernie here, he's nosey, aren't you, boy?' She held her hand out to him, then smiled as he lipped her palm and turned his head so she'd scratch his favourite spot. She couldn't help but notice that he kept one eye firmly on Rick. Not that she blamed the little donkey.

'He's cute. Totally reel-worthy. Can he do any tricks?'

'Like sniff out a sugar cube anywhere on you?' Angela didn't like the question.

'I was thinking more . . . showy than that? Like count? Or jump over stuff? Maybe pull a little cart with something cute inside, like a bunny?'

'Why would he need to do something like that?'

'Coz it would get lots of stars and kudos.'

Angela shook her head. 'I'm pretty sure every word in that sentence was English, but I still don't understand it.'

'You know, kudos and stars. Likes and ratings?'

Angela shook her head again.

'Social media? YouTube, TikTok, Insta. You upload videos people like, and they give you stars and likes and kudos.'

'What's the point of that?'

'Money.' Rick laughed at her.

It didn't make sense to Angela, who shook her head again. 'My animals don't do circus tricks.' Ernie added to her disdain with a huffing grumble aimed in Rick's direction.

'So he lays around eating all day with three women at his beck and call?' He reached out a hand towards the donkey. 'You got it made, mate.' He yanked his hand back when big yellowed teeth snapped where his fingers had just been.

'Ernie works really hard.' Angela grinned. 'He's great at teaching people to mind their manners.'

'So I see,' Rick replied wryly.

'He also helps disengaged children learn how to read, and helps people with mental health problems. And this—' she leaned down to breathe gently in the donkey's nostrils '—is how you say "hello" to a donkey.'

'Are you having me on?'

'Nope.' She could feel him watching her for a few seconds while she focussed on Ernie, letting him snuffle her all over before turning his attention to Rick. 'Gently.'

After a few more moments, he leaned over to follow her advice, blowing on one of her favourite residents, who snuffled, wheezed and then huffed back at Rick. After a few seconds he head-butted him, shoving his nose under Rick's hand. 'Guess maybe he thinks I'm not that bad.' Rick grinned.

'So it seems.' Angela tried not to feel offended at how easily Ernie had taken to him. It was probably novelty value. She'd had to reduce a lot of the sanctuary's business over the last few weeks, which meant she wasn't getting the funds in, and the animals weren't getting their usual visitors.

She gave herself a mental shake. Ernie might be happy with his new friend, but she had other animals who needed her.

* * *

Rick took a few shots of himself with Ernie, who had grinned obligingly, seemingly enjoying the attention. He flicked through them quickly, picked out his favourites, and uploaded them. He briefly looked for the sanctuary's links to hashtag them, but gave up when he couldn't find it easily. Instead, he flipped over to his own feed and started scrolling through comments. He was so involved in his feed that he didn't hear or see Angela return.

'I know your phone is utterly fascinating, but I'm pretty sure whoever is on there can wait. I'm here with you, and we have a patient. If you're really going to be here to help, then it would be easier if you put the dumb phone down and paid attention — otherwise I might be tempted to drop it in the duck pond.'

'It's waterproof.'

'Would you like to test that theory?' She put down the bag of straw she'd been carrying and limped back out.

Whatever. He shook his head and tucked the phone away before turning his attention back to the little donkey. 'So how exactly do you help people with depression and reading?'

'It's called Donkey Supported Activities.' Angela hobbled back into the barn, this time with only one of her crutches, carrying the not-a-duck in what he now knew was its transport cage. Feeling guilty, he disentangled himself from his new donkey friend and went over to help. He didn't complain when Angela shoved the cage into his arms, making it easier for her to open it and retrieve the not-a-duck.

'So what are they?'

'It's actually pretty simple. People come and help out, caring for some of the animals — like Ernie and his ladies here — and they take them on walks, spend time with them, and even read to them.'

'And that helps? People, I mean.'

'Yeah, it really does. There we go Miss Moorhen, your five-star accommodation for a few days. Room service will be along to check on you tomorrow and top up your food and water, but I'm afraid no baths for a couple of days.' Rick watched as she tucked the moorhen — he'd have to try to remember that term — into the pen.

'How does that help people, though?' He thought it sounded like a bit of a scam, really. Angela got help, and people paid for the pleasure of cleaning up after her stinky animals.

'There's a whole raft of studies and science behind it,' Angela explained as she locked up the moorhen. 'When people are around animals, they release more happy hormones — serotonin, prolactin, oxytocin — things that help you relax and destress. And that can help reduce symptoms of depression. Personally, I think being around animals is just good for people. Animals don't judge you like people do.' She hobbled over to where Ernie stood, watching and apparently listening, and rubbed his nose. 'So long as you're kind to them, they're usually fine with you. They'll only attack if they feel scared, or threatened, and they don't play games, or try to manipulate you. With animals, what you get is what you give — give them your love and your trust, and you'll get that back in the purest possible form. And that—' she grinned as Ernie whickered in agreement '—is really something very powerful.'

'Wow. And Ernie does all of that?'

'And more.' Angela nodded. 'Ernie's especially good with children recovering from trauma . . . the types of things you'd pray no child ever experienced. The thing is, he understands them. His background before he came here . . . it wasn't good, Rick. We don't talk about it.' She pressed her face against the little donkey's, hugging him to her. 'But Ernie knows what it's like to be hurt by someone you should be able to trust, and he gives those kids his understanding, and his support, and he helps them to heal. And maybe they help heal him a bit more too.'

'Ernie was abused?' The lump in Rick's throat made it hard to get his words out, but he found it so difficult to believe. The donkey seemed happy and friendly to him.

'Like I said, we don't talk about it. It will never, ever, *ever* happen again. He — and his drove — are safe and loved here, and they know that.'

'Right.' Rick had to swallow hard to be able to speak. 'And the reading thing?'

'Oh, that's much simpler.' Angela petted her grinning friend, picking bits out of his tufty mane. 'When kids are reading, or adults learning for the first time, they're often being judged. There's someone there waiting to helpfully correct you or help you when you struggle with certain words or get your letters in a muddle. While that's how most people learn, for some it makes things harder, because you get stressed waiting for the next correction, and then the words and letters jump around a lot more.'

'You sound like you know what you're talking about.'

'I do.' Angela met his eyes squarely. 'I'm dyslexic.'

'Oh, I'm sorry to hear that.' He wasn't sure if it was the right thing to say, but how else were you supposed to respond when someone told you they were disabled?

'What are you apologising for?' Angela laughed at him. 'It's dyslexia. Not like I just told you I'm dying of some painful, terminal disease.'

'Sorry.'

She laughed at him again. 'Would you apologise to me for my curly hair?'

'No, but . . .'

'Or the fact that I need glasses when it gets late and my astigmatism acts up?'

'No, but . . .'

'But nothing, Rick. It's exactly the same. Part of how I'm made.'

'Right.' He wasn't totally sure what to say to that, so instead he changed the subject by holding up the empty moorhen cage. 'Where do I put this?'

'Blankets come inside for washing, cage gets disinfected and then goes back with the others.'

'Then tea?' He was already ready for a break.

'For the animals, yes.'

'Right.'

'Furred, four legs, feathered and scaled get fed before humans round here. I hope you're not squeamish.' He didn't think he was, but something about her wicked grin made him take a step back.

He soon learned why she'd grinned. Over an hour of cleaning, chopping, prepping, carting food and bowls back and forth from the makeshift kitchen, and he'd had more than enough. He dreaded to think what the smudges on his jeans were, or whether the splodges on his boots would ever come out.

He'd quite liked the ferrets — with their sleek fur and quick, smart moves . . . right up until he'd learned how disgusting their diet was. And he found it difficult to understand how Angela could go from feeding the birds she was rehabbing from various wounds in different cages and aviaries, to feeding chicks complete with their feathers to the ferrets and weasels.

'It's nature.' She'd shrugged and moved onto cleaning down the preparation area. 'It's not as if I'm the one who killed them. I don't like it, but critters need to eat.'

By the time they'd fed the rabbits, the mice, the hedgehogs, two squirrels, the goose missing feathers down one wing, and the barn owl, Rick had had more than enough. He hadn't prepared so many vegetables since the last time he was on a juice cleanse. And after the ferret and owl food . . . yuck, he might not eat for another week.

'Are we done now?' he asked hopefully as he wiped the last chopping board and handed it to her.

'Nearly, just the donkeys and goats to go.'

"Just" turned out to mean lugging over a large bag of surprisingly heavy feed to the impatient, noisy gang who hollered and stamped — letting him know in no uncertain terms that they thought he was too slow. He was hungry, smelly and really regretting his late night. His head thumped and span with random nonsense thoughts — as he tried to empty the bag into the feeding trough, he could imagine the donkey's huffing and wickers as laughter at the slow, clumsy new guy in his grubby trousers and stained shoes.

'That's it.' Angela, who had been supervising his every move, closed the barn door.

'And you do this every day?' Rick was impressed.

'They need feeding every day, so yes. Twice a day for most of the guests, with a full clean through of all habitats in the morning. Is there any chance I might see you before tomorrow morning becomes the afternoon?'

'Ah, yeah.' He felt slightly sheepish. He was well aware he needed Angela to confirm his hours, and report back favourably to the probation office, so he did his best to apologise — and mean it. 'I'm sorry about that. Didn't get home until late last night — or rather this morning. Overslept.'

'Who goes out on a Tuesday night?'

'Someone being paid to show up.' His tiredness, and the thumping in his head, made him more honest than he would usually be. While sponsored appearances weren't exactly a secret, he usually tried to be more discreet than that.

'You get paid to go clubbing? By who?'

'Clubs. Promoters.' He saw the look on her face and tried to explain. 'I chat about my plans online, take a few pics and vids of me in the club, add a few tags, and it means more people want to pay to be there.'

'And you really get paid for that?'

'Yeah. Pretty well.'

'Wow. You really do live in a different world.'

'Yup.' He grinned cheerfully, thinking how awesome his life really was. It wasn't until a few hours later when he was eating dinner — in an exclusive new restaurant, natch — that it occurred to him Angela hadn't exactly agreed with him. And now that he thought about it, she hadn't sounded all that impressed when she'd said it.

But he shrugged it off, pasted on his toothpaste-advert-worthy smile and flashed it around the place.

* * *

Angela shoved away her miserable microwave meal and tugged her blanket over her knees. She wasn't cold, exactly, but she liked the comfort and warmth it gave her. And it would offer some protection if Ruby, or one of the cats, wanted to snuggle with her later. The newest kittens hadn't exactly learned that their claws were supposed to stay in when they were playing.

She was so tired and aching that all she wanted to do was curl up in bed, but her brain was racing and it would keep her awake if she tried to sleep now. She couldn't wait until she was properly back on her feet. She wouldn't have thought the partial, temporary loss of one leg would have made almost every job feel like it took twice as much energy. That just didn't add up in her mind.

Even the administration side of the charity — which she hated — seemed to take more effort, because of the effort it took to get into a comfortable position where her leg wasn't complaining. Or her arms would ache from using the crutches all day. She certainly had a deeper respect for the amputee animals she had worked with in the past — and *her* injury would heal!

She didn't want to look at her admin tasks — then she'd end up looking at bank accounts, and they weren't going to make happy reading. She really needed to get the business side of things back up and running. Jake and her volunteers had done their best keeping things going while she'd been in hospital and off her feet — and she was beyond grateful that her animals had been looked after — but she needed to crack on with arranging more fundraising, and sorting things like the Donkey Supported Activities, which she'd been forced to temporarily cancel. In order to get that all reinvigorated and running again, she was going to need more help. Which brought her back to her latest problem: Rick.

Rather than think about that, Angela unlocked her phone and dialled her mum.

'Hello, darling, how are you?'

'I'm OK.' Angela tucked her feet up onto the couch — mindful of her knee and leg.

'Are you sure?'

'Yeah. Just tired.'

'You're not working too hard are you?'

'No more so than usual.' Angela didn't want to worry her mum. 'How's the seaside?'

'Wonderful.' Cathy sighed happily. 'I can understand why they used to send people to beach towns to convalesce. The air here is different.'

'Probably the salt.' Angela rubbed her eyes tiredly.

'Maybe. That and it's nice to be looked after for a bit. I've barely been allowed to lift a finger since I got here.'

'And neither should you!' her aunt said, and Angela laughed at the voice in the background. 'Ask her how her new helper is working out.'

'All right, give me a minute.' Cathy laughed. 'So, you heard her. How's it going?'

'Well . . .' Angela thought carefully before answering. 'He was *some* help once he'd settled in and put his phone away. He helped prep some food and set up a rescue pen. But, honestly, he was late and probably did less work all day than Summer or Sarah do in one evening.'

'I guess they're more enthusiastic too.'

'Definitely,' Angela agreed. 'They turn up on time and do actual chores.'

She chatted to her mum for a few more minutes before saying goodbye. She prodded her uninspiring dinner a couple more times, before returning to thoughts of the sanctuary and her latest "helper".

If Rick — she refused to use his ridiculous nickname — was going to be of any help, she'd have to find a way to get him more interested in caring for the animals than posing with them . . . which gave her a horrible thought: the video from that morning. Surely he *wouldn't?*

She grabbed for her phone and searched quickly. It took her longer to remember her login details than it did to find his account — *1.8 million* followers! Who on earth was this man, and what did he do to have so much interest? She shook

her head at people's silliness and carried on scrolling. Oh *no* .
. . that looked like . . . yep. It was her street. She watched in
horror as Rick chatted to his camera, swinging it around, then
sauntered up her driveway and smacked the bell.

At least he hadn't mentioned Bill's by name, or the village
. . . but oh *NO*, there she was, peering through the top half of
the gate. Naturally her hair was a crazy wild mess after she had
just chased a squirrel out of it, and she was in pain from having
just limped across the courtyard at high speed, thinking she
was receiving a patient.

She winced when the version of herself on the screen
told him to jump off a pier and slammed the gate on him.
She groaned and covered her face, horrified and embarrassed.
Maybe she could ask him to take the video down. She grimaced
when she saw the number of views the video had already gained
— more than the population of Broclington . . . many times
over.

She shook her head and swiped to the next video, and
nearly dropped her phone laughing. Grinning out from her
phone was Ernie, showing all his teeth while Rick petted him.
She paused the video to check something as Ernie whuffled
happily . . . squinting and zooming in, and yeah, he was actually getting his ears scratched. That was surprising — she knew
how sensitive their ears were, and how much trust it took for
most animals to put themselves in a vulnerable situation like
that, and especially one with Ernie's background.

She'd always claimed her animals were usually a good
judge of character. True, they were cheeky, forthright and
demanding — but they did usually seem to know how to
read people.

She hit play again, watching as Ernie leaned happily into
Rick. It was confusing — she knew who Rick was: the selfish
idiot who had gotten into a car after he'd been drinking and
smashed into the village café, nearly killing her, her mum, a
little girl and the other guests. And then turned up late for his
court-ordered community service and didn't even bother to

apologise — for being late, or anything else. Not to mention posting videos — *of her!* — without her permission. He was a nuisance, and bound to be more trouble than he was worth.

And yet, as she watched Ernie happily grumbling and sighing his big donkey whistles, she couldn't help but wonder what he'd seen in her new "helper".

* * *

Rick shook off the gloves he'd been wearing, and tried not to gag — again. After two coffees and the promise of an expensive dinner, Yvette had finally deigned to crawl out of his bed and drive him to the sanctuary — wearing her traditional "disguise" of bright pink, skintight yoga pants, teamed with an eye-watering ly white vest top and trainers from the latest brand sponsoring her, topped off with huge sunglasses and a baseball hat.

She'd been quite disappointed when she hadn't spotted a single photographer or fan on the whole journey, despite her looking for them at every opportunity — and had nearly ploughed his car into a hedge when she thought she'd spotted one, who turned out to just be a normal cyclist who'd flipped them the bird.

He'd tried to explain why he wasn't 'gramming the sanctuary all over the internet — he didn't really want his fans turning up and getting content of him literally shovelling shit. Hardly on-brand with the glossy, on-trend, you-either-wanted-him-or-wanted-to-be-him image that was Maverick. But as much as Yvette should have understood influencer life, she still grumbled about the lack of attention.

When they'd reached the place, she'd given him a perfunctory kiss on the cheek, her glossy lips barely grazing his skin. He'd understood — there wasn't an audience, so no need to perform. Not that their relationship was a performance . . . exactly.

They knew each other before Yvette's agent carefully and gently suggested perhaps they might want to consider a public dinner or two . . . and she was absolutely fucking stunning, regularly topping sexiest or hottest celeb charts. And the sex was pretty good. Which was a much more pleasant thing to think about than the heaping pile of shit Angela had him clearing out of the barn.

He dragged another barrow load over to the great pile that sat in the corner of one of the paddocks, trying not to gag at the smell. Or the thought of what it was. He'd had no idea the cute donkey who garnered him so many likes, retweets and stars was so full of shit — although if he said that out loud, Angela would probably scowl and correct him to "poopy-de-whoopy" or something equally weird. He shook his head and dumped the barrow over, into the heaping pile of crap that was now quite literally and viscerally and stinkily in front of him.

He heaved the wheelbarrow back across the yard, cursing the squeaking, wobbling wheel. The more time he spent at Bill's, the more impressed and surprised he was. As well as the sheds off the small courtyard, the rescue centre spilled out into paddocks and fields that sprawled across the back of the neighbouring houses.

He was shattered, which was ridiculous — he hit the gym at least three times a week to keep in shape for his fans and sponsors. He could party until it was so late that it became early, and then keep going until early became late again, and not feel as tired as he did after a few hours of cleaning up after animals who weren't exactly grateful to have him poking around.

He'd just taken a break, leaning against the barn wall and lighting a fag, when Angela hobbled out of the tiny lean-to that served as her office. It was ridiculous how tiny that room was — his bathroom was bigger. Heck, his shoe cupboard was bigger. Maybe that was why she was so grumpy all the time, being squashed up in that windowless room.

'Do you mind?' She glared at him.

'About what?'

'The cigarette.'

'You don't like smoking?'

'Not around my animals, no.' Her words were short and clipped. Yet again he'd managed to annoy her.

'Sorry.' He stamped it out on the ground.

'Pick it up please. There's plenty of silly critters around here who would happily try eating it.'

'Oh. Sorry.' He stooped to pick up the offending remnants of his break, looking up to come face to face with a pair of curious gold eyes peering at him over a ginger-and-white muzzle.

'Is that a fox?' He'd felt silly asking. Ginger fur, white belly, pointy ears and fluffy tail. It looked like the foxes he'd seen before — mostly on TV or in reels, but he'd never seen one skipping around someone's ankles like a dog.

'Yes. This is Ruby. Ruby, stop showing off.' She pulled what looked like a dog toy out of her pocket and sent it bouncing out of the barn, the fox flying after it, giving her the space to work.

'You have a pet *fox*?' Rick's eyes were incredulous as Ruby bounded back in, proudly holding her toy aloft.

'Absolutely not. Ruby's a rescue too. Just like all the animals here. Foxes make terrible pets. They're messy, destructive, noisy and territorial. And they like to scent-mark their territory too — which stinks. They need a huge amount of space and mental stimulation, otherwise they get into all sorts of trouble. Unfortunately Ruby's previous owners didn't realise any of this until she'd well and truly imprinted on humans.'

'She seems happy.' He watched the fox roll around with her toy.

'Yes, but she shouldn't be. With two people standing here, talking, she should be nervous — watchful at the very least. Instead she's showing off.' She secured the door on the moorhen's new coop. 'Rehabilitation was tried, but she failed miserably. She can't ever be released.'

'So what do you do with her?' He really wanted to get some footage of her. A cute fox that jumped and played like a dog? That would go viral for sure!

'She has a bed in one of the other sheds. The donkeys tolerate her, but I don't think they'd like her sharing their space too closely. I feed her, keep an eye on her, and she pretty much comes and goes as she pleases. Sometimes she invites herself into the office, but I try to discourage her from the main house.'

'Why?' Rick quite liked the idea of snuggling with a fox in front of the TV. Yvette would probably love it.

'You can't house-train a fox like you do a dog.'

Maybe not then. 'Hey Ruby-ru.' He crouched down, stretching out his hand to her. 'Wanna play? Are you friendly?'

Angela shook her head. 'She can be, when she wants to be. But she's as likely to try and bite you as she is to let you pet her.'

'Thanks for the warning.' He stayed in position, and was rewarded when a wet nose and fuzzy snout investigated his fingers. After a few seconds, he carefully rubbed a pointed ear gently, prompting the fox to lean against him, making a soft clicking noise. He didn't know what it meant, but it sounded happy. 'I don't think you're going to nip me, are you?' He murmured the words softly. 'I think you might even like me, don't you?' He sighed. At least someone did.

CHAPTER THREE

Angela watched as Rick finished carefully sweeping out the huge pen she'd nicknamed "guinea garden", and started laying out the different tubes, blocks, bales and other toys that kept her cavy crew amused while they waited for adoption.

'Stop it, Ruby, the piggies don't know you only want to play. They're worried you're going to eat them. It's all right, ladies, Ruby's well-fed. Just ignore her.' He sent a ball bouncing across the yard, which Ruby gleefully bounded after. When he caught Angela watching, he grinned and, for a few moments, she found herself wanting to grin back.

After a couple of seconds, he shrugged and went back to his work. 'All right, lads. Your turn next. Let's see what stinky surprises you've got for me.'

It was impressive how fast he'd settled in. He'd learned the ropes and won over most of the animals in just a couple of weeks. And he'd been ridiculously excited when they'd been able to release the moorhen — the first time he'd helped release any animal.

It *was* impressive — but in some ways, it annoyed Angela too. He was supposed to be being punished, but instead he seemed to have landed on his feet, taking to it better than a duckling in a pond for the first time. For some reason that irritated her almost as much as rubbing Ernie's fur the wrong way bothered him.

She decided not to think about it, instead forcing herself to go back into the office and start ploughing through the paperwork she'd been letting pile up.

She'd barely made a dent when the phone rang with the type of call she didn't like. She made some quick notes, then dialled the number for Badger's Hospital. She didn't like to disturb Jake, but if he didn't have a full schedule, he would often help — and she didn't think she'd be able to manage by herself. Unfortunately her luck wasn't in that day, and he was in surgery, then had a busy list of patients for the afternoon.

She drummed her fingers against the desk, thinking. A trapped animal wasn't a call for Harry, and her mum was away recuperating. Evelyn would be busy at work. She didn't want to leave an animal in distress — and from the phone call, that very much was the case — which meant she only had one choice. She hobbled back to the courtyard. 'Rick, how do you feel about a field trip?'

It only took them a few minutes to gather up the equipment she thought they might need, and a few things she hoped they wouldn't — like the cat grabber and dog noose pole. They were useful tools, and protected rescuers from nasty bites, but despite being properly trained to use them safely and Jake's reassurances, she couldn't help dislike how much more they seemed to stress animals out.

A few minutes later and they — well, mostly Rick — had loaded up her big, battered, old car. She tried not to focus on how the old V70 estate, with her quirks, rattles and squeaks, would compare in Rick's mind to the expensive sports car she often saw him dropped off in. She shook her head. It didn't matter what he thought — he wasn't a permanent fixture in her life, and her car more than did the job she needed it for. The massive estate boot meant she could fit all her equipment and cages easily into the car, and the four-wheel drive function had got her out of more than one tricky situation that would have stranded a lesser vehicle. And, more importantly, the automatic gearbox meant she could still drive despite her injured leg. Still, she was more aware than ever of the slight clunk whenever she turned left. She didn't know what it was, but she hoped it wouldn't be too expensive.

The woman who had called was waiting when they arrived. 'I've tried calling it, and I put down some food, but it hasn't come out and just keeps yowling. I think it might be a cat. I'm afraid my dogs might have chased the poor creature down there. But I've no way to get access, so had to call you. If my boyfriend were home, I'd get him on it, but he's away for work — and I can't listen to the poor thing cry for two days.'

'You did the right thing.' Angela offered reassurance. She followed the yowling into the garden — the raised decking angled away from the slope and turned into steps down into the back garden. 'Oh dear.' The problem was immediately obvious: while there were gaps enough for an animal to squeeze through, there wasn't anywhere near enough space for her or anyone else. 'Is there any chance you'll let us remove some of these boards?' She crossed her fingers as she asked. Despite being a so-called nation of animal lovers, in the past she'd had people refuse or need a lot of convincing.

'Of course. If I had more confidence, and the tools, I would have tried it myself. But I'd probably make a dreadful mess.'

'Well, I will try my best to be neat.'

'Shouldn't be a problem,' Rick called from near the stairs. 'If I can get these screws out, I'm pretty sure we can slide these rear slats out without damaging anything. I think a couple might be a bit tricky from this angle, it looks like they were put in before the steps were built, but I can always drill them out and just reattach slightly further along. It would only be a couple of centimetres. You probably wouldn't know if I hadn't said anything. Is that OK?'

'Really?' Angela felt her eyebrows jump up. She hadn't expected Rick to be so . . . helpful.

'Yeah.' The woman was nodding, not paying attention to Angela at all. 'I don't mean to be rude . . . but you are who I think you are, right?'

'Depends on who you think I am.' Rick flicked his sunglasses down to peer at her and flash a smile.

'Oh my God! It *is* you. You're Maverick Star!'

Rick flicked his fingers in a complicated salute, which made the woman laugh.

'How come you're here? Is VettyBaby with you? I'm a huge fan of hers. That's why I recognised you. Her style is just amazing. Is she as gorgeous in person? Is she really lovely? I bet she is. She seems so *nice*.'

Rick laughed and held up his hands. 'I'm here helping out my friend Angela. Yvette's not with us today, but I'm sure she'll be thrilled to hear I've met you. She loves hearing from her fans. Yes, she is gorgeous in person, and yes, she can be really lovely—' he leaned forward, adding conspiratorially '—when she wants to be — but she can be a real grump when she's hungry!'

'Oh my God, VettyBaby gets hangry!' The woman seemed thrilled with the information, but Angela couldn't figure out why . . . or what Rick had meant.

'Would you mind if I took a few pictures while you're here?'

'Tell you what,' Rick gave her that super bright smile, 'once we get kitty out, I'll even pose for some selfies. As thanks for you letting me take apart your garden. How's that?'

'That would be *awesome*. I'll go grab you some drinks. And maybe run a brush through my hair.'

'Drinks would be great. Personally—' he flashed another of *those* grins '—I think you look gorgeous, but we've got things here if you did want to pop indoors.'

'Yeah. OK. Great.'

Angela waited until the woman disappeared back into the house. 'What was that all about?'

'Sounds like Yvette has a fan. And I might just have gained a new follower.' He laughed. 'Don't suppose you've got a really long-handled Philips in your box? I think I'm going to need as much torque as possible to avoid rounding the heads. It's all right, kitty. We're coming to get you. Just settle down.'

Wordlessly, Angela handed over the requested tool, still reeling a bit from discovering that Rick apparently knew one end of a screwdriver from another, and he knew it wasn't just a cocktail. She wasn't sure if that surprised her more than the fact that the trapped cat had apparently decided to listen to him and settle down. Weird coincidence.

Another few minutes later, and Rick shifted the last plank, grinning at her — not the flashy bright smile he'd given the homeowner, but the cheeky, slightly shy grin that she found herself wanting to return. 'You're surprised I'm handy, aren't you?'

'Honestly, yes.' For some reason she felt a bit guilty.

'Turns out I'm more than just a pretty face, huh?' There was that irritating, persuasive grin again. 'I used to mess around in my dad's shed. I'm not really into it anymore, but this was simple enough. Do you want to hand me the torch?'

'Why?'

'So I can find our latest rescue.'

Angela looked at the gap he'd created, momentarily tempted to let him do all the hard work. But when the cat yowled again, she shook the thought away. 'No. If the animal's injured, I'll need to come down anyway. I might as well crawl in to start with.'

'OK.' Rick nodded. 'After you? You'll probably have to duck, but I don't think you'll need to crawl.'

'Right, sure.' She wasn't going to think about it. She was just going to do it. She slipped on her head-torch and handed the larger, heavier handheld one to him. She grabbed a heavy pair of gloves and passed a carrier to him, followed by a fleece blanket — soft and fluffy to comfort scared animals, but also safe and free from any loops that could easily catch claws or toes.

It wasn't as dark as she'd feared: the boards Rick had so efficiently removed let in quite a bit of light, which pooled across half of the under-decking area, but naturally she couldn't see her latest rescue target. The rest of the area stretched out like a dark cave, with only slivers of light creeping through cracks in the decking.

'Kit, kit, kitty?' Rick called out, clicking his tongue as he shone the torch around. 'Talk to us, help us find you.'

The strangled yowl came from the back of the decking, where it was darkest. Of course the critter would be in the darkest spot possible. She took a deep breath and forced herself to take a couple of steps. As soon as she stepped outside of that puddle of light, she felt as if someone had poured cold water over her. Goosepimples raced over her body, and she started to feel sick as her breath came short — her whole leg started to throb.

She swallowed hard. *Breathe. Just breathe, find the moggy and get out. Breathe, find the moggy and get out. Breathe.* She could do this. She had to, even though she could feel icy sweat trickling down her back, and her stomach rebelled, threatening to invite her breakfast up.

She looked around, her headlamp light seeming too pale and watery to be of any comfort.

'There you are!' Rick's triumph echoed against the wood above her head. *Close above her head.* And she had to fight back the panic that clawed at her throat, threatening to choke her ability to focus on the reason she was down there. 'Angela, I've got her. Poor thing seems stuck, though.'

Of course it was.

'Stuck how?' Angela edged closer to Rick's pool of torch-light, taking her further from the entrance than she was totally happy with.

'Oh dear. This could be tricky.' She stared at the feline butt sticking in the air, the tail twitching back and forth angrily, despite Rick's hand stroking slowly down its back. She peered around, trying to understand exactly what she was looking at. It looked like, at some point, there had been trellising running up the side of the house, and the decking had been built straight over the top of it. And, for some reason, the cat had tried to climb through it and gotten firmly stuck.

What she couldn't figure out was what the H-E-double-hockey-sticks to do about it.

'I don't think I can break this trellis thing,' Rick admitted, his tone quiet and calm as he petted the stricken feline. 'At least, not without hitting it really hard — much harder than I'm happy to with her stuck in there.'

'That has to be the very last option. If we can get our hands round the other side, it might be possible to turn her enough and push her head back through.'

'There's not much room, and the wood is pretty rough.'

'So splinters are going to be an issue. Not great.'

'Any chance you have a saw in your toolbox? If I can cut here, here—' he pointed to the wooden joins around the cat '— here and here, I think we might be able to lift her out, bringing the trellis with her, and then figure this out in daylight.'

'And if needs be, take her to Badger's Hospital and have Jake sedate her and cut her out. Sounds like a plan. And yeah, I'm pretty sure there's a hacksaw in my box.'

'Great. Do you want to stay here with her, rather than you climbing back and forth?' He flicked his light over to her when she didn't answer, and squinted. 'Angela, are you OK? I don't mean to be rude, but you look like shi . . . something she could have dragged in.'

How on earth was she supposed to answer that? 'I . . . umm . . . I'm not too keen on dark spaces.' There, that was honest enough.

'Oh, right . . . do you want me to stay here and you grab the tools then?'

'Yeah.' She almost toppled herself over with her eagerness to escape. She wasn't being a wimp — not really. It was just that the cat was obviously already calm-ish with Rick, and it made sense not to risk causing any more stress.

A few minutes later she steeled herself to re-enter the dark. Not that it was dark, dark . . . there was light there, just not enough of it. It didn't help that it had a similar dusty rubble smell to the café that day, which hadn't been pitch black either. And this time was different — this time she was the rescuer, not the rescuee. She focussed on that as she clambered back down carefully — a heavier blanket and saw in hand.

'Hey.' Rick held his torch up high, illuminating as much of the area as possible. 'Do you want to just give me that and wait up top?'

Wow. Did she really look that bad? She felt pretty awful, but still . . .'No, I'm all right.' If she said it with enough conviction, she might make herself believe it as well as him. 'And I think this is going to be a two-person job.'

'You're the boss.' He took the saw from her.

'We're going to have to cocoon her.' She held up the blanket. She wondered how long the little cat had been stuck down there before starting to yell, and how long it had called before the homeowner had heard. She bit down on the inside of her cheek to stop herself from crying.

'OK.' Rick took the blanket from her gently, watching Angela for a few seconds. 'All right, Miss Kitty, I'm just going to pop this over you, then Angela here is going to tuck you in nice and cosy, and then we're going to get you out of here.' He kept his hand moving across the cat's fur as he positioned the blanket.

Angela watched as Rick soothed the cat, and found herself thinking he was a natural. 'So, is there a special way to do this cocoon thing?'

'Yeah.' Angela leaned over to show him, wrapping the blanket around the cat carefully, making sure all paws and tail were tucked gently but firmly inside. The last thing they wanted was the cat getting stressed and lashing out — hurting itself or them.

'All right, let's do this.'

'OK.' Angela held the cat secure as Rick wound his hand around the trellis before starting to cut.

'Well, that's annoying,' he commented after a few seconds.

'What is?' She tried to concentrate on him and the cat rather than where she was and how much she didn't want to be there.

'It's actually a pretty solid trellis. And the saw isn't the sharpest.' He glanced at her, saw still continuing its journey to free the mischievous moggy. 'This might take a few minutes. Kitty's wrapped up bug-snug, I think I can handle it if you want to go?'

Oh, she so, so desperately wanted to take him up on his offer, but as she saw it, she had a responsibility to the cat and to Rick. 'I'm OK.' She wasn't sure if she was trying to convince herself or him, but either way he wasn't buying it.

'Can I help?'

The offer surprised her in how genuine it sounded. 'You should probably concentrate on freeing this silly blighter.'

'You know, it's a fallacy.'

'What is?'

'The idea that only women can multitask. I'm actually perfectly capable of cutting through wood and holding at least a semi-coherent conversation.' He grinned at her, and even in this dusty torch world she could tell it was a proper smile and not the slick, flashy one he wore so easily.

'Sorry.'

'Nothing to apologise for.' He broke through the first part of the trellis and grinned triumphantly. 'One down, three to go. Good thing she didn't get stuck any higher up, otherwise we'd be having to cut all around her. So, talk to me.'

'About what?'

'Anything. How come you run a rescue centre?'

'Honestly, I think I just got really lucky.'

'This sounds like it could be a good story.' He glanced at her. 'Tell me?'

'Well, I've always loved animals. Mum always likes to tell the story of how, when I was about five years old, I found a baby blackbird after a storm. Not that I knew what it was then. We assumed it had been knocked from its nest by the wind. Apparently I came running back in from the garden with this sopping wet bundle of squealing feathers. We dried it off and warmed it up. We couldn't find the nest or parent birds, so Mum drove us to a rescue centre miles away. Apparently I cried all the way home because I didn't want to leave that little bird so far away from its nest. Even though, now, I know it was probably destroyed in the storm. Silly, really.'

'I think it's actually pretty sweet.' He grinned as the next trellis gave. 'Two down. Halfway there — of this stage, at least. What happened to the bird? Did you find out?'

'Yeah. We called the rescue every day, and it was successfully released shortly afterwards. That's why I don't mind update calls . . . even though they take time. I know some people really care about the critters they bring me.'

'I guess that's nice.' He concentrated on getting the position right for the next cut. 'So, how does five-year-old you and one storm-rattled blackbird turn into a full rescue centre?'

She knew what he was doing — trying to distract her — but she didn't mind. In fact, she felt quite grateful for it. 'After that, Mum says I developed a knack for finding strays and injured critters. So she learned — and taught me — the basics. How to feed a baby bird safely, when to intervene and when to just pop them back in the nests, or leave for parents to deal with. I grew up knowing I wanted to work with animals, but I didn't have the grades, or interest in university, to go into veterinary medicine. My grandparents got involved, and my grandad set up his old shed as a mini rescue centre. He was so amazing. He insulated the whole building and got a couple of old incubators from a farmer, and my nan came up with a pattern and crocheted little nest bowls for the rescue birds — I still have a few of them that are serviceable, she made hundreds over the years.'

'How old were you then?'

'Probably about eight or nine.' She smiled at the memory. 'Then Nan decided she wasn't that bothered about having a greenhouse anymore, so Grandad turned that into a pre-release aviary.'

'Third one down. One more to go.' He hesitated, then looked at her. 'Hang on. The funny-shaped aviary at Bill's, is that the one your grandad built?'

'Yeah. When Grandad built something, it stayed built.'

'So, Bill's is your grandparent's old home?'

'Yeah, they left it to me. I wouldn't have been able to afford it otherwise.' She didn't mention that she still struggled to a lot of the time. 'Mum already had her own place and business, and Grandad thought I'd do a lot more good in the world expanding the rescue than in any other job he could think of for me. We started running it together after Nan died — partly to keep him busy and partly to keep me out of mischief. When Grandad joined her a few years later—' she swallowed hard, the loss painfully raw even after so many years '—I decided there couldn't be a better tribute than keeping it going.'

'So Bill was your grandad. Makes sense.'

Angela looked at him oddly for a few moments, then laughed. 'No. Bill's a badger.'

'One of your first rescues?'

'No, he's fictional. He was Rupert the Bear's best friend. You know, like the cartoons and annuals?'

'So you named your rescue centre after a cartoon badger?'

'Yeah.'

'Why?'

'Why not?' Angela countered. 'Nan used to read me all the stories, and bought me the new annual every Christmas.'

'Well, why not a squirrel or fox? Or Rupert?'

Angela shook her head. 'You've not realised yet?'

'Realised what?'

'Broclington. Brock is the old word for badger. It's literally "Badger Town". A lot of the local businesses here have badger references in their names. There's Badger's Hospital — the vet — the Brockle's Retreat, which is the pub and the café, the Brockle's Paws . . .'

'You're right, I hadn't. I might have to do a reel on that.'

'Why?'

'Because people will think it's cool, and probably watch the video and share it lots.'

'And that's good . . . because?'

'Because it makes money. You really don't know how this works, do you?'

'Not a clue,' Angela admitted cheerfully. She didn't understand it, and didn't really want to.

'Phew.' The last bit of wood gave. 'We're done. Let's get this little girl out of here and see about removing her new fashion accessory.'

Gratefully, Angela hugged the cat against her, peering at the dusty moggy's face, who decided that was the perfect moment to resume her yowling complaints and start to wriggle.

'Here.' Rick held out the saw, blade down. 'Swap you? She looks like she's not going to make it easy for you.'

After a moment's thought, Angela handed the cat over. He was right. And it seemed the cat agreed — she stopped fussing the moment she was in Rick's arms.

* * *

Rick blinked in the light as he handed over the cat to Angela, who popped her straight into the waiting carry-basket, still cocooned tightly in the blanket, and still with her head stuck.

'It's just for a minute. I just need . . . a minute.'

He eyed her with concern as she sat down on the decking steps. He'd thought she looked pale before, but had assumed it was just the bad lighting. Now he could see she was still pale, and looked sweaty too. Damn, he was glad he'd kept her talking down there, because she looked about ready to burst into tears. And he hated it when women cried — a fact that Yvette seemed to use to her advantage. He put her out of his head to focus on Angela, and sat next to her on the steps.

'I don't mean to be rude, but do you need a hug? I mean, you look like you do, but maybe not from me.' She didn't respond, so he nudged her elbow with his. 'Angela?'

When she looked at him, her eyes were overly bright.

'Hey, come here.' He wrapped one arm awkwardly around her shoulder, and realised she was shaking. 'You did great, Angela, really great. We got her out, and once she — and you — have had a little break, we'll figure out how to get the thing off her neck, and then figure out who she belongs to. OK?'

'Yeah.' She nodded slowly, her curls bouncing back and forth in the ponytail she'd tossed it into before rescuing the cat, who was sitting calmly in the basket, watching them with interest. As those curls bounced he noticed a lump of cobweb, and what looked like dead flies, caught in them.

'Here, hold still a second.' He reached out, and she jerked back a few inches. 'You've picked up some cobwebs.' He decided not to mention the deceased inhabitants.

'Oh.' She relaxed again. 'Thanks.'

He wiped the cobwebs away, teasing them gently from her brown curls, which were a lot softer and silkier than he might have guessed. If he'd spent time thinking about them, which he obviously hadn't. But, for a moment, she was very close and very warm in his arms. He found himself wanting nothing more than to cheer her up, to see her eyes flash at him again, the way they did when she was annoyed with him, or amused at something Ernie and his jennets or Ruby had done.

He dropped his hand and forced himself to look away, but kept his arm around her shoulders, reasoning that it seemed to be offering her some level of comfort, and had nothing to do with that sweet-hay, summery-evening scent below the dust.

'So, this "not being keen on dark spaces" thing. You had that all your life? Or do you have some cool story to go with it? Did you get stuck down a hole rescuing a badger or something?' He shot her one of his most winning smiles, trying to make her feel better.

'No. It's pretty new.' It sounded like she was gritting her teeth. She tensed against him briefly, then shoved him away, glaring as she struggled to her feet. 'Come on, we've got a customer.'

He was missing something, and he knew it, but he couldn't figure out what it was, so he followed her lead and turned his attention back to the dusty, mottled cat. 'Right then, little missy, let's have a look at you.'

'Why do you keep calling it that?' Angela watched the cat as he opened the crate.

'What?'

'I couldn't see the sex down there, but you keep calling it "miss" and "her" like you're sure.'

Now she mentioned it, he realised she was right, although he had no idea why. 'Well, it seemed rude to call her an "it", and I have even odds on being right.'

'Fair enough.' She was still watching the cat, but he had a feeling it was less about the trapped animal and more to avoid looking at him. He studied the cat, and the wooden-trellis necklace she wore. 'You know, if you had a coping saw, I could probably get it in there and be able to cut through the wood above her head and then we can just drop it off.'

'You are not using a saw that close to a live animal!' Well at least the flash was back in her eyes.

'I said "coping saw". I wouldn't do anything to risk hurting her, especially when we worked so hard to get her this far,' he reassured Angela, and the listening cat. 'Coping saws are the ones with skinny, removable blades. I thought I could — very carefully — reverse the blade and slide it alongside her neck, where there's plenty of room, and then reconnect it to the frame and cut her free. It might rub her slightly, but the back of the blade is smooth anyway, and it's got to be safer than knocking out an animal whose medical history we don't know.'

'It would be quicker, too. Jake is in surgery, so it would probably be a while before he could get to her.' Angela nodded, still avoiding his gaze. 'OK, let's try it. I think I've got one of those saws in the box. I just thought they were called fret saws.'

'The smaller ones are. But the larger ones are usually coping saws. Either should work for this job, unsticking Miss Kitty here.'

He got to work quickly, petting the cat and tucking his fingers alongside the space around her neck, so he could slide the blade into position and started sawing against wood. He struggled for room, and hesitated, wanting to keep his fingers between the back of the blade and the cat. Even though her neck was skinny, he didn't have enough room.

'Here.' Angela rested her cool fingers on his wrist and tugged gently. 'Let me.' She pulled his hand out of the way, and replaced it with her own, much slimmer fingers.

'Thanks.' He smiled and set to work, slightly surprised at how easily they worked together. At the same time, he felt a bit sad. If they'd met under different circumstances — not that he could really picture *how* they might have met — he thought they could have been friends.

Oh, *shit*. His brain caught up with his train of thought: she didn't like dark, small spaces and it was a "pretty new" thing. Shit. He completed the first cut, and carefully wriggled the blade along for the next, his brain still reeling. How the hell was he supposed to broach this? He wasn't even sure if he really should, but now that his brain was screaming at him to pay attention, he wasn't sure that he could ignore it anymore.

Angela had clearly been scared — sweat-causing, hand-shaking, stomach-churningly *terrified* — and she'd still clambered under the decking to rescue an animal she didn't even know. He couldn't help but wonder how many other times she'd done things like that. She'd spent her whole life helping animals — creatures who would never be able to tell her thank you — and she did it for free. If anything, it seemed to cost her money, judging from the amount of food and bedding Bill's went through every day.

He'd never met anyone like her.

The judge had been right. There was Angela, doing her best and fighting every day to make the world a bit kinder for animals, and there he was — a menace to society. He'd never disliked himself so much as he did in that moment.

He really was a total fucking moron of the highest degree.

* * *

Every so often Rick's warm fingers brushed against hers as he worked to cut the silly kitty free. He'd wrapped his first two fingers around the frame of the saw and edge of the blade, using them as a cushion so he didn't knock the metal against the wood as he worked. Angela really appreciated how much care he was taking over this rescue. It was things like this, and how he interacted so easily with her animals — and how they reacted to him — that she struggled to reconcile with the idiot who caused so much damage to her village, to herself and to some of the people she loved the most.

The way he thought about her animals' comfort was completely at odds with the so-cheeky-it-bordered-on-obnoxious persona that she saw in his videos. Not that she was following him or anything — she just thought she should keep an eye on what was being said, and to who, about Bill's and her. Obviously she scrolled past his other videos. Though not quite so quickly that she hadn't caught a few glimpses of Yvette, who looked like a supermodel in most of the videos — glammed up to levels that wouldn't have looked out of place on a red-carpet premiere. Far different from the glimpses of the track-suited, dark-glasses-wearing woman she'd occasionally seen drop Rick off before zooming away too fast in a bright red sports car.

'Done.' Rick lifted away the piece of wood that had trapped the cat, putting the saw to one side. Instead of sounding happy they'd finally wrestled the kitty out of its predicament, he seemed deflated. When she looked up, his eyes were darkened by some heavy emotion.

But she didn't really have time to think about it. Instead, she slipped a spare collar over the cat's head — last thing she wanted was to risk losing it to another dangerous situation — and gently unwrapped the cat, keeping a firm hand on the new collar.

She needn't have worried. The cat was calm as she examined her, and she was relieved to find no serious injuries. She gently scooped the cat up and slowly rolled it over to check the stomach, then grinned. 'Well, you were right. She is a little missy. And a very friendly and lucky one.'

'You think she'll be OK then?'

'Yes, I think she'll be fine. Just a bit dirty and dehydrated.' She turned the cat again and petted her, using the motions to wipe away the worst of the dust and dirt. Gently, she probed between the shoulder blades. 'And I think I can feel a microchip too, so we can get Jake to scan her and hopefully reunite her pretty fast with her family.'

'Good.'

Maybe she'd read him wrong, but after so much effort, Angela had expected a bit more enthusiasm at the success of his first proper rescue. He hadn't even mentioned videos or reels once. Maybe he was just tired and a bit overwhelmed. She tucked the cat back into her basket, where kitty kneaded the blanket for a few moments before flopping out, exhausted by her adventure. Maybe that was Rick's problem too.

'Angela? I'm sorry.'

She looked up, surprised at his words.

'I know it's not even close to good enough after what I've done to you, your friends and your community, but I really, really am very sorry. I know you probably hate me — you have every right to. I'm pretty sure I'd hate me in your position. But, if you're willing to let me, I'd like to spend every minute of the rest of my six hundred hours doing my very best to make up for even a small part of the hurt and distress I've caused you.'

What the fuck? The fact that she swore — even mentally — showed how shocked she was. He'd worked alongside her for three weeks, easily ninety or so of his hours — and now he wanted to apologise. What had prompted that? After years of working with animals, she prided herself on being quick to respond to surprises, but this one left her not knowing what to say.

'It's because of what I did . . . to you, and the café . . . that's why you don't like dark spaces, isn't it?'

Angela had to swallow hard before she could speak. 'Yeah, it is.'

'Like I said, I know it isn't even close to good enough, but I really am truly very sorry.' His eyes were earnest, with no trace of his usual cheek and swagger.

'I'm not going to lie to you.' Angela felt he deserved honesty. 'What you did really was shit.' She saw him baulk at her swearing. 'Yeah, that bad. And you're right, saying you're sorry isn't even close to good enough.'

'Angela, I—'

'No,' she interrupted, taking a deep breath. 'I think now it's my turn to talk.'

'Of course.'

'Just *saying* you're sorry — and especially in this case — isn't always enough. Sometimes people use it too easily, and it becomes a fairly meaningless platitude. But in this case, I think I believe that you really mean it. Because things like today—' she gestured to the cat '—things like how you are with Ernie, it means something. And I want to believe you when you say you're sorry.'

'I do mean it,' he promised. 'I know I have a lot of work to do, but I really will try to help you. And—' he took a deep breath '—I want to change for the better. Which is something I've never felt or said before. So, do you think you might be able to find me another five hundred or so hours' work at

Bill's? Even if it's just mucking out and chopping food and carrying stuff. I know you probably need time to think about it, but would you? Think about it, I mean.'

'I don't need to.' Angela already knew the answer. 'You're definitely welcome at Bill's.'

'Really?'

'Really.' She nodded firmly.

'Thank you.'

'Oh, you'll probably want to withhold your gratitude. I can line up *a lot* of chores for you.'

'None of them can be as bad as the ferrets' food and cleanup.' He shuddered, and Angela had to suppress a laugh. She knew exactly how gross that job could be.

'Seriously, thank you. I'm not going to let you down.'

'I believe that.' She took another deep breath and held her hand out to him.

He took it, wrapping his fingers around hers. They were warm and strong, and reassured her that she'd made the right decision.

'Hey, you got it out!' The homeowner skipped back down to them, and Angela couldn't help but notice that she'd changed and now wore a full face of make-up. No wonder the drinks had taken so long. 'Is it OK?'

'She's absolutely fine.' If Angela hadn't been looking right at him, she'd have missed the moment the slick, overly bright smile clicked into place. 'Did you still want to take some photos?'

CHAPTER FOUR

'But, baby, you're spending all your time with those dull animals.' Yvette pouted at him.

'Some of them are actually pretty cool. It was really awesome when we got the cat back to her family — the little girl had been really worried about her.'

'It's just a cat.' Yvette rolled her eyes. 'And you didn't even vid it.'

It hadn't seemed right to record a crying child — but he wasn't going to try explaining that to her, so changed tack. 'I didn't, but you saw how much love the one with Ernie got.' He grinned, thinking of his donkey friend. The way the donkey grinned, stomped and rolled his eyes, whistling whenever he saw Rick, made him feel warm and gooey inside. It was very clear he'd decided that he liked Rick, and wanted his attention. It was a little odd to Rick, used to only getting likes and follows in response to carefully planned, edited and sometimes even . . . not scripted, exactly, but maybe a little *staged* videos. Whereas he was sure Ernie didn't give a stomp about social media. When he'd tried to show Ernie his own video during a break, the donkey had hawed in what he was convinced was laughter, then mouthed Rick's hair.

'You're not even listening to me, are you?' Yvette stamped her foot. Rick struggled not to compare her behaviour to Ernie's, and briefly found himself thinking it was cute when the little donkey did it.

'Sorry, babe, I'm just tired.'

'You're always tired.' Again the pout. 'And you're no fun anymore. You just want to sit around and Netflix — you didn't even want to chill last night!'

'The sanctuary is hard work.'

'I thought you said it would just be cute fuzzy animals with lots of reel potential.'

He couldn't remember saying that, but wasn't in the mood to argue, so just shrugged. 'I guess I was wrong.' He shot her one of his best smiles. 'I have just had the best idea. Why don't you come down to the sanctuary one day? Then you can meet the animals and see some of the work Angela does. It really is quite amazing.'

'Can't you just quit?' She ignored him. 'It's not like they're paying you.'

He sighed heavily. 'You know I can't. It's court-ordered.'

'So?'

'So,' he explained very slowly, 'I have to do it. If not, they might send me to jail.'

'You'd probably be happier to see me if you were in jail.' She huffed and slammed out of the room, swishing her hair back and forth. He found himself thinking that she must have put a lot of effort into stomping up the stairs to make the lights rattle and flicker as much as they did. He sighed and opened up his computer to edit and upload his latest vids.

Barely ten minutes later the lights rattled again as Yvette all but threw herself down the stairs.

'I can't believe you! I can't believe you would let me go off upstairs so upset and not even bother to come after me!'

What the hell? 'Yvette, I thought you went upstairs because you were mad with me and didn't want to be near me. I was just trying to give you some space.'

'You want space from me? Is that it? What type of man upsets a woman and then leaves her to cry by herself?'

Even while he struggled to explain himself, part of him gave a mental thumbs up to her latest make-up sponsor. If she really had been crying — and why would he doubt her? — her mascara was still flawless.

'But if you really loved me, you wouldn't want to see me upset at all,' she reasoned, flicking her long extensions over her shoulder, doing that thing with her arms that made her boobs pop out.

'You're right, I'm sorry.' He reached out to her.

'Well come on then, you need to get ready.'

'Ready for what?'

'The club, silly. I'm going to go change, just as soon as the votes are in on which dress I should wear. They're both pink — natch — but so, so totally different. Maybe you could wear that salmon shirt I got you for your birthday. You know, the one with the zips and rips. It's just so on trend.'

'Yvette . . .' He pulled away, settling back into the couch that somehow managed to look a lot more inviting and comfortable than it actually was. 'I told you, I don't want to go out tonight. I'm really tired. And I need to be at the sanctuary on time tomorrow, and if you're giving me a lift . . .'

'Giving. You. A. Lift?' Her tone was vicious, her usually pretty face pulling into an ugly scowl. 'Why would you think I'd do that?'

'Because that was what you'd agreed. You said you'd be happy to help drive me around . . .'

'Yes, but I didn't mean like every day. I thought it would just be a couple of days with some content ops.'

'Nope. It's six hundred hours.'

'Ugh, that's so unfair!'

'Actually, I'm starting to think I got off lightly.' He thought back to the conversation with Angela — his stomach twisted again.

'What do you mean? The judge was mean. You should have just had a fine or something. You have so many more important things to do with your time.'

Did he though? He wasn't so sure after the cat rescue.

'Can't you just, like, make them some reels and get six hundred hours of views? That would work, wouldn't it? They'd still get their hours and you could come back to living a proper life with me. What do you think?' She pouted again, widening her eyes until she looked almost like one of the filters she used. 'Come out with me, and you can make content tomorrow, and then get your other hours . . . with your online presence, you could hit that in a few days.'

He didn't like to tell her he'd already done that — and more — with the video of him and Ernie pulling faces at each other. 'Yvette, I'm not going out tonight.'

'So you'll let me go out by myself, even though I'm really upset?'

'Sorry.' He shrugged, not really meaning it.

'Well I'm still going!' She snarled the words at him.

'Then, I guess have a nice night.' He reached for his phone, and she smacked it away, sending it spinning across the floor before turning on her heel and storming out. A few minutes later he heard the growling chug of a car — his car — start up and roar away. He shook his head and opened up his taxi app. Somehow, he didn't think he could rely on Yvette tomorrow, and he definitely wasn't going to let Angela down.

* * *

'Ready for some lunch?' Angela held up the bag she'd picked up from the village café. 'I've got cakes.'

'Don't have to ask me twice.' Rick finished stacking the dishes he'd been cleaning and washed his hands before joining her. Much to Angela's amusement, he almost inhaled the first half of the sandwich without pausing to speak.

'Guess you're hungry then?'

'Yeah. Sorry, I should remember my manners. My mum would give me a right clip round the ear. Thank you for this, it's bloo . . . ming good.'

'You're welcome.' Angela laughed, knowing how hard he found it to not swear, and appreciating the effort he made around her. 'I thought today deserved some sort of mark.'

'Really?'

'Yeah. As of about half an hour or so ago, you're one hundred hours into your time here.'

'Really?'

'Yeah.' She laughed at the look on his face. 'Did you not think you'd make it this far?'

'Honestly, no. At first I was just planning to try and figure out the quickest way out of it. And then, when the village council told me where they wanted to assign my hours, and then I realised who you were, I didn't think there was any way you'd want me here.'

'I didn't at first,' Angela admitted.

'What changed your mind?'

'Desperation,' she admitted. 'And some not-so-gentle nagging from friends. You know how physical it can be around here. I wasn't keeping up as well as I needed to be. Things were slipping. To be honest, in some ways they still are.' She didn't know what it was that prompted her to admit it.

'How do you mean? It looks pretty good round here.'

'It costs a lot to run Bill's. The fundraising work I do and events I run have almost all stopped at the moment.'

'Because of your injuries.'

'Yeah. Anyway, I don't want to talk about it now. I want to enjoy cake. Are you joining me? Or watching me eat two slices?' She got out the cake box.

'Depends on what cake it is.'

'Really? There's cake you wouldn't eat?'

'Not a big fan of carrot. The whole vegetable masquerading as dessert is just a bit wrong to me. And don't even get me started on beetroot or, worse, courgette in cakes.'

'Relax, it's Brockle cake.'

'And what's that?'

'A local speciality the Brockle's Paws café is famous for. It's chocolate and vanilla sponges, with a cherry jam, on a sort of pastry, shortbread base.'

'Sounds delicious.' He took the box happily and scooped out a chunk of the cake. 'Oh wow, that *is* delicious.'

'And probably like a thousand calories in every bite.' Yvette clipped into the too-tiny office, looking as made-up and glamorous as she did in the videos Angela tended to scroll past. From the high heels to the silky-looking dress and bright pink fur coat — which had blooming well better be fake! — Angela wasn't sure she'd ever seen anyone so *dressed up*, even at a party. She looked down at her tie-dye hoodie, slightly fuzzy after the attentions of the new baby badger who had come in — far too small to survive winter and in need of lots of feeding. It really was a different world she inhabited.

'Yvette, what are you doing here?' Rick had frozen, his cake halfway between box and mouth.

'I've come to see you, Ricky baby.' Angela had never actually seen someone pout and bat their eyelashes in real life. 'You did say I should come to this little place and meet some of the animals.'

'Did you, indeed?' She could feel her hackles rising. If she'd been a dog, her lip would be curled in warning. While she opened to members of the public to raise funds, she wasn't happy that Rick was issuing invites like he owned the place.

'Yvette was upset about how much time I'm spending here, and I thought if she could see some of the amazing work you do, she might be a bit happier,' he explained to Angela with an apologetic shrug. 'But that was last week.' He turned back to Yvette. 'And I didn't think you were interested. You did say no.'

'Of course I'm interested in your work, baby.' She purred the words and strutted over to wrap herself around Rick, climbing into his lap. 'And I wanted to meet this Anthea woman you're spending so much time with.'

'It's *Angela*.' She honestly didn't know why she bothered. She didn't really want to be forced out of her own office, but she'd already had enough. It was very clear to her that Yvette had wanted to check "Ricky baby" was behaving himself. Honestly, she couldn't have been any more obvious than if she'd peed or pooped in front of Angela, marking Rick as "hers" like Ruby would have.

'Look, apart from the guineas,' Angela added, 'none of my animals are pets. If you try to stroke them, they may well bite. That's the only warning you're getting.'

'Oh, I'm sure Ricky will protect me,' she simpered as Angela hopped off as quickly as her crutches allowed. If she didn't get away from them she was in danger of regurgitating her lunch.

* * *

'I thought you said there were lots of cute animals.' Yvette pouted and stomped her foot. 'All the ones you've shown me smell.'

'They were only cleaned a couple of hours ago.'

'Well they still smell!'

'They're animals. What did you expect?'

'Can't you, like, spray them with something? They make doggy deodorant and breath mints. Can't you give them some of them.'

As much as Rick thought Ernie and his jennets might like some mints, the thought of making such a suggestion to Angela terrified him. 'I'm not sure Angela would like that.'

'I'm not sure it should be up to Anthea.' Rick rolled his eyes, ignoring Yvette's comment. He didn't like her when she got catty. 'Anyway, where are all the cute animals? Like the puppies and kittens.'

'It's not really that type of rescue centre,' he tried to explain. 'It's a wildlife rescue. Angela only takes in cats and dogs when there's no other option.'

'Well where are all the baby animals? The sweet little chicks and bunnies and things?'

'Most birds have finished nesting and are fully feathered and flown off by now, and the bunnies are fully grown rabbits. We have some hedgehogs who are a bit small.'

'But you can't really snuggle a hedgehog.'

Rick bit back a sigh, starting to feel a bit frustrated with her unannounced visit. But he knew arguing, or logic, rarely worked with Yvette — she'd spent too much of her life doing what she wanted, when she wanted, and being spoiled by everyone around her. He had to admire her confidence, but if he was honest with himself . . . it could get a bit grating at times.

'What about Ernie? You've not met him yet.'

'The funny donkey who got you all the views? Yay!' She did a happy dance, clapping her hands together like a little girl, skipping along as he led her through the courtyard. He couldn't be sure, but for a moment he thought he heard Angela snort with laughter. But by the time he turned to look at her, she was busy feeding the guineas, stooping over their "garden".

'Ernie?' Rick whistled and clucked his tongue in his best impression of donkey talk — he was not going to heehaw in front of Yvette! — and grinned when the little donkey stuck his head into the barn. 'C'mere, boy. I've got someone who wants to meet you.'

Ernie, displaying typical donkey stubbornness, stomped his hooves and snorted loudly, but didn't move any further.

'C'mon, mate.' Rick whistled again. 'I've got an apple for a well-behaved donkey. Do you know any well-behaved, polite donkeys who might like an apple?' He grinned when Ernie trotted happily towards him, his ears pricked forwards. 'Here you go, mate.' He handed the apple over, rubbing his fuzzy ears while Ernie chomped happily and messily.

'It smells funny.' Yvette wrinkled her perfect, purchased nose in distaste.

'He probably thinks you smell pretty odd too,' he replied without thinking.

'What the fuck does that mean?' She snapped, glaring at him.

'Just that he probably hasn't ever smelt couture perfume before,' he tried to recover.

'True enough round here.' Yvette laughed. 'And I bet they don't even know what caviar crème is.'

Rick wasn't sure that he knew what it was either, but so long as she was distracted and happy, he wasn't going to argue. It was just easier for everyone that way. Instead he petted Ernie, scratching the bridge of his nose the way he liked best. Ernie whuffed at him, shuffling his feet and edging closer.

'Hello, smelly donkey.' Yvette stuck her hand on his mane then yanked away. 'Ugh, he's not very soft, is he? Maybe they need more conditioner.'

'I don't think they use conditioner.'

'That'd be the problem then.' Yvette rolled her eyes and looked around. After a few seconds of fiddling with Ernie, she turned and boosted herself onto the fence, her heels scrabbling against the floor. 'Take some footage for me, babe.' She shoved her phone at him, already attached to a mini-tripod.

Whatever made her happy. He stepped back and took a few stills while Yvette posed and pouted. 'Ernie!' He whistled and the little donkey turned to look at him. Perfect. 'OK, reel in three, two, one . . .' He was pretty sure Angela was watching them from across the yard, but he didn't want to turn to look at her. He wasn't at all sure how Angela would react to even more videos of Ernie — particularly ones not featuring him. He wasn't worried about Ernie at all, not when the donkey so happily posed and showed off whenever he had a camera pointed at him.

At first, Rick had felt silly trying to explain things to Ernie — but after the success of the first video he'd felt like he owed the donkey that much. So he'd shown him some reels and some of the comments he'd gotten, politely asking if he'd liked to do more — in exchange for bellyfuls of carrots and apples and plenty of itches. He'd been worried trying to talk to the animal like he was human would make him feel like the ass, but Ernie had appeared to listen, before hamming it up on camera even more than before.

Yvette preened in front of the camera, hitting all her best angles like the pro she was. After a few more photos, Rick balanced the tripod at the right height, hit record and leaned back against the wall, watching.

She tossed her hair, flicking her extensions around. Irritated by the hair in his face, Ernie tossed his own head back and forth. Ignoring the donkey's discomfort, Yvette wrapped her arm around his neck, squashing herself against him, her hair swinging back and forth across Ernie's eyes and irritating his sensitive ears.

'Yvette, maybe we should stop.' He didn't like the way Ernie was starting to shift back and forth, and the way he was rolling his eyes.

'Why? This is brilliant.'

Ernie disagreed — tossing his head to shake off Yvette's enforced affections — but because Yvette was who she was, and not good at taking hints, she automatically tightened her grip, ignoring Ernie's grumbly huff.

'Yvette, that's enough.' He didn't get more than two steps forward before Ernie, agreeing with him, stepped firmly back. If Yvette hadn't been balanced so precariously, or holding on so tightly, or if — for the first time in as long as he'd known her — she'd being paying attention to another being's feelings, it might not have been so bad.

* * *

Angela jumped up at the squeal that echoed from the courtyard. The action sent shards of pain screaming up her leg, but she grabbed for her crutches and hobbled outside to see which animal was in pain. What she didn't expect to find was

73

a screeching blonde sitting in the donkey pen, howling and squealing while Ernie stomped and huffed, stuck in the corner between the fence and Yvette, his eyes rolling and sides heaving. Rick was between them, trying to calm the scared donkey while Yvette clawed at his legs.

'Ernie!' Angela sent an ear-piercing whistle across the courtyard, hoping it would cut through the racket and panic. Thankfully, Ernie at least had the sense to listen, his heavy grey head swinging to look at her, pleading in his eyes. 'C'mon boy,' she flung the crutches down and leaned against the fence, placing one hand along the side of his muzzle, pulling him towards her as she stroked up and down the bony length of his nose, making soothing noises. She really hoped it would work, because her balance was still dodgy — if Ernie pushed in the wrong direction, she'd probably end up on the floor, likely injuring herself further.

'Sort her out, would you?' She forced herself to keep her tone calm and even, despite feeling anything but. She knew she should have felt some level of sympathy for Yvette, but she was making a ridiculous fuss and — worse — she was terrifying one of Angela's animals, and potentially undoing years of work.

She kept her whole focus on Ernie, petting and soothing and trying to reassure the terrified animal, while Rick tried to reason with his girlfriend, before giving up and manhandling her out of the pen, depositing her none-too-gently on the floor.

'Is he all right?'

'I think so.' Angela coaxed the donkey closer to her, so she could run a soothing hand along his sweat-soaked withers. The poor little thing was shaking. 'It's just bad memories, isn't it Ernie? You know you're safe here, don't you?'

'You're worried about *him*?' Yvette screeched, breaking what seemed to be Ernie's last nerve and sending him bolting out of the barn. As much as Angela wanted to run after him, she knew he'd be all right with his jennets, and it was more than likely that he'd had enough of people right now. Especially as Yvette clearly hadn't finished her histrionics. She tried to find some sympathy for the woman who — despite being only a few years younger than Angela, according to her online profile at least — was behaving a lot like a child having a tantrum.

She clung to Rick, who had sunk to his knees, and sobbed against his shoulder, meaning Angela struggled to make out more than the odd word as she fumbled to pick up her crutches.

'He didn't mean to scare you,' Rick soothed, stroking Yvette's hair and trying to calm her.

'Scare me?' Yvette choked the words out between sobs. 'He tried to kill me!'

'Don't be silly. Why would he want to hurt you? Donkeys don't even eat meat.' Rick tried to reason. 'Tell her, Angela.'

Ugh, she so didn't want to be drawn into this, but the look Rick was giving her was pleading, so she muttered something vaguely agreeing.

'See?' He stroked Yvette's hair.

'It dragged me into that . . . pigsty, and tried to stomp on me,' she whined.

'What exactly did happen?' Angela asked, needing to understand to figure out what had upset Ernie so much. And how she could try to undo any damage the blithering idiot might have done.

Yvette hung off Rick's neck, tugging at him as she whimpered and fussed. As much as Angela wanted to help, she was worried her temper would only make things worse. She didn't know why she found it so much easier to show kindness to animals than some people. Then again, animals rarely tried to con her out of anything more than the odd extra treat. Not that she was accusing Yvette of that — even in her head — but she couldn't help but notice, for all the noise the woman was making, her make-up was still better than Angela's would have been if she'd spent an hour trying to follow a tutorial. If she'd been as upset as Yvette was acting, she'd have snot and tears all over the place.

She shook her head, trying to understand the mumbled, breathy gasps.

'You're fine, baby. Nothing happened. You're OK.' Rick soothed before rolling his eyes at Angela. Apparently he was used to this behaviour. 'Yvette was posing with Ernie, and I think he'd had enough of being a social media star. She was sort of hugging him while sitting on the fence, and when he stepped backwards, she toppled in. But—' he stroked her hair again '—no one got hurt. You're fine. Ernie's fine. It's all OK, isn't it?'

'He could have kicked me,' she argued.

'But he didn't,' Rick reassured, sticking up for the donkey.

'He tried to,' she insisted.

'I highly doubt that.' Angela stuck up for him. 'Ernie is one of the gentlest creatures. I'm sure he wouldn't have tried to hurt you. He was probably just scared.'

'Why would he be scared of me? He's the huge, vicious animal!'

Angela sighed, feeling the nagging of a headache behind her eyes. 'The only thing Ernie poses any danger to is carrots. And my neighbour's apple tree when he escaped last year.'

Yvette ignored her, still clinging on to Rick. 'Baby, will you please take me home.'

'Of course.' He shot a helpless look at Angela. 'Is that OK?'

'Of course . . .' She didn't even get to finish before Yvette interrupted with a screech.

'Why are you asking her? Why would you listen to her instead of me!'

'Well, she is kinda my boss while I'm here.'

'It's fine. Really.' Angela was more than happy to have Yvette far, far away from Bill's before she could upset any more of her animals.

'See, baby. She said it's fine. Not like you needed permission. Take me home now,' she demanded.

'OK. Thanks, Angela.'

'Humph!' Yvette snapped upright and stomped across the courtyard. She got halfway to the gate before spinning on her high heel. Angela had to admit she was impressed. She'd barely be able to stand in shoes that high, let alone perform a manoeuvre like that without ending up on her backside. 'Come on, baby. I need you to drive me home.'

'I can't drive you anywhere, babes. Driving ban, remember?'

'But I'm upset!' She stamped her foot hard on the cobbles, and Angela saw Rick wince as Ruby shot out of her favourite napping spot, blurring into a russet streak in her eagerness to get away from the squawking, screeching, stamping human. Angela couldn't really blame the fox for wanting to escape — she was already seriously regretting not locking the gate.

'You can't expect me to drive when I'm this . . . this . . . traumatised!'

'Then I'll have to call for a lift,' Rick offered.

'Don't be silly. You can just drive me. It's an emergency.'

Angela bit her lip, trying not to lose her cool with the woman acting like a spoiled brat. As much as she wanted to read her the riot act, she suspected it would only make her squeal louder and upset even more of Bill's residents. They needed calm, understanding and peace — not the blonde banshee act.

'I don't think my probation officer would see it like that,' Rick tried to mollify.

'So don't tell him. Duh.'

Angela actually felt bad for Rick. And incredibly awkward, trapped watching the conversation — and partly involved, thanks to him — unable to figure out how to extricate herself from it without drawing Yvette's attention and putting herself in the line of fire.

'It's not really that simple,' Rick argued, sounding tired.

'If you loved me, you'd drive me.'

Youch. If Angela had thought she'd felt awkward before, she needed a new word to describe how horrifically embarrassed she felt now. She wished she could freeze and disappear into the foliage like so many of her birds could. Or that the ground would open up and swallow her whole. Either would do, she just really wanted the conversation and situation to be over with.

* * *

Rick stared at Yvette, struggling to figure out how to placate her this time. Usually he gave in to her demands — it was easier than arguing and putting up with her sulks — but he wasn't willing to break the law for her and give the judge a chance to make good on her threat to have him locked up. It would be so *easy* to give in to Yvette — like he had done a thousand times before — but this time he could feel Angela's eyes on him, and knew she was waiting to see what he was going to say and do.

And much to his surprise, he found himself caring about what she thought. She wasn't just another Rickhead, following his videos and posts, or a sponsor paying to tell him what to think, or at least what to say publicly. But Angela? Despite how badly he'd hurt her, she trusted him with her precious animals. With Ernie, who was loving and trusting despite the background Angela hinted at but wouldn't discuss. Oh crap, he really hoped Yvette — and he, by his own hesitant inaction — hadn't done anything to hurt his grinning, gentle donkey friend. Oh, he really might have screwed up.

He felt awful. He couldn't remember the last time someone had trusted him with anything more important than some product they were flogging.

'Well?' Yvette stared at him, her foot tapping on the floor.

He looked at her — so, so beautiful and perfectly made-up — and looked back to the now-empty space where Ernie, with all his scruffy smelliness, had bolted from. Ernie, who trusted him and asked for nothing more than clean bedding, food and water, and in exchange gave him so much love. The way the little dude would whinny and whistle and race to the fence to meet him did something funny to his stomach. Oh shit, he hoped he'd be forgiven.

'*Well*.' Yvette's tapping grew louder and more impatient as she folded her arms, pushing her tits up as she did so. 'Did you hear me?'

Something inside him snapped. 'Yeah, I heard you,' he answered coldly.

'So, let's go. Take me home.'

'You know what, Yvette? No. I'll happily call you a ride, and make sure you get to your place safely, but afterwards I need to come back. I'm working here.'

'It's not like it's real work.' She pouted. 'And she said you could go.'

'But she still needs help and, actually, I think this might be some of the "realest" work I've done in years.' And he still had to work out how to apologise to Ernie, but he highly doubted that would be a smart thing to say.

'If you loved me, you'd drive me home *now*.'

How many times had she done that to him? Brandished the phrase "love" around as if it was a weapon? And, more to the point, how many times had he let it work? So desperate to please her and not upset her, he'd done things that were against his better judgement, often causing him trouble. It had been Yvette who begged him to stay out the night before the accident — not that he blamed her, it was his fault, and he was willing to take responsibility for that, but this time it was all on her.

'Then I guess maybe I don't. I'm sorry, Yvette.' As harsh as the words were to say, they felt incredibly true. 'If you loved me, you wouldn't ask me to break the law,' he told her mildly. 'And you'd respect my decisions. As I said, I'm happy to call a ride and make sure you get home safely, but afterwards I'm coming back here. To work.'

The screeching noise Yvette made was hideous and filled with anger. A few weeks ago he might have called it animalistic, but even a scared cat screaming for rescue hadn't sounded so awful as she did. 'You have no idea what you're doing. This is your last chance, *Rick*,' she snarled.

'Actually, I think I do.' Rick stood firm. 'I think it's best if you leave here.'

'Oh, believe me, I'm going.' She stormed out of the gate, sending it crashing back against the wall.

Rick let out a long breath he hadn't realised he'd been holding. He turned to look at Angela, suddenly feeling incredibly embarrassed. She shouldn't have had to witness any of that, and he worried what she was going to think of him. He was pretty sure her opinion of him was already far from the best.

'Are you OK?' She watched him with wary eyes, like she was approaching an animal she hadn't had time to win over yet.

'Huh. I think I might have just broken up with my girlfriend.' Saying the words aloud just sounded weird.

'I . . . um . . . hate to say it, but I think you might be right.' Angela pulled a sympathetic face.

Rick winced as he heard his car, with all its beautiful, expensive engineering, screech out of the road. Maybe he should have demanded the keys back, but he wasn't that much of a bastard — regardless of what Angela probably thought of him.

'I'm really sorry you had to see that.' He shook his head, feeling embarrassment scorch his cheeks.

'It doesn't matter.' Angela shrugged. 'And it wasn't exactly your doing. To use your own words — do you need a hug? Because you look like you do.'

'You know, I think I actually might.' He wasn't sure what surprised him more: that she'd offered, or that he really wanted to take up her offer.

She held her arms out to him, and he had the odd experience of being wrapped in a fuzzy rainbow that smelled warmly of hay and something sweet — a bit like the summer picnics he remembered from childhood. Only without the ants. She squeezed him tightly — warm, firm and yet oddly soft in his arms. She was all curves and warmth against him, compared to the bony angles, gym-honed and surgically perfected firmness of Yvette.

He felt instantly bad for having thought it, but it was one of the best hugs he'd had in ages. Angela didn't flinch or pull away, or get distracted by someone else walking by who just "had to be greeted", or stop to flick her hair and worry about her angles in case there was a photographer nearby. She just hugged him — worried about nothing more than making him feel better.

The lump that had started when he'd realised how much he might have upset Ernie returned, doubling in size and threatening to choke him.

When she pulled away, she didn't immediately smooth her clothes or pull out her phone. Instead she just looked at him, one hand still resting on his forearm. 'You OK, or at least as OK as you can be?'

'All things considered, I think so.'

'Right. Then I think it's time for a brew. You in?'

'Yeah, please.' He hesitated, remembering an obligation. 'But I need to go and apologise to Ernie first.'

The smile she gave him filled him with warm approval. Obviously he'd done something right. 'I'll put the kettle on. You know where the carrots are.'

* * *

Ernie had lived up to the phrase about how stubborn mules could be — and it had taken Rick a lot longer than he'd expected to get the little donkey to begrudgingly accept the carrots from him, and even longer before his ear scratches were permitted again.

When he'd finally made up with Ernie, and apologised to Angela again — who'd just waved it away — it was getting late and he had to wait longer than usual for his ride home. But not so late that he couldn't call one of his favourite people in the world.

She answered on the fourth ring. 'Hey, bro, how's it going? You behaving yourself and not bothering the local cops?'

'You do remember that you're the younger sibling, right, Moggy?'

'Ugh, don't call me that. And don't ignore my question. Are you staying out of trouble?'

'Yes, I promise I'm behaving. I'm not even drinking all that much.'

'Seriously?' His sister sounded impressed.

'Yeah,' he promised.

'And how are you getting on with all the animals? Been chased by any crazy kittens yet?'

'Hey, that thing had sharp claws — and I was only ten. And I was wearing new jeans.'

'It was a kitten, Ry-no.' Imogen cackled. 'A sweet, fluffy little kitten — the type that people put in teacups and take pictures of.'

'Shut up, Moggy.'

'You called *me*.' Her laughter echoed through the phone. 'Seriously though, how's it going?'

He thought about it for a few seconds before answering, picturing Ernie's grin, and the way Ruby bounded over so cheerfully to greet him.

'It's going good. I've not been chased by any kittens, but I did help to rescue a cat.'

'Really?'

'Yeah. It got stuck under some raised decking.'

'Poor thing.'

'It's all right. We got her out and reunited with her family. Cute little girl was very, very pleased to get her back. And I helped release a moorhen who needed antibiotics and rest after she got hurt.'

'Wow, sounds like you're really making a difference.'

'It's a lot more fun than I'd expected,' he mused aloud. 'And . . . um . . .' He hesitated. 'I sort of broke up with Yvette today.'

'Oh wow. I'm really sorry to hear that.' Anyone else might have believed her — but other people hadn't known her as long as he had.

'You almost sound like you mean that.'

Her huff of irritation made him smile, and he could picture her rolling her eyes. 'Fine. I'm sorry that you've had another relationship not work out, but I'm not going to suddenly pretend that I liked Yvette. You know it's not my style to lie. Especially to you.'

"Yeah. You're annoyingly honest.'

'I prefer to think refreshingly so,' Imogen teased him. 'How are the parentals?'

'You know, you could call them yourself and ask.'

'But asking you is so much easier, and so much less likely to cause arguments. I didn't stop loving them. I just . . . don't really know how to talk to them anymore. It's easier to leave it to birthday cards, texts and whatever and just asking you. Last time I actually spoke to them, Dad asked me when I was going to come to my senses. It's the twenty-first century — you'd think they could try to be a little more open-minded.'

'I know, Moggy.' As much as he adored his parents, he was still torn over how badly they had treated his sister when she'd introduced her first girlfriend. 'But they're OK. Plodding along. Planning another holiday and grumbling about work. Same old, really.'

'Yeah. They don't really change much, I guess.'

'No. So . . .' He changed the subject. 'How's your love life? Met anyone gorgeous to fall in love with yet?'

'No. Mine's about as quiet as yours just became.'

'Ouch. You wound me!'

'Easy target. Besides. My wanderings were more about figuring out what I want to do next and finding myself, rather than finding a relationship with someone else.'

'And how is that quest going? You are looking after your-self, right?'

'Yes Ry-no.' He could hear the frustration in her voice, but that didn't stop him asking. She was his little sister, and that was more than enough reason to look after her, before considering other things. 'I'm looking after myself perfectly fine. And I'm still enjoying pottering around the country. How are you taking to country life? You've been quieter online than you usually are. Everything OK?'

'Yeah, it's fine. I'm actually quite enjoying things. Bill's — that's the name of the sanctuary — is hard work, but at the same time it's a calm and quite soothing place to be. I can understand why the animals like it here.'

'Yeah, I saw the grinning donkey video. Is he really like that or did you get lucky?'

'Nope, he's really like that. I've made friends with him and his mini-harem of donkey girls. And a fox.'

'A fox?' Imogen laughed.

'She chases toys and begs for treats, a lot like a dog. You know, if you came down, you could meet them,' he wheedled, hoping the lure of meeting wild-ish animals would entice her into visiting.

'Maybe. My contract runs for a few more weeks, then I have another one lined up in Yorkshire after that — then a few weeks on the south coast.'

'You're really enjoying this whole nomad-finding-your-self-thing aren't you?'

'I really am.'

He settled back into his seat. 'Go on then, tell me what you've been up to.'

'You know, same job, different patients, different days. Doesn't matter which physio team I'm working with, there's always a couple of patients who seem to "forget" their exercises the second they walk out the door, always at least one who pushes too hard too soon, and the one who doesn't want to listen.'

'Gold star pupils?'

'Yeah, I've got a few nice ones as well.'

'And how's the complementary side going?'

'It's good.' He could picture her smile as she got started on one of her favourite topics. 'I've been allowed to practice it a bit more up here — the lead therapist here is experienced with reflexology so happy for me to recommend. And I've started selling some more spell bags and crystals online.'

'And you'd sell a lot more if you let me do reels about you.' It was an old argument that he knew the answer to, but he wasn't going to stop trying to help her.

'And I told you before that I really want to do this myself, at my pace — I can't keep up with your speed. I'd probably make myself ill trying.'

'OK, OK. Tell me more about the slow lane then.'

CHAPTER FIVE

Angela grimaced as she looked out the window at the rain cascading down in a torrent. It felt like it had been raining non-stop for the best part of a week, and she hated it. It was only just November, but winter had well and truly landed with a vengeance. The rain had turned the courtyard into a slippery rink that threatened to dump her on her behind every time she had to cross it.

Her jacket dripped over the washing-up bowl in the corner of the room, and she sighed as Ruby slunk in, bringing a pungent, musty damp smell with her. Angela wrinkled her nose and slid slowly and carefully to the floor, holding out an old towel to the grumbling vixen.

'Come on, you and I both know you hate being wet,' Angela coaxed. 'Almost as much as I hate you being wet indoors. Please be a nice girl and *don't* shake!' She just about got the towel over the little fox before she grinned and shook. 'You really can be a brat, you know?' She laughed as she briskly rubbed the little fox dry while she squirmed happily, rolling on the floor and enjoying the attention for a few minutes before deciding she'd had enough, letting Angela know in her usual, ungrateful way — a growl and nip at her fingers. She flopped out in front of the stove, filling the small room with her pungent foxy funk.

It had to stop raining soon. Even the ducks had had enough.

* * *

The rain lashed down hard, flooding out the small roads as the drains gurgled, struggling to handle the ongoing downpour. The news had threatened storms, and to Rick it felt like the clouds were trying to dump an entire season's worth of rain onto the little village in a few days. He'd splodged his way up the path to Bill's, regretting his expensive shoes that seemed no more effective than sandals at keeping his feet dry. He'd gotten drenched the day before in trainers, so had switched to boots that had purported to be "all weather, all terrain". A good sales line, but a terrible product. He'd already realised they were much better for posing in than actually using. He wondered if he'd somehow used them wrong, but that was ridiculous. How could anyone use boots incorrectly?

He squelched into the office and peeled off his equally expensive jacket. At least his top half was dry. He was glad he'd taken Angela's early advice of stashing a bag of clean clothes in the office — changing might be the only way he could stay warm and dry today.

'Hang it over the bowl.' Angela pointed to the corner where, sure enough, the washing-up bowl was now in position under a hook. 'I'll stick the kettle on.'

'Thanks.' He set about taking off his shoes, grimacing at the feel of the wet laces. Sure enough, his socks were soaked through, so he peeled them off, wrung them out into the bucket, and shoved them next to the coat to dry. 'What is that *smell?*'

'That would be madam ungrateful.' Angela flicked a finger towards Ruby, lying spread out in front of the flickering wood burner, her white belly spread out towards the ceiling. 'You could always shove your socks in the washing machine.

I've got a load of cloths and towels to go on this morning,' Angela offered.

'No, it's fine thanks.' He dreaded to think what had dirtied the towels, but at Bill's it probably wasn't anything too pleasant. 'They're hand-wash only, anyway.'

'Hand-wash socks? Are you serious?'

'Cashmere.' He shrugged.

'You hand-wash your socks? What, like in the bathroom sink?'

'No.' He laughed. 'Dry cleaners.'

'Wow.' She shook her head at him. Really slowly. 'Coffee?'

'Please yes. It's been a bit of a day already. My ride was late, apparently some of the roads flooded and the detour was a huge traffic jam.'

'Still no sign of Yvette then?' He couldn't help but notice Angela busied herself with the kettle, not looking at him as she asked.

'No. I've not seen her since her visit here. She did text me though. My car is being delivered and she wanted her things back. She said she's going to stay with a friend while she "gets over me". Some friend called Jean with a yacht off some Greek island or somewhere. Corfu, maybe. They go away like this pretty often.' He didn't really care. Eight months of dating, and apparently all he deserved was a brief message nearly a week after she'd stormed out on him. He suspected that if he didn't have one of her favourite, limited-edition handbags in his flat, he wouldn't have heard from her at all.

He wondered what it meant that he wasn't particularly upset. Sure, he missed the fairly energetic sex, but in honesty his agent had seemed more upset than he felt at the split.

'Cashmere socks, yachts and Greek islands.' Angela shook her head. 'A far cry from instant coffee and stinky damp fox.'

'Yeah.' He laughed. 'For someone so cute, she is pretty pongy.' But despite that, he surprised himself by realising that he actually wouldn't change anything today. Well, apart from the road-flooding rain and maybe some air-freshener . . . not that Angela would let him spray the little vixen. But to pet and play with a wild fox? That was pretty awesome, and worth a bit of discomfort. Besides, the Rickheads *loved* her. Then again, they didn't have to smell her!

But the video of him throwing a ball for her, and getting her to do tricks like sitting, speaking and shaking "paws" on command — in exchange for bits of sausage — had drowned out any speculation regarding the picture of Yvette's skinny knees and perfectly polished toes against a backdrop of the Med. He supposed he should be grateful for that.

The most hideous noise echoed around the courtyard and into the office, freezing his thoughts in their tracks. Rick glanced at Angela, waiting for her reaction to understand his own. It sounded like something was being murdered, but he'd already learned — courtesy of the foxes — that sometimes the most horrible of noises was "normal" around animals. But the worry paling her face didn't do much to reassure him.

The sound was followed by a weird shrieking, not unlike a car alarm, before reverting back to the hideous screeching that made the hairs on the back of his neck stand up. Ruby shot across the small room, bolting to her favourite hiding spot behind Angela's desk.

'What the he . . .' He caught Angela's glare and quickly changed his tune. '. . . Heck. What the *heck* is that noise?'

'I don't know. But I can't imagine it's anything good.'

Rick grimaced as he shoved his bare feet back into his still-wet shoes, following Angela outside. He grabbed the umbrella from by the door, doing his best to hold it above Angela's head. When she shot him a grateful smile, he just shrugged. He was already pretty damp anyway, and it wasn't like she could easily manage the umbrella with her crutches.

They found the source of the noise at the end of the driveway: an old crisp box, already collapsing in on itself from the rain. Angela struggled to kneel down, hampered by her crutches and the slippery stones beneath their feet, and shot him a pleading look.

'You're kidding me.' He shook his head and made a point of holding the umbrella a little higher. He was there and he was helping, but he wasn't sure he fancied sticking his hand into a dark, collapsing box that was howling like something out of a horror film.

She rolled her eyes, carefully balancing herself against the wall, and nudged the lid of the box open with one end of a crutch. An angry growl emanated from the box, followed by dark, evil-sounding muttering.

Rick stared at Angela, his eyes wide in horror as his heart pounded. 'If you believe in karma and things like that, do you believe in evil and demons too?'

The box let out another screeching yowl, and this time Rick definitely heard swear words.

'I didn't.' Angela swallowed hard, then shuffled closer to the box, before it told her, in a grating and squeaky voice, to drop dead. 'But I'm starting to think we should have grabbed a cage.'

'I suppose it's too late for me to volunteer to go back and get one?' Water dropped off the brolly to land in his collar, trickling coldly down his neck.

'You suppose right.' She shook the water out of her hair. 'Right, I've had enough of this. On three?' Her eyes locked with his.

Damn it. If he said no now, he'd be admitting to having less cajónes than a woman on crutches. He had far more pride than that, so he took a deep breath and nodded.

'All right then. One.'

'Two.'

'Three.' She flipped the flaps of the box open, and leaned back.

Dark scaly talons gripped the edge of the box, followed by a vicious looking hook attached to the strangest looking creature Rick had ever seen. It grumbled and hissed before snapping at Angela, who had stooped to look at it.

'What the hell is that?'

'I think it's a parrot. A very wet and bald one.' She reached towards the alien-looking thing, then yanked her hand back when it snapped and hissed at her.

'Are you sure?' It looked like an oven-ready partridge to him — far too small and too grey looking to be a chicken. If not for the wet clumps on the head and dirty feathers sticking out from bony wings, it would have been completely bald.

'Yes, see this hooked beak . . . ?'

'The one trying to take lumps out of you?' He manoeuvred the umbrella so he could crouch to look at the thing without smacking Angela in the head. As soon as he was near the hell-creature its demeanour changed — it tilted its ugly head on one side, as if looking at him from underneath a messy mop of something.

'Yeah.' Angela laughed. 'Only parrots have hooked beaks like that.'

'Eagles have pretty sharp, hooked beaks.' He was sure he'd seen that on a nature reel.

'Different shape. Parrots' are much broader and stronger, so they can bite into nuts. Raptors tend to have much smaller, sharper beaks for tearing into flesh.'

'Wonderful.' He shuffled his feet. 'So now we've established that it's a probably-parrot, can we go back inside and dry off?'

'I'm not leaving it here. Poor thing must be terrified. And freezing.'

'I wasn't suggesting we should.' Despite what she might think of him, he wasn't that heartless. 'But can't we just grab the box or something?'

'I'm pretty sure that disgusting thing will disintegrate when I touch it. And there's no way it can fly when it's this wet and partly bald. If the box collapses, it'll hit the ground hard. We're going to have to pick it up. Poor critter must have been here for hours. Didn't you notice it on your way in?'

'Obviously not.' He'd had his head down, ear buds in, too busy trying to drown out some of his misery to take notice of his surroundings. He felt a little guilty — if he'd been a bit more focussed he could have brought the thing in sooner. 'Can't you just grab it or something? I'm getting cold.' If he hadn't already been feeling it, her glare would have frozen him through. 'I meant, I'm getting cold and I've got a coat on. Unlike this . . . thing.'

'You're not a thing, are you? You're a gorgeous parrot, aren't you? Don't listen to the silly man.' She reached out to the bird again, making little cooing noises as she did so. The thing seemed calmer and edged towards her. 'Come on, sweetie, let's get you inside and we can warm you up and give you something nice to eat.' The little "Sweetie" edged closer still, and Angela slowly petted the mess that passed for feathers on the top of its head. 'There, there, it's all going to be OK . . . it's all going to be — *sugar-plum fairies and custard! Gerroff!*' she screeched as it chomped down on her thumb.

'Hey!' Without thinking, Rick dropped the umbrella and shoved his fingers into the sides of the hell-bird's beak, pressing hard at the point when skin met . . . whatever beaks were made of . . . He glared at the bird like it was a hostess who had messed up his reservation at the latest must-be-seen-at joint. 'Enough of your nonsense. *Behave!*' Much to his shock and relief, the critter released its grip on Angela and dropped its head into his hand. Was it snuggling with him? A bright black eye peered up at him, and for a second he could have sworn the thing purred.

'Well, it seems to like you better than me. I don't suppose you want to try picking it up?'

He hesitated. No, he absolutely did not want to pick up that demon-chicken with the huge beak, which it was obviously more than happy to use. He looked up at Angela, cradling her bitten hand against her chest, and had a sudden flash of worry. Exactly how strong was that beak, and how much damage had it done to her and her usually quick, nimble fingers that were gentle enough to hand-feed tiny baby mice?

He sighed, knowing he didn't really have a choice.

He pulled his coat sleeve as far over his hand as he could, and tucked his fingers into a tight fist, hoping it would make it harder for the bald devil to get hold of him. 'Come on, you ungrateful brat.' He channelled his sternest former teachers. 'Up you get, and no more of your nonsense.' *Don't bite me, please don't bite me.* He repeated the mantra in his head while offering his wrist to the hellion hen.

Much to his amazement, and slight horror, one scaley foot followed the other to step onto his wrist. He stood up slowly, gingerly, not wanting to disturb what had to be the ugliest living creature he'd ever seen. And, judging by the way Angela was still cradling her hand, one of the meanest. 'Are you all right?'

'It's not bleeding too badly, but I'm not sure I can bend my thumb. Hardly surprising as someone here—' she leaned closer, giving him a whiff of that oddly compelling sweet-hay scent that she seemed to carry with her '—tried to crack my knuckle like it was a walnut.'

As soon as she was close enough, the featherless heathen lunged for her again, beak wide and hissing like an angry snake, and Rick had to fumble to keep it from crashing to the floor. Not that he wasn't sure it would have been deserved. Angela was one of the nicest people he knew, and this . . . goblin of a thing . . . was attacking her, dancing up and down and lunging and cackling.

If he'd stopped to think, he would never have done it — it was utterly stupid — but as usual he didn't think, instead acting on the instincts that had so often led to him doing stupid things. He tapped it hard on the beak. 'Stop it, you. We're trying to save your ungrateful, naked butt. If you keep biting I'll put you back in the box to freeze or drown. I mean it.' The fugly thing froze, its head tilted to one side as it looked at him, appearing to think. After a moment it wriggled its creepy wings and edged along his arm to sit in the crook of his elbow, looking up at him.

'Right, looks like it's decided it likes you. Let's get back inside where we can all dry off and warm up. And hopefully we can find something to feed it other than my hand.'

* * *

Angela eyed the parrot warily. She needed to examine it, but had the feeling it wasn't going to be an easy task. It seemed quite content sitting on Rick's elbow, mouthing — or beaking — his jacket. She didn't know all that much about parrots — a visit to Jake would definitely be in order — but she did know birds, and knew this one needed help. She needed to check it over for injuries, warm it up and find something to feed it to start with.

'Right, let's be having a look at you.' She approached the bird slowly, one hand tucked behind her back and the other stretched out, palm up so her fingers couldn't be mistaken for claws or talons. After all, parrots were prey animals. As soon as she was within range, the bird lunged at her, hissing and snapping at her fingers. 'OK, towel it is. Sorry, but I need to look you over properly.'

With a deftness brought on by years of practice, she dropped the towel over the hissing, bobbing head and soon had the bird swaddled up, pinning the wings gently so as to avoid injury. The bird was a lot stronger than the ones Angela commonly dealt with, and it put up more of a fight than the moorhen — wriggling, squawking and muttering dark, rude words.

'Can I help?' Rick reached out for the angry bundle and snuggled it back against him, laying it against his arm as if it was a baby. 'Now come on, you, stop your silliness. Angela's just going to take a quick look at you and make sure you're OK, then we'll find you something nice to eat. And besides, you're soaking wet. We need the towel to dry you off. I might not know what you are, but I'm pretty sure you're not a duck!'

To Angela's utter shock the bundle stopped swearing and started making happy clucking noises. 'What did you do?'

'Don't know.' Rick chuckled. 'But it seems to have worked.'

'Right, as you seem to be the chosen one, want to help?'

She watched as Rick thought about it, staring at the bird before looking up at her and nodding slowly. 'Tell me what to do.'

'All right.' He followed her instructions, carefully unwrapping bits of the bird, keeping it happy and calm while she examined its feet, wings and head. The poor thing looked skinny to her, but she wasn't sure how an almost-naked parrot should look. But she did know the bloody red hole under one wing was wrong in any bird.

'Do you think she'd been attacked by something? Do we need to take her to your vet friend?'

Angela wasn't sure when Rick had decided the bird was a hen, but she wasn't going to argue. He'd been right about the cat. 'I think she does need a visit to Jake, but I don't think it was a cat or predator that's had a go. I think this is self-inflicted, sadly.'

'She's done this to herself?' His eyes were wide and pained. 'Animals can self-harm?'

'Yeah, they can. It's not uncommon with parrots, sadly. Especially if they've been abused or neglected.'

'You mean someone made her so miserable she attacked her own skin?' Rick's voice had dropped to a low, dangerous level.

'Sadly, yes. She probably pulled her own feathers out too.'

'If ever I meet the person responsible for causing her so much pain, I'm probably going to end up with a lot more than community service.' He carefully unwrapped the towel, and grinned when the parrot walked up his arm and snuggled back against his chest.

'Can't say I don't share the sentiment, but let's not tell Harry, OK?' She winked at him. 'I think the local constabulary have enough to worry about without telling them things like that!'

Rick laughed with her, and once again Angela found herself pondering on how much he'd changed.

'Guess I should give Jake a call, see if he can fit her in today.'

'When you take her, do you think I could come too? I mean, I understand if you don't want me there, but . . .' He peered down at the parrot who had stuck her head inside his jacket. 'I know it sounds stupid, but I think she might want me there.'

Angela laughed. 'I think you might be right. And I'm not going to argue with anything with a beak that big!'

* * *

'Parrots are not my speciality.' Jake popped the bird back in the carry crate they'd transported her in, and she immediately waddled to the corner nearest Rick, climbed up and hung off the bars nearest him, demanding his attention with clucks and whistles.

'Hush. I'm trying to listen, to learn about you.' He stroked one scaly foot, feeling oddly protective of the fugly creature.

'Well, it seems to have taken to you.' Jake pursed his lips as he watched Rick.

'She.' Rick couldn't help it.

The vet laughed. 'Even I can't tell. Cockatoos aren't sexed visually. Few parrots are. Some people think you can tell with eye colour, but if that's true I'm not experienced enough to do it. We'd have to do a DNA test to know for sure — unless it decided to lay an egg.'

Rick shrugged, feeling a bit silly.

'Then we might as well call her "she". It's better than "it", isn't it?' Angela shot him a wink.

'Fair enough,' Jake agreed.

'You said she's a cockatoo. Can you tell what kind? There's more than one, isn't there?' Rick asked, casting his mind back to a recent visit to a zoo where they'd filmed reels. He wished he'd spent more time paying attention, and less time acting like "Maverick". He would have valued the information now. He wondered if he might be able to get some help from some of the keepers there. Then again, he'd been a bit of a pain in the arse and he wasn't sure how happy they'd be to hear from him again.

'From her crest, I'd say she's a Moluccan cockatoo. They're the only ones this size with pink feathers.'

'How is she?' Rick worried over the bird, who had clearly been through so much, but still nibbled his fingers so gently. It was crazy that he was letting her so close to him when he'd seen what she'd done to Angela, but he found himself trusting her. Plus, she was so damned ugly she was actually kind of cute. It didn't make sense to him, but then again neither did those stupid handbag dogs that so many of Yvette's friends carted about. He personally thought most of them looked more like overgrown, shaggy rats than dogs — but they cooed over them like they were babies. Which was how he was starting to feel about the half-bald bird — not that he thought it was a baby, obviously, but certainly something he felt oddly protective of. 'Angela thought she'd done this to herself.'

'Sadly, she's probably right.' Jake washed his hands before sitting at his computer. 'Parrots aren't easy pets to keep. At least, not to keep happy and healthy. Some people think they can just shove them in a cage and look at them. But in reality, they're very, very clever creatures who need a lot of love, understanding and care. We'll need to find a specialist rehab for her. There's a couple of good avian vets I've consulted with in the past. I'll pull their numbers for you, and they can direct you to an appropriate rescue centre. In the meantime, I'll print off a proper diet sheet for you.'

'Thanks, Jake.'

Rick didn't bother to listen to much more of the conversation. Instead he picked up the little cage containing the fugliest animal he'd ever seen, itching her head through the bars. 'Do you hear that? We're going to find a specialist who can properly look after you and get you better.' He knew he was probably imagining it, but for a few moments those big eyes — which he now realised had dark brown irises and weren't completely black — looked sad. But it would be fine. She needed a proper expert to help her, and that's what they would find.

* * *

Two days later, Angela watched as Rick bounced the cockatoo up and down on his arm, the thing cackling and bobbing her head as she whistled and blew kisses.

'See, she likes this game,' he told Paul, the man from the parrot sanctuary. 'I think maybe it feels a bit like flying does.'

'Quite possibly.' He nodded.

'And you're sure you can help her?' Rick asked again as the bird he'd nicknamed Chicken-butt hopped up his arm to rub her beak against his cheek.

'It's not the first cockatoo we've had like this. And once it's been tested for viruses and quarantined for a few weeks, it can be released into one of our aviaries, and go about learning how to be a happy bird again.'

'Sounds good.' Angela nodded, happy to have the little biter going somewhere she'd be properly cared for. She and Rick had done their best for the last couple of days, but it was very clear the bird didn't like her, and they weren't really set up to deal with parrots at Bill's.

'Do you think she might fly again?'

'It's possible.' Paul nodded. 'I've seen other birds in similar condition learn. If it stops picking, the feathers could start regrowing in anything from a few weeks to a few months, if it hasn't damaged the follicles. But it's usually a long process, and not all of them recover fully. But, whether it doesn't or not, it can live happily with us. Right, do you want to step up for me?' He held out his wrist, but the bird backed away, edging around Rick's neck and to his other shoulder. 'All right then, can you pop it in the cage for me, please?'

Rick did as he was asked, pushing the cockatoo gently but firmly down his arm and into the waiting cage, which he had to admit looked a lot sturdier than the wire crates they'd been using.

'Thanks, Paul, it's a relief to be handing this one over to a specialist.'

'Not at all.' He offered Angela a handshake that was dry, but slightly limp. 'It's been nice meeting you. Next time someone asks me what to do with a fox or donkey in need of a home and rehab, I'll know who to call.'

'Sounds fair to me.' Angela laughed. 'And thanks for coming all this way to collect her.'

Paul shrugged. 'A hundred-mile round trip seemed easier for me than you. And I've driven further for smaller birds. Hope the leg gets better soon.'

'It already is, thanks.' She waved the man and bird out of the door. 'Well, that's one good job well done.' She turned to Rick. 'Are you OK?'

'Yeah, just . . . I dunno. Feeling a bit sad to see her go.'

'You know, Paul's much better qualified to care for her than you or me. And she'll have other bird friends in a few weeks.'

'Yeah, I know.' He sighed heavily, still looking miserable. 'And it's the best thing for her. I know that. But . . . do you think she seemed a bit reluctant to go? I felt like I was having to really shove her into that cage.'

'Would you want to be pushed in a little travelling box when you didn't know where you were going?' Angela reasoned. 'It doesn't look nice, but it really is the safest way for her to travel.'

'I suppose so. And Paul was very highly recommended by Jake's colleague.'

'Just still feels a bit miserable, doesn't it?'

'Yeah.' Rick shoved his hands deep into his pockets.

'The good thing about this, over other rescues, is you can always call Paul in a few days and see how she's getting on. We don't get that when it's hedgehogs or moorhens being released.'

'No, I guess not.'

'And, maybe when she's settled, we could go visit.' Angela didn't know why she'd made the offer, but the way Rick's eyes lit up, she knew it was the right thing.

'Really?'

'Sure. Fifty miles isn't that far, and I'd quite like to see these aviaries Paul mentioned. Maybe I'll get some ideas to improve the ones here.'

'Yeah, maybe.' Rick had gone back to being quiet and pensive again.

'Hey, this really is a good outcome for her,' Angela promised, wanting to see Rick's smile again, but not fully understanding why it meant so much to her.

'Yeah.' Rick was still looking at the floor.

'Hey.' Angela rested her hand on his shoulder. 'This really is for the best.'

'I just never expected to get so attached to that bald chicken-butt so fast.' He looked at her hand on his shoulder, then up at her. When his dark eyes locked on hers, a shock of heat flared through Angela. What on earth was that about?

Thankfully, Rick didn't seem to notice, shrugging and heading towards Ernie's pen.

* * *

Three days later, Rick looked up as Angela joined him in the food prep room, a solemn look on her face that worried him. He'd seen her happy, angry, sad, scared and when she was concentrating — focussing all of her attention and efforts on an animal — but he'd never seen her looking quite so . . . defeated.

'Rick, can I have a word?'

'Sure, what's up?' He washed his hands, skipped around Ruby, who was trying to wrap herself around his ankles like a cat, and headed over to where Angela was standing. The closer he got, the more his stomach churned with worry. The way she held herself, the look on her face . . . worry flooded him. 'Seriously, Angela, what's wrong?'

'I've had a call from Paul at the parrot rescue. It's not good, Rick.'

'My little cockatoo mate? What happened?'

'Paul and his team aren't really sure. But she's refusing food. Their vet can't find anything wrong to explain it. They've crop-tubed her twice — force feeding her — and they're going to try that for a couple more days, but if she doesn't start feeding herself soon . . .' She shrugged sadly.

'If she doesn't start feeding herself soon then what?'

Angela took a deep breath. 'Then they'll let her go.'

'What does that mean?' He had a good idea, but surely it couldn't be what he dreaded to think.

'It means they'll put her to sleep. I'm sorry, Rick.' Her hand was warm on his forearm, but he yanked away, not wanting comfort right then. 'You have to understand, if she can't or won't eat, she won't have any quality of life. It's kinder just to let her go gently.'

'She was eating fine when she was here with us,' he argued, wanting there to be some sort of mistake. 'Hell, you saw her stealing the biscuits off my plate.'

'She ate with you. Me she just bit. It could be that shock and infection set in, or something like that,' Angela guessed. 'It just happens sometimes.'

'Right. Thanks for letting me know.' That seemed the polite thing to say. 'I'll go finish off with the donkeys.' He didn't wait for her reply before storming away. It was so bloody unfair. The little bird had been so sweet — with him, at least — and lively and funny. She'd been through so much, and finally found somewhere that she should be safe and loved, only to give up and die. It was just so fucking stupid.

He dragged his hand across his burning eyes, before angrily stabbing at the donkey's hay and chucking it into their pen, breaking up the bale with vicious jabs. He dumped the food into the trough, not caring that half of it ended up on the floor. He was pretty sure Ernie and his jennets would take care of it.

'I'd be lying if I said it got easier when rescues don't work out the way we hope.' Angela was waiting for him when he stomped back into the shed. 'But it does get . . . I don't know . . . more bearable.'

'It feels pretty damn awful.' He shoved his hands into his pockets. 'I just don't understand what's happened.'

'We don't always get to understand.'

'I'm not sure I know how to accept that.' He sighed, then made his decision. 'Would it be a huge pain in the a . . . behind if I finished early today? Obviously I'll make the time up. There's something I need to do. Somewhere I want to be.'

'Are you sure you want to do what I think you're going to do? It probably won't change anything except make it harder for you.' The gentle sympathy in her eyes made him realise that she really did understand.

'Yeah, I think so.'

'All right. I'll call Paul. So long as you're sure.'

'I am.' He was already opening the app to arrange a car. 'Thanks, Angela.'

* * *

Rick didn't really know what to expect from another sanctuary — but the parrot rescue was a lot different from Bill's. Instead of the cute, converted home that he was used to, the Parrot's Perch was a huge, custom-built site with a visitor's centre, café and at least six aviaries he could count at a quick glance.

'We've been here for close to fifty years,' Paul explained when he met Rick at the entrance. 'We've got around thirty people working here, all in, plus more volunteers, and somewhere around three hundred birds — depending on the season.'

'Wow.' Rick's mouth gaped open as he watched a couple of bright red macaws swoop down, one skimming the top of Paul's head, who just laughed and carried on walking.

'As you can see, we free fly a lot of our birds too.'

'Don't you worry about them flying off and getting lost?'

'No, we acclimate them slowly, and they know where the food is. And they have caged roosts at night to protect against predators.'

'What about the threat from eagles and things? Wouldn't they try to hunt them? I mean, it's not like they camouflage well here.' Rick followed him past another large aviary, an area where more parrots than he'd ever seen before hopped around branches and ropes, squawking, whistling and chatting loudly. He didn't know parrot body language, but if it had been Ruby or Ernie, he would have said they were showing off for their human visitors and begging for treats.

'The trees give good canopy cover, so raptors can't see the birds to attack. And if they did get down here, they'd struggle to take off again. As you can see, there's plenty of people around. Our parrots love people, it's great mental stimulation for them — wild raptors don't.'

'I guess.' Rick wasn't convinced, but what did he know? The setup was impressive, and busy — on another day, he might have been thinking about reels and content for his channel, but he was too worried.

'How's . . .' He hesitated, not wanting to call her Chicken-butt in front of this busy, experienced professional. He already felt silly enough having trekked there, when clearly they knew far more about what they were doing than he did. 'The bird. How's the cockatoo?'

'Not doing well, unfortunately. It happens sometimes.' Paul frowned as he stopped at a door and punched in a code. 'This is one of our clinics. We have another over the far side of the park for injured birds and babies. This one is mostly used for quarantining rescues. Your bird is in here.' He picked a few things off shelves by the door and handed them to Rick.

'These go on over your clothes, shoes and hair. And you'll need to disinfect on the way out. When you're dressed, knock on the window and our duty worker will let you in.' He checked a clipboard. 'It's Nancy in today.' He tapped on the window and waved at the woman working in the small room.

'You're not coming too?' Looking down at the stack of protective clothing, he started to feel really nervous.

'No, I've got a staff meeting in ten minutes, so don't have time to garb up. Besides, we try to keep these rooms quieter. When you're done, out the door on the other side, and make sure you follow Nancy's instructions.'

'OK.' Rick nodded. 'And Paul? Thanks. I know you're busy, and I appreciate this . . .' He trailed off, not quite knowing what this was. A chance to say goodbye? He didn't know, but it did matter to him.

'Not a problem.' Paul grinned. 'And if you ever want to visit on a less sad occasion, as your Maverick self, just let me know. We could always use a bit more help with exposure and attracting donations.'

Rick nodded, feeling quite proud that this busy, important person knew who he was. Clearly he was doing better expanding his brand than he'd realised. Perhaps world-wide domination wasn't that far behind, and maybe even a chance at the Influencer Marketing Awards would be within his grasp. 'I will do.' It was the least he could do.

'Great. And if it's a weekend or school holiday that would be even better. It's my daughter, you see. Apparently she'd be the envy of her entire year if she could get a selfie with you.'

'Of course.' He made sure not to let the Smile fade. 'How old is she?'

'Thirteen.'

Yeah, that sounded about right.

He pulled on the long white coat, faffed a bit trying to get the plastic shower hat thing on, before realising it was one of a pair of shoe covers — idiot. He finally got things the right way on and tapped on the window.

'Hi.' A woman buzzed the door, letting him in. 'I'm Nancy, one of the aviculturists here. I understand you're here to see the little cockatoo?'

'Yeah.' Rick nodded and held out his hand. 'I'm Rick.'

'Nice to meet you, but you'll have to forgive me the handshake. Disinfectant gel is by the door — and be liberal with it please.'

Rick did as he was told, covering his hands in the pink, acrid gel. 'How's she doing? I mean, I know it's not good, but did you get her to eat at all?'

'I'm afraid not.' Nancy sighed. 'I've crop-tubed her this morning, but she didn't fight me too much — which isn't a good sign — and she hasn't really shown any interest in anything. Nothing has come back on the blood work, and we didn't find anything in the droppings either. There's a few tests outstanding — like the PBFD one, but we don't think it's that.'

'What's that?'

'A particularly nasty virus, and the main reason we're both in protective gear. It's called psittacine beak and feather disease. It's a bit like HIV in that it destroys the immune system of birds, making them susceptible to lots of other diseases. Only there aren't really any treatments, and it can spread through their droppings, even feathers or dust, as well as bodily fluids.'

She must have seen the look of horror on his face. 'But don't worry. Like I said, we don't think it's what she's got, and it's only a problem to parrots. It can't hurt you. All this—' she gestured to their gear '—the hand sanitiser, the shoe wash you'll walk through on your way out, and the air purifiers in here are all to protect our other birds. Thankfully, it's quite rare in the UK, but sadly not unheard of, and potentially devastating to a sanctuary like this, so we take precautions very seriously.'

'That makes sense. But you don't think that's what she has?'

'No.' Nancy shook her head. 'She doesn't have any obvious symptoms. Her beak, claws and skin — apart from under her wing — look fairly normal, and the pattern of feather loss combined with her wounds look more habitual than disease-led. Are your hands dry yet?'

'Yeah.' He held them up to show her.

'And you're sure you want to do this?'

'Yes, please.' Rick nodded firmly. 'I know it's silly — but I just wanted to . . . I don't know . . .' He didn't have the words to finish the thought he barely understood himself.

'It's not silly. These birds, they're special . . . I think more so than other animals. They're so incredibly intelligent and loving, and they sneak their way into our hearts and change us somehow. I'm glad that, after everything this little one has been through, there's someone who cares about her enough to want to make a hundred-mile round trip to see her, who feels as bad as you do that she's losing her fight.'

'There's really nothing more you can do for her?' Rick had to ask one more time, even though he felt a bit guilty doing so. Especially when Nancy sighed sadly.

'We've been trying to get her to eat since she got here. All the usual foods and some treats. We've changed bowls, tried spoons, had other birds eating at the same time on the other side of the window, and tried playing videos in case she was lonely. I've even sat in here with my lunch in the hope it triggered her interest. We could try anesthetising her and X-raying, but there's no guarantee she'd survive the procedure at this point, or that we'd find anything we can treat. Our vet is reviewing her tomorrow, but he's questioning quality of life at this point.'

Rick nodded, glumly. He knew what that meant.

Nancy held open another door for him, and a blast of warm air hit him. 'She's in here.'

'Thank you.'

At first, he didn't see the bird in the large, wide cage in the corner of the room, filled with toys and perches. She was huddled in the corner on a fuzzy cushion, facing away from the room, her scrawny, mostly bald wings loose against her sides, her head flopped down on its side. He could see her ribs and tail moving with every breath — but that was the only sign of life. He had to swallow hard twice before he could speak. How could this pathetic scrap of feathers and skin be the same obnoxious bird who had sworn so gleefully and made Angela yelp with nips.

'Oh you poor little bald Chicken-butt.' He laced his fingers through the cage bars. 'This just isn't fair. Why have you stopped eating, you silly thing? Don't you realise you're in the best place possible? You could be so happy here if only you'd try.' It was stupid to be so upset. He'd only known this ugly bird a few hours, and his life wouldn't change at all if it died tomorrow. If he hadn't been forced to volunteer at Bill's he wouldn't have even met her. But in that moment, he wanted nothing more than to see her chowing down on some food, or hear her mutter dark, evil-sounding noises and rude words. He had to close his eyes against the burning tears he didn't want to shed in front of a stranger.

He didn't see the dark brown eyes blink slowly open, or the little head bob up and down a couple of times. He didn't see, or hear, the little bird wobble slowly across the cage, using her beak to pull herself the last couple of inches to shove her head under his fingers.

'Oh, Chicken-butt.' He rubbed his fingers through her velvety crest of feathers. 'You are a sorry-looking state.'

The bird nibbled his finger gently, and tilted her head to one side to look at him, then whistled softly.

He turned to Nancy — who was watching, her eyes wide with shock. 'Can I get her out? Maybe try to feed her?'

'Umm, yeah. Feel free. But try not to get your hopes up too much. The only way we've gotten her to eat so far was forcibly with a syringe.'

'Doesn't sound like much fun.' Rick opened the cage and stuck his hand in, and was gratified to see the bird try to stand a little taller. 'Hello, you bald, ugly chicken.' He rubbed the few feathers she had on her head a couple more times, before resting his hand on the bottom of the cage.

After long, painful moments the bird looked at him and very, very slowly lifted one scaley, grey foot onto his wrist. She stretched out, digging that big, black beak into his sleeve and using it to hoist the rest of her skinny self onto his arm. Moving very slowly, scared of unbalancing or scaring her, he lifted her out of the cage and cradled her against his chest.

'Hello, Chicken-butt.'

The bird mumbled and muttered, turning herself slightly to bury her head in the crook of his elbow, and he felt the lump in his throat grow, threatening to choke him. She muttered some more, and he leaned in closer to try and hear what she was saying.

'Fuckerfuckerfuckerfuckerfuckerfucker.'

Rick burst out laughing. 'Still got no bloody manners, I see.' He turned to Nancy. 'Got some of this food she's been refusing?'

'Sure.' She handed over a dish.

'Right, you bad-mouthed, poorly mannered, bald little chicken, are you going to behave yourself and try eating something now? Because right now it wouldn't even be worth plucking what's left of your feathers to roast you, you're so scrawny. Honestly, the size-zero heroin-chic look hasn't been in fashion since the nineties. It's just so uncool.' He picked some of the mush out of the bowl and shoved it in front of the bird's beak, already knowing what was going to happen.

'Wow.' Nancy breathed the word. 'I've heard of parrots bonding to someone so strongly that they refused food from other people, but I've never actually seen it. How long did you know her?'

'Not even three days.' Rick shook his head and hooked out another blob of food.

'You're kidding.'

'Nope.'

'Fucker,' Chicken-butt growled happily before shoving her beak into the dish, smothering herself and Rick in the mush.

CHAPTER SIX

Rick looked at the heavy-duty carrier sitting next to him and wondered, for about the hundredth time in the last few days, what the hell he was thinking. He was wearing clothes he'd bought — much to his surprise — from a supermarket, which had been the only place still open when he'd left the bird park, and had spent a small fortune online having a list of items the length of his arm special-delivered to his flat.

After two days of joyfully watching Chicken-butt pig out on everything he'd offered her, and — heartbreakingly — reject food from every other source, Rick had given up and spoken to Paul and Nancy. After much discussion they'd reached an agreement, then spent the next day giving him a crash course on everything they could think of that he needed to know to care for a parrot.

Angela had been incredibly understanding about him missing days at Bill's, and had even gone so far as offering her login details to one of her suppliers, so he could get the charity rates on some of the equipment he apparently needed. He'd refused — feeling guilty because he could easily afford it — but was still shocked at the total. After the past couple of days he was well aware parrots were special creatures with specialist care needs, but he couldn't help wondering if the same was true for a lot of Bill's residents, and how Angela managed to cover their bills.

When finally he paid the driver, stumbled out of the lift on his floor and let himself into his flat, it was dark and he was knackered. He nearly brained himself tripping over a large box, fumbling with the cage and bruising his arm so as not to drop his expensive, new, pain-in-the-butt pet. She showed her gratitude by chomping down on his finger. Hard.

'Knock it off, you arse.' Rick balanced her on the sleek console that held his expensive — mostly designer — shoes and flicked on the light. Stacked up semi-neatly were large boxes. He'd have to send some chocolates or something to the building caretaker for making sure they got to the right flat.

He looked at the boxes again, a sinking feeling hitting his stomach. None of them looked big enough to be the cage he'd ordered . . . unless . . . oh shit, cages came flat-packed? He sighed and dragged one of the boxes towards him. Yep, just as he feared: cages didn't come pre-assembled. He rummaged around his random crap drawer hopefully for a few minutes, before sliding down the wall to sit on the floor, admitting defeat. He knew damn well he didn't own a screwdriver anymore. He used to be good at things like this, but lately he'd just paid people to do the stuff in life that he considered "boring". Who was he kidding, bringing the bird here? He couldn't even manage the basic task of sorting out a cage. What the hell was he supposed to do?

'Shitty shit fucker shit.'

'You said it, Chicken-butt.'

* * *

Angela was just peering into her freezer, trying to figure out what to throw at the microwave when her phone rang. She glanced at it, hoping she wouldn't need to go out this evening. 'Bill's Sanctuary.'

'Hey, it's me.'

'Hey, Rick. Are you and the ungrateful little biter home and settled?'

'Sort of.' He sighed.

'Long day?' She'd never heard him sounding so down.

'Yeah, and still not over. Umm, can I ask you something without you judging me too harshly?'

'Sure.'

'I'm pretty sure I know the answer to this, but there's no chance I can leave Chicken-butt in the travel cage overnight, is there?'

'I'd advise against it, unless you really have no other choice. Oh—' She closed the freezer as a thought hit her. 'Did your delivery get messed up?'

'No — well yes, sort of. I didn't realise the cage would arrive flat-packed.'

'Oh dear, is it missing parts?'

'I don't know. I don't think so.'

'What's the problem then?'

'I have no idea what I'm doing! I'm in way over my head, I have no idea why I agreed to bring her home. I've got no idea how to look after her, or what I'm supposed to be doing and when. I don't even know how the hell to build her bloody cage.'

'All right, take a breath.' Angela let the swearing slide and focussed on getting to the root of the problem. 'Cages look a bit unwieldy, but they're really simple. So long as you know how to use a screwdriver and spanners, you're pretty much fine.'

'And if you don't even own a screwdriver?'

'You're kidding, right?'

'You're judging me, aren't you?'

'No, no, not at all,' she lied. 'I was just surprised, that's all. You were so good getting the cat out . . .'

'I learned messing around in my dad's shed years ago. Using his tools. But I haven't really bothered with anything like that in years. It's easier just to pay someone else to do it.' He hated admitting how useless he was nowadays. 'Do you see what I mean? I don't even own a basic toolkit. How the hell am I supposed to look after a special-needs cockatoo?'

'Surely a neighbour or someone has a toolkit?'

'Yeah, I guess . . .' He didn't sound very convinced. 'You said these things are really easy, right? I've never tried to build anything like this . . .'

'Yeah. Did you look at the instructions yet?'

'I did. They're all in Chinese. And German. I think I saw Spanish or French, and maybe Danish too. Pretty much every language other than the one I need. I guess I can try a translation app on my phone . . . and see if I can borrow a toolkit.'

He sounded so defeated that the words jumped out of her mouth before she'd even realised she'd thought them. 'Do you want me to come over?'

His sharp intake of breath made her think she'd overstepped the mark. 'Are you serious, Angela? Because if you are, that would be amazing.'

'Message me your address.'

'Do you really have time for this?'

'Yeah. I was just about to make some food.'

'I'll order in,' Rick offered. 'At least I can do that, right? Chinese, Indian, Italian, Greek, Turkish . . .'

'Anything veggie and not too spicy,' Angela interrupted before he could run through the United Nations of food options. 'If it's my choice, I'd pick aromatic over hot.'

'I think I can manage that. But are you sure you've time for this?'

'Yeah, it's fine, Rick. You've just agreed to take on a bird who, with all good luck, will be with you for years. I think I can spare a couple of hours to help set you up and make sure your first few nights go well. Besides, takeout and cage-building sounds like a better Friday night than the microwave meals and paperwork I had planned.' And the misery of her budget.

'Well, if you're sure . . .'

'I am.'

'Thank you, Angela. As much as you hate me calling you this, you really are something of an angel.'

'Hush your silliness and go order some dinner,' she ordered him, thinking that maybe she didn't mind being called "angel" quite as much as she'd complained about before.

* * *

Rick met her in the underground car park. 'I really can't thank you for this enough.' He took the heavy toolbox out of her car and guided her to the lift.

'Wow, this is really *nice*,' Angela exclaimed.

'I suppose it's OK, for a lift.' He looked around.

'It has parquet flooring and what looks like walnut inlay. And uplighters.'

He'd been about to reply when they reached his floor, but a horribly familiar noise echoed through the lift doors and bounced around. Bloody hell, how loud was she? As soon as the doors opened, he raced down the corridor and flung his door open.

'It's OK, it's OK, we're here, we're here. You don't need to scream the whole building down. Please hush.' He opened the crate and had to fumble to catch the bird as she launched herself at him, scolding, puffing up the few feathers she had, muttering rudely.

'Guess she really doesn't like that cage.' Angela leaned against the wall in his hallway.

'I guess not. Please, come in.'

'Thanks.' She took a few steps in, then hesitated. 'Wow, this place really is amazing.'

'Thank you.' Rick smiled proudly. 'It's one of the first things I bought when I made it big as Maverick. Well, that and the cars.' He grinned again. 'Here, can you hold Chicken-butt while I get the toolbox?' He handed the bird over, ignoring the squawks of complaint from both of them.

By the time he got back, the bird was on the console, and Angela was cradling her hand.

'She bit you again? I'm so sorry. I'm going to have to work out how to train her. Bad Chicken-butt!' He scolded the bird.

'I'm not sure scolding her afterwards will work. She probably doesn't realise what she's done.'

'Oh, if she's smart enough to choose who she accepts food from, I think she's smart enough to learn this concept. You—' he tapped the bird on the beak '—do not bite people. Especially Angela, who's here to help build your cage so you can stay with me. You should apologise to her.' He glared at the bird, who waddled from side to side, clacking her beak as she shifted from foot to foot.

'Rick, I don't think she understands.' Angela started to look a bit awkward.

'I think she can. And if she doesn't yet, then she can learn. Paul says they're easily as smart as a three or four-year-old child. And kids are old enough to understand.' At least, he thought they probably were. He stuck his hands on his hips, remembering what Nancy had said about birds fluffing up to look bigger when they were facing off for a fight. 'Say you're sorry to Angela.'

He felt like a complete idiot, standing off against a bird who didn't have a clue what he was doing — if Angela was right, and she usually was about things like this. But something inside him told him he was right, and now he'd committed. He'd look a real tit if he backed down. So instead he glared at the bird, waiting for it to respond. After a few, painfully long moments in which he questioned his sanity, Chicken-butt tilted her head and let her crest fall back into its relaxed position. After a few moments more, she sidled up to Angela and whistled softly, then blew a couple of kisses and bowed her head for itches.

'Wow, did that actually just happen?' Angela reached out a slow, wary finger and gently ruffled a few feathers. 'Oh! She's so soft.'

'There's a good girl, Chicken-butt.' She ran back towards him, fluffing her crest feathers and bobbing her head. He held out his hand and she ran up his arm to his shoulder.

'I can't believe that just happened.' Angela laughed, stepping closer to look at the bird. So close that he could see flecks of blue deep in her eyes. 'But are you really going to keep calling her Chicken-butt?'

'I probably should think of something better,' he mused, still distracted by that blue . . . or was it turquoise? . . . playing at the edge of her pupils. 'I just hadn't really thought about it.' He was hit by another pang of guilt. No proper cage, no previous experience and not even a proper name. There was no way he was the right person for this animal.

'Hey.' Angela rested a hand on his arm, the warmth from her palm soaking straight through his jumper to his bare skin. 'If you're doing what I think you're doing, you should stop right now.'

'And what do you think I'm doing?'

'Starting to panic. Maybe even feeling a little guilty. Thinking you're in over your head.' If she'd read his mind she couldn't have been more accurate. 'You might feel like you don't know what you're doing, but she does. I've seen it happen a lot with rehomes, when an animal picks their humans. There was one just a couple of months ago, a very sweet little Jack Russell who a friend offered to foster while I was recovering. I'm pretty sure he's going to be staying with her and her family now. This bird . . . whatever you're going to call her . . . has made it very clear that you're her choice. She trusts you.'

'But what if I fu— screw up?'

'You probably will. You're going to make mistakes. Just try not to make them terrible ones and she'll probably forgive you. What do you think, pretty bird?' She reached out her hand again, but backed off immediately when Chicken-butt hissed at her. 'OK, so I'm only allowed to touch you on your terms. I can respect that.' She laughed good naturedly, but Rick found himself staring at the spot where her hand had rested on his arm, already missing the contact.

'I guess we should get on with madam's cage,' he said.

* * *

115

'What about Rosie?' Angela asked as she lifted the last panel into position — the cage was now nearly as tall as she was.

'Well, she's definitely got some thorns about her.' Rick grinned as he started bolting the panel into place. 'What do you think, are you a Rosie?'

The rude noise from the bird made Angela laugh. They'd been trying out different names, calling them out to the bird for most of the time they'd spent building the cage — although it was so big Angela thought an aviary might have been a better description. She was pretty sure she could lie down in it without braining herself — if she'd wanted to try.

'Don't think she likes that one.' Rick laughed. 'What about Nugget?'

Angela laughed. If a bird could have rolled her eyes, she was sure this one would have. 'Peony?'

'What's that?'

'Another flower. Usually pale pink with lots of fluffy petals.'

'So you're basically just naming after pink plants?'

'Well, you said Paul and his team thought there was a good chance she'll grow her feathers back, in which case she'll be pink.' It made sense to her.

'I'm not sure I think she's very floral though . . .' Rick looked at the bird, who watched them with interest from the spot she'd claimed on the sofa in the large living room. 'What do you think, Chicken-butt? Are you a pretty flower?' The bird cackled in answer.

'That sounded like a no to me.' Angela laughed.

'Yazoo?'

'Like the milkshake?' She screwed up her nose.

'Yeah? Actually, maybe not. What about Floss, like candy floss?' He pulled over a box filled with perches, ropes and toys, and Angela winced, mentally totting it up. It didn't look like Rick had spared any expense in this setup. She was pleased he was taking things seriously, but part of her was a little jealous — she only wished she had these sorts of resources when it came to Bill's.

She set about securing some of the perches in place, bouncing them up and down to check they would be safe to hold the weight of a cockatoo. 'I've got it. What about Flump?'

'Like the marshmallows?' Rick tapped two perches together thoughtfully.

'Pink and fluffy . . . and not a flower.'

'I like it. But I'm not sure it's quite right. What do you think? Are you a pink fluffy marshmallow?' The bird hopped along the counter, then started to whistle. 'Well, I think she likes it. But it might be a bit of a mouthful . . . or a beakful. It would be nice if she had a chance at learning to say her name, and maybe a few words that aren't rude.' He glared at the bird who clucked and bobbed, rattling her beak in parrot laughter. 'What about Mallow? Do you think you might be a Mallow?'

He had to dive across the room to catch the bird as she launched herself off the counter.

'I guess we have a winner?' Angela asked, giggling as the bird bounced up and down excitedly, trying to climb onto Rick's head.

Rick caught her and lifted her down gently before offering her a treat. She crunched on it happily, and he offered another — but as she reached for it, he tossed it into the open cage. 'Go on, our food will be here soon, and you might as well get used to your new cage. You can't be hopping around like you own this place. There's far too much trouble you could get into.' The bird — Mallow, he had to get used to that — eyed him suspiciously before walking slowly down his arm and stepping delicately into the cage. 'There's a good girl.' Rick didn't close the door, instead leaving her to look around.

* * *

'I really can't thank you enough for this,' Rick said again as he held the door open for Angela and picked up the toolbox.

'It really isn't that big of a deal.' Angela smiled at him. 'And I'm happy to help.'

'Well, I really do appreciate it. I'd like to say Mallow does too, but I think she's still got a way to go with learning manners!'

'You got her to apologise — I never thought I'd see that from a parrot. I might believe you're capable of anything after that!' She hit the button to call the lift.

'Yeah, I think I'm almost as surprised as you are that it worked.' He ran his spare hand through his hair. 'Do you think she'll be happy in the cage?'

'Rick.' She touched his hand. 'I already told you, Mallow — which is a much better name than Chicken-butt, by the way — chose you. And I can only imagine how much you spent on the cage, all the toys and perches and equipment . . .'

'And replacing half my cookware,' he added. 'And my iron. Pretty sure my straighteners are going to have to go too.'

'What?' She tried not to focus on the fact that he'd admitted to owning hair straighteners.

'Non-stick surfaces. Apparently it's deadly to parrots because of how their lungs and stuff work.'

'Oh, right.' Angela nodded.

'I know it's a lot of money, but — and you can call me crazy for it — I think she might be worth it. And like you said, with luck, she's going to be with me for many years. So it's really not that much, if you pro-rata it across years.' He shrugged.

'I guess that makes sense.' Angela liked this side of Rick. If she was honest, there were a lot of sides to him she liked — a lot more than she'd imagined when she'd first met him.

He followed her down to her car, putting the toolbox back in the boot. 'So, I guess I'll see you Monday. Have a good weekend, Angela.'

'You too. Thanks again for dinner.'

'And thanks again for your help.' He grinned at her, and she found herself thinking how nice his smile was. Not the fake, flashy one that he used in a lot of his videos — although, she'd noticed it wasn't so prevalent in his recent videos shot at Bill's — but the real one that he wore right then . . . it made her feel gooey in a way usually reserved for kits, cubs, pups and chicks.

'I actually had good fun.' She smiled when he held the door open for her, then offered his arm to steady her while she faffed with her crutches and settled into the driver's seat. She couldn't help but miss that firm, reassuring hand when he let go and closed the car door.

* * *

Sweat trickled down Rick's chest. His heart crashed against his ribs and his arms ached from where he'd bolted upright at the crash of clanging metal . . . and something else. He still wasn't fully awake, but strained his ears for that eerie, nightmare sound. When it echoed around his bedroom again the hairs on the back of his neck jumped to attention.

What the hell was it? It sounded like an animal being murdered. From inside his house. Gathering his courage, he threw back the covers and tiptoed to the door. A howling screech tore through the wood, jolting his heart-rate higher. The door creaked as he opened it, and he cursed under his jagged breath. The howling stopped and was replaced by claw-like clattering that drew closer.

Holding his breath, Rick stretched for the light switch. 'Mallow?'

'Hello, pretty!' A maniacal laugh and wolf-whistling soothed his frazzled nerves. There was only one living creature who made a noise like that. Sighing, Rick flicked on the rest of the lights and followed the soft clucking noises. Moments later, he peered under the couch to a dusty black beak and intelligent brown eyes watching him.

'C'mere you little brat. Up!'

Reluctantly, one scaly, almost Jurassic, clawed foot followed the other, and the culprit was pulled out of her hiding spot.

'Why aren't you in your cage?' He looked around the living room and grimaced at the grubby pink footprints now decorating his formerly white rug. That would teach him to not take his plate away after dinner. 'Maybe I should call you Houdini, you ungrateful little brat.' He stroked a finger through what soft, pink feathers she had, and groaned when he saw the cage door on the living room floor — removed from its hinges by a clever beak. 'It's a good thing you're cute, the amount of trouble you cause. I'll have to do the bolts up a lot tighter next time.'

Mallow just snuggled against his neck and made kissy noises. She knew she'd gotten away with it!

'I'm going to have to text Angela.'

* * *

'I am so sorry,' Rick apologised again as he strode into Bill's a few hours later.

'It's all right, I got your text. What's going on? Is Mallow OK? You said she's why you're late.'

'Yeah, she's fine. But she took the cage door off its hinges first thing this morning. And it took me a while to get it back on, and when I eventually did I was already running late.' He didn't even bother to mention the mess of footprints — though he had taken a quick reel of them, with the culprit looking very pleased with herself. He'd probably get a few thousand hits from it, and hopefully some cleaning advice.

'She took the door off her cage?'

'Yup.'

'Did we not fix it properly?'

'Apparently not tightly enough. She undid the bolts on the hinge. Must have taken her all night.'

'Clever little madam.'

'Yeah. And then, as soon as I tried to leave this morning, she started screaming. I went back and settled her twice, but the third time I locked up I could hear her calling three floors down. So, I . . . umm . . . I brought her with me and I've just put her in the office. Which in itself made me even later, because my first lift wouldn't let me in the car with her, so I had to call another one. I really am very sorry.'

'It's fine, Rick. Is everything sorted now?'

'Umm.' He wasn't totally sure how she'd take the answer. 'Depends on how much you mind her being in your office.'

'In her cage?'

'Her travel cage, yes.'

'Rick, you can't leave her in that cage all day, it's far too small.'

'I know, but I couldn't leave her screaming, and I didn't want to let you down either. I didn't know what to do. I mean, I know Paul and Nancy said I'd have to make some lifestyle changes to look after Mallow, but I didn't realise I wouldn't be able to leave my flat! I can hardly even leave the room before she starts screaming. By the time I'd showered this morning, the neighbours probably thought I was committing murder.'

'Well, she can go in the bathroom with you, so long as you're not spraying things. The steam will probably be good for her feathers and skin, but that's not really a long-term solution.'

'No.'

'She's probably scared,' Angela explained. 'It's obvious that whatever happened in her past, she's been traumatised. And it's equally obvious that she feels safe with you. She's probably scared that you — the only person she trusts — might disappear and leave her alone again.'

'Yeah.' Rick nodded sadly. It made him angry to think of what Mallow might have experienced before being dumped in the rain. 'Nancy called it separation anxiety.'

'Poor Mallow.' Angela sighed. 'Come on, let's see what we can come up with to keep her ladyship happy today.' She hobbled back towards the office.

'Thanks, I really appreciate this.'

'You're welcome.' She studied him for a moment. 'Can I ask something though? You said your ride wouldn't accept her. Are you still using taxis every day?'

'Yeah.'

'But you live miles away. Isn't that costing you a fortune?'

Rick shrugged. 'I don't really have much choice. It's not like Yvette is going to give me a lift anymore. I mostly just use the time to catch up on social media and check in with my Rickheads.'

'And edit videos of Ruby and Ernie and the others?'

'I *knew* it!' he crowed triumphantly. 'You *are* a Rickhead!'

'Hardly.' Angela rolled her eyes. 'I just thought it was a good idea to keep an eye on what you're posting.'

'Of course.' He had to bite his lips together to keep from smiling.

'Shut up.' She laughed, giving him a nudge.

'What? I didn't say anything!'

'You didn't have to.' The look she gave him was so filled with amusement that he couldn't help grinning back.

'I really appreciate you not sharing the details of Bill's, by the way.'

'You're welcome.' Rick shrugged. 'At first it was a bit of self-preservation. I didn't really want my fans finding out I was only here because of a court order. But then I got to know you, and Ruby and Ernie and the others, and I realised you probably wouldn't want a bunch of strangers poking about.'

'True enough.' Angela smiled, making him feel that warmth in his chest when she approved of something he did. 'But still, thank you.'

It took them nearly an hour, but with some ingenuity and swearing — not just from Mallow — they managed to turn one of the pens into a temporary cage, with enough space for a couple of perches and the toys Rick emptied out of his bag. He grinned when Mallow strutted across the floor of the makeshift enclosure, throwing toys until they were in what she clearly thought were their "proper" position. Given that she'd been tapping on death's door a few days earlier, he was delighted to see her filled with so much spunk and attitude.

Angela laughed as one of the more expensive chew toys — which Mallow was supposed to attack instead of her own feathers — bounced off the wire and was followed by a prolonged raspberry noise.

'You know she's got you wrapped round her smallest claw, right?'

He did, and he didn't really care. 'I know I've said this a lot in the last few days, but again — thank you, Angela.'

'You're welcome.' She smiled at him, and the approval in her eyes warmed him right through. 'Can I be honest with you, Rick?'

'Yes.' He swallowed hard, hoping it wasn't going to be anything too difficult to hear.

'I'm starting to think she might be rehabilitating you as much as you are her.'

'Really?' That was one of the last things he'd expected to hear.

'Without putting too fine a point on it, could you have seen yourself rearranging your living room, and parts of your life, for a bald cockatoo a few months ago?'

'I guess it is a bit different for me.' He shrugged. 'But maybe it's not such a bad thing?' he mused aloud.

'If you're waiting for me to argue with you on that, you're going to have a really long wait.' She gave him one of those smiles that made her eyes sparkle.

'So, you're saying you like this version of me better?' He knew he shouldn't tease her — it was verging on flirting, which was probably an even dumber move than rescuing a swearing, bald, biting cockatoo. But he couldn't resist.

'More than the version of you who turned up on the first day, shoved a camera in my face, and did almost nothing helpful at all? Yeah, I like this version better. What are you grinning at?'

'The fact that you said you like me.' He couldn't keep the smile from his face.

'Fine, I like you.' Angela grinned. 'But I could go off you pretty fast, if we end up having to work late.'

'Yes, ma'am.' He flicked her a cheeky salute before peering at Mallow. 'And you, you had best behave!'

Mallow just whistled innocently. If it was possible to grin with a beak, he was sure she would have.

CHAPTER SEVEN

'What on earth are you doing?'

Rick had just raced past the office door for the umpteenth time, whooping as he ran through the courtyard, his arms outstretched and Mallow balanced on a perch.

'Well, um . . .' He blushed as he stood in the doorway, dishevelled and puffing, cradling Mallow against his chest on a thick, short perch. She'd come in with him every day for the last two weeks, and had made good progress with not screaming every time he left her sight. It had been a rough few days at first though, with panicked cockatoo screams echoing around Bill's, as he'd taught her again and again — for longer and longer periods — that she could trust him to come back if he left her.

'Oh come on, I'm itching to know.'

'I saw a video online. It was another rescue centre, one in Indonesia or somewhere like that, and they had these flying squirrel things they were rescuing. And it was really cute. Even though some of them couldn't fly anymore, because they were injured or too old or whatever, the volunteers would pick them up and sort of let them pretend "fly" around the centre . . .'

'And you thought you'd try it with Mallow.' Angela covered her mouth with her hand.

'You probably think it's stupid. It probably *is* stupid . . .'

'I think it might be one of the sweetest things I've heard in a while,' she told him honestly. 'Do you think she likes it?'

A huge grin swept across his face. 'At first I don't think she could figure out what I was doing, but now I think she likes it. She's usually pretty good at letting me know when she's not happy about something. And when I offer her the flying perch, she jumps up pretty quick.'

'Well, if her ladyship has had enough of her "flying lessons", there's something I'd like to show you. Pull up a chair?'

'Sure.' He did as asked.

'So — and no judgement please, as I know it's terrible — but this is Bill's website. I had a go at updating it while I was laid up, but I think I've made it worse. Half the images seem to have moved.'

'I have to admit, I struggled to find it when I looked.' Rick leaned forward. 'And when I did find it, I did find it a little . . . messy.'

Angela looked at him, then laughed. 'Saying the site is a bit "messy" is like saying Madam Mallow here can be a "little" noisy! I know it's bad, but I was hoping you could help? You seem to be pretty good with this type of stuff.'

'Well, I can't promise anything, but I'm happy to take a look.' He scooched closer and settled Mallow onto his shoulder, looking like the strangest pirate Angela had ever seen. She couldn't help but smile as he leaned over and reached for the mouse.

It took a few hours, numerous rounds of tea and the best part of a packet of ginger nuts — which Mallow happily begged a few bites of — but eventually Rick pushed the keyboard away and pulled out his phone. 'Angela? Do you have time to have a look at this?'

'Definitely.' She took his phone and flipped through the screens, feeling more and more impressed with each one. 'This is brilliant, Rick.'

'Really?'

'Yeah, you've made it look so much more professional. I'm amazed you did it all so quickly.'

He shrugged easily. 'Most of the content was there, though I did add a few things I've created while I've been here.'

'I can see that.' Angela tapped on another video. 'This really is very good, Rick.'

'You really think it's OK?' Angela was surprised to see that Rick seemed genuinely uncertain.

'Yes, I really do. Thank you.' She grinned as a thought occurred. 'In fact, I think it's so good that we deserve to celebrate.'

'Let me guess, you want me to put the kettle on and find some more biscuits.'

'You could.' Angela grinned, realising how easily they'd fallen into step with each other. 'Or you could come to the pub with me tonight.'

'You want *me* to come to a pub with *you*.'

'Yeah.' Angela nodded. 'It's quiz night. It's good fun, and the Brockle's Retreat put on a great spread as part of the cost of entry — which is only a tenner. And there's prizes for the winning team. It's a good laugh.'

'Right, you mean with a group of people?'

'Yeah, of course.'

'*Riiiight.*' Rick laughed. 'For a minute I thought you were trying to ask me on a date or something crazy like that.'

'That really would be crazy. As if someone like you would ever date someone like me. Ridiculous.' Angela shook her head.

'What do you mean by that?' Rick gave her the oddest look.

'Well, I met Yvette, so I know what your type is. And believe me when I say I don't think I could be any more different if I tried.'

'Maybe true. But that's not necessarily a bad thing.' He watched her with an odd look on his face, which did something

126

even odder to her stomach. For a moment, she couldn't have looked away from his gaze even if she'd wanted to — not that she was sure she did. What on earth . . . ? Then, as quickly as the moment arrived, it was gone.

'What about Mallow?'

'She's been doing a lot better at being left. And sooner or later you're going to have to be more than a few hundred yards away. She seems happy enough here, and if she's going to complain, maybe better here than in your flat.'

'That's true.' He chuckled. 'She's already made herself known to my neighbours. I hadn't realised how bad the soundproofing was until taking her home.' He hesitated. 'But what if she gets upset?'

'We can set up some foraging toys for her to keep her busy, plus it's not until this evening, when she should be settling down for the night.'

'I can set the computer up as a monitor too, if you don't mind me linking it to my phone.'

'Not a problem.' Angela was glad he was warming to the idea.

'Are you sure me coming along is OK? Wouldn't it be a bit weird, me inviting myself onto an established team?'

'Well, for one, you're not inviting yourself — I'm inviting you. And for two, the team is pretty flexible. It's whoever is around on the night. You'll be welcome. We're meeting about half seven. I've got to stop by the doctor's surgery after we're done here. You could meet me at the pub?'

'Yeah, I think I'd like that.'

It wasn't until he'd said yes that she realised just how pleased she was he'd accepted the invitation.

* * *

Rick hesitated at the door to the pub, suddenly feeling nervous — which was weird, because he was famous for never "feeling the fear!" and jumping headlong into things without a thought. Weird. Beyond getting their likes and stars, he didn't usually care what people thought about him. He'd learned early on in his career as an influencer, playing Maverick, that there were plenty of haters — people with strong opinions on what he did, who were waiting to troll and criticise him at every opportunity. So he'd just stopped listening or caring.

But when it came to Angela . . . he shook his head and tried to clear the thoughts he didn't fully understand before heading inside. And it was awesome, like something off a film set, with all old beams, crackling fires in huge hearths, and big, heavy-looking tables that seemed like they'd been in use for longer than he'd been alive. Totally Insta worthy. But, even as he pulled out his phone and hit the quick-launch camera button, he hesitated, unsure whether he actually wanted to be Maverick. He felt totally out of place. He'd just turned to leave, already mentally writing an apology ping to Angela, when a familiar whistle pierced the cosy noise of the pub.

'Rick, we're over here.' Angela waved to him from a table in the corner, and for a few moments the noise seemed to fade from around him. He couldn't remember how to get his feet to work — he did a double take. Her hair, which was usually pinned or tied up with numerous scarves and clips, cascaded down her neck and shoulders in a cloud of soft curls, and she'd left her usual tie-dye fleeces at home and wore the most beautiful long jumper or dress thing he'd ever seen. It was fluffy and grey — a colour he'd usually reserve for the most sombre of suits and occasions, and even then under complaint — which faded from the softest pearly colour at her shoulders to almost black at her knees. Looking at it on her, he'd never liked grey so much.

Knowing Angela, he guessed it had probably come from a charity shop, or been given to her, but he couldn't help think-ing she wore it better than Yvette did some of her most expen-sive couture outfits. He immediately squashed the thought. He didn't want to be thinking of his ex tonight, and Angela definitely deserved better than to be compared. Even if it was no competition. She was sweet, funny, kind and driven, and quite literally — as of that moment — stunning.

Oh *shit* . . . the thought ricocheted around his brain. Did he have a thing for Angela? That would not be a smart move.

'What are you waiting for? You've already had an invitation — I'm not gold-plating one for you!' He laughed as she stood and waved at him again. 'Come on.'

He made it halfway across the bar before realising she wasn't using her crutches, and that he couldn't see them nearby. 'Given your sticks the night off? Or have you been pulling a fast one this whole time?' He couldn't resist teasing her, even though he knew it was probably one of his dumbest ideas.

'Yeah, I'm lazy really. Just wanted some strapping hunk to do all my heavy lifting for a while.' Her eyes sparkled when she grinned at him. 'But apparently he wasn't available, so I got you instead.'

And she was teasing him back. This was dangerous territory. 'Seriously though, if you're off the crutches, do I get time off for good behaviour?'

'Well, maybe if you can actually behave and stop teaching my fox to do tricks for your videos . . .'

Oops, he hadn't realised she knew about that. He'd been careful to be discreet with his filming — not because he thought Angela would mind, but because he didn't want to be seen as slacking off. She'd admitted to having seen some of his videos, but he'd not uploaded any of Ruby's tricks for nearly a week. Maybe she really *was* following him online. He grinned at the thought.

'Just for the record,' a blonde woman with green eyes — so bright they had to be contacts — waved a finger at Angela, 'you are not officially "off the crutches". You are supposed to be slowly rehabilitating your leg with the walking brace.' Now that it had been brought up, Rick let his eyes wander lower, and took in the brace that wrapped around Angela's calf and knee, disappearing up her leg and beneath her dress.

The bright green eyes turned to him. 'And you, mister, had better be sure she's not overdoing things. Especially as it's your fault she's in this situation in the first place.'

Rick gulped hard, guilt flushing through him.

'Evelyn, please don't. If I can forgive him, you can at least try.' Angela held up her hand, half-laughing.

Wow, Rick didn't know what to say to that. He'd hoped that she'd been thinking about his apology from when they'd rescued the cat, but he hadn't really dared to hope that she might accept it. Which apparently she had, to the point that here she was defending him to her friends.

'Besides—' she shot him that sparkly-eyed, mischievous grin '—I'm planning on putting him to work. Hoping he can make up for my complete uselessness on the music rounds.'

'Oh, if he's good at music, I want him to play. That round destroyed our chances last month,' the other woman — another pretty blonde — held out her hand. 'Hi, I'm Liv. Evelyn you've just met, and Callum and Jake — our respective intendeds — are at the bar.'

'Liv and Cal got engaged a couple of months ago.' Angela answered his quizzical look. 'And he's already met Jake.'

'Oh, you're the one with the bald parrot?' Evelyn asked, those strange green eyes pinning him against the seat he'd just taken. 'How is the poor little thing?'

'Hopefully tucked up asleep and not screaming down Bill's.' Rick flicked open his phone. 'In actual fact, I should probably check. Yup—' he showed the phone to Angela '— looks like she's sound asleep.'

'Hopefully she'll settle as well at your flat.'

'Hopefully.' He was still musing on that thought when one of the last people he wanted to see pulled out a chair.

'Evening, Sergeant Brown.' He tried not to feel guilty, but just the policeman's presence reminded him of how he came to be there. That, combined with Evelyn's somewhat accusatory welcome, made him feel about two inches tall, which he probably deserved.

'Evening, Rick. Surprised to see you here.'

'Apparently he's our secret weapon for the music and pop rounds.' Evelyn grinned at him.

'Oh, thank goodness for that. And it's Harry when I'm out of uniform. You any good at soap operas? My wife usually picks up those questions, but she's visiting her parents with the littluns this weekend.'

'Awww no, no Marie? We're doomed!' Liv leaned forward. 'And how is my little namesake?'

'Growing out of clothes quicker than we can keep up. Want to see some new pictures?'

'Obviously.' Liv reached for the phone that had appeared in Harry's hand.

Starting to relax, Rick sat back.

'Make some space, please. Hi, Rick.'

He looked up to see Jake towering over him, carrying two brightly coloured pitchers. Behind him, with a stack of glasses, was the man he assumed was Callum.

'Right.' Putting the glasses down he held out a hand. 'Nice to meet you, Rick. You joining us for tonight?'

'Yeah, Angela invited me.'

'Apparently he's going to help us on the music, pop and soap rounds.' Liv placed a quick kiss on Callum's cheek as he sat next to her.

'Red jug's alcoholic, yellow is soft — for those of us on call.' Callum grinned down at Liv. 'Which one of us is it?'

Rick watched, slightly bemused as they played rock, paper, scissors, Liv triumphantly wrapping her "paper" around his "rock". 'Red for me please. Whatever it is.'

'Pomegranate iced tea.' He poured her a glass, then glanced to Rick. 'We're both doctors at the village surgery. So far from the hospital, we're never really completely off-call.'

Rick nodded, thinking it must take a lot of dedication to never be able to go out and party.

'Pretty much the same when you're the only vet in the place.' Jake took a sip from a red glass before handing it to Evelyn. 'Bit sweet for me anyway.'

'Yay for being a district nurse surrounded by other medics. Cheers.'

'You can pour me one of those while you've got it.' Harry grinned. 'I'm off duty and there's no risk of me being woken up by a teething tot in the morning.'

'What about you?' Jake asked, and Rick was aware that the conversation had stopped — all eyes were on him.

'Yellow.' Without question, and he didn't even care what it was. He'd barely touched a drop since he'd started volunteering with Angela, at least after that first night. Even the last argument with Yvette, which would have usually sent him straight to the nearest bar, hadn't been enough to tempt him. It just didn't seem worth it.

And the approving smile Angela shot him warmed him far more than even a dozen glasses of pomegranate-whatever-it-was could.

* * *

'I still can't believe we won!' Angela shoved her curls back from her face, laughing.

'Well, it's taken us long enough!' Evelyn placed a goodnight kiss on her cheek. 'I meant what I said. Take it easy on your leg and quit jumping around. I do not want to see you in my re-enablement clinic ahead of your next planned appointment.'

'Yes, ma'am!' Angela giggled and gave her friend a big hug.

'Are you going to be all right getting home?' Liv checked.

'Yeah, it's only a couple of streets.' Angela was touched by her friends' concern.

'I can walk back with you,' Rick offered.

'Great idea,' Evelyn agreed. 'G'night, secret weapon!' They waved goodbye and headed off in the opposite direction.

'I really am fine. No one needs to make a fuss,' Angela insisted. 'I'm perfectly capable of walking myself home.'

'It's hardly a fuss.' Rick grinned at her. 'And I've got to pick up Mallow anyway.'

'Oh right, the biter. But you'll be quicker if you don't wait for me, and your jacket doesn't look anywhere near warm enough.' Angela didn't know why she was complaining so much — she'd actually really enjoyed his company.

'It's not that cold,' he argued good naturedly. 'And I have to admit, I might just be a bit scared of your friend.'

'Oh, Evelyn's fine!' Angela said, grinning back at him. 'She's just a bit protective of her patients. And family. And apparently soon-to-be family.'

'She's nice. They all are. Thank you for inviting me this evening. I had a really good time.'

'Me too,' Angela told him honestly. 'And we won!' She wasn't used to the weight of the brace, and her toes caught on the kerb as she skipped up it. Almost before she realised she was falling, Rick's arms were around her waist, holding her firmly, keeping her safe from harm.

He held her tightly as she regained her balance, and she found herself hoping he wouldn't let go right away. His hands were so warm around her, and so comforting, that she had to fight the urge to lean in closer and rest her head on his shoulder. As it was, she could feel his heart thundering beneath her palm where it rested against his chest. He'd pulled her close to keep her from face-planting. It would be incredibly easy — almost natural — to lift her other hand, slide it round the back of his neck, to . . .

'Are you all right?' His eyes were intense on hers, and she could feel her own heartbeat racing in time with his. 'You're not hurt, are you?'

'No, I'm fine.' Her words came from far away and took a lot more effort than they usually seemed to. It was so hard to focus on anything but the weight and heat of his hands on her waist.

* * *

133

Damn, she felt so *good* gathered up against him that he didn't want to let go. Even through the fuzzy warmth of that grey dress, which was just as soft as it looked, he was sure he could feel the heat of her skin against his palms. *Focus, man.* 'You're absolutely sure you're OK?'

'Yeah.' She gave the tiniest of nods, not breaking eye contact with him, but not making any effort to move. What the hell was happening here? He couldn't be reading this situation right . . . there was no *way* Angela would think of him like *that*, not after everything he'd done. At best they were friends, and he definitely, absolutely would not do anything to risk changing that. He'd never had a friend like her — someone who would drop everything on a Friday night to help out with anything, for nothing more than a cheap takeaway. He was only just starting to realise how important she was to him.

But those grey eyes with their flecks of blue — how had he never realised what a stunning colour grey was? — stayed locked on his, darkening with a heat that he knew was reflected in his own gaze. Her fingers curled against his chest, tangling in his shirt beneath his open jacket. He was scared to speak, or even breathe, in case he broke the spell. But at the same time he knew that what he wanted to do — what his body was screaming at him to do — would be dumb beyond words.

He knew that, but couldn't help himself, and he couldn't stop the hand that reached up to touch her curls and brush them away from her face. Just like he couldn't resist stroking her cheek with his thumb.

When she pulled away slightly, closing her eyes and lowering her face — her lips and breath scorching against his palm — he had to bite back a groan. He'd never realised how much of a turn-on such a simple thing could be.

He ground his teeth together, trying to will his heart to stop jumping quite so much.

'It would be stupid of me, wouldn't it . . .' he spoke against her hair, his nose almost touching the soft, sweetly scented curls '. . . to tell you I want to kiss you right now?'

'Yeah.' Her words tickled his palm. 'It probably would.'

'Probably really, really stupid, in fact.'

'Monumentally.'

'Probably one of the dumbest things I could do.'

'Yup.' When she looked back up at him there was a glint in her eyes, and he knew he was in a huge amount of trouble. 'But I can't help wondering if it might be less stupid if I were the one who kissed you.'

He didn't have time to catch his breath or process her words before her lips were against his, hot and insistent and completely delicious. When she pulled back for a second to look at him, he did the only thing that made sense and wove his fingers through her curls, pulling her back close again.

She pressed against him, so warm and welcoming that the crisp, cool air disappeared, and the world around him dulled into nothing while he lost himself in her kiss. She didn't hold back, instead weaving her fingers through his hair and tightening her grip on him while moulding her body against his.

In the glow of the streetlights, their breath puffing around them in an icy cloud, time slowed down and the world closed in to focus just on her — and in that moment every stupid, cheesy, overblown, hyped-up romance made sense to Rick. Angela invaded all of his senses, leaving him unable to think of anything else — not that he'd want to. It was unlike anything he'd experienced before — utter, perfect bliss. And he couldn't get enough of her.

'Oi, oi! Get a room!' The wolf whistles and jeers forced them apart, and Rick felt his blood boil for another reason.

* * *

Feeling a bit unsteady, Angela buried her face against Rick's shoulder, trying really hard not to laugh. What in the he . . . screw it . . . what in the hell was she thinking, kissing Rick of all people?

Rick, the arrogant idiot who'd been stupid enough to get into a driver's seat drunk, destroy the café and seriously injure her — and she was making out with him in the street? She must have taken leave of her senses. It must be the stress of everything catching up with her — the usual challenges of running a charity, of trying to stretch impossibly tight finances further and further every week. It couldn't be more than that.

Except . . . her lips still tingled and her body still thrummed from his touch, and she was pretty sure his arms around her waist were the only thing keeping her upright. She didn't think she'd ever been kissed in a way that was so raw, or so real, which made it even harder for her not to laugh — the idea that the *realest* kiss in her life had come from someone who introduced himself by a screen name was too utterly ridiculous for words. But she couldn't deny the fizzing excitement spreading through her from that kiss.

She didn't resist when Rick, his arm still on her waist — no doubt keeping her from falling on her face — guided her gently into movement again. He didn't say anything, and neither did she — mostly because she didn't know what to say. But that didn't stop a hollowness from settling in her stomach. She couldn't help feeling that she was on the verge of missing out on something important. But rather than ponder on that, she tugged Rick's arm.

'Penny for your thoughts?'

'Bloody teenagers,' he grumbled. 'Just thinking how much I'd like to dump them in the duck pond for ruining that moment.'

'Maybe they had a point.' Angela paused, not sure she trusted herself to focus on the conversation as well as the pavement, which had already tried to trip her once.

'How do you mean?'

'Well, we were stood there in the middle of the street, necking.'

'Did you actually just say the word "necking" without even a trace of irony?'

'Yes, I did.' She looked up, challenging him to be stupid enough to comment further, hoping he would ignore the blush she could feel heating her cheeks. 'Problem?'

'Yeah.' He stroked her face with cool fingers. 'You're so bloo . . . ming adorable that I want to kiss you again.'

The thrill that raced through her was electric — it short-circuited her mind, wiping out all sensible thoughts. 'Are you still waiting for your gold-plated invitation?'

His arm tightened around her waist, pulling her deliciously firmly against him, while his other hand slid up her spine and wove fingers through the curls at the base of her neck, tilting her mouth to the perfect angle. His lips brushed hers so gently that she could have imagined it, but his breath was hot against her skin. 'Tell me to stop, Angela.'

She didn't know if the harsh whisper was a plea, a dare, a tease — but she knew how she wanted to respond. She nuzzled against him, letting her nose run along his as her lips teased the edge of his, brushed against his cheek and whispered, 'But what if I don't want you to stop?'

She was so close that she felt his smile before she saw it. He drew back to look at her, checking before he lowered his lips to hers, fizzing, thrumming tingles exploding throughout her. When his tongue hit hers, she moaned, unable to hold the sound back any more than she could stop the shiver that raced through her when he gently nipped at her lips. He drew her more tightly against him, and the sensation when his fingers traced down her neck made her shiver again.

He drew back slowly — hopefully reluctantly — and smiled at her. Properly, the way she liked. 'You're cold.' He rubbed his hands up and down her arms.

'Am I?' She hadn't noticed.

'You're shivering.' He peeled off his coat.

'Put that back on.' She giggled.

'Why?'

'Because otherwise you'll be cold. I'm a big girl, and I'm wearing a great big jumper dress and this big wrap.' She tugged her woolly cape back around her. 'It's practically a blanket by itself. Really, Rick, I'm fine.'

'You know, I was trying to be sweet. Maybe even a bit charming.'

'Yeah, I got that.' She caught his hand, twisting her fingers through his. 'Come on. If we stand here much longer we'll be in danger of turning into icicles.'

'Your hands are cold.' He fell into step beside her. 'Will you at least take my gloves? I'm not even wearing them. Please?'

It was the "please" that did it, and the look he gave her as he handed over a ridiculously soft pair of gloves. 'You know—' Angela didn't look at him as she tugged them on; too big really, but incredibly warm and sweet all the same '—I'm starting to think maybe the suggestion the kids made might have been good advice.'

'What suggestion was that?'

'The one about us "getting a room" of some sort.'

Rick froze to the spot, his feet seeming to forget what they were supposed to be doing.

'For a second you actually had me there, but you're just teasing.'

'Am I?' She bit her lips together, trying not to laugh.

His eyes were still locked on hers, the heat in them suggesting this wasn't a laughing matter.

'Why not? Last I checked we're both free, single adults. I like you, and I'm pretty sure after that kiss that you like me too.' She tried to play down her nerves. She didn't put herself out there like this and — as casual as she forced herself to sound — it was scary. But she didn't want to put pressure on what was becoming a good friendship. 'But, hey, if you're not interested, it's not like it's a big deal or anything.'

He was on her in a heartbeat, his bare hands cradling her face to plant another scorching kiss. 'Angela, if I was any more *interested* I would throw you over my shoulder and carry you off, caveman style, to the nearest bush.'

'Nah, too cold for that.' She twined her fingers back through his. 'And if Harry has to arrest either of us for indecent exposure it'd just make things really awkward. Besides, my bed is a lot comfier and warmer.'

The grin he gave her sent little zings of warmth through her again, and she could barely feel the cold.

* * *

Rick let his hands drop from Angela for long enough to let her slide his coat down his arms and fumble his scarf to the floor, and even that was longer than he wanted to let go of her for. He gathered her back against him the moment he could, sinking his fingers into those soft curls while he kissed her, still not quite believing that it was happening.

She was soft and warm, all sweet and tempting curves as she moulded herself against him easily, fitting perfectly, naturally. How anything — anyone — could feel so easily familiar, and at the same time so new and exciting was beyond him, but he certainly wasn't going to complain as her hands drifted down his chest, and shoved him backwards onto her bed. He grinned as she wriggled out of her dress, pulling the soft grey and black fabric up over her hips until she could pull it over her head, leaving her in leggings and some sort of lacy vest.

His mouth went dry as he hooked his fingers into her waistband, drawing her back close, spreading his knees so she could stand between his legs and he could slide his hands around her back, pushing the lace out of his way to get his hands on her soft, bare skin. She leaned down to kiss him, gently moving her lips over his, tracing her fingers over the features of his face.

'You are absolutely stunning,' he told her reverently, meaning every single word. 'Is it bad of me to tell you I can't wait to get you totally naked?'

'Very.' She laughed and her breasts jiggled in a way that just demanded he give them attention. 'And you're pretty well positioned to help with that.'

'Really?' He forced himself to look away from those gorgeous, inviting curves.

'Uh huh. Make yourself useful while you're sat down there.' The look she gave him was pure mischief, spurring him on. How had he forgotten how much *fun* it was to laugh with your partner?

He rucked the lace up and placed a kiss on the warm skin just below the hem of her bra, enjoying her shiver. He kissed lower, working his way down to her belly button, taking his time and enjoying making her squirm. He stroked along the top of her leggings, fully intending to peel them down, when her hands caught his wrists. 'I didn't mean *that*. I meant the brace.'

Right. His brain snapped back into focus as he moved his hand down to her thigh. 'Should we be doing this?' Damn, that hadn't come out right. 'I mean your leg. Is it all right, are you sure?' He didn't want to think about her injury in any more detail than that. So long as he didn't think about it, it would be OK.

'I only need to be careful when I'm bearing weight.' She didn't make any attempt to pull away, thank the lord. 'Which means you're going to have to do most of the work.' There was that wicked look of mischief again that sent his blood pulsing south. 'You can start with the Velcro.'

His hands shook slightly as he undid the straps one by one, working down to her ankle. She kept her hands on his shoulders as he worked, balancing against him as he slid the brace from her thigh and it dropped to the floor. He slid his fingers along the top of her leggings, chasing goosepimples across her skin. 'These now?'

'I think so.' She grinned — he couldn't tear his eyes from hers as he slid them down her legs, then held her firmly while she dragged them off her feet. She sat next to him on the bed, swinging around to drape her legs over his lap and wind her arms around his neck, pulling herself tightly against him for another deep, scorching kiss.

His hands wandered up and down her legs, before catching on roughened, raised skin that made her flinch in his arms.

Reality slammed into him, cold and unwelcome, as he looked down at the shiny, reddened, raised scars.

'Oh hell, Angela, this is what I did to you.' It wasn't really a question, but she nodded anyway. He leaned down to study the horrors he'd wreaked on her. His stomach rolled and twisted. He didn't know how she could bare to have him touch her when he'd hurt her so badly. 'I'm so, so sorry.'

'It's OK.' She tucked her hand alongside his cheek, turning his head to look at her. 'It's fine. Well, it's not fine, but it will be. *I* will be.'

'I don't understand how you're not angry with me.'

'I was,' Angela admitted quietly. 'For a while. But you apologised, and I believe you genuinely meant it.'

'It's that simple for you?' He wasn't sure it would be for him.

'Yeah.' She drew him close for another kiss. 'The way I see it, you made a mistake. A really, really stupid decision, but you're learning from it, and you're trying to change. And if I didn't believe in second chances, I'd be in the wrong line of work.' She watched him closely. 'Am I wrong?'

He thought about his answer for a few moments, then shook his head. 'No, you're not. I really am trying to be a better person.'

'I think you're doing pretty well. From my point of view, you've changed quite a bit since we met, and — in case you didn't notice — I quite like this version of you.'

'I think I like this version of me better, too.' He stroked gentle fingers over her leg again, wishing he could take back the pain he'd caused. 'Does it hurt much?'

'It did at first, but it's getting better all the time. And it will be perfectly fine.' She grinned at him, that irresistible glint of mischief back in her eyes. 'But in the meantime, I can think of a few ways you could make it up to me.' She nipped his neck, teasing again.

Well, if she wanted to play, he definitely wasn't going to complain. He teased his fingers up her side, sliding the lace with them. 'So, how can I make things up to you? I bet you have lots of ideas . . .'

'Uh huh.' She squirmed against him as he stroked up her ribs. 'Lots of heavy lifting and manly things like that, plenty of animals to feed . . .'

'It's dark now, though.' He slid her top higher, loving the feel of her skin.

'True.' Angela gasped when he hit a sensitive spot, near the middle of her back, which he teased gently, making her squirm even more. 'Most of the animals will be asleep. You'll have to think of another way to start making amends.'

'I can be pretty creative, you know.' He peeled the top over her head and teased his lips over her newly bared skin, eliciting a delicious, breathy sigh from her.

'Oh I bet you can, Rick.'

His fingers made deft work of removing her bra, and he lay her back against her pillows, taking a moment to admire the frankly mouth-watering view, before fumbling for his wallet and one of his trusty friends. His redundant driving licence winked at him, putting an unexpected thought into his head as he stared at it for a few heartbeats.

'Everything all right?' Angela propped herself up on her shoulders, and he had to force himself to remember to breathe. She was absolutely stunning — her hair tumbling every which way in a crazy mess. He couldn't wait to bury his fingers in those curls while he buried himself in her. 'Rick?'

He dropped his wallet, along with his jeans, back on the floor and crawled onto the bed. He started at Angela's feet, stroking, kissing and teasing up her calves and thighs, ignoring the scars he felt so much guilt over. He took his time, enjoying the soft sweetness of her skin and the gentle sighs that drove him crazy, telling him he was doing exactly the right thing.

He could have happily lavished attention on her breasts for hours, marvelling at their warm, natural beauty, and the way she moaned and pushed them more tightly against his lips and fingers, but he had something else on his mind. As much as he was throbbing and aching to make good on his promise of making things up to her, there was something else he wanted to do first. It surprised him, because it hadn't bothered him in the nearly ten years since he'd adopted the character, but it felt different with her. Like it mattered. More than the throbbing ache between his legs.

'Angela?'

'Uh huh.' Her eyes were closed, in what he could only hope was pleasure, so he placed a kiss on her lips, waiting until her eyes fluttered open and locked on his.

'You were right, the first day we met.'

'How so?'

'When you refused to call me Maverick. You were right, it's not my real name.'

'Well, duh.' Even though she was almost naked beneath him, squirming under his touch, and he was pretty sure ninety per cent of the blood that should be in his brain had relocated, she could still make him laugh with her snark, which somehow made her even more exciting.

'It's Ryan. My name's really Ryan.'

'Hello, Ryan.' She wrapped her arms around his neck, pulling him down against her. 'It's really, really nice to meet you.'

* * *

Angela bolted awake, her heart thumping and not knowing why. Rick — no, *Ryan* — was warm against her as he shifted in his sleep, and she smiled and snuggled closer, relaxing again. Her leg twinged a bit, and she ached in the most delicious way that only really, really good sex achieved. She propped herself up on her elbow and looked at him, contemplating kissing him awake. After last night, she was pretty sure he wouldn't object.

A wailing siren cut through her thoughts, jerking her out of the sleepy, relaxed state. Right, that was what had interrupted her dreams. She sighed and flopped back on the bed.

'Shit, is there a fire?' Rick sat up, shoving the covers back, and she didn't have the heart to complain about his swearing. 'Shouldn't we be doing something?'

Angela laughed, flicked on the bedside lamp, and yanked the duvet back over herself. 'That's a problem for you, not me.'

'What?'

'My fire alarm beeps, so I'm pretty sure that wailing is your lovely little parrot doing a very good impression of someone else's alarm.'

'Oh crap.' He caught her eyes. 'Sorry. I just realised I'm going to have to get my flat soundproofed, aren't I?'

'Probably.' She laughed, trying not to think about how expensive a task that would be, and gave him a shove. 'Go on, go and sort your Chicken-butt out.'

'I thought you didn't like me calling her that?' He yanked on his jeans.

'It's barely light. She's definitely not being marshmallow-sweet right now.'

'That's true.' He leaned down to brush a quick kiss against her lips, which made her tingle, and winced as the wailing stepped up a notch. 'All right Chicken-butt, I'm coming. Try a little patience.'

Angela grabbed the pillow he'd slept on, and pulled it over her ears. It smelled of Ri . . . Ryan, and she inhaled deeply, then hugged the pillow to her, thinking. The caterwauling had stopped so quickly that she guessed Mallow had shut up as soon as she'd spotted him. As annoying as it was to be woken at ugly-o'clock in the morning, Angela couldn't really blame the little cockatoo. She'd obviously had some fairly awful experiences in her life, and if Ryan made her feel safer, she couldn't really resent her that. Especially when she'd so recently learned how good being the centre of his attention could be.

He walked back into her room a couple of minutes later, shaking his head. 'Silly thing had managed to knock over her water bowl. The way she dived in it, you'd have thought she'd been dehydrated for days, not a couple of hours. Little diva bird I've found myself there.'

'Yeah, but she's cute most of the time.' Angela sat up, still snuggling the covers against herself.

'So what do we do now, Angela?'

'About what?'

'This.' He gestured between them. 'Us. How do you want to handle this? Do you want me to gather up the rest of my clothes and the diva-brat, and on Monday we pretend this didn't happen? Or do I go downstairs and make you tea and breakfast?'

She had a few ideas herself, but couldn't resist the impish urge to tease. 'Well, I did just get woken up by your feathered alarm clock.'

'You did.' He smiled as he watched her. 'Probably something I should apologise for.'

'Definitely.' She folded her arms across the duvet. 'And I really am not a person who likes being woken up.'

'So I've got a lot of "making up" to do?'

'Absolutely.' She tried not to grin. 'A huge amount.'

'Probably going to take me ages then. Hours.' She tried not to shiver at the promise in his voice as he grabbed the end of the duvet and started to pull. She fought for a few seconds, a ridiculous game of tug-of-war she didn't even really want to win, and tried not to laugh as she lost.

'That's better.' He gathered her up in his arms, making her squeal as his cold hands hit her warm skin.

* * *

'So, this whole Rick-slash-Ryan thing, what am I supposed to call you?' Angela asked while chewing the sausage and mushroom sandwich he'd made for them both. He'd struggled a bit with the idea of vegetarian "sausages", and they'd looked really quite weird when he'd poured them out of the box from the freezer, but they'd cooked up pretty well and were surprisingly tasty.

'For the last few years, pretty much everyone has called me Maverick or Rick. I adopted the persona nearly ten years ago, but it's really taken off more recently.'

'Doesn't answer my question.' She watched him over the top of her sandwich.

'Sorry, I guess I'm trying to figure it out myself.'

'Fair enough.' She shrugged and went back to her breakfast. 'But let me know when you've figured out what you prefer me to use, otherwise I might have to resort to "Oi"!'

He watched her in surprise, unable to help thinking how different it would have been if he'd said similar to Yvette. She would have nagged, pushed and badgered at him for an answer, unable to accept that there was anything in his head he wasn't willing to share. He shook his head irritably, not wanting to give Yvette any space in his thoughts, especially when he was sat opposite Angela, whose hair was still tousled from his fingers.

She shoved the last of her sandwich into her mouth and sat back with her tea. Another hugely refreshing difference to someone who barely ate and would lecture him on the evils of carbs.

'What? Do I have sauce on my face or something?' She wiped her mouth.

'No. You're perfect.' He caught her fingers and kissed their tips, making her blush. Bloody hell. After what they'd done last night she blushed at that.

She sat quietly with her drink, absent-mindedly petting Ruby, who had come scrounging for titbits, while he sorted through his thoughts from the night before.

Eventually, he felt like he'd shuffled them into something close enough to order. 'So, the Maverick-slash-Ryan thing?'

'Yeah?' She smiled at him, encouraging.

'Maverick was the screen name I used when I first started uploading content ten or so years ago. It was something fun to do to distract me from the string of fairly rubbish jobs I had after finishing my studies. And I thought Maverick sounded cool, and a bit clever, and that it would make me stand out like I was something special. In honesty, I was a bit of an arrogant idiot. Don't worry, I'm not expecting you to argue with me.' He shook his head at himself. 'You know how every school has a class clown? That kid who's a bit cheeky, and rude, and irreverent, but just smart enough to walk the line between funny and getting into serious trouble?'

'That was you, wasn't it?'

'Yup. For most of my life. Then I made a few videos and stuck them online, and people seemed to like them. I made some more, and then more, and somehow I ended up in the right place, filming the right thing at the right time, with the right opinions that everyone else seemed to agree with — and I ended up going viral. "Maverick" stopped being just a screen name, and blew up into an entire brand, one that's pretty valuable, and has been really good to me. I found an agent who gave me the right advice and support to turn those first few videos into a full-on career as an influencer. It's set me up really well for life, and meant I could buy my flat and car, and not really worry about money.'

'Sounds nice.' Angela sounded wistful for a moment, and again he wondered how expensive running Bill's was. 'Why do I feel like there's a "but" coming?'

'Maybe because you pay attention.' He fidgeted with his cup. 'But sometimes, especially in these last few weeks, I've started to wonder if being "Maverick" is all it's cracked up to be. If it's who I really want to be anymore.'

'How do you mean?' She rested her chin on her hand, giving him her full attention.

'Like taking risks I'm not always comfortable with, doing things I probably shouldn't, and making decisions I'm not totally happy with — all because I'm trying to keep up with the brand. And I know it's the brand I created, but, for a while, I've been starting to think that it's gotten so big that it's grown a life and personality of its own, one that really isn't me. And that hasn't bothered me until recently. I was happy to play the role.'

'So what happened recently?'

'You did.' He answered honestly. 'When I'm here at Bill's, I feel different. More grounded. Like this is the most real place I've ever been.'

'Well, you can't get much more real than mucking out donkeys and cleaning cages. The ferrets alone will ground anyone pretty quickly.' Her eyes sparkled with amusement.

'It's not just the animals,' he added, feeling nervous. 'It's you too, Angela. You make me feel more grounded too. I suspected, the day I met you, that you weren't going to put up with any nonsense from me, and you didn't. You've held me accountable for my actions, but in a way that was kind, and supportive, and gave me the space to take a long, hard look at myself. You're one of the most amazing people I've ever met.'

He paused. 'Last night — us — it meant something to me, because I really, really like you, Angela. And I wanted it to be real. That's why I told you my real name. Does that make sense?'

'Yeah, it does. And, for the record, I really like you too, Ryan.'

'You do?'

'Yeah, I do.'

'Does that mean you might agree to go out with me?'

'Like on a date?'

Ryan shrugged. 'I know we've done things a bit backward, but yes, sort of. I'd love to take you out.'

'Yes please.' Angela giggled. 'But I do have one question. What do you have in mind? Because I've seen some of your videos, and there is no way I'm up for any of your daredevil activities, and I don't think leg braces and crutches are club wear.'

'So I should cancel the abseiling then?' He chuckled at her expression. 'That sounds more like a Maverick date to me.

I was thinking something a bit simpler. How about you, me, a roaring fire somewhere, a stack of crunchy roast potatoes, and whatever it is you eat instead of roast beef? Tomorrow?'

'Sunday lunch sounds lovely. Do you want me to give the Brockle's Retreat a call? They get pretty busy, so it's a good idea to book.'

'As lovely as I'm sure that would be, maybe somewhere a little further afield? Where it can be just you and me?'

'Sounds good.'

CHAPTER EIGHT

As soon as her two favourite helpers — Summer and Sarah — were settled in the guinea garden, and Ruby had been reassured that Tilly was far too polite and well-behaved a dog to attack her, Angela caught her friend's arm. 'Can I get your opinion quickly on something indoors please?'

'Of course.' Evelyn turned to the girls. 'Summer, can you keep an eye on your cousin please? We'll only be a few minutes.'

'Yeah, Mum.'

'It's OK, Auntie Evie, I'll be good,' the little girl promised solemnly.

'Auntie Evie?' Angela asked as her friend followed her into the main house.

'I know, adorable, right? She decided she didn't want to wait until after the wedding to call me that.'

'Precious.'

'Precocious, more like, but she's such a sweetheart. And Summer takes her role of "big cousin" so seriously, and she's so good at it . . .' Something in her friend's tone grabbed Angela's attention, distracting her from her inner turmoil.

'Are you telling me you're bringing the wedding forward, shotgun style?'

'No, no, I'm not pregnant.' Evelyn laughed. 'But, between you and me, it might not be something Jake and I have ruled out completely. He's such a wonderful father to Summer, but I sometimes can't help picturing him with a baby in his arms.'

'Oh, you're a gonna.' Angela was thrilled for Evelyn.

'You don't think I'm crazy, do you? Or too old?'

'No, not at all. And I really hope it happens for you.' She squeezed her friend's hand tightly, meaning every word. 'You're one of the best mums I know, and you, Summer and Jake, you deserve every bit of happiness in the world.'

'Thank you.' Evelyn smiled back. 'So, what is it you wanted my opinion on?'

'I have a date this afternoon, and I don't know what to wear!'

'That's unlike you. You don't usually worry about things like this.'

Angela knew her friend was right, but that didn't stop the tornado of butterflies quickstepping around her stomach. 'This feels different.'

'Really? Who is it? Someone you met on an app?'

'No. Not an app.' She picked up the three outfits she'd brought down for consideration. 'This is what I've narrowed it down to.'

Evelyn studied the choices. 'What type of date is this?'

'Just a late Sunday lunch.'

'Well these are all lovely, but do you think they might be a little . . . dressy for Brockle's Retreat?'

'It's not the Retreat. It's some country hotel. And I get the impression it definitely isn't a jeans type of place.'

'Really? That's an impressive-sounding first date.'

'What makes you think it's a first date?' She held up an outfit.

'Hmm. Don't love that one.' Evelyn wrinkled her nose. 'I just didn't expect you to be worried about a date that wasn't a first one. Plus, you hadn't mentioned seeing anyone.'

'How about this?'

'That could work.' Evelyn nodded. 'But don't think I've noticed you ignoring my other question.'

Fiddlesticks and sugar-plum fairies. Angela had really hoped that had slid past Evelyn. 'It's Rick.' She winced.

'Rick, like smashed into the café, put you in that leg brace and is here under court orders Rick?'

'Uh huh. Do you think I'm crazy?'

'Well, no more so than usual.' Evelyn smirked. 'He was a good laugh down the pub, and did help us win the quiz — so there's that in his favour. But really, Rick?'

'Yeah. I think I really like him, Evie.'

'Would you accept some advice from a friend?'

'Always, when it's you.'

'Just . . . be careful. I wouldn't want to see him cause you any more hurt. Maybe take things slowly. You're still healing.'

'Yeah, I know. And so does he. But he's been really careful about my leg. I think he would have carried me to bed if I would have let him.' She smiled brightly and held up the last outfit option. 'How about this one? I'm not sure if it's a bit too much for a lunch date.'

'I've always thought blue looked good on you, but I can see what you mean — hang on, when you say "carried you to bed", do you mean . . . ?'

'Yeah.' Angela laughed, covering her mouth.

'I take it back. You might be a bit crazier than usual.'

'I know.' Angela shook her head, still laughing. 'I'm not sure what came over me, but . . . wow . . . I'm so glad it did.'

'Really?'

'Oh yeah, really.' Angela could feel the heat rising in her cheeks.

'Good for you.' Evelyn gave her a hug. 'I'm not the only one deserving some happiness. You spend so much of your life looking after your animals, making sure they get their happy-ever-after homes. It's about time you had some of your own. So, a first date after the morning after the night before?'

'That's about it, yeah.'

'Definitely the blue, then. Give him something to really sit up and pay attention to.'

'You think I should?' She fingered the blue dress, wondering if she really could.

'Absolutely, I do.' Evelyn grinned. 'Now, I should probably go see what the girls are up to.'

'Yeah, it has gone a bit quiet.' Angela smiled, knowing that she had nothing to worry about, apart from them wanting to claim all the animals as their own. Well, except for one thing. 'Hey, Evelyn? Is it OK if we keep this between ourselves?'

'You don't mean from Jake too, do you?' A small frown tugged at the edges of her friend's mouth.

'No, Jake's fine. It's just this . . . whatever it is . . . between me and Rick . . . it's really new, and I'm still trying to . . . I mean, we haven't really talked about what it is, or what it might be, and . . .'

'And you don't want the whole village weighing in with their opinions until you've figured it out?'

'Exactly.' She breathed a sigh of relief, glad Evelyn understood.

'Especially given that you met in less-than-ideal circumstances, and that gossip in this place could outrun a greyhound in full sprint.'

Angela nodded.

'And especially because your mum is probably going to have a few things to say about it when she gets back. I'm assuming you haven't talked to her about him yet?'

'No, not really.' She wasn't looking forward to that conversation at all.

'OK.' Evelyn grinned. 'But you have to keep me up to date on the gossip.'

'Obviously.'

'And you realise that if he puts so much as a single toe one step wrong, I'll be in serious danger of breaching my Nightingale pledge and doing him some "harmful or injurious mischief". And you know I mean it.'

'I do. And I'm lucky to have a friend like you.'

'Right back at you, Ange. Even if you do conspire against me with Jake and Summer to increase our menagerie!'

* * *

'This place is beautiful.' Angela gasped as she walked over the bridge that spanned the moat — an actual moat! 'It's more like a castle than a hotel.'

'Apparently it was. The original parts of it date back to the fifteenth century.' He'd made a point of memorising some facts he hoped she'd find interesting. He felt more nervous about this date with Angela — and more worried about impressing her — than he had done in years. With Yvette, it hadn't really been proper dates, and most of them — certainly the first ones, at least — were organised by agents and managing companies. All he'd had to do was turn up, smile for the cameras and turn on that "Maverick" charm. Which might well be why he felt so edgy; for the first time in a long time, that charm and persona wasn't going to impress at all, and he was dating as Ryan.

'Wow, that's really cool. I wonder if it's haunted.'

He gave himself a mental pat on the back. 'Apparently it is. People have reported hearing footsteps, seeing strange lights, and there's one corridor where a maid sometimes appears and disappears.'

'Did you look that up for today?'

'Umm, maybe?' he admitted reluctantly, not wanting to seem geeky, or overly eager.

'That's really sweet of you.' Angela tucked her hand through his arm and smiled at him, making him feel ten feet tall. The way she looked at him made him rethink all his worries — she wasn't judging him, or measuring him up against expectations based on his videos, because she already knew him as Ryan. Which was equal parts strange, and somewhat scary — he didn't have his big, showy persona to hide behind.

'Oh wow,' Angela breathed the exclamation as they followed the discreet and elegant signs to the dining room, where they were met by a hostess who could have easily doubled as a model on her days off. He automatically scanned the room as they were led to their table, checking for anyone he should probably say hello to, then froze when his eyes landed back on Angela. She'd slipped off her coat — which he belatedly realised he should have offered to help with — and handed it to the hostess.

His breath caught in his throat as he took in the sky-blue dress that wrapped around her, crossing over her chest and tying tightly at her waist, before flaring out to float down to below her knees. His eyes caught on the bow at her hip, and for a moment he had to really focus on not thinking about wrapping his fingers around the silky-looking fabric and tugging it undone. Despite being starving when they'd entered the place, he suddenly found he couldn't care less about food.

He held his arm out to her, steadying her as she sat — still feeling that flush of guilt for the brace she had to wear. Within moments they'd ordered drinks, and he could turn his attention back to her.

'This place is so beautiful,' she whispered to him as she glanced around. Was she nervous? He wasn't sure he'd ever seen Angela lacking confidence in anything. 'I have to admit, I feel a bit under-dressed.'

'You look perfect,' he told her, honestly. 'How can you think anything else?'

She beckoned to him, leaning across the table conspiratorially. 'You know this dress came from a charity shop?'

'You're kidding.'

'Nope, and not just a charity shop, but the bargain bin too. It was ankle length, but it had a big hole — probably where the former owner had caught their heel or something — and had these huge, flared seventies-style sleeves. But I loved the colour, and Mum taught me to sew years ago, so I bought it, reshaped the sleeves, and shortened it.'

'Then you are as talented as you are fair and beautiful, and I wish I had a drink to toast you.'

She watched him, her lips twitching for a few moments before she snorted and burst out into giggles, which she hastily muffled with her napkin. 'Sorry, sorry.'

'Are you OK?'

'Yeah.' She nodded and took a deep breath. 'Can I be honest with you?'

'Of course.'

'I know you're probably just trying to be charming, and I appreciate it — I really do — but you don't need to try so hard to impress me. I'd much rather we just relax and be our normal selves, rather than talking like we've stepped out of the pages of a Jane Austen novel.'

'I'm being a bit over the top, aren't I?'

'You brought me flowers to my front door, refused to let me drive here, and have brought me to one of the most stunning places I've ever eaten. I'm already impressed, Ryan.'

'Sorry. It's been a while since I've actually done this — and even longer as . . . well, as myself. But since we're being honest . . . ?'

'Yeah?'

'I'm really starting to like the sound of my name on your lips. Or is that cheesy too?'

'It's a bit cheesy.' Angela grinned at him. 'But at least it's a bit more honest. Though I suspect if I followed it up with something like "it's time to muck out the donkeys", you'd be a bit less happy to hear me call your name.'

'Maybe true.' He laughed.

If the waiter had heard their odd exchange, he did well to hide it. 'Would sir and madam like to peruse our menus, or are you here for our Sunday repast?'

'I'm all about the Sunday roast today.' Ryan grinned, looking forward to a stack of roasties. 'What about you, Angela? Do you want the main menu?'

'Do you have any vegetarian options?' Her question sent a wave of panic through Ryan. He'd been so busy checking how prestigious the place was, pulling the few strings he had to get them a late reservation, that he'd completely forgotten to check if Angela would actually be able to eat there.

'Of course, madam. The non-meat option today is a hand-pulled seitan en croute with chicken o' wood and caramelised red onion duxelles, finished with a black truffle jus.'

Well, at least there was *one* option.

'I'm sorry, did you say chicken?'

'Chicken of the wood, madam.' The waiter leaned forward. 'It's a mushroom that grows locally. Our chef harvested them in the grounds this morning.'

'Thank you, I'll have that please.'

'Make that two, please.'

'Very good. Your drinks will be brought over shortly.'

'Thanks.' Angela waited until he'd left, then leaned forward. 'Do you know what it is I've just ordered?'

'You mean you don't?' He tried not to laugh.

'Well, I think I ordered the only vegetarian option. I know what seitan is, and apparently chicken of the woods is a mushroom. But I can't remember what en croute is. Don't laugh at me.' She glared at him.

'Sorry, I'm only laughing because I'm not totally sure what it is either,' Ryan admitted. 'En croute is basically beef Wellington, only in this case, apparently the beef has been made from something that sounds like yanked devil. What is that?'

'What?' Angela stared at him in confusion, before finally cracking up with laughter. '*Seitan*, not Satan. It's a vegan protein made from gluten. It's fairly bland on its own, but really good at taking on the flavours of other things. Why did you order it if you didn't know what it is?'

'I didn't want to be rude.'

'How would you be . . . Oh, right, because I'm vegetarian, you don't want to eat meat in front of me.'

'Exactly.'

'Because you think it's rude?'

'Isn't it?'

'I've seen you eat ham sandwiches before,' she pointed out.

'Yeah, but that was before we were dating.'

'So that's what we're doing now, is it?'

'Isn't this a date? I'd sort of hoped it was.'

'But one date is quite different from dat*ing*.'

Now he'd put the words out there, he might as well be honest. 'Yes, but I was hoping this one date would lead to a lot more.'

'Really?' Her smile and the warmth in her eyes sent his pulse rocketing.

'Yeah, really.' He reached across the table to grasp her fingers. 'And I'm kind of hoping you feel the same.'

'Maybe I might. Depending.'

'On what?' Whatever it was, he was pretty sure he was going to agree to it, or do it, or figure out a way to make it happen.

'On whether or not you order what you really want to eat.' She squeezed his fingers. 'If you want to change the way you eat, then I'm happy to offer you any advice and recipes or whatever. But you should only do it because you want to, not because you think it would make me or anyone else like you better.'

'You're really OK if I sit here and eat beef in front of you?'

'I appreciate that you asked, but I really am OK with it. For goodness' sake, you've seen what some of my residents eat. I'm really not that squeamish, and I really would like you to relax and enjoy yourself. And *be* yourself. I'm here because I like *you*, Ryan. It would be nice to get to know you better.' She looked up as the waiter returned with their drinks. 'I don't suppose it would be too late to change our order, would it?'

* * *

Angela looked at the dessert and tried not to laugh. Just like the main it was beautifully plated, incredibly elegant and utterly tiny. She had no doubt it would be delicious, but honestly, half a sliced apple, three walnuts and a spoonful of oats was not what she considered an apple crumble. Even if it was deconstructed. And anytime custard was served in an egg cup — albeit a cut glass and incredibly elegant one — it wasn't going to be anywhere near enough for her liking.

Even taking extra time between bites, she finished the dessert in record time and reached for the coffee that had accompanied it — ironically served in a cup big enough to have bathed one of her hedgehogs in.

'There is absolutely no way you're paying for this.' Ryan pulled the smart leather bill-holder out of her reach before she could look at it.

'I'm happy to go halves,' she argued, while wondering whether they'd be charged half-price for the less than half-sized meals. Probably not.

'Please, you're my guest. It's my pleasure, honestly.'

'Ryan . . .' she started to argue.

'Nope.' He held it out of her reach. 'I'm not letting you pay.'

'You're not letting me? Really?'

'Really.' He grinned at her. 'And you can glare at me all you want, it's not going to work, and I know you're faking. You're not really annoyed with me.'

She folded her arms across her chest. 'Is that what you think?'

'Yeah, because you have a tell.' He wriggled his eyebrows at her, and she had to try really hard not to laugh. 'Right here.' He stroked her cheek, making her shiver. 'It's not quite a dimple, but a sort of mini one. And it appears when you're trying not to laugh. You get the same look when you're trying to tell off Ruby or Mallow.'

'I didn't know that.'

'Well how often do you look in a mirror when you're trying to scold a fox?'

'Not often.'

'So you're going to let me pay for dinner, right?' He continued stroking her cheek, and the shivery sensations made it more difficult to concentrate. 'Say yes, Angela. Just for once, let someone look after you. Please?'

'All right. Yes. Thank you.'

'You're more than welcome.' He signalled to the waiter, paid, then tucked a cash tip into the folder.

Angela blanched at the notes he'd folded and left. Either he was an incredibly generous tipper, or the meal had been far more expensive than she wanted to know.

'Are you ready?' He held her coat out for her, helping her into it, then offered his arm as they walked back down the long corridor.

'There's something I feel like I want to tell you,' he murmured as they stepped into the now-empty reception.

'OK.' Angela turned to look at him.

'It's a bit of a confession, really.'

'I'm starting to feel a little worried. Should I be?'

'No, not worried. Although I have to admit I'm feeling kind of nervous.' His shy smile was so unlike the smarmy, cocky grin when he'd first shoved a camera in her face — she couldn't help but think about how much he'd changed.

'Tell me then, if you think it will help.'

'Well, it will either help or I'm going to fall flat on my face.' He stroked her fingers where they still rested on his arm. 'Because, the thing is, I'd really like to kiss you right now.'

Relieved laughter bubbled up inside of her. 'You've kissed me before. You've *more* than kissed me before.'

'Yeah, but I didn't spend ages thinking about how much I wanted to do it first. And, technically, if I were being really accurate, the first time, you kissed me.'

'I think I'm suddenly feeling a bit nervous too.' Angela could feel her breath coming more quickly, as her pulse stepped up its thumping.

'So what do you say? May I kiss you, Angel?'

'Angel, huh?' She found herself liking that name more and more.

'Yeah.' He stepped closer towards her, crowding her in the most delicious way, as he brought up one hand to cup her cheek. 'I'm waiting for your answer.'

The warmth in his eyes and his soft smile made her feel like she was still sat in front of the fireplace, and she had to swallow a couple of times to find her voice. 'Yes please.'

The glow of the fairy lights and glistening sparkle of the early tinsel seemed to explode into fireworks as he lowered his lips to hers and kissed her, gently easing his lips against hers and filling her senses. When he parted her lips, he tasted of the rich, dark, spicy coffee they'd both enjoyed, and the even more decadent dark chocolates they'd been served with. It was all she could do to remember they were in a public place, and not moan into his mouth and pull him even closer than he already was. She just about resisted the urge to bury her hands in his hair as he teased his lips and tongue against hers, sending shivers of desire through her.

He took his time, exploring her mouth slowly and gently until she could think of nothing else but him, until nothing mattered but that moment, that kiss.

When he eventually pulled away, slowly and reluctantly, she couldn't stifle a small moan, which just made him smile and kiss her again, only this time with such sweet gentleness that it stole her breath and turned her voice into a whisper. 'Wow.'

'Yeah, definitely worth the nerves.' He stroked her cheek once more, making her giggle, before taking her hand. 'Do you think maybe we should wait outside? Our ride should be here soon.'

'Yeah, probably. I certainly feel like I need to cool off.'

* * *

"How would you feel about a selfie?"

Angela looked at him suspiciously. 'For what?'

'Just for me. And maybe to send to my sister, if you're OK with that. But I promise it won't go online.'

'You've told your sister about me? About us?'

'Yeah.' Rick nodded. 'Don't worry. All good things.'

'OK. But I get to veto any pictures I don't like.' She smiled and leaned into him, fitting so perfectly that for a brief moment he felt like she belonged there, and didn't want her to move again. He held the phone out and took a few quick shots.

Angela didn't move, instead staying cuddled against him while she swiped back and forth through the photos. He couldn't have cared less which she picked — as far as he was concerned, she looked gorgeous in all of them.

They were halfway back to Broclington when his phone started buzzing and chiming. The first time he muted it without even looking at the screen. There were far more interesting and important things for him to focus on than whoever was on the other end of his phone. The second time he glanced at the screen and sent it to ignore. If it was important, his building caretaker could leave a message. It was probably just another leaseholder query about the colour of the hallways — like he cared.

When it rang a third time, Angela looked at him, her eyebrows raised. 'You know, you can answer the call. I'm not going to be offended.'

'I didn't want to interrupt our date with unimportant things,' he told her honestly as the phone rang off.

It started again almost immediately. 'It sounds like whoever it is thinks the call is important. It really is fine.'

'Thanks. I'll keep it short.'

He could only just make out the voice at the other end of the call. Mallow, on the other hand, he could hear so clearly he had to hold the phone away from his ear. 'Yes, yes, I can hear the problem. I really am sorry. I know. Yes, I appreciate that. Yes, I have requested quotes. Yes, I know. Yes, I'll do my best.' He hung up and turned to Angela, his joy turning to disappointment. 'I'm afraid I'm going to have to cut things short. Mallow . . .'

'I heard.' Angela nodded and squeezed his fingers.

'I'm going to have to go home and sort this out.'

'I know.'

'I really would have rather spent the evening with you.'

'You still can.' She shrugged easily and settled back into the seat. 'Just give the driver your address, we can go straight there.'

'You're sure?'

'I wouldn't have said it if I wasn't.' She gave him a smile that was so reassuring he felt all the tension drift away. He redirected the driver.

'You really are an angel at times.' He kissed her on the cheek and settled back.

'Oh no, this has underlying selfish motives.' This time her grin was wicked and full of cheek. 'I really, really want things to work out for you and Mallow.'

'So do I,' he admitted. 'I love that little chicken-butt. But how is that selfish?'

'Because at least part of the reason I want it to work out is I'm scared, if it doesn't, she'll end up living at Bill's. And I'm not sure my fingers would survive!'

'Don't worry, I'll protect you from the big, bad birdie.'

'Too right you will.' She shifted to rest her head on his shoulder.

In that moment, everything felt right with the world, and he was filled with a sense of calm and peace.

It didn't last long.

They were met at the building foyer by a small crowd of people — most of whom he vaguely recognised, but none of whom looked particularly happy. If a screaming cockatoo wasn't enough to ruin a brilliant date, then a mob of angry neighbours definitely was. He apologised, again and again, and again, while slowly making his way towards the lift. Then, just for a change of pace, he apologised even more while waiting for the blasted thing to arrive, as it seemed to have halved its usual speed.

Yes, he knew he was a bloody nuisance, no he didn't know how hard it was to get a baby back to sleep, no he didn't really know what he was doing, yes he'd already gotten quotes for soundproofing that would be installed as soon as possible and yes, he really was very sorry for disturbing everyone's weekends.

It was a relief when the doors finally opened and he could dart into the lift.

'Wow, that was intense,' Angela murmured a little shakily.

'Yeah.' He dragged his hands through his hair. 'Usually when I have that many people yelling at me it's because they want a photo.'

'Wow, you're really that popular?' Her eyes were wide.

'What can I say? People love Maverick,' he quipped, before wincing as he heard Mallow for the first time. 'Oh shit, she is really loud.'

He raced down the corridor as soon as the doors opened, slamming his key into the lock, expecting to see blood or terrible injuries from the racket she was making. He half-feared that one of the neighbour's cats had gotten in and was slowly killing her based on the blood-curdling screams. But he froze when he saw her: locked safely in her cage, running from one side of it to the other, angrily smacking the bars and screaming.

He yanked the door open to examine her, and she threw herself into his arms, clucking and cooing as if she hadn't been pissing off half his building seconds earlier.

'Is she OK?' Angela caught up, limping slightly in the brace.

'I can't see anything wrong.' He held her up, turned his wrist back and forth to study her. He forced himself to stay calm, knowing it would help relax her too. 'What's wrong, Mallow? You've been doing so well lately, and I was only gone for the afternoon. It's not even getting dark, and the sensor lights would have come on if it was. You've managed without me for a few hours at Bill's, and this cage is so much bigger and nicer.' He tried to reason with her, to figure out what had gone so wrong.

'Do you think it could be this?' Angela held up an empty food bowl. One of the ones that was usually bolted firmly to the cage.

'Well, is it?' He took the bowl from Angela and showed it to Mallow, who stuck her head inside his jacket. 'You broke your dish, dumped your dinner on the floor and decided to scream down half the bloody block?' He gently rubbed the bird's crest. 'Bloody hell, Chicken-butt, you're going to get me kicked out of here!'

'I thought you owned this place?' Angela took the bowl back and peered at the cage.

'I do — the flat at least.'

'Then how can you be kicked out?'

'Because I don't own the freehold, which means there are still rules and tenancy agreements. Ones that you—' he cuddled Mallow against him '—are currently breaking with all the noise.'

'Oh. I didn't realise. I've never had to deal with leaseholds before. And I guess my neighbours are more understanding than yours.'

'Lucky you.' He tucked Mallow into the crook of his elbow. 'Let's see what you've done.' He fiddled with the cage for a bit, then pulled out the cleaning tray that sat beneath the grate. 'I don't believe it. She's undone the bloody nuts.' He held up the evidence. 'It's supposed to be a parrot cage, I'd assumed that meant it was parrot-proof. She's not even that big by parrot standards!'

'Maybe we just didn't do them up tightly enough,' Angela suggested.

'Maybe. Right, let's get this sorted. And as for you, missy—' he bounced Mallow up and down on his arm, making her cackle and laugh '—you and I need a little chat. For one thing, this—' he tapped her beak gently with the nut '—is very naughty. For two, you're not going to starve. You had plenty of other food you could reach — look, here's your pinecone pick, and the lovely fresh breakfast I chopped you up. And you have treats if you can be bothered to get off your perch and learn to forage for them. And third — and this is very important. If you keep screaming like that, you will get us kicked out, and then we'll both end up living in a box.'

He looked up at Angela, who watched him with interest.

'I don't know how much she understands or not, so I decided just to talk to her normally. I'm not really one of those googa-wooga oogie-boogie type of people.'

He filled up Mallow's bowl — a task made a lot harder and messier by her insisting on "helping" — and put her, and the dish, back into the cage. 'I really am sorry about this, Angela.'

'I already told you, there's nothing to apologise for. It was a lovely meal.'

'But?'

'Did I say there was a but?' Her eyes were too wide, and that adorable little dimple thing had reappeared.

'No, but I thought I heard one anyway.'

'Nope.'

'Right. So you weren't thinking the portions were at all stingy.'

'I might have said "delicate" rather than stingy.'

'But if I offered to make something to eat — like toasted cheese — you wouldn't be at all interested in that?'

'All right, you got me.' She laughed. 'I know I'm probably supposed to be playing it coy or something, and pretending that I'm stuffed after half an apple and an egg cup full of custard, but I could demolish a round of cheese on toast. Especially if you've got Worcestershire sauce.'

'Obviously. Only thing you should put on it.'

'Well, onions or mushrooms can be really nice. But I agree. If you'd suggested ketchup I'm not sure I could have coped with that,' she teased.

'That would have been a dealbreaker then?'

'Ketchup on cheese on toast? Definitely.' She nodded firmly.

'I'll have to make a note of that. Screaming, bratty, bald chicken-butt birds you can handle, but ketchup on cheese is a dealbreaker.'

'Exactly.' She grinned, and he leaned over, wanting to kiss her. She wound her arms around his neck, rubbing her nose against his, brushing her lips against his gently then pulling away. It drove him crazy, and he wrapped his arms around her waist.

'Hey.' She wriggled, teasing him more. 'You promised to feed me.' The way she smiled as she bit her lip sent his desire to another level.

'I'll feed you in bed, if you like.'

'Hmm.' She tapped her finger against her lips, making him want to kiss her so badly it actually hurt. He couldn't ever remember wanting anyone as badly as he needed Angela. 'I might be able to be convinced . . .'

'I'm so glad you said that, otherwise I might have had to fall on my knees and beg.'

'Well, I wouldn't want to put you in that position . . . I mean, others, maybe . . .' And there it was again — that glint of mischief that made him realise he was in the very best type of trouble.

* * *

Angela winced as Ryan dragged his fancy coffee table across the hardwood floor, making a shriek that even Mallow complained at. 'Sorry.' He looked around, then grabbed a couple of cushions from the second couch and gently raised her leg up on top of them.

'Are you comfy? Warm enough?'

'I'm fine.' Angela shook her head, trying not to laugh. Even after her stay in hospital, and weeks of her mum's care, she still found it strange to be looked after, especially by someone she'd just been naked and very, very happy with. 'You really don't need to fuss.'

'Is it really fussing to try and look after you?'

'Maybe a bit.' Angela shoved the sleeves of a borrowed hoodie further up her arms.

'You look adorable, by the way.' He leaned over her, bracing himself on the back of the sofa to kiss her.

'My hair's a mess, you kissed off my lipstick, and I'm pretty sure the rest of my make-up isn't much better,' she complained, always the first person to criticise herself — it was just easier that way. 'I probably look awful.'

'Shut up, would you?' He kissed the tip of her nose.

'Excuse you?'

'Excuse yourself. You're the person being less than kind to someone I care about a lot. I'm not going to stand here and let you diss one of the most awesome people I know.'

'You're not making any sense.'

'Learn to accept a compliment, Angel. You're due a lot of them.' He kissed her on the cheek and stood. 'Now, what type of cheese on toast do you want?'

'Uh, cooked. Ideally with Worcestershire sauce.'

'Well that's a given.' He laughed. 'But what type of cheese? Cheddar, mozzarella, goat's, Gouda, brie . . . I might have some Swiss as well.'

Angela gaped at him. 'How much cheese do you have?'

'I like cheese. Yvette used to complain it made my breath smell, and now . . . I'm enjoying what I missed.' He gave her a look that was so hot, for a second, Angela thought he could have melted the cheese with it — then laughed at herself, glad that he couldn't read her thoughts. Even in her own head, she sounded cheesier than his menu selection.

'Chef's choice.' She shrugged.

'Combo then.' He rubbed his hands together gleefully. 'And tea?'

'It's fine, I can come make that.' She put her feet down.

'Nope, you're my guest, and I'd really like you to stay there. Plus, your friend told you that you need to be careful on your leg still. And I did tell you I'm a little bit scared of her.'

'Oh, Evelyn's lovely.'

'She seems it,' Ryan agreed. 'But I also get the impression she's not someone I would want to annoy, say, for example, by letting you set back your recovery at all.'

'That's true,' Angela conceded.

'So, in the interests of me not annoying your friend, and supporting getting you back on your feet as soon as possible, will you please just stay here — looking adorable in my hoodie — and let me look after you?'

'All right, all right, I give in. But do you want to let Mallow out to keep me company? I think she and I need to work on being the type of friends who don't bite each other, right, Chicken?'

By the time Ryan came back, Mallow had edged along the back of the couch to within arm's reach of Angela, and was delicately taking treats from her outstretched fingers, chuckling happily every so often.

'Well, at least no one is screaming.' Ryan grinned. 'Come on, Mallow. Back to your stand. No scalding cheese for you!'

'Yum, this looks delicious.' Angela picked up a slice and grinned as the cheese fell in long strings. She caught them, twisting them round and then sucking them off her fingers.

'Yeah, pretty damn tasty.' Ryan was watching her as she licked her thumb clean.

She giggled and blushed. 'Stop looking at me like that.'

'Like what?'

'Like *that*.' She was interrupted when his phone rang. 'It's OK if you want to get that.'

He reluctantly answered the call. 'Hello? Yes, thanks for calling back . . . OK, yes, yes, that sounds fine . . . Yes, please, pop that over to me in writing . . . And how long? Really? Oh, that's longer than I'd expected . . . No, no, of course, that makes sense. Yes, yes please. Brilliant. Thanks . . . Yes, include those details please. Thanks . . . Bye.'

'Everything OK?'

'Yeah, just a quote coming back for the soundproofing here. I was pretty happy with this firm, so will probably go with them.' He sighed. 'I just hadn't expected that it would take so long.'

'How long is long?' Angela asked around a mouthful of cheese.

'Weeks not days.' He shrugged. 'I knew it was a big job, but I hadn't really appreciated how big or how messy. They'll have to install it all, re-plaster, which apparently takes time to dry, and then redecorate.'

'Well, I guess you can look at it as an opportunity to add some more colour to the place.'

'What's wrong with it?'

She clapped her hand over her mouth. 'Nothing, it's fine. Lovely.'

'Fine.' He nodded. 'Go on, tell me what you really think.'

'No, I was being rude. I'm really sorry.'

'Now I really want to know. Go on,' he dared her. 'Be rude and tell me what you really think.'

'Well . . . for me — and you have to understand this is completely personal . . . it's just a little beige.'

'It's not beige. It's Moroccan sandstone.'

'Clearly.' Angela bit back a grin.

'I guess it could be a bit brighter.' Ryan looked around again. 'You know, now you've said that, I'm not sure why I don't have more colour in here. Something to think about, I guess. Getting the work done is going to be a problem though. I can't exactly move into a hotel with the mini banshee here.'

'No, and being around dust probably wouldn't be good for her.'

'No. It wouldn't. I guess I'll have to find a short-term let somewhere. Who wouldn't mind a parrot.' He shot her a cheeky grin. 'I don't suppose you know anyone looking for a short-term tenant? I can be really quite charming.'

'Oh, I know . . .' She hesitated. 'You know, actually, I think I might know somewhere. Let me make some calls?'

'That would be great. Thanks, Angel.' He placed a kiss on her cheek, filling her with warmth.

CHAPTER NINE

Ryan paused at the door of the cutesy little stone and slate cottage and peered at the nameplate: *Aosán Taigh*. He grinned. He'd never lived anywhere that had a name instead of a number, and made a note to ask Angela what it meant. Or her friend Liv. After all, she'd apparently lived there until moving in with her fiancé a few weeks ago.

He let himself in with the key from the agent, resisting the urge to pull out his phone for some quick shots. Honestly, all it needed was a dusting of snow and a wreath and it would look like the perfect Christmas card. A tiny hallway with stone floors — so different from the grand entrance to his flat, designed to impress people — led to a small living room that was painted the colour of really good custard. The limited space in there was taken up almost completely by a squishy brown sofa that looked far more comfortable than his designer one, and a huge stone fireplace. If he rearranged a bit, he'd just about have space for Mallow's cage.

The kitchen couldn't have been any less like the one installed in his flat, but it was cute all the same, with one of those expensive Aga things he so often saw in design magazines. He peered out the window at the large garden — definitely

171

a step up from his balcony. Even in winter it looked pretty. He followed the instructions to turn on the heating — he wasn't sure he wanted to risk an actual fire yet — and headed back to the waiting moving van. There wasn't much in it — just his basics, computer gear and Mallow's stuff. Hopefully it wouldn't take too long, and the driver would be minded to help him for a few extra quid.

He'd just given the driver a hefty tip and waved him off with "Merry Christmas" wishes, when a very familiar, battered old estate pulled up. He sauntered down the garden path — still slightly surprised he even had a garden path, because the whole situation was feeling very surreal.

'Hello, gorgeous.' He offered his arm to help her out the car. 'Your timing is perfect.'

'Let me guess, you need help building a parrot cage?' She kissed him — the gesture so natural and easy that he wondered why it had taken them so long to get together.

'Actually, no. We just got it through the door. It was tight at the flat, but that can be repainted, and the back door here is huge. You—' he kissed her again '—are just in time for my first cuppa here. Thankfully I found an electric kettle in one of the cupboards, because I'm not totally sure how to use an Aga. Going to have to YouTube that!'

'They're not so hard.' Angela smiled at him. 'But if we're having tea, you might want to grab the box from the passenger seat.'

'Did you bring me a house-warming gift?'

'Of course.' The smile she gave him was sunshine itself. 'Even though it's just temporary, it seemed a good idea. Besides, Brockle cakes are almost always a good idea.'

'Agreed.' He leaned in to grab the cakes. 'Thanks, Angel. I would say "come in and I'll show you round", but given your friend lived here, I suspect you know this cottage better than I do.'

'There may have been a few hours spent here.' She held onto his arm, her hand settling comfortably in the crook of his elbow as they walked up the garden path.

'Do you know what it means, by the way?'

'What?'

'Ayosan Tiger.'

'What?'

'The name of the house.'

'Ooh' She giggled. 'It's pronounced more like *ow-sin tay*. It means the fairies' house. It even has an old fairy well in the garden. At least, if you listen to the stories, it's supposed to be a wishing well.'

'Oh, you're going to have to tell me some of these stories.' He wondered if his Rickheads might like them. Probably. It sounded like it might be pretty unusual, and they usually liked that.

'If you really want to know the tales, you should ask Sarah and Summer.'

'Your little helpers?' He'd met them a few times.

'Yeah, they're really into the old stories about the village. Especially the fairy ones. Quite possibly they know even more than I do. I'm pretty sure if you agreed to help with cleaning the guineas they'd tell you lots of stories. They're also easily bribed by cake. Especially Brockle.'

'Can't blame them for that! I'm still amazed this place was available. It's like an Insta-reel made into reality.'

'It is pretty idyllic.' Angela nodded. 'But, maybe it was meant to be. Even if it is just for a few weeks.'

* * *

A few days later, Angela looked up from the badger enclosure at the sound of a bell, followed by cheerful whistles and cackling. For a second she couldn't believe what she was seeing.

'Morning, gorgeous!' Ryan called out cheerfully, as if the bizarre sight was perfectly normal.

'I'm definitely awake still, right? I didn't fall or bang my head or something?' She shook her head as she walked over to kiss him, keeping her dirty hands away from him.

'I know it looks a bit crazy, but it makes sense.' Ryan laughed as he got off the bright purple bike, which looked better sized and shaped for a teenage girl than it did him. He held it upright so it didn't disturb Mallow, who was dancing up and down on the handlebars, bobbing her head quickly as she chattered happily.

'Go on . . .'

'Well, remember the "flying" lessons I was giving her?'

'I remember you running around with her on a stick . . .'

'Well, the bike's faster. And she seems to like it.'

'So I can see. And the outfit?' She eyed up the fluorescent pink jumper that appeared to have a tutu attached.

'I didn't want her to get cold. And I think she likes it.' He offered his arm to the bird. 'Show Angela your pretty dress.'

She laughed when Mallow turned in a circle on his arm and spread her wings, flapping them. 'Yes, it's a very pretty dress. You're a pretty girl, Mallow. I think her feathers are looking a lot better too.'

'Yeah, she's getting some pink feathers on her chest. Not just fuzzy grey down anymore.'

'That's great,' Angela enthused. 'But, seriously? A tutu?'

'It's called a Polly Pullover.' He rolled his eyes. 'They're specially made in America for each bird. And I wanted it quickly, and the only ones they had ready in her size were Halloween leftovers. It was ballerina or scary pumpkin. And she is supposed to be pink, so I figured tutu it was. I couldn't keep shoving her inside my hoodies for warmth.'

'Hey, I wasn't complaining. I think it's adorable. Let me just finish with the badgers and we can have a drink.'

'I'll go settle this one.' He bounced Mallow up and down. 'And I'll stick the kettle on.'

'Perfect, thanks.'

He came out a few minutes later. 'Phone call for you. Marston's Feeds.'

Damn. Not a call Angela particularly wanted to take. She was quite sure it was going to put a dampener on her good mood. 'Thanks.' She scrubbed her hands under the hose before taking the phone.

After a few minutes she hung up, trying to regain her composure. It wasn't as bad as she'd feared, but it was still more than she could stretch to afford. She sighed sadly. She'd figure it out, she always did. But each time it took more and more out of her, leaving her further and further down.

Still, things usually worked out, one way or another, and almost always for the best. She'd have never guessed Ryan — the person sent to her as punishment for the harm he'd wrought on her and Broclington — would end up being so important, or bringing so much joy. With that thought, she smiled and headed into the office.

'Hello.' Ryan wrapped his arm around her as soon as she entered the room, kissing her and sliding one hand up her spine, teasing her lips until she was breathless. 'Sorry, I just really wanted to say "good morning" properly.'

'Yeah, that's something you don't ever need to apologise for.' She tried to get her brain working again.

'Coffee?' He stepped away, then handed her a steaming, very welcome mug.

'Thanks, really need this.'

'Is it really that bad already? Couldn't sleep without yours truly?' he quipped. When she didn't laugh, he looked at her more closely.

'Don't worry about it.' She hobbled to her tiny desk. Worrying and figuring it out was her job, not his.

'What's wrong?' He steadied the office chair for her as he did all the time, making sure it didn't shift or roll away. She wondered if he even thought about it, or if it was just automatic. 'How can I help?'

'It's just the same old nonsense on a different day.' Angela shrugged, hoping he'd drop the topic.

'Problem shared is a problem halved?'

'But does that actually help the problem?' Angela pondered aloud. 'Or does it just spread it out a bit more?'

'Well, they also say misery loves company.' Ryan nodded. 'I've got loads of these silly old sayings and adages. Want to tell me what's up or shall I keep going? They say it's always darkest before the dawn . . . and that every cloud has a silver lining.'

'I could do with finding that cloud.' She sighed into her coffee. 'That was one of my feed suppliers. Price increases. It varies a bit from product to product, but it's going to equate to around twelve per cent on my usual order. Another hundred-ish a month.'

'A hundred isn't that bad, is it?'

'It wouldn't be if it was just the one supplier.' Angela felt her throat tighten with frustration and misery. 'But it isn't. All my suppliers are putting their prices up, some more than others. Everything is starting to cost more, and donations are dropping off because people are having to make harder choices.' She rubbed at her eyes irritably. 'And I've had to take time out from fundraising since . . .'

'Since I hurt you.'

She hadn't wanted to say the words, to put the blame on him, to put the ugliness of how they met between them again, but there it was. 'Yeah.'

'Right.' Ryan dragged over a chair. 'Do you want to show me what it is you — we — are dealing with?'

'Ryan, you don't need to do this. It's not your problem.'

His hand found hers, warm and reassuring. 'I'm here to help, remember?' His eyes met hers, level and serious. 'And it's more than just the court order, Angel. I want to help. Please?'

'You really don't have to. It's fine. I'll sort it out. I always do.'

'I don't doubt that.' Ryan squeezed her fingers again. 'I know you're completely capable, and I fully believe you when you say you'll sort it. But I also mean it when I say I want to help. Anything I can do to make your life a bit easier I want the chance to do. OK? And that's not me saying that I think you need help, because I don't. It's just me wanting to offer it.'

As supportive and kind as her friends, and her mum were, she was used to dealing with things like this by herself. 'Really?'

'Yeah, really. Let me help you, Angel.'

'OK.' She slid her hand up his arm and tugged him closer so she could kiss him. 'Thank you.' She slid the blue folder — her folder of misery — across the desk.

* * *

For about a week, Ryan loved his new — albeit very temporary — life in Broclington. Maybe it was because he knew it was temporary, but it had that wonderful, holiday-esque feel to everything. It was calmer and quieter than his flat, and he'd just about worked out the weirdness of the Aga — with some careful and very enjoyable instructions from Angela. He slept better, got up later and still had time to walk — or cycle the ridiculous purple bike — to Bill's most mornings, in time to join Angela for a round of coffee before they started work. When he didn't walk there with her from his cottage, or wake up next to her.

And he'd found time, in between the never-ending rounds of feeding, medicating and cleaning, to set up some fundraising links for Bill's and create online shopping lists to help guide people's donations. It wasn't enough, but it was just the start of his ideas and plans . . . he just knew he had to tread carefully so as not to risk stomping all over Angela's toes. Bill's was her baby, and he knew and respected that. He had to prove that his smaller ideas might work before trying to sell her on the bigger ones — including the one he hadn't mentioned to her, despite starting weeks ago.

He looked down at Mallow, her wings stretched on the handlebars, as he peddled carefully along the street, making sure not to jolt her over any tree roots. It would be better once he got to the winding path in the park, which was well-maintained, and he could push down harder on the pedals, so

Mallow could really spread her wings and feel like she was fly-ing. She'd thrown herself off the sofa again last night, thump-ing heavily to the floor and scaring him. He'd have to figure something out about that.

He was just wondering if you could buy some sort of room-wide crash mat — and what the hell you'd type into a search engine to find them — when he cycled past the cricket pavilion and brought the bike to a slow stop. Mallow whistled at him, tilting her head to look at him, wondering what he was up to and why her fun had been cut short.

'I just want to see what's going on.' The usually quiet, locked-up pavilion had been thrown open, and half a dozen large vans were spilling out equipment all over the usually serene park.

Mallow squawked at him again, this time less patiently, ruffling the feathers she'd grown that were sticking out of her latest pink outfit. Regardless of how nosey he felt like being, she was very clearly wanting to start her morning business of begging treats from Angela while being told how pretty she was.

'All right, you impatient brat.' He rubbed his fingers against her cheek and ear, in the spot that usually made her fluff up even more and pin her eyes happily. 'Let's get your royal feathers over to Bill's.' He pushed down on the pedals again, allowing Princess Mallow to spread her growing flight feathers and pretend she was flying.

He pulled into Bill's a few minutes later, Mallow dancing and cackling happily, and was thrilled to see Angela waiting for him. It could have been coincidence — most likely she'd just been into one of the many sheds, checking on one animal or another, and hadn't specifically come out to greet him. But he liked the thought that maybe she had heard them.

'Well, it's about time. I was starting to miss you.' His heart filled with warmth at her words. 'Hello, my darling, aren't you looking spectacularly beautiful today? Another new outfit?' She swooped down and scooped up Mallow, who immediately started fluffing her feathers and bowing her head in play-flirting.

'As much as I'm glad you two have gotten past the knuckle-cracking stage, I'm starting to feel a little left out,' he grumbled half-heartedly as he put his bike out of the way.

'Oh, you poor boy. Do you need your ego stroking?' She pouted and fluttered her eyelashes at him, but in a way that was designed to tease him.

'Well, if my ego is the only thing of mine I can convince you to stroke . . .'

The grin that got from her was worth the smack to his arm. He loved teasing her, making her eyes flash with mischief, and he loved it when she teased him right back.

'I can't believe you would say something like that in front of such innocent, easily corruptible young ears.'

'Whose?'

'Mallow's of course.' She held her hands as if ready to cover the bird's ears. 'How can you possibly pollute her ears with such things?'

'You know she could well be older than either of us? And, as smart as she is, I'm not sure she understands innuendo.'

'Of course she does, don't you, sweet girl?'

Naturally, she agreed with Angela, bouncing up and down, scolding him while she climbed up to Angela's shoulder.

'It's a good thing you're cute, you little traitor.' He grabbed her beak, play wrestling with her gently as he leaned around to kiss Angela. 'Morning, gorgeous.'

'Good morning.' She kissed him right back, wrapping her free arm around his neck.

Just when things were about to get really interesting, he felt a non-too-gentle nip to his ear, followed by a loud cackle. 'Lazybastardgettoworkhahahahahaha!'

'She is right.' Angela pulled back reluctantly. 'We have work to do.'

'I could go off you.' He glared at Mallow and grabbed her beak again, making her cackle loudly. 'Never thought I'd be bullied by less than a kilo of feathers! Can't think why I put up with you.'

She fluffed up her feathers and waved her foot at him. 'Upupupupupup!'

'Yes, your majesty.' She waited until she was level with his face, before blowing him a big kiss. 'Oh yeah, that's why. You're cute.'

'Right, when you two have finished your love-in, we need to get to work.'

They were so busy, it wasn't until a few hours later that he remembered to ask about the park.

'They'll be setting up for the Christmas Tree Dance.'

'Which is . . . ?'

'Oh, it's lovely. It's a Christmas dance we've held here for years, and it's gradually got bigger and bigger. The whole village goes, and everyone dresses up and the WI make lots of food, and most of the businesses who are able to bring food do as well — pot-luck style. And there's a few hours of family fun, before the kids go home and the adults dance the night away.'

'Sounds amazing.'

'It is.'

'So it's something you usually go to?'

'Of course.'

'Are you going this year?' His mouth was suddenly drier than it had any business being.

'Planning to, yes. I'll probably just meet my friends there.'

'Would you, maybe, want to go with me?' He was sure his heart thumped loudly enough that she could probably hear it.

'With you, like with you, with you?'

He nodded, struggling to unstick his tongue from the roof of his mouth.

'A public date in the village?'

'Yes. I mean, I'll understand if you don't want to, because this is your home, not mine, but . . . I'd love you to be my date for the Christmas Tree Dance. If you want to.'

'So we'd be going public as . . . a couple? In Broclington?'

He couldn't tell what she was thinking. Maybe it was too big of a thing to ask, but he really hoped she understood what it meant to him.

'Yes. I'd like to.'

'OK.' She gave a tiny nod.

'Really?' He couldn't believe his luck. He was going to have to buy a lottery ticket after this.

'Yes, really. Unless you don't want to?' She looked like she was starting to doubt her answer.

'Angela?' He caught her face between his hands and kissed her gently. 'I'd be really proud to be your escort. To be your date.'

CHAPTER TEN

Angela ran her fingers through her hair again, spreading the serum through her curls, and looked in the mirror. She hesitated, peering at the box on her dressing table, then shrugged and thought: why not?. It was the Christmas Tree Dance, after all, so she wove the sparkling twisted pins amongst her hair, and dusted shimmering gloss across her lips. A silver-grey pashmina and she'd be ready.

She wasn't a model-skinny social media starlet, and she wasn't all that sure the pretty-make-up-and-dresses thing was really her — but she had to admit, she did scrub up pretty well. And, as much as it annoyed her to admit it, the dress her mum had gifted her for Christmas the previous year was perfect. It wasn't anything that she would have ever chosen: a handmade dress that started off smooth over her shoulders and chest, fitted closely against her in dove grey silk, before flaring out at the waist, shading into soft blues and bringing in different fabrics and shades of blue that turned into a full skirt, which swished and swirled as she moved. And she did, twisting back and forth and enjoying the soft sigh of the fabrics. Although her still recovering leg meant heels weren't an option — she wasn't sure that wasn't more of a handy excuse

— so she was wearing purple biker boots that she'd glammed up with some sparkly laces. They'd have to do. Not exactly elegant or glamorous, but comfy, and very her.

She didn't think anyone would comment on it, but if anyone didn't like it — they'd just have to lump it. And that went as much for how she looked as it did for whose hand she'd be holding. She didn't think any of her friends would have real issues — they'd been welcoming enough at the pub — but other people, and her mum . . . she wasn't so sure.

She'd spoken to her mum about it a few days before. She'd put it off for as long as she'd dared after Cathy had gotten back from staying with her sister — but she hadn't been able to avoid it forever, knowing how Broclington was, and how fast news would spread. So she'd done her best to reassure her mum — explaining that she really did like him, and that he'd changed a lot from the man who'd caused them both so much hurt — but Cathy had pulled a face, warning her daughter that she should be careful. She didn't trust that he wouldn't hurt her again. She had a very low opinion of him, and wasn't afraid to share it. It hadn't been an argument — not exactly — but it had left Angela feeling a bit out of sorts, and at odds with her mum. It wasn't a feeling she liked, and she hadn't yet worked out how to deal with it.

Thankfully, Ryan's knock at the door interrupted her thoughts before they took a path she didn't really want to follow. It was a few minutes to get down the stairs to open the door, and when she did, she had to remind herself to close her mouth. Ryan looked . . . like his online persona. His dark hair was slicked back neatly, making his dark eyes seem even deeper and brighter than usual, and his slick, dark blue tux fit like it had been made just for him.

Part of her wanted to pull him into her house then and there, locking the door firmly behind them, but the other part held back, slightly unsure of the gorgeous, polished man who stood in front of her. He reached for her hand, raised it to his lips and gently kissed her fingers, his eyes not leaving hers.

'You look spectacular, Angela.'

She had no idea how to respond to that, and felt a flush creeping up her cheeks. Rather than think about it, she wrapped her arms around him in a warm hug, mindful of her carefully applied make-up. And wow, he smelled amazing — something stronger and spicier than usual, but utterly delicious. She was tempted to bury her face in his neck and stay right there.

'Oh wow, are these for me?' She couldn't miss the flash of colour behind his back.

'Right, the flowers.' He grinned, looking less like Maverick and far more like the Ryan who'd turned his life upside down for a bird. 'I'd forgotten. You really are stunning.' He pulled the flowers from behind his back. 'For you.'

She gathered them in her arms, inhaling their sweet scent — a beautiful mix of creamy white roses, mixed with frosted pinecones and bright, glossy red berries. She struggled to remember the last time a man had brought her flowers before Ryan, yet here he was again, with another beautiful bunch. 'They're beautiful. Thank you so much.' She leaned forward and kissed him on the cheek. 'Please, come in while I find a vase. You really didn't have to do this.'

'I know. But the way they made you smile, I'm really glad I did.'

And just like that, she couldn't care less about her make-up — she wrapped her arms back around his neck and kissed him deeply, breathing in his scent and loving the feeling of his hand nestling in the small of her back, pulling her closer, while the other slid around the back of her neck.

* * *

Ryan was used to a certain level of attention, and even expected it — after all, that was how Maverick made his money — but the quiet ripple that went through the crowded cricket clubhouse when he walked in, Angela on his arm, was something else.

'I think we might be public now,' he whispered to her.

184

'I'm good with that.' She brushed a kiss against his lips, smiling as she did so. When she pulled back, she winked at him. 'Just in case anyone had any questions.'

Damn, she really was amazing. For a few seconds, she eclipsed everything and everyone else in the room.

'There you are, you look gorgeous, Ange!' Liv gave her a brief hug as they walked into the ball, leaving him time to look around at the shimmering winter wonderland that had been created inside of the cricket clubhouse, which spilled out into a marquee that had been added onto the back.

'Evening, Rick. Good to see you again.' She gave him a bright smile. 'Nice entrance.'

'Good to see you too, Liv.' He wasn't sure how he was supposed to respond to her other comment, so ignored it. 'You look lovely.'

'Thank you.' Liv smiled. 'You scrub up pretty well yourself.'

'Thanks.' He nodded, still not knowing how to reply.

'Certainly better than when you're elbow-deep in Ernie's leavings.'

'Well, at least I'd like to think I smell better now.'

'True enough.' Liv laughed. 'I should go find the girls. Have a good evening.'

'Thanks.' Angela kissed her friend on the cheek before sliding her hand into his.

He smiled at her as they headed further in, walking down a red carpet edged with snowflakes and fairy lights that shimmered and flickered in a game of chase. It was far from the fanciest carpet he'd walked, but with Angela by his side, he was pretty sure it might be one of his favourites.

They were stopped again by an older woman who had Angela's stunning eyes, and curls streaked with grey. Rick gulped, hoping that his nerves weren't making his palm sweaty in Angela's hand, as the woman he'd dreaded meeting looked him up and down.

'So you're him.' Her tone of voice and expression gave nothing away.

'Yes, ma'am.'

'And you convinced Ange to be your date.'

'Yeah.' He looked at Angela, watching her when he answered. 'She very kindly and graciously agreed to give me another chance. She's pretty amazing.'

The smile that spread across Angela's face lit up his world.

'Yes she is.' Her comment snapped him back into the room. 'And you'll do well to remember that.' She looked Rick up and down again — he had to fight the urge to squirm. 'I've heard a lot about you. Most of it a lot less bad than I would have expected, given how you quite literally crashed your way into our lives.'

'Mum, please don't.' He felt Angela's fingers tighten around his, and he looked down in surprise. The last thing he'd expected was for her to defend him.

'I really am very sorry about that, Mrs Turner. And I *am* doing my best to turn over a new leaf.'

'Are you really?'

He nodded earnestly, not breaking eye contact.

'Mum, please . . .'

After a long moment, the older woman smiled, the expression incredibly similar to Angela's. 'Don't worry, I'm not going to start anything. I just wanted to tell you how lovely you look, and to meet your young man.' She held out her hand.

He took it gratefully. 'Ri—Ryan Finnegan, ma'am.'

If she noticed the hesitation, she didn't comment. 'Cathy.'

As soon as his hand was released, Angela threw her arms around her mum. 'Thanks, Mum.'

'Have fun tonight. And you—' she pinned a look on him '—I've always thought Angela had a beautiful smile.'

'I won't argue with you there. And it's easy to see where she got it from.'

'Hmm. Very slick.'

'I was trying more for charming,' he admitted.

'My point was I've always thought my daughter looked prettiest when she's smiling, so you better do your best to make sure she doesn't have a reason not to.'

'*Muuuuum*,' Angela complained.

'*Whaaaat*?' Cathy responded in the same tone, forcing him to bite back a grin. 'I only said you had a beautiful smile. Anyway, you'll have to excuse me, I was headed to the bar when you came in, and just wanted to say "hello". Have fun tonight.'

'Thanks.' Angela kissed her mum on the cheek, giving her a brief hug before sliding her hand back into his. 'You too.'

'Why do I feel like I've just been through some sort of test?' He waited until he was sure Cathy was out of earshot.

'Probably because you have.' She smiled gently. 'But if it helps, I'm pretty sure you passed.'

'Really?'

'Yeah, with flying colours.'

'Well, that's a relief.' What he didn't add was that most of the relief was based on the fact that Angela clearly approved. Her opinion mattered so much to him. It would be easy to be scared of how much he cared about what she thought — far more than anyone else in his life. Of course, he cared about his parents' and sister's opinions — but they loved him no matter what. Even through his more stupid moments they still loved him — even if his sister Imogen had made it clear that she didn't always like him. But Angela . . . he really, really did care about her opinion — it was worth more to him than ten thousand likes.

And when he thought about that — the idea that her opinion was worth more to him than the people who kept Maverick in business, it bothered him a lot less than it should. Especially when her hand was warm in his, and she smiled at him like that.

'So, how does it feel to be the centre of attention?'

'There are quite a few eyes on us right now, aren't there?' Angela pulled a face and scanned the room again, flicking her fingers in a wave to a few people. 'But I think it's you everyone is interested in.'

'That's where you're wrong.' He leaned down to whisper in her ear as he pulled a seat out for her. 'It's *us* they're all interested in. And it's you they're looking at, because you are absolutely, breathtakingly stunning, and I am one of the luckiest men on the planet to have you by my side tonight.'

Her skin was warm as she slid her hand around the back of his neck to pull him closer, twisting in her seat to be able to kiss him sweetly and slowly. The noise, the lights, the party and all the people around them disappeared as he lost himself in her scent, the feel of her skin and the taste of her lips. When she moaned against his lips, it took every bit of self-restraint he had not to grab her and behave in a way that would definitely earn him a place on the naughty list.

When she drew away, to catch her breath, her fingers stayed tangled in the hair at the base of his neck, and her eyes locked with his. What he saw there, in her gaze, felt even more intense than kissing her, and the world around him slowed even more, until the space between each of his heartbeats stretched out for short eternities, filled with a realisation that eclipsed everything.

It took a blindingly familiar flash of light to drag his attention back into the current moment. He blinked, seeing stars as Angela did the same.

'Sorry.' Summer shrugged, not looking the least bit apologetic as she lowered the phone. 'You just looked so happy. Look!' She waved the phone at them. 'Mum's letting me take all the pictures and videos I want.'

'I'll forgive you if you send me a copy.' He flashed the Smile at her, really wanting to get another look.

'I can send it on your Insta.'

'Thanks.' He sat down next to Angela. 'But just to me, yeah? Not my public feed.'

'Sure. Whatever. There you go.'

His phone beeped. 'Thanks.'

'No problem.' She skipped off happily to wave her phone at other people, capturing other moments.

* * *

Angela watched Ryan with building confusion. She'd thought — hoped — for a moment that she'd seen something wonderful and only slightly terrifying in his eyes. Then Summer had interrupted.

She shook her head, wondering why Ryan would ask for a photo, but not want it shared with anyone else. He shared everything, so what did it mean that he'd want that held back? Was he ashamed of her? Was that why he didn't want the picture out in public — because she wasn't good enough for Maverick?

She watched as he unlocked his phone and opened the picture with a smile.

'Here.' He scooted closer to her.

The moment Summer had captured shone out from behind the screen — Angela's breath caught in her throat. What she'd thought she'd seen in his eyes, the raw emotion that she'd felt surge, was there, captured forever and pinned behind the glass. Undeniable. She swallowed hard, feeling totally side-swiped and not knowing what to say. 'Wow.'

'Don't worry, I'm not going to share this one unless you tell me I can. I just . . . wanted to have it. It seemed important.'

She cradled the phone, her hand wrapped around his, looking at the tiny, glowing image in front of her. When had the tingling heat turned into something that looked like *that*? How long had he been looking at her this way? Like something out of a film.

Maybe that was what scared her — that Ryan, or more accurately Rick — had built an entire career out of videos and films online. Out of convincing people that he was a different version of himself, and he'd done it so convincingly that he'd even fooled himself a bit. She studied the image a few moments longer before finding the strength to look up at him and meet his eyes, her heart in her mouth. What if what she thought she saw on the screen wasn't really there? What if he didn't feel the way she did?

'Ryan?'

He smoothed a loose curl away from her cheek and stroked his fingers down the sensitive skin there. 'I see it too.' The smile he gave her was full of promise and hope that drove away the fears darkening her mood. 'I feel it too. We should talk about this.'

'Yeah.' She looked around the busy room filled with half of her community.

'But . . . probably later . . . because there is something here to talk about, isn't there?' His eyes were dark and intense, and she had to swallow before she could find her voice properly.

'Definitely.' She smiled at him.

'Definitely,' he agreed, and leaned forward to kiss her, flooding her with reassurance and heat and want, and a dozen other things she wasn't sure she knew how to understand. But it was OK, because "later" they'd figure it out together. 'But how about, just for now, we enjoy the party.'

'That sounds like a good idea,' she agreed happily.

'Do you think you could manage a dance? If we were careful and took it slowly?'

'I'd love to dance with you.' She tucked her hand into his, letting him steady her as they stood and he led her to the dance floor. He slid his other hand around her waist, and she felt the heat of his palm so intensely through the silk of her dress that it was almost like she wore nothing — which brought up a lot of delicious memories, and heat rushed into her cheeks. The look in his eyes didn't help the heat recede at all.

She could have worried about all the eyes that were on her — on them — and what people were thinking about her, how they were judging her for taking up with the man who'd done so much damage to the village, herself and her mum. She could have worried about the phones and cameras she knew were pointed at them, and all the images of Maverick — and herself — that would doubtlessly be hitting the web soon, and the comments they would no doubt produce, and whether or not she was heading for another awkward conversation with her mum.

But, instead, she stepped closer, letting herself melt into his warmth, ignoring everything apart from the fairy lights sparkling around them, and the sensation of being wrapped up in his arms as he guided them carefully and gently around the dance floor.

* * *

'You're sure you're warm enough?' Ryan held her hand tightly, not wanting her to slip on the icy paths. The gritters had been through, but it was still cold and frosty underfoot. And incredibly beautiful. Everything seemed to shimmer and sparkle around them, like the village had been dusted with glitter and Christmas magic.

'I'm fine.' Angela smiled up at him. 'Really. And it's been a lovely evening.'

'Yeah.' The words weren't even close to describing how good of an evening it had been. He was stone-cold sober, heading home before midnight, which was when he'd usually just be getting started on other nights out as Maverick — but he couldn't remember the last time he'd felt so happy and content. And it was that last word that made all the difference to him. Of course he'd been happy before, and felt pride at his achievements, and he'd been excited, and high, and drunk . . . but there was always that undercurrent of restlessness too — the pressure and expectation of what he'd do next, the next reels, the next ambition, the next project, the next sponsorship deal to drive his brand even higher.

But right in that moment — and he realised a lot of the moments he'd spent in Broclington — he felt content as well, and happy with who he actually was, which was bit of a new idea to him, actually being happy exactly as he was.

Angela nudged him out of his thoughts when she tugged him towards the village centre instead of the street that would take them back to Bill's. 'The wishing tree will be lit up,' she explained. 'And it's really pretty. Unless you're too tired and wanting to head home?'

'No, I'm fine.' He lifted her fingers up to kiss them through her gloves, which made her smile at him in the way that made him feel better than his latest reel going viral. The word "home" bothered him a bit though, because for him that really meant his flat miles away from the sweet little village. And as much as he loved his sleek, expensive flat, he couldn't help feeling a bit . . . less than excited . . . at the thought of going back there. Which was another weird idea for him.

He stopped in front of the huge Christmas tree that twinkled with lights and decorations. 'Wow.' It was at least thirty feet tall and sparkled with fairy lights that reflected off shiny baubles in every colour imaginable. In the darkness, it glowed softly and looked almost ethereal. If he'd still been a child, it definitely would have made him believe in magic. He looked at Angela, staring at the tree, spellbound. The lights kissed her skin and caught in the sparkly things in her hair, making her look like part of the magic. He couldn't resist whipping out his phone and taking a couple quick snaps of her.

'Hey,' she complained. 'If you're going to do that, you should be in it too.'

'OK.' He looked around, and spotted a post-box nearby. That would do. It was the work of a few seconds to switch the camera lens round and turn the case into a mini stand. He raced back to her, beating the camera timer with just enough spare seconds to gather her against him and grin down at her, as his phone started its flurry of shots.

'Come here.' She reached up to kiss him, her breath and lips so hot that she melted all thoughts from his brain. How she did that so easily and so often he still didn't know, but he loved it. Just like he loved how easily and comfortably she fit against him — like she was meant to be there. And he wasn't sure he wanted to let her go, even when she drew away. 'Pretty magical, huh?'

'Yeah. It's pretty much perfect. I'm amazed there's no one else here.'

'Well, it is kind of late. And getting cold.' Angela smiled. 'But I think it's worth a little cold for moments like this.'

'I couldn't agree more.' He took a deep breath, knowing he probably wouldn't get another opportunity this good for a long time. 'Angela, that talk we agreed we should probably have?'

'Yes?'

'I think it's probably "later" now, don't you?' He stroked her cheek, knowing it would be smooth and soft even through his glove. She nodded, not breaking eye contact with him. 'Angela, I really, really like you. The last few weeks here, with you, have been nothing like I expected. They've been amazing, and I really don't want it to end when my court-ordered time is up, because I really, really like being at Bill's, and I really, really like being with you. But it's more than that. I like who I am when I'm around you, and the animals. I think you bring out the best version of me I've ever been, not because I feel like you're trying to change me or anything bad like that, but because you're just so amazing in so many ways that I want to do — and be — better for you.'

'Ryan, I'm really not that special.'

'You really are, Angel. You're incredible and kind, and sweet, and beautiful and stubborn and driven and passionate — and possibly the only thing bigger about you than your hair—' he teased one of her escaping curls '—is your temper when you think someone is hurting an animal . . .'

'Well, they need people to stick up for them.'

'And your heart. And it's all those reasons, and dozens more, like the way you fit so well against me and how adorable you are when you're getting irritated with another stupid thing I've said or done and trying not to show it, and that you have no fear in telling me exactly what you think of me, but almost endless patience when I'm being an idiot — which I'm aware is a lot of the time. All of those things, Angel, are just some of the reasons I think I'm falling for you.'

'Falling for me?'

'Yup.' He took another deep breath and put it all on the line, knowing nothing less than honesty would work. 'Head over heels, completely and totally. And I'm not telling you this because I expect you to feel the same or—'

'I do.'

Her words filled him with awe and joy — and disbelief. How could Angela — so amazing in so many ways — feel the same. 'You do?'

'Really, I do.' She did that thing that he loved so much, stretching up to kiss him, bracing herself against his shoulder to keep her balance. He really hoped she'd keep doing it when her leg was fully better, because he was planning and hoping with everything in his being to still have her as a part of his life then. 'It's crazy, this whole thing is utterly insane . . . the speed with which everything has happened, how we met, who you are . . . but, Ryan, I'm falling for you too.'

He smoothed her hair away from her face, cradling her cheeks between his hands to kiss her again, completely and totally losing himself in her. He had no idea how long they stood there, wrapped up in each other, sharing a moment so sweet, so filled with hope, that it was almost unbearable — almost, because Angela soothed everything.

* * *

Slowly and reluctantly she pulled away, shivering as her breath puffed into the air, mingling with his, but she didn't know whether it was the cold making her quake or the intensity of Ryan's kiss.

'Now you're cold.' He chafed his hands up and down her arms.

'Maybe.' She smiled, not really caring about that, especially when he slid his arm around her waist. 'You know, you couldn't have picked a better time or place for this conversation.'

'I don't know, somewhere a bit warmer might have been nice.' He snagged his phone from the pillar box. 'But it is very pretty here.'

'It's not just that,' Angela explained to him. 'It's what the tree stands for.'

'Right, you called it the "wishing tree". I assume there's a story in that name somewhere. Some ancient tradition?'

'Well, I wouldn't say it was ancient, exactly — but it's definitely a tradition, if something that's been happening for less than twenty years can be classed as tradition.' They slowly circled the tree.

'It's not even twenty years old? It looks a lot bigger than that.'

'We planted it . . . we being the whole village. One of our first group fundraising efforts. It wasn't exactly a tiny tree when we did it, but we've come a long way as a community since then.'

'You mean the Summer's Christmas thing?'

'Yeah. We've made some pretty big wishes come true as a community, and it all started here.' She stroked one of the tree's branches gently, feeling the cold spike of the fir through her gloves. 'We had a tree here before, but something happened, some sort of tree illness, and it was declared unsafe and had to be cut down. Apparently there wasn't enough money to cover a decent-sized tree, and the Christmas tree was a big part of village festivities, so the community came together to raise money for a replacement.'

'And let me guess, that was the first Christmas Tree Dance?'

'Yeah.' Angela nodded. 'But now it's a lot bigger, and raises a lot more money. All for charity, of course.'

'It's a good event.' The smile he gave her, even just by the light of the tree, was beaming, flooding her with warmth. 'Possibly one of my favourite nights out ever.'

'Really?'

'Really.' He squeezed her hand where it rested on his arm.

'If you believe local legend, the tree is on a magical spot. The one before it was big and old, and there were lots of stories. Give them half a chance and Summer and Sarah will tell you all of them, because most of them involve fairies and magic . . . which they love.'

'And you don't, of course,' he teased.

'Nothing wrong with believing in magic.' She smiled, thinking it had certainly played a big part in her life recently.

'And sometimes I think magic comes from inside of people, and all they need is something to help them focus — a symbol to believe in. And that's what the tree became.'

'Your wishing tree?'

'Broclington's wishing tree. Not just mine.'

'Go on then, tell me the ancient fairy story.'

'What makes you think I know it?'

'Because I know you, Angel. Because you believe in magic, fairies and sometimes even demons . . . even if they do turn out to be balding chicken-butt birds.'

She laughed at that. 'I suppose you think I'm silly.'

'No. I think you're wonderful. And only a little bit silly about your animals sometimes.' He laughed as she thwacked his arm. 'Come on. Tell me your fairy story while we head back.'

'Well, like a lot of the things round here, it goes back to a history so old that it's practically myth.'

'A lot of the best stories are.'

'So, there's this old, like ancient Celtic old tradition, in which certain trees were beloved by fairies, and people would make offerings to those trees, or the spirits and fairies that lived in them, in the hope they would bless them and make their dreams come true.'

'Offerings like what?' He flicked on his phone's torch as they headed up the street to his cottage. Now they were away from the village centre, it was much darker.

'Summer or Sarah would probably be able to tell you better than me, but I think people tied ribbons or cloth to the trees to hold their wishes, and when the wishes were granted they go back, untie the knot and leave a gift for the tree. Or the fairies.'

'You can't tell me that's an ancient tree. Not when you said the village planted it.'

'No.' She laughed. 'Of course not. But our tree has its own magic, in a way. It brought a community together again, and you know the amazing things we've pulled off working together in the last few years. The wishing tree has kind of

196

become the symbol of modern-day Broclington. You probably couldn't see them in the dark, but some of the decorations aren't really decorations . . . they're wishes.'

'People still make wishes on the tree?'

'Yeah, they do. I mean, sometimes they're more like prayers than wishes. For hope, for healing . . . but sometimes they're wishes for things too. And when they come true, the person who made the wish comes back, undoes the knot and replaces it with a star. Every year we put the decorations up, there's a few more stars than last year.'

'That's really sweet.'

'Yeah.' She smiled. 'It really is. I mean, it's fun for kids, but there is something a bit special about it too.'

'It sounds it.' In the near darkness she could see him watching her. 'Angela? Have you ever put a wish on the tree?'

'That would be telling.' She laughed as she walked up the path to his front door. 'Why, are you thinking you might like to tie on a wish of your own?'

'No.' His eyes met hers in the porch light, sending her pulse racing. 'Right now, I can't think of a single thing I would wish for. Everything I want is right here.'

* * *

Ryan rolled over in bed, grinning at the mop of curly hair peeping out over the top of his duvet. He couldn't resist smoothing her curls and sliding his arm carefully around her waist. He didn't want to wake her, not exactly, but he missed her — which was another bizarre concept, the idea that he could miss someone just a few inches away from him. She mumbled something and shifted sleepily, snuggling closer to him, tucking herself into his arms, deliciously warm and soft in all the right places. Even in her sleep she welcomed him, which was another experience he'd not had in far too long.

He lay there, cuddled against her, losing track of time for long minutes, thinking how much his life had changed so recently, and how much he'd really meant what he'd said the night before — that he liked this new version of himself. He felt happier, and calmer, and more free to be himself than he had for a very long time.

He wasn't totally sure what that meant for Maverick — obviously he still needed to make a living, and he had contracts to fulfil, but after that he was planning quite a few changes — hopefully involving the woman curled up next to him, who snored gently, making soft snuffling noises that he found adorable. It was hard to resist reaching out and waking her up.

As if knowing he was thinking about her, Angela's eyes flickered open and she smiled up at him. 'Hi.'

'Good morning.' He smiled back at her, brushing her curls from her eyes before leaning over to kiss her. 'Did you sleep all right?'

'Really well, thank you.' She stretched happily and giggled. 'Despite waking up twice, I don't feel even a little tired.'

'Yeah, I woke up a couple of times too, but feel pretty good as well.' He grinned, thinking of the last time he'd woken and she'd pulled him against her.

'What time is it?'

'Nearly nine.'

'Pity. I could have happily stayed here a lot longer, but . . .'

'. . . but you've got animals to feed and care for. Medication rounds to do.'

'Yeah.'

'Do you think they can wait an hour or so?'

'Why, do you have something in mind?' The glint of mischief in her eyes almost made him change his mind and pull her beneath him again.

'I was thinking I could make you breakfast, then come help you at Bill's.'

'Hmm.' She propped herself up on one hand. 'You're not supposed to be on today, but I guess I could add it to your payback hours.'

'You don't need to. I just want to spend the day with you. Even if we spend part of it in piles of excrement.'

'You really mean that?'

He thought about it for a few moments before nodding. 'Yeah, I really do. So what do you say — breakfast with me? I've even got some of those meatless non-sausage things you like.'

'Yes please.'

* * *

'What have you done in here?' Angela dug a toe into the weirdly springy living room floor, not totally sure of her footing.

'Oh, they're play mats.' Ryan took her plate and cup, then offered his arm to steady her. 'You know, like for kids?'

She concentrated on getting her footing right, making sure she didn't put too much pressure on her leg. 'So, erm, why have you replaced your flooring with kids' play mats?'

'Because her royal highness over there has been trying to fly. I was worried she'd hurt herself crashing.'

'Mallow's flying?' Angela was amazed.

'It's not really flying yet, more jumping off things haphazardly and terrifying me.'

'You've worked wonders with her.'

'I'm not really responsible, she's mostly done it herself.'

'I'm sure that's not true.'

'Well, I might have encouraged her and teased her a bit with treats and toys.'

'You gave her the confidence to safely take the leaps she needs to, and then motivated her to do it. You might be a natural at rehab.' Angela thought of all the ways he reached out to help her, usually without even appearing to think about it. 'I bet when you were younger you wouldn't ever have guessed you'd be teaching a pink, hoodie-wearing, bald cockatoo how to fly.' She laughed at Mallow's squark of complaint. 'Sorry, sweet girl. When I said "bald", I obviously meant beautiful, sweet and clever.'

Mallow rattled her beak in cockatoo laughter, blew a kiss and bowed on her perch — spreading out her wings and showing off her new feathers.

'Yes, you're very pretty.' Ryan laughed. 'You're also pretty cheeky, pretty demanding and a pretty big pain in the behind.' She whistled again, fluffing her feathers up. 'Yeah, and you're pretty damn cute.'

'So, is she coming in with us today?'

'I don't know.' He shrugged. 'I'm tempted to set her up with some foraging toys and leave her here while we're there. You know . . .' he reached out and took her hand '. . . Mallow's not the only thing I would never have guessed. I could never have imagined, never even dreamed that I would find someone like you . . .'

'Biiiiiig kissy!'

'Smart bird, your Mallow.' Angela smiled as Ryan took the cup out of her hand and put it carefully on the table.

'Yeah, she is.' He whispered the words against her lips as he tangled his fingers in the curls at the nape of her neck and she lifted her lips up to his.

His kiss was so sweet, so demanding and so full of promise for the future it might have been scary — except that his arms were easy and reassuring around her, letting her know she was safe and could trust him. And just like the half-bald, battered bird bouncing up and down on her pink perch, Angela really did trust him. She knew her heart — and future — was safe with him. He wasn't going to let her down. She could believe that promise.

CHAPTER ELEVEN

'So this is where you've been hiding.' Yvette sashayed across the yard, dressed in skintight leather trousers and a huge, puffy coat. 'You haven't returned any of my calls, Ricky baby. And when I went to our flat, it looks like a bomb went off.'

'I'm having work done at *my* flat. And you never called me.' He could feel Angela's eyes on him, and he still had her perfume in his nose from kissing her just a few moments earlier. 'We broke up.'

'No we didn't, silly. And I called you lots. You just never answered.' She pouted. 'But I forgive you, baby.'

'For what?'

'For being naughty and not calling me back.' The pout deepened to full-on photo pose and she flipped her hair.

'Yvette,' he kept his voice firm. 'You texted me something about being on a yacht with your girlfriend Jean. And that was it. I've not heard from you in two months. And I didn't expect to, because we broke up, remember?'

'No we didn't, silly. That was just a little lovers' tiff. We're so much better than that, baby.' She wrapped a hand around his arm, her perfectly manicured nails clawing into his jumper. 'Come on, let's leave this smelly place and these stinky animals and go somewhere to catch up and talk.'

'Yvette.' He gently peeled her fingers off his arm one by one. 'As far as I'm concerned we have nothing to talk about.'

'But of course we do, darling. We have to talk about our future.'

'Yvette, I don't know how to make this any clearer, but we don't have a future.'

'Of course we do, Ricky.' The name and her simpering tone made his teeth clench.

'No. We don't.' He shot Angela an apologetic glance over the top of Yvette's head. He had no idea what his ex wanted — that was very firmly, very clearly all she was to him — and he really hoped Angela understood that too. The only other person he needed to convince was Yvette.

'But of course we do, Ricky. We need to talk about the baby.'

The bottom dropped out of his world as her words penetrated his brain. She couldn't possibly be saying what he thought she was saying. They'd always been so careful . . . Even after swallowing twice, the words were a half-squeak that sounded nothing like his usual voice. 'What baby?'

'Our baby, of course, silly.' She unzipped the huge coat and thrust out her stomach. 'Our baby.'

'You . . . what . . . how . . . ?'

'Come on. We need to talk about our future. About our family.' She rested her hand on the tiny but life-changing bump. 'Take me home.'

'Angela . . . I'm . . .'

'It's fine.' She was ashen, her voice shaky, and she wouldn't look at him. 'Go.'

'But . . .'

'Just go, Rick.' She still wouldn't meet his gaze.

'Come on, baby. You heard what she said.' Yvette's claws wound back around his arm, dragging him away from where he really wanted to be. They were halfway down the drive, him being dragged away from Bill's and Angela, before he realised what was really bothering him and turning his stomach: Angela had called him Rick, not Ryan. And that really left a bad taste in his mouth.

He listened to Yvette prattle away as he walked back to the cottage, his feet moving automatically as she whittered about getting his car out of storage, painting rooms and names for the baby he really didn't want to have — not with her. Obviously he'd step up, look after it and support her — he wasn't a total arse. At least, not anymore, but how the fuck had this happened? Well, he knew how it happened, but he knew he'd always been careful . . . hadn't he? And she was supposed to be on something. He definitely remembered seeing her pills in his bathroom. To have two lots of birth control fail — what were the odds against that?

'When do you think this happened?'

'What?' She looked at him, confused for a moment.

'When did it happen? I mean, we were always careful . . . I was trying to figure out where we . . .' He trailed off, not wanting to say what he was thinking. 'I mean, when it happened.'

'Before your accident. Don't you remember? I changed pills.'

Did he remember that? He wasn't sure.

'Oh my God this place is so cute!' Yvette squealed as he opened the front door, snatching away his train of thought. 'Why haven't you been 'gramming this cottage? It's like out-of-a-film-set cute!'

'Yeah, I suppose.' He wanted a drink. A very big, very strong one.

'It'll be the perfect setting to announce our good news to everyone. We'll have a big party, and do a gender reveal reel, and then announce our engagement. I'm picturing lots of pink and blue balloons, and maybe a giant cake, or we can get the new Land Rover customised . . . that would be adorable. We could have one of those bright white ones, and have LEDs run underneath it that light up pink or blue to tell us if we're having a baby Ricky or a baby Vetty. Wouldn't that be adorable?'

His brain was slowly catching up. 'Land Rover?'

'Well, obviously we can't keep the Lamborghini. That won't be any good for a baby, and we'll never get the iCandy and nanny in it.'

'A nanny called Candy?' He supposed it was good she'd found someone already. He was mentally running through his finances — a pounding headache and something else nagged at his brain.

'No, silly. An iCandy stroller. They're the best ones there are, and obviously our baby will have nothing but the best.'

'Obviously,' he agreed, not hearing her and still desperately trying to catch up. He was worried about Angela. She'd looked so pale and shaky. He needed to call her, to make sure she was OK, to let her know he still cared about her . . . To beg her to forgive yet another fuck-up he'd made as Maverick.

'Ricky?' The name was like nails on a chalkboard to him now. 'Why is the living room floor squidgy?'

'It's for Mallow.'

'What?'

'The bird. My bird.' He pointed to the cage where Mallow sat, unusually quiet, her head cocked to one side while she studied the new incomer.

'You got a bird?' Yvette tottered over to the cage, her ridiculously high heels sinking into the squidgy flooring. 'Eww. It's really ugly. Couldn't you find a prettier one? Disgusting thing.'

'She's not ugly, don't say that. She's gorgeous, and special, and clever.'

'If you say so.'

'I do.' The thing was still nagging at his brain, desperate for attention, but he couldn't focus properly. All he could think about was the look on Angela's face as Yvette dragged him away.

* * *

The last thing Angela wanted to do was respond to the knock at her door. It was the door to her private entrance, meaning it was someone she knew and not an animal needing help — and she really wasn't in the mood for company. She'd finished off her unavoidable daily chores, trying not to think — but now she didn't know what she was supposed to think. What were you supposed to think when your . . . what . . . boyfriend's — she supposed — ex turned up pregnant by him? She didn't know how to handle all the emotions twisting up her stomach, but she certainly didn't feel like being friendly at the moment.

'Ange?' The knocking was louder this time. 'It's Mum.'

Great. One of the last people she wanted to see right now. She loved her mum, but the thought of having to deal with her right then, listening to her being all smug and right, was unbearable. For a few moments she contemplated ignoring her and doing what she really wanted: pulling a blanket over her head with Ruby, and possibly the tub of chocolate-brownie ice cream from the back of the freezer.

Her phone started to ring, and she pounced on it — hoping it was him, calling to explain. But it was just Mum. With a huge sigh she heaved herself off the sofa and limped over to the door. 'Mum.'

'Ange, sweetie, I had a few hours spare so I thought I'd drop by. I brought cake.' She was in the kitchen, already filling the kettle before she looked properly at her. 'Have you been crying? What happened? Did you lose the hedgehog babies?'

'No, no, the hogs are fine.' Angela rubbed at her eyes.

'What is it then?'

She forced herself to take a deep breath. 'Rick's ex turned up.'

'That dreadful blonde girl?'

'Yeah.' Angela nodded. 'She's back. And pregnant.'

'Oh.'

'And when she asked him, he left with her.'

'Oh, sweetie.'

205

'And if you're about to turn around and tell me that "you told me so", I swear I'm not going to be able to deal with it. I'm just not. So please, Mum, just don't.'

'I wasn't going to, sweetie. But do you need a hug?'

'Yes please.' She leaned against her mum. There really wasn't anything quite like a "mum hug" when you were feeling sorry for yourself.

'Tell me.' She stroked her hair, rocking her gently. 'Tell me, whatever you need me to hear. Tell me how I can help. Tell me what I can do to make this better for you, sweetheart.'

'I don't know, Mum, I really don't know.' Tears crowded into her throat, choking her. 'I thought we had something . . . that he cared about me. I thought he'd changed. I thought . . . Then she just clicked her perfectly manicured fingers, tossed her perfect blonde hair and he followed her perfect, skinny arse. He barely even looked at me.'

'Then he's an idiot who doesn't deserve you.' She hugged her fiercely.

'I told him to go, Mum.' The tears streamed hot and angry down her cheeks. 'He should have argued. He should have called. If he really did care about me, wouldn't he have stayed?'

'I don't know, sweetheart, I really don't.'

'I got him so wrong, Mum,' she bawled, not caring that she sounded like a whiny child. 'I thought he was so much better than he really is. I've made such an idiot of myself. I should have listened to you.'

'I'm so sorry, sweetheart. I've honestly never wished I was wrong about something, or someone, as much as I do right now.'

* * *

'So what happens now?' Rick rubbed his eyes tiredly. They'd been talking for hours — well, she'd been talking, and he'd been trying to pay attention and find something to care about in what she was saying. In truth, his eyes and attention kept being dragged back to the tiny bump that was apparently housing his son or daughter. The idea was utterly bizarre and amazing to him. How could there be a mini version of him in there that would be a living, breathing actual human that he would have to take care of in a few months? Who he would be responsible for, and have to care for, and teach things to, and look after.

A living being that would tie him to Yvette for the next two decades — if not forever. A scary thought.

'Well, obviously we'll move back in together, film a pregnancy announcement, let all our fans know we're back together — which should easily go viral. And then I think we should capitalise on that to announce our engagement, although obviously we won't have the wedding until after I've had some time to get my figure back.'

'What? No.'

'I'm sure it would only be a few weeks. I'll get a personal trainer and chef. Don't worry, darling.' She stroked his arm, making him cringe. 'I'll be looking fabulous again in no time. I'm sure I'll just snap right back.'

She was completely misunderstanding, and Rick needed to stop all of this immediately. 'Yvette, I'm sorry if I've misled you, but we're not getting married.'

'I know we're not, darling, not until after the baby is here and I've got my shape back. Didn't you hear me? And how sweet to have our little baby at the wedding. I've already checked, and Dior do some just adorable baby dresses and suits.'

'No, Yvette,' he tried to explain. 'We're not getting married.'

'Of course we are, baby. We're Maverick and VettyBaby, and we're having a baby. We're going to go beyond viral. We'll be blasting into space. Isn't it wonderful?'

'Yvette.' He caught her hand in his, mostly to get her to stop stroking him like a pet. 'I really, really need you to listen to me, and focus. Yvette, we can't get married.'

'Of course we can, silly. People do it all the time. And I am pregnant with your baby.'

'Yes, I know other people get married all the time. People who are in love.' He tried to find the words to explain.

'Exactly, people like us. I mean, I *am* carrying your baby,' she repeated, more firmly this time.

'Yes, I know that, but . . .' He took another deep breath. 'Yvette, we were over. If you hadn't found out you were pregnant, would you even have bothered to talk to me again?'

'Of course I would, Ricky baby.' She pouted. 'And I don't know why you keep saying we were over. I was just on a little holiday while you were doing your animal thing. I was always coming back. It's you and me, baby. And we're going to be huge! Online, I mean. I'm not going to get huge,' she tittered. 'I'll just be one of those girls who has a cute little bump, then snaps right back — don't you think?'

'Sure, whatever.' She probably would be as well. 'But Yvette, there isn't a "we", there isn't an "us" anymore.'

'I don't know why you're saying such unkind things.' Her eyes filled with tears. He hated it so much when she cried. 'Of course we're in love and getting married. I wouldn't be having your baby if we weren't. I wouldn't be able to cope with that.'

There was something in the way she said it that sent chills down his spine. 'What do you mean by that?'

'Just what I said.' Yvette glared at him. 'I don't know how I could go through it all if you weren't with me. I'm not sure if I would want to go on without you. I need you to help me cope with this, because if you push me away, I won't be able to. I can't go through a pregnancy and get fat and have a baby by myself. I won't do it.'

He had never seen her look so cold and calculating, and would never have thought she was capable of what she was hinting at. What she was threatening. To his child. He felt sick. He took another deep breath, trying to quell the nausea he felt as he opened his arms to her. 'Yvette, I promise that you don't have to go through this alone. I'll take care of you. Both of you.'

'Good.' Yvette snuggled against him, appeased, and he wondered what the hell he'd just committed to. 'Shall we go to bed? Celebrate?'

He guessed what they said about pregnancy hormones must be true, because her change in mood was so abrupt he felt like he had whiplash. She stroked her fingers down his chest in a way that — a few months ago — would have produced the result she wanted, but now it just made his skin crawl.

'I think you need your sleep. I'll make you up the bed in the spare room.'

'I don't want to sleep in the spare room. I want to sleep in your bed.'

'Fine, I'll change my sheets for you and I'll sleep in the spare room.'

'But I don't want to sleep by myself. And I'm not that tired anyway.'

This time the pout wasn't going to get her what she wanted. 'Yvette,' he said gently but firmly, pushing her away. 'I'm not sleeping with you or sharing a bed with you.'

'Are you sure? We always were pretty good together,' she purred.

'I'm sure.'

'Is it the belly? Do you think I'm not sexy enough?' Again with the pouting.

'No, Yvette, you're still beautiful,' he told her honestly. 'And you hardly have a belly.'

'So why don't you want to fuck?'

'Because I just don't feel that way about you anymore, that's what I've been trying to tell you.'

'Is it that Anneka?'

'Angela,' he corrected automatically. 'But yeah, I'm involved with Angela.'

'Were.'

'What?' He looked at her, not sure what she meant.

'You were involved with Anna. You had a little thing, but I'm back now, and we're having a baby together. It's OK, I can forgive your little hook-up.'

'Right.' He wasn't sure he had anything that he needed to be forgiven for, and he was damned sure Angela was a lot more than a "little hook-up".

'Besides, you're having a baby with me, and you left that smelly little farm with me.'

'Animal sanctuary.'

'Whatever. The point is you left with me. She told you to leave, and you did. I think she made it pretty clear that she doesn't want to be with you now anyway.' With that she stood and sashayed out of the room, leaving him with ugly, unpleasant thoughts.

* * *

'Don't you dare answer that!' Liv grabbed the phone from Angela's hand as soon as she saw his picture flash up on screen, then stuffed it under the cushion on Angela's couch where they were all sitting. 'He's had two days to call or text or message, and you've not heard a thing from him since he walked out with *that* woman.'

'But he obviously wants to talk now . . .'

'Too little, too late, and Evelyn agrees with me. Don't you?'

'I agree that nearly midnight, when we've been drinking for the last three hours, might not be the best time to have whatever conversation you and he need to have.' Evelyn shrugged. 'But, I think you and Rick probably do need to talk.'

'About what?' Liv demanded. 'What could he possibly have to say after walking out of here with his ex, then not bothering to call Ange for two days, after telling her he was falling for her. He obviously can't be trusted.'

'You're being a bit harsh, Liv.'

'I just don't want to see Ange hurt anymore. She deserves a lot better than that.' Liv slipped her arm around Angela's shoulders and squeezed her tightly, making her feel loved and supported. She was so, so grateful for her two friends who had dropped everything to be with her, to listen to her complain and offer equal amounts of comfort, bitching, alcohol and chocolate. Liv's fierce protectiveness offset with Evelyn's pragmatic, sympathetic calm was exactly the balm she needed.

'Neither do I,' Evelyn agreed.

'And if he really did walk out with that . . .' Liv hesitated, knowing Angela's views on swearing '. . . harpy, without a word of explanation . . . and move her into *my* old cottage — of all the cheek! — then he needs to come on his freaking knees before Angela gives him so much as the time of day again!'

'I did tell him it was fine, and that he should go.' Angela tried to complain, not totally sure why she was defending him. 'And you did move out of the cottage.'

'Humph. I still feel sorry for my little fairy cottage. Besides, even if you did tell him to leave, did you really want him to?' Liv's question was gentle, but it still hurt.

'No. I wanted him to tell her to stuff the H-E-double-hockey-sticks back off to wherever she's been.'

'But if she's pregnant with his baby . . .'

'Oh, she's pregnant.' Try as she might, Angela couldn't get the image of that bump out of her mind. Why was it that she could easily forget important things — like to pick up more milk — on a regular basis, but couldn't get rid of that image, no matter how hard she tried. Even her brain was betraying her.

'Well, then he has a responsibility to her. And to that baby,' Evelyn reasoned.

'He has a responsibility to Angela too,' Liv argued. 'And waiting two days to call her, especially when he's not been turning up for his community service, makes him a heel . . . and a lot of far worse things that Ange will tell me off for saying!'

'I really am lucky to have you two as friends.'

'We're lucky to have you, too. Even if you do end up palming your rescues off on us both!' Liv laughed.

'Can I help it if you fell in love with Sparks?'

'No she can't.' Evelyn joined in the giggling. 'But you could maybe stop showing our girls all your cutest babies.

Summer announced she wants ferret kits for Christmas. But that it can't be just one, because they have to be kept in groups. So, thanks to you, she wants a bundle of ferret babies and has written to Santa to tell him that.'

'Does she even believe in Santa anymore?'

'I honestly don't know,' Evelyn admitted. 'I mean, she's nearly eleven, so most children her age wouldn't, but she's not really most children, is she?'

'That's true enough. Most children don't have Santa turn up in August to help save their life . . .' Angela nodded.

'And I don't want to do or say anything that might break the magic.' Evelyn drained the rest of her wine.

'And this *is* Broclington,' Liv added thoughtfully. 'A lot of the time the "normal" rules don't seem to apply here. Sometimes, with some of the things — some of the coincidences — I've seen happen, well . . .'

'What do you mean?' Angela looked at her friend, who was studying her also empty glass.

'Well, I'm not sure I'd want to admit this too publicly . . . given that I'm a doctor and woman of science, and I've probably had too much to drink . . .'

'But . . . ?' Evelyn prodded her.

'But do you ever think our girls might be right? About the fairies, and wishing well?' Liv blurted out.

'And the wishing tree.' Angela grinned.

'Yeah. That's pretty magical.'

'Sometimes.' Evelyn smiled. 'I'd certainly like to. And I think if there is anywhere in the world that magic like that really does still exist, it's probably here.' She reached for the wine bottle. 'More wine?'

'Definitely.' Angela held out her glass, pondering her friend's response. 'So, if you believe in magic, do you believe in fate too?'

'I believe things happen for a reason,' Evelyn replied. 'If my marriage hadn't ended, I probably wouldn't have come back to Broclington. So I wouldn't have met Jake, and

Summer and I wouldn't have been here when she got sick again and . . .' She swallowed hard.

'. . . and it if hadn't been for Jake, she probably wouldn't have ended up on a trial in America that cured her cancer,' Liv finished quietly.

'Exactly.' Evelyn smiled. 'So as bad as my marriage break-up was, it put me in the exact place me and my daughter needed to be, at the right time. So if that's what fate is, then yes, I really do believe in it. And am grateful for it.'

'And if it was fate that left me needing a new home and job, right when the surgery needed a locum, then I'm pretty grateful to it too,' Liv added.

'And just when we really needed someone with some crazy ideas on saving our surgery . . . there you were brimming with ideas.' Evelyn grinned. 'Like a modern fairy godmother with all the answers.'

'I wouldn't go that far,' Liv said.

'No, she's more of a roll her sleeves up and drag everyone else on-board type than *bibbity-bobbity-boo*!' Angela laughed. 'Though some days I could totally see you with a magic wand instead of your stethoscope.'

'Well, I'm pretty sure Sarah's part fairy, so I could find one without too much difficulty.' Liv laughed. 'But if anyone in *this* room has fairy-tale magic, it's you, Angela. Talking to animals, giving them their happy endings.'

'It's not all happy endings at Bill's.' She frowned, thinking of all the stresses and sadnesses she'd faced — the animals who she didn't get to soon enough, the never-ending pile of bills. Not to mention her own presently tattered and battered heart.

'No, it's not always happy endings in medicine either.' Liv sighed.

'True enough,' Evelyn commiserated, then she lifted her glass with a smile. 'But there's a lot more good outcomes, thanks to the two of you, than there would be if you weren't here.'

'Thanks to the three of us,' Angela corrected, squeezing her friend's fingers.

'Then here's to us.' Liv raised her glass in salute. 'To as many happy endings as it's possible to create outside of fairy tales!'

'To happy endings.' Angela chinked her glass. 'And probably fairy magic.'

'And to Angela getting the happy ever after she deserves.' Evelyn squeezed her fingers tightly.

'Oh yeah,' Angela agreed, 'I'll happily drink to that.'

* * *

It had been over a week since Yvette had sashayed back into his life, and it had been one of the worst weeks of his life. She'd been busy dragging her "essentials", spreading their news all over social media and working with their agents to set up what felt like back-to-back appearances, shoots and opportunities. He'd done his best to avoid most of the calls — and just responded to his agent with brief messages. He didn't really want or know how to engage — because everything seemed so impossibly surreal.

Part of him was glad to be swept back into the crazy, non-stop world of Maverick and VettyBaby, where his time was filled with being seen eating at the best restaurants, appearances at the hottest new places, and making videos of them jointly testing expensive baby gear — sent by companies who hoped to use their rocketing popularity to build their own sales. He was quite gratified to see that some of his animal videos were doing better than the new happy-expectant parent ones, but he didn't dare tell Yvette that.

He was mostly just glad to not have to think. When he did, everything started to fall apart. He'd avoided answering calls from his family and friends — just sending them brief messages to let them know he was OK. And he was, at least as much as it was possible to be, OK. The irony was the only person he really wanted to hear from seemed to be the only person in the world who didn't want to talk to him.

Angela hadn't returned a single one of his calls or messages, and he hadn't been back to Bill's. He'd sent her a long, apologetic message trying — and probably failing — to explain everything, but although he could see that she'd read it, she hadn't responded. Not that he could blame her.

And when Yvette had found out, she'd gone through the roof — screaming and crying about how she couldn't trust him, and that she needed to feel safe, secure and loved to bring their baby into the world, and that she needed to be calm because stress was bad for growing babies. How could she possibly feel those things when he was trying to contact the woman he'd been screwing. Her entire life was changing — and she was giving up her body to give him a child — obviously *she* had to be his first priority.

He'd felt so guilty after she'd finished crying. And Angela hadn't replied, so it had all been pointless anyway.

He really had fucked everything up — or at least his drunken, stupid Maverick persona had. He assumed it had been when they'd been drinking, as he was always careful otherwise. As much as he'd enjoyed being with Yvette, he'd wanted to avoid exactly this situation. The fact that this was all happening now, just when he'd started to get his life going in the way he'd wanted — and having found someone he really, really cared about — was beyond unfair. But he'd made his bed, he'd created this situation, so he would man up and deal with it, and he would make damn sure his child would be happy and loved, and have everything they needed and wanted that was within his ability to give them.

The only thing that gave him any real joy at the moment was playing with Mallow, helping her to strengthen her wings and teach her new tricks and words. Inspired by the mess she'd created during one of her Houdini moments, he'd invested in some non-toxic paints and art pads, and Mallow appeared to love creating her "art", running around, splodging through the different colours, nibbling the edges of the pages and creating multi-coloured chaos, all while cackling and whistling joyfully. When she had picked up one of her favourite balls, dumped it in the red paint, and threw it happily across the paper, he'd grabbed his phone and started filming, turning their game into another reel.

He hadn't bothered to involve Yvette, or even tell her what he was doing, because as much as he'd tried to encourage them to get along it was pretty clear they didn't like each other. Yvette couldn't seem to see past Mallow's odd looks, while the bird didn't help matters by lunging and snapping at the woman at every opportunity. So, instead, he just uploaded them to his separate animal account — the one he'd set up for Ruby and Ernie and their friends, and hadn't told Angela about, let alone Yvette — and which was growing in popularity nonetheless.

'Are you ready?' Yvette bounced into the room, wearing a tiny top that showed off her neat little bump. 'We need to leave now if we're going to get to the scan on time.'

'Right, yeah.' The scan — the first time he'd get to see his child. He knew he should be excited, and on some level he probably was, but he couldn't help feeling that it wasn't the way it should be — or with the person he should be with.

'And that's what you're wearing?' She scowled at his hoodie and jeans combo. 'You do realise there will be photos and maybe even fans?'

'Why would there be fans?'

'Because people care about us, and our baby.' She rolled her eyes.

'I know that, but how would they know where to find us?'

'Because I posted about it, obviously. So you're changing, right?'

He took a deep breath — thinking that he was spending a lot of time practising deep breathing and counting to ten, and all the other things he tried to do to extend his rapidly thinning patience. He reminded himself, yet again, that it was important to try and avoid stressing out pregnant women, so he smiled and nodded. 'Yeah, I'll change. Just give me five minutes.'

'OK.' Yvette peered into a mirror, already distracted with her preening. 'But don't make us late.'

* * *

It had been over a week since Angela had told Ryan — or Rick — to go, and since he had left . . . with that woman. She couldn't really blame him, not when there was a baby involved, and it wasn't like he'd cheated on her . . . whatever *that woman* had said, she'd been there to witness their split, and it had seemed a pretty solid break-up to her. She tried to comfort herself with that thought, telling herself that it meant whatever she'd shared with him — whatever she'd thought they had shared — was real. But it didn't really help her mood as she dragged Ernie's food across the yard.

Rick — it was easier to think of him like that rather than Ryan — had tried to call her a couple of times the next day, but she hadn't been able to face hearing him tell her that he'd chosen Yvette over her — which of course he would. She was beautiful, much more involved in his online world, and they had history together — and the future of the baby. And when she hadn't answered his calls, he'd sent her a long message explaining what she basically feared — that he had to try and figure things out and work out how to support Yvette and his future child. Exactly what she'd expected — but that didn't make it hurt any less.

Ernie looked up when he heard her coming, and hmphed at her before hanging his head again. 'Yeah, I'm not too thrilled that it's just me either.' She sighed and petted his nose. 'I miss him too.' She swallowed hard against the pain that the words brought with them, forcing herself to get on with her chores and look after her animals. They were innocent in this situation and didn't deserve to suffer her moodiness.

Not that she deserved the pain either. She dumped the food in for the donkeys, and dragged the back of her hand — which was a bit cleaner than the rest — across her eyes and nose. She wasn't crying, not really, it was just dust, or some other irritant escaping from the animals.

It wasn't really anyone's fault, so she didn't have anyone to blame or be angry at, and she couldn't decide if that made things better or worse. But it definitely didn't make it any easier, or make it hurt any less.

Things with Ryan had been so lovely: he'd cosseted her, looking after her and fussing over her in much the same way that she did her animals — but in a way that was just so simple and easy that it didn't make her feel awkward or indebted, as it did when other people tried to help. Ryan made her feel special, and like she deserved to be cherished, and she missed that feeling. She missed him, and his easy-going humour, and damn it, she even missed Mallow — despite the cockatoo still being overly quick with her beak when it came to Angela's fingers.

The other thing she missed was his skill with computers and the website. She'd tried to make some edits to add some more information about the fundraising event she was planning, and instead had managed to crash it. She'd have to find someone who was a bit more tech-savvy to sort it out, but she kept hesitating. It was silly, because she knew it needed doing, but actually making the call felt like she was giving up on Ryan and the promises that they'd made to each other — and the future she'd been hoping for and starting to believe might actually be theirs. And even though she knew that that future was someone else's now, it still hurt to let go of that dream and those hopes.

And it was really hard to sleep at night, in the bed that now felt a bit too big. She knew it was silly, but at 3 a.m. the bed felt a bit more empty than it had before.

* * *

'Oooh, it's cold.' Yvette squirmed on the couch as the gel was applied. 'And remember, we want the gender in an envelope so we can have a big reveal party.'

'Yes, you mentioned that. A couple of times.' The sonographer smiled and nodded. 'Right, are we ready to meet baby?'

'Yes.' Yvette grabbed for his hand, and he held hers tightly, suddenly feeling excited. He was going to meet his son or daughter. If it had been his choice, he'd walk out of the room today knowing which, so he could start painting rooms, buying toys and picking out names. For the first time since Yvette had come back into his life, he actually felt excited by everything that was happening.

'So, we don't have any notes on you yet, but I understand this is your first scan with us?'

'Yeah.'

'All right, so we'll get a look at baby, check them over, and then take some measurements to work out your due date. How does that sound?'

'Good.' He nodded, his eyes already glued to the screen. A rapid thudding filled the room, taking him by surprise. 'Is that . . . ?'

'Yes.' The sonographer nodded. 'That's your baby's heartbeat.'

'It's so fast, is that normal? Are they OK?'

'Yeah, that's normal.' A nod and smile of reassurance. 'And everything looks as it should. Ten toes, eight fingers, two thumbs — one of which is currently being sucked. Here.' She used a finger to draw on the screen.

'Ooh, look how cute she is!' Yvette crooned.

'She?' He stared at her in surprise. 'I thought you wanted to do the big gender reveal.'

'I do, but look at that little nose — it's definitely my nose.'

Given that he knew her current nose wasn't the one she'd been born with, he decided not to comment. 'I'm not sure it works like that.'

'It doesn't.' The sonographer chuckled. 'And even I can't tell right now, because baby is feeling modest and hiding from me a bit. But that's OK, we can give them a poke and see if they'll move a little. But right now, I need to get the date measurements, OK?'

'Of course.' He nodded, still not wanting to take his eyes off the tiny, blurry figure on the screen.

'You don't need to do that,' Yvette replied. 'I'm sixteen weeks. We conceived in August, didn't we Ricky? *Ricky*?'

'Huh? Oh yeah. August.' Before the accident. Before the courts. Before Angela. He sighed and looked back at the screen.

'You can skip straight to the gender,' Yvette insisted.

'Sixteen weeks?'

'Yeah.'

'Are you sure?'

Rick was so busy staring at the screen that he barely heard the exchange.

'I know I should have had the scan sooner, but I was away.' Yvette smoothed her hair. 'Corfu. You can probably tell from my tan.'

'Right, a nice babymoon break then?'

'No, but that's an awesome idea. Don't you think, Ricky? We should have a babymoon before I get too fat. Ricky, don't you think?'

'Huh? Sure.' He wasn't sure what he was agreeing to — he was far too caught up in the image on screen. In his baby.

'Right.' The sonographer clicked a few buttons. 'Are you sure about your dates? Because the baby definitely looks closer to twelve weeks to me. If you're certain about your last menstruation date, then I need to call in a specialist to consult, and we'll probably want to keep you in for some more tests.' Though her tone was gentle, it sent slivers of ice through Rick. 'You shouldn't worry unduly, but we should check this out.'

'Oh, I'm sure it's nothing to worry about.' Yvette's blasé attitude surprised him, and worried him a bit. Was she going to be like this when the baby actually arrived?

'Yvette, if the doctor thinks this is what's best, then this is what we should do.'

'Oh, it's not like she's a proper doctor.' Yvette shrugged and tossed her hair.

He stared at the sonographer in embarrassed horror, not entirely sure what to say or how he was supposed to respond to that. 'I am so sorry. Yvette, that's rude.'

'Oh I'm sure it's fine. And she knows what I mean.'

'Your partner is right.' The sonographer cleaned the probe and handed tissues to Yvette. 'I'm not a doctor.'

'See.' Yvette shot him a smile that seemed to border on relieved. He really didn't know what had gotten into her. Surely the hormones weren't going to make her like this throughout the whole pregnancy?

'But what I am,' the sonographer continued, 'is an experienced midwife, with extensive training in the field of obstetrics radiology. And while I understand that it can be very frightening to hear that your pregnancy might not be going exactly as planned, it's much better for us to investigate these things.'

'I'm sure there's nothing wrong. I'd know if there was anything wrong with my baby. It's just small because I am, that's all. It's not like I'd have a *fat* baby,' Yvette argued, making him wonder what her problem was. He couldn't believe she'd be so vain . . . at least, he didn't want to believe it.

'That's not really how these things work. So, if you're sure about your dates, I do need to bring in a colleague.'

'Ricky, baby?' Yvette turned to him with a bright smile. 'I'm feeling really thirsty — absolutely parched — could you be the sweetest and pop out to the vending machine and grab me a Diet Coke?'

'Right now?'

'Yes.'

'Yvette, I'd really like to hear what they have to say. You know, about our baby.' Something, but he wasn't sure what, flickered across her face. It only lasted a moment — not even a blink — but it was long enough. He folded his arms across his chest, watching her intently as the thoughts formed properly in his mind.

'Please, baby. I'm so thirsty my throat hurts.'

'There's a water machine there.' He glanced to the corner of the room.

'But I want fizzy. Still makes me feel sick.'

'I want to hear what you're about to say.' He glanced at the sonographer. 'I'm really sorry about this.' He felt awful for her, having to witness what he was starting to suspect would be a very embarrassing and awkward conversation.

'It can be a very emotional time.' She smiled sympathetically. 'And it is important to try and be accurate about these things.'

'Yes.' He glared at Yvette, thinking that he couldn't possibly be right about his suspicions. She had done some things in the past he'd questioned — behaved in ways he didn't exactly agree with — but surely he'd got something wrong. He had to be wrong — and he'd doubtless feel like a total jerk afterwards — but he had to know. 'Yvette, answer the question. How sure are you about your dates?'

'Ricky . . .' She reached out to him, but he shifted slightly away.

'Yvette, please just answer the question. How sure are you about the dates?'

She didn't actually need to say the words. He could see it in her eyes, in the look of defeat that crossed her face. She wasn't worried about the baby being too small, because it wasn't too small. It just wasn't his baby. And from the look on her face, she had known — or at least suspected that — all along.

The sonographer watched them both expectantly — waiting to do her job — and again he felt a flash of guilt for involving her in this silly drama Yvette had created.

'I . . . umm . . .'

'Just answer the question.' He ground the words out, forcing calm into his voice that he didn't feel.

'There might be a slight — tiny — possibility that . . . umm . . . I got my dates muddled.'

'By a month?' He glared at her.

'Maybe.' Yvette studied her nails. He wasn't surprised she didn't have the guts to look at him. He didn't want to look at her either. She might well have ruined the single, best thing in his life, and he was never going to forgive her for that.

He sat through the rest of the appointment in seething silence, which continued as they walked back to the car — to his car — which he would be taking the keys back to immediately. If he could have legally driven, he would have taken them then and there, but he couldn't. And even if he could have, he wouldn't have been such a bastard as to abandon her. Even if she did probably deserve it.

'Ricky . . .'

'Are you OK to drive?'

'I think we should talk.'

'I asked if you are OK to drive.'

'Yes, but I want to talk. We need to talk.'

'Actually, Yvette, no we don't. I don't need or want to talk to you right now. I just want quiet please.' With that he shoved his earbuds in so far that it hurt, and turned up his music loudly enough to make his teeth vibrate. It still wasn't enough.

CHAPTER TWELVE

'Can I come in?' They'd sat in the car on the driveway in the same silence that had lasted the whole drive home. 'I could really use a bathroom. Please?'

'Fine.' He nodded tersely before stomping into the cottage and into the living room. He whistled briefly to Mallow, who bounced up and down on her perch, rattling her beak against the cage bars. At least she was pleased to see him, and she was completely clear with what she wanted from him. He opened the door, and she raced out, climbing to the top of her cage and the play stand attached to it. He held his fingers out to her, itching her growing feathers and tussling with her beak.

Eventually, when his patience was almost at its limit, Yvette appeared. She hovered awkwardly in the doorway, looking pale beneath her perfectly applied make-up. 'Ricky, can I . . .'

'No. Whatever it is, you don't get to ask anything of me right now.' He folded his arms across his chest. 'What you get to do now is answer my questions.'

'Of course. Whatever you want.'

'What I want, right now, is some honesty from you.' He steepled his fingers, pressing them against his lips, while he figured out what he wanted to ask first. 'Did you always know? That it wasn't mine? Did you know from the start?'

'Well, it's not like you wake up and suddenly know you're pregnant.'

'No, I assumed that.' He'd stay patient with her and keep his cool. Regardless of whose baby it was, she was still pregnant, and he still had to do his best to not cause her stress. 'But given that we know the baby was conceived while you were supposedly at the spa with your friend, I assumed you would be able to remember whether or not you had a period while you were there.'

'Well, you know things were really busy, and I was stressed, and . . .'

'Stop making excuses, Yvette. Just answer the fucking question. Did you know from the start that the baby isn't mine?'

'Yes.'

'So when you stopped getting periods because you'd "changed your pill to make things better for us both", you were already pregnant?'

'Maybe.'

'Right. So while I was recovering from the accident, and preparing for court, you weren't really at a spa getting your face plumped up . . . you were cheating on me.'

'I wouldn't really call it cheating.'

'You wouldn't? What would you call it then?'

'A silly mistake that made me realise how much I really loved you.'

'A silly mistake?' He forced another deep breath, searching for some level of calm, but failed miserably to find it. 'So what? You tripped and accidentally impaled yourself on another man's dick?'

'No, I mean . . .'

'Oh please, do tell me what you mean. Mallow and I are just itching to know.' He folded his arms across his chest, waiting for the answer she didn't have. 'So go on then.' He couldn't help his curiosity. 'Who really is the father?'

'Well, you *could* be. No one would know apart from us.'

'Let me rephrase that. Who were you fucking while claiming to be in love with me?' He felt a pang of guilt when she winced at his words. Oh well, not his problem.

'You remember my friend with the yacht? Who I went to the spa with?'

'Yeah. Jeannie or something like that.'

'Jean,' she corrected him, using the continental pronunciation. 'As in Jean Charles.'

'Wow. So the friend "Jean", who you let me assume was a woman, was actually the guy you were shagging.' He shook his head in disbelief. 'And not just once either. So it's not really a mistake, is it? Not when it happens again and again.'

'You're picking on me.' She threw the accusation at him. 'You're trying to confuse me and my pregnancy brain. It's not my fault I've never been as smart as you.'

'I'm not "picking on you", I'm just stating facts. And don't think flattery will get me to change the subject.' He ignored her pout. 'You fucked him, at least twice, while supposedly in a relationship with me. You must have had a really good laugh at my expense.'

'I wasn't laughing at you. I was lonely. You weren't giving me enough attention. You were so busy being all stressed about things . . .'

'Right, so it's my fault is it? Life got a little bit too real, so you had to run away to another man? You really do have some nerve.'

'We can move past this,' she pleaded. 'We're so good together. Vetty and Maverick—'

'So what was your plan?' he interrupted her, not wanting to hear any more about his stupid online persona. 'Not that it matters now, but I'm curious. If it hadn't been so obvious on the scans, would you have just worried everyone by pretending the baby was premature?' Her lack of response was answer enough. 'Did you ever intend to tell me the truth?'

'Honestly?'

'Yes. Honesty is about the only thing I'm really interested in hearing.'

'I don't know.'

'So you were prepared to let me support you, meet a child who wasn't mine, fall in love with it and bring it up, and you were never going to tell me.'

Again, she didn't answer, telling him everything he needed to know.

'That's what I thought.' He shoved his hands into his pockets, trying to keep himself from clenching them into angry fists. 'Will you tell me why?'

'Because I didn't have any other choice.' She shrugged as if it was obvious. 'Come on, Maverick and Vetty? We're a power couple, made to be together. We're like soulmates or something. I couldn't let you throw that away.'

'Me? You think it was me . . .' He shook his head in disbelief, then realised that he didn't care. 'It doesn't matter.'

'You're right.' She seized on the words. 'It doesn't matter. None of it matters. We can just go back to being how we were, and have the baby. And they'll grow up calling you daddy and we'll be incredibly successful and rich, and we'll make money from all over the world, living in the best resorts and the best hotels in every country. It's going to be so amazing. Can't you just see it? Our baby is going to be a star.'

'But it's not my baby, and that's the point, isn't it? You've spent all this time lying to me. You don't do that to someone you love. When you love someone, you treat them better than you do yourself, because their happiness becomes yours.'

'Of course we're in love. I just made a silly mistake. When you love someone, you forgive them their mistakes. We'll be fine, baby. Better than fine.'

He really hoped that was true, and he really, really hoped that Angela would forgive him his stupidity. He doubted that she would, and he knew she probably shouldn't — but he also knew that he'd do everything possible to convince her to give him another chance.

But if his time with Angela, and Mallow, and Ruby, Ernie and even the stinky ferrets and guineas had taught him anything, it was that love didn't come with conditions — it had to be built on total trust and honesty. If you lied to an animal — if you broke their trust — they would hold it against you and see you as a threat, often with teeth, beaks, claws and hooves to protect themselves. But if you treated them with love and respect . . . well, you got something so pure it was almost magical, and incredibly valuable and worth cherishing. Like Mallow. And that was just with the animals. With Angela . . . oh, he really hoped he hadn't screwed that up beyond redemption, but he wouldn't blame her if she never wanted to speak to him again.

'So we're all good then?' Yvette asked him, snaking closer to him. 'We still love each other, and we can bring the baby up like it's yours. No one will ever know. I love you, Ricky.'

'Yvette, no.' He caught her wrist as she reached out to him, stopping her hand in mid-air. He didn't squeeze or twist — he wasn't like that. As much as she'd hurt him, he didn't want to hurt her. As Maverick, he might have pushed her away, shouted and sworn and acted like an idiot. But as Ryan — as himself — he just didn't really want her to touch him. So he gently released her hand, and stepped away, taking him closer to Mallow — and maybe closer to the version of himself he actually liked.

'What do you mean, *no*?' She pulled a face, like the word tasted bad. Perhaps it did to her — it certainly wasn't one she heard very often.

'I mean no,' he replied calmly. 'No, we're not "all good". No, I don't want to be a family with you and your baby. No, I don't think there's a big, bright, glittering future between Maverick and Vetty. And no, I don't think you really do love me. I'm not sure what we had was even really love.'

'What do you mean?' Her voice hissed angrily between her teeth. 'We were good together.'

'Yeah,' he agreed. 'We were good together, and we made great content and had great sex. But outside of videos and the bedsheets, I don't think you ever really loved *me*, Yvette. Because if you did, you would have treated me a lot better than you have.'

'So now what?' She jumped to attack mode. 'Are you saying I abused you or something?'

'No. I'm saying you cheated on me, and lied about it. And that if you hadn't got caught today, I think you would probably have carried on lying about it. Even now, you're standing here trying to convince me that somehow this is my fault, to make yourself the victim, so I have to be the one to apologise and make things right. Well, I've got news for you, Yvette. I've moved on. And you're going to have to do the same.'

'Where am I supposed to go?'

'Why not go back to the actual father? Go back to Jean.' He spat the name out.

'He's not interested in me like that.'

'Well clearly he was . . . more than once. Can't you work it out with him?'

'I doubt it. His wife doesn't know about me.'

'Wow. You really are the lowest of the low.' He couldn't help the comment slipping out. He didn't really want to be mean to her, but he was so angry at what she'd done to him. And apparently he wasn't the only one having his relationship torn apart by her selfishness.

'So where do I go?'

'What's wrong with your own flat?'

'It's not as nice as yours. I don't like it.' She pouted. He didn't think he'd ever come so close to losing it with someone. Really losing it. Instead, he took yet another deep breath.

'To use your own words, "that really sounds like more of a you problem than a me problem". You're not homeless or penniless, Yvette. You still have your brand and your money. You're just not tagging it onto mine anymore. I really don't care where you go, or what you do, so long as it's away from me.'

'You know what?' She folded her arms, squishing her boobs up a bit higher. 'If you take that back now, I'll forgive you.'

'I'm not asking for your forgiveness. I'm not the one who's done anything wrong.'

'You didn't make me your priority. That's why I ended up making a mistake with Jean.'

A mistake. She actually thought of it like that. 'You know what? I've held my tongue this long, but now I just don't care. I'm going to say this to you without any expectation that you'll listen, but in the hope that you might. Because I don't think anyone else is going to say it to you, and because you need to hear this. You're not that great, Yvette. You're not the special little princess that you think you are, and the world does not revolve around you! You're not that pretty, or that clever, or even that nice. But you are about to become a mother, and your entire world outlook needs to change, because if you carry on with your manipulative, bullying, selfish ways then your baby will end up hating you. I don't care what your excuse is, or how you grew up, or how other people have treated you. For the sake of that growing little life you're carrying inside of your body, you need to do better.'

She stared at him, mouth hanging open.

'And know this — when you walk out of my door you're probably going to forget about all this. But I won't. I'll think of you every so often, and hope that you're doing OK. And I'll send some positive thoughts out into the world for you, and I'll make sure I finish any of the contracts with companies who still want to work with Maverick and Vetty. Because you're going to need every bit of luck there is.'

He wasn't surprised that she didn't listen.

'It's that Abigail bitch, isn't it?'

'Angela.' He corrected her automatically. Again.

The noise Yvette made was almost as bad as the screeching of fighting foxes: vicious, angry and barely human. 'I hate you, Rick! I hate you, I hate you, I hate you!'

'Yeah, well, I'm not too keen on you at the moment either,' he snapped back, his cool and patience well worn out. 'I'd like you to leave. Now.'

'And where am I supposed to go?'

'Not really my problem. Just go back to your flat or whatever. And leave my car keys.'

'You really are a fucking arse! You want your precious car back so much, here you go! Not that you can drive it, you pisshead arsehole!' She threw the key at him, putting all of her anger behind it. He was too slow to catch it, and instead it rocketed past his ear.

Mallow let out a gasping squawk before slamming to the floor, where she stayed, flopped behind her cage, her wings hanging loose by her sides.

'Mallow!' He dived behind the cage. 'Are you OK? Oh, little baldy-butt, please come here . . .' She still didn't move, so he jammed his shoulder against the heavy cage and shoved it out of his way to reach her. She didn't complain when he scooped her up, which sent icy fear racing through him. She was hardly ever quiet. If something scared her — usually the postman or similar — she was obnoxiously loud and rude in her complaints.

'Get the fuck out of my house.' He didn't take his eyes off Mallow, who stayed flopped in his hands, heaving heavily as she breathed — her whole body moved with the effort, her tail and wings bobbing as she gasped. That, he knew, was something to worry about.

'Are you seriously more interested in that hideous monster than me? I'm upset here. Ricky!' Yvette stamped her foot.

'The only ugly thing I see here is you.' He glared at her briefly, eyes filled with hate, as he made up his mind. He scooped his keys off the floor. 'You're hideous, Yvette. All the way through ugly. Mallow might be a weird, half-bald chicken-butt, but her feathers are already growing back. She could probably bite through my finger if she wanted to, but she never will. Because, despite the pain she's been through, she still has the sweetest, most trusting, loving heart. And that's what makes her beautiful.' He zipped the bird carefully into his hoodie, taking a few extra seconds to snuggle her against him safely and soothe her. 'I don't expect you to understand that. You're pretty on the outside, but you don't have a single redeeming feature. You're toxic and rotten to the core — shallow and selfish. There's only one hideous monster here, and it's you.'

'Ricky . . .'

He ignored her, talking to Mallow instead. 'Come on, sweet girl. We need to get you help. Just hang in there.'

'But Ricky . . .'

'Get out of my way.' He stormed past her, cradling Mallow against his chest. 'I really do feel bad for your kid, Yvette. I hope for their sake you sort your shit out.' He stopped to grab a scarf, looping it around his neck and draping it over his chest, trying to give Mallow some extra warmth.

'You can't drive, you're banned still. I'll drive you.'

'I'd rather risk arrest than spend another second near you. Make sure you're gone before I get back.' He slammed out of the cottage, zapping the Lambo open and climbing into the driver's seat as quickly as he could manage. 'Come on, Chicken-butt. Just hold on. We'll go see Jake and he'll fix you right up.' He really hoped he was telling her the truth. He didn't think he could bare it if he wasn't.

He'd only made it halfway across the village — far too quickly — when blue flashing lights appeared in his rearview mirror. The very last thing he needed was a run-in with the police, but it looked like he'd developed the very worst type of luck today, having attracted the attention of Sergeant Brown or one of his colleagues. Swearing and trying not to burst into tears, he pulled up on the side of the road and rolled down the window, tucking the scarf around the bird-shaped bump in his hoodie.

'Good afternoon, seem to be in a bit of a hurry . . .' Harry's stern face darkened even more when he saw who was behind the wheel. 'Mr Finnegan, would you care to explain why you're speeding through Broclington while on a driving ban?'

'Harry . . . Sergeant Brown . . . I'm sorry, but it's an emergency. Please, it's Mallow . . . I think she might be dying.'

'Who?'

He unzipped the top of his hoodie so Harry could see the pathetic bundle of feathers inside.

'Oh, poor little mite. Is Jake expecting you?'

'Not yet.' He realised he should have called ahead, but he hadn't stopped long enough to look for his phone.

'Get out of the car, Rick.'

'Harry, please just let me get her to the vet. Then you can confiscate my car. Have it towed. Have it bloody crushed if you want. Please just let me get her help.' He didn't care that he could feel tears dampening his cheeks.

'Rick, you're on a driving ban. And even if you weren't, you're in no fit state to drive. Hop out and jump in my car.' He unlocked his phone and handed it to Rick, then jogged back to his car. 'You call, I'll drive.'

'Thank you.' Rick jogged to the cop car as quickly as he dared, cradling Mallow against his chest with one hand.

When they drew into the vet's car park, Jake was already at the door waiting for them with a fluffy blanket. 'What happened?'

He explained quickly, aware that Harry was still watching him closely.

'Give her here.' Jake held out the blanket.

He unzipped his jacket, gently and carefully lifted her out. She didn't complain or struggle when Jake wrapped her up in a towel, burrito-style, which worried him even more. 'Come on, Mallow. Let's go see what we're looking at.' Jake headed back into the surgery, leaving him to turn to the policeman.

'Sergeant Brown, I'm so sorry . . .' he started.

'Call me when Jake's finished with her.' He handed over a business card. 'You'll probably have to come into the station, formally present your identification, and we'll have a chat, but I'm pretty certain this is extenuating, life-or-death circumstances that you will not *for any reason* repeat, am I right?'

'Yes, sir.'

'Go look after your bird.'

'I will do. Thank you.'

'It's all right.' The policeman winked at him.

'Hey, Harry? Coppers can drive any car, right?'

'For constabulary business, yes.'

'Like relocating a car driven by someone on a ban that was abandoned on a street somewhere?'

'Arguably, could be.' Harry nodded, grinning as he caught on.

He chucked his keys to Harry, guessing the copper would enjoy the car, and raced inside to see how Mallow was.

'I can't palpate anything broken, and her air sacs look to be intact. There could be internal bleeding, but I'm reluctant to anesthetise her to take an x-ray. And, if I'm honest, if there's something wrong internally, there's not a huge amount I can do. You know parrots are not my specialism, Rick.'

'I know.' He nodded tensely. 'What do you suggest?'

'Painkillers, supportive fluids, warmth. I can nebulise her in the hospital cage too, and call one of my colleagues who has more avian experience. But I think . . . I hope . . . it's a bit of shock and bruising.'

'But she's going to be OK, right?'

'I'm optimistic.' Jake nodded. 'But you know birds can be trickier to work with than other animals. If she's all right overnight, she can probably go home with you in the morning.'

'Thanks. Can I put her in the cage?' He just wanted to give her a quick snuggle, and he wasn't going to think on it any more than that — doing so would mean he'd have to admit that there was a possibility he might really be saying goodbye. So he snuggled Mallow, giving her a quick itch and ruffling her crest in the way she usually liked, before snuggling her into the cage that Jake held open. She looked so forlorn and tiny that he wanted to cry, but he wouldn't. Instead he forced a smile, and petted her head once more. 'There you go, Chicken-butt. Luxury accommodation for you for the night. Feel better, and I'll come get you tomorrow.'

'Thank you for seeing her.' He pulled a face, knowing how close Evelyn and Angela were. 'I can imagine I'm not exactly your favourite person right now.'

'Mallow's health is more important than that.' Jake shrugged. 'It's not the same duty of care as the Hippocratic oath for doctors, but vets make a very similar commitment to our patients.'

'Still, thank you,' he told Jake sincerely as he followed him to reception. 'I'm really sorry, but I rushed out without my wallet or phone. Can I call you later to settle the bill, or pay you tomorrow when I collect her?'

'Or I can add it to the rescue's account. She is a rescue, after all.'

'Thanks.' He nodded, and took a deep breath before asking the question he dreaded, but also needed to hear the answer to. 'How is she? Really?'

'Stable. Like I said, I'm optimistic about her prognosis, and can call you with an update later today.'

'Thanks. I'm sure she'll be fine — Mallow's a fighter. But I was wondering about Angela.'

'You know I've worked with her closely for years, and that I consider her a good friend as well as a colleague? And that she's one of my fiancée's best friends?'

'I do.'

'So you also know that I'm not going to betray Angela's trust.' Jake folded his arms across his chest and watched him for a few seconds.

'Which I respect. I just . . . I wanted to know how she is. I'm not asking that you to tell me anything personal, I just want to know if she's OK.'

'In honesty, no, not really. She's really upset still. But, she's got good friends and family around her, and she's got Bill's, and she'll be OK. It's just going to take her some time. I understand why you did what you did, and had to make the decision you did, and I'm not going to judge you for it. But I'm not going to lie and tell you Angela's OK when she's not. At least, not yet.'

'I appreciate your honesty.' He gave Jake a half-smile. 'And if I can be honest back—' he waited for the other man's nod '—this isn't what I wanted, or what I had planned. Or what I expected. This whole thing is such a fucked-up mess.'

'Not really wanting to be judgemental, Rick, but that might not be the best way to describe your future family — however you feel about it right now.'

'Not my family, Jake.' He hadn't had time to think about what he would say to people, but it was going to come out sooner or later. 'She lied. The baby isn't mine.'

'From the way you said that, I'm guessing it's not a misunderstanding or mistake.'

'Nope. Definitely not.' He was still reeling. 'But, anyway, I've taken up enough of your time. Thank you again. I'll talk to you later about Mallow.' He tapped the top of the counter before heading to the door, not really wanting to leave. It wasn't like he was abandoning Mallow — Jake really was the best person to try and help — but he still hesitated, worried that he might not see her again.

'Hey, Rick?'

'Yeah?'

'I've got a bit of time. Want a cuppa?'

'Sure. That'd be good.'

* * *

'Wow, that's a lot to take in.' Evelyn drummed her fingers on the kitchen counter as she studied Jake. 'And she really knew all along? She was lying to him the whole time?'

'That's what he said.'

'That's absolutely hideous. What type of woman would try and trick a man into bringing up a baby that wasn't his?'

'The very worst type.' He shook his head. 'It's disgusting, despicable and really quite abhorrent behaviour.'

'What a total bloody bitch.' She shook her head, pulling a face.

'Evelyn!'

'Sorry, but it's true. She ruined what could have been a really good relationship by being a lying, nasty, manipulative wretch. Did she honestly think she would get away with it?'

'Apparently so.'

'So, what are we going to do about it?'

'Do?'

'This lie broke Angela's heart. Maybe the truth could help heal it?'

'So you *do* think we should tell her?'

'I think I'd want to know.' Evelyn nodded firmly. 'And sooner rather than later. We could invite her for dinner tonight.'

'Liv, Cal and Sarah are coming,' he reminded her.

'I don't think that's a problem. I'll give her a call and we can talk to her together.'

'Apparently it's not as uncommon as you'd think. Or hope.' He pulled a face. 'Three point seven per cent of fathers are conned into situations like this, bringing up children they don't know aren't theirs. At least, according to John Moores University.'

'Of course you looked it up.' Evelyn laughed.

'I was curious.'

'I love that about you.' She leaned in to give him a kiss. 'And for the record, if we're lucky enough that I get pregnant, I promise you it wouldn't ever be anyone else's but yours.'

'For the record,' he gathered her up in his arms, '*when* we get that lucky, I wouldn't question it for a heartbeat. And I love you too.'

* * *

'Angela! Angela!' The excited yells were followed by even more exciting yapping. Quickly, she sat on the bottom stair.

It was either that or risk being knocked flying by the exuberant greeting.

'Hello, hello. You're all acting like you've not seen me for months. It's only been a couple of weeks.'

'Yeah, but we missed you,' Summer explained, Sparks and Tilly joining in and trying to climb into her lap, taking turns washing her face hello. She giggled beneath the over-excited girls and dogs.

'Well, this isn't exactly the ideal welcome.' Jake grinned down at Summer before grabbing his niece Sarah, lifting her up and throwing her over his shoulder. He tickled her, making her squeal and squirm. 'You, fairy, are getting too big for me to do this much longer.'

'Nuh-uh,' she said through her giggles.

'Come on, Summer, let Angela in the door. And take Tilly and Sparks with you.' He reached down a hand to help Angela back to her feet. 'Welcome to the mad house. Like I said, sorry about the greeting.'

'You know what?' Angela grinned at him as the girls ran off. 'It was exactly the "hello" I needed this week.'

'How are you doing?'

'I'm . . . getting there.' The breath she took was shaky, but at least it wasn't followed by tears, so there was that to be grateful for.

'Sure about that?'

'Most of the time, yeah.'

'And the rest of the time?' He watched her with concern.

'And, sometimes I feel like I've been really silly, that I'm still being really silly, but other times I think that there was something real there . . . Maybe the big thing, like you and Evelyn, and Callum and Liv have. And then I think I really must be crazy, because if that was true, he wouldn't have been able to walk away so easily.'

'It wasn't easy for him, and he's regretting it. If that helps.'

She turned to look at him. 'You've been talking to Ryan . . . Rick?'

238

'Yeah. He brought Mallow in earlier today.'

'What happened?'

'A fall.' He shrugged. 'She knocked herself a bit silly.'

'But she's going to be OK, right?'

'I think so.' He nodded. 'She was already picking up when I left, and the nurse will check on her again when she does the final rounds of the night.'

'Good.' Angela breathed a sigh of relief. 'She's a sweet little thing — when she's not trying to bite. She deserves a chance at happiness.'

'She's not the only one.' Evelyn joined them in the hall-way. 'Sorry, I wasn't eavesdropping — not exactly. Just wondered if you're actually coming in. Liv and Callum are in the kitchen too.'

'Yeah, I figured from the greeting.' Angela laughed and hugged her friend. 'And it's not really eavesdropping when it's your own home, and a friend.'

'Glad you feel that way.' Evelyn hugged her back tightly. 'Because I mean it. If there's anyone more deserving of a chance at happiness, I've not met them.'

'Well, there's you and Summer . . .'

'Doesn't count. We've already got ours in Jake. Which reminds me, I need to ask you something. A bit of a favour, really.'

'I'll go start mashing the spuds.' Jake headed back through. 'So what's this favour?'

'Well, given that we've been friends for years . . .'

'Probably since the sandpit in pre-school.' Angela grinned.

'Yeah. I definitely remember you getting me in trouble with Mum for daring me to decorate my dress with poster paints!'

'Oh gosh, I'd forgotten about that.'

She laughed. 'Anyway, it is sort of dress related. Will you be one of my bridesmaids?'

'I thought Summer and Sarah were?'

'They are, but there's quite a difference between adult bridesmaids and child ones. I've asked Liv too, as we're basically going to be family, but . . . it wouldn't be the same if you weren't there by my side.'

'I'd love to.' She linked her arm through Evelyn's as they headed into the kitchen together. 'But maybe one condition?'

'Let me guess. No pink taffeta?'

'Exactly. I love you, but please don't ask me to wear pink taffeta!'

'Come and have dinner. Jake's probably done with the mash by now. And you can consult with the dress designers. They've been favouring ruffles and stars in the recent designs.'

'Wonderful.' Angela tried not to roll her eyes, already knowing that she'd wear anything Evelyn asked her to.

'It's not so bad. There's been quite a few rainbows featured too.'

'Now that sounds more like my style.'

'Yeah, I thought you'd like those.' Evelyn rolled her eyes now. 'Guess I'll have to rely on Liv.'

'Hey, Angela.' Liv looked up from where she was colouring with Summer and Sarah. 'What am I being relied on for?'

'Beautiful and elegant bridesmaid dresses.'

'Oh, I don't know, the rainbow thing might be growing on me,' she teased.

'Evening, Angela.' Callum appeared in the kitchen. 'Right, you mucky mischief makers, time we all went and washed up for dinner. Liv, are you coming to help? I might need an extra pair of hands to get rid of all the glitter. Which is mandatory for anyone wanting dessert.'

'Of course. And it might be best to make sure we don't flood Evelyn and Jake's bathroom too.'

'I only did that once,' Sarah huffed, rolling her eyes and tutting, making her seem far more like a teenager than the sweet little girl she was.

'Shift, go on. Otherwise Tilly and Sparks can have your dinner. I'm pretty sure they'll both like toad in the hole,' Jake threatened.

'We're going, we're going.' Summer raced from the room. 'Come on, Uncle Callum!'

Angela smiled as she watched the girls run ahead, giggling and whispering. She adored these random Macpearson family dinners she often got invited to. They'd started years ago, when Jake, Callum and Kim were still young — and their mum had happily scooped up and fed anyone who happened to be around at the right time for dinner. Being practice manager and receptionist at the Macpearson's GP surgery there weren't many people in the village their mum didn't know. Angela was glad the meals had been continued — random, rarely planned and as fun as they always were.

'So quick, before the girls come back, how are you doing, Angela?' Evelyn squeezed her fingers.

'I'm OK.' She sighed sadly. She didn't miss the look that flitted between Evelyn and Jake. 'What's going on?'

'When Rick came into the surgery today, he stayed and had a bit of a chat.'

'And? I'm not bothered if you want to stay friends with him. It's not like that.'

'Good to know.' Jake nodded. 'But that wasn't why I was telling you.'

'OK.' Angela watched him expectantly.

'The thing is, well . . .'

'Just tell her,' Evelyn urged.

'Tell me what?'

'That it turns out Yvette is a huge bitch,' Evelyn answered.

'That seems a bit harsh,' Angela said, not really knowing why she was defending the other woman. Habit, she supposed.

'It turns out that the baby isn't Rick's,' Jake added gently. 'And it seems that Yvette knew all along.'

'Wow.' Angela didn't know what she was supposed to say or feel about that. 'Are you sure?'

'He seemed pretty certain.' Jake nodded.

'Huh.' Angela chewed her lip while she thought.

'Well, what do you think?'

'I think that it doesn't change anything.' Angela sighed as she worked it out. 'As much as I want to believe that it does, let's be honest about it, he walked away from me too easily.

Apart from a couple of calls I didn't — couldn't — answer, and a rambling message about how sorry he was and how he needed to work things out, I've not heard from him.'

'Did you reply to the message?'

'Wasn't really anything to say.' Angela shrugged. 'What was I supposed to do? Beg him to pick me and a few weeks of good sex over the woman he has history and a future with?' She knew she was probably being unfair, and massively down-playing what she thought she'd had with Ryan, but it didn't matter. Maybe she'd been wrong all along — maybe Ryan was the illusion, and the real version of him really was the slick, designer-clad Maverick. 'Besides, it's not like I can compete.'

'What do you mean?'

'Come on, guys, don't be naive. She's model-beautiful and they had a life together, long before he smashed into the café. One filled with fancy restaurants, designer gear and all things glamorous. Compared to what? Endless piles of manure, cold damp mornings that start too early and dona-tions that never reach far enough to balance the books?'

'Compared to you.'

'Some big whoop I am.'

'Angela, you shouldn't talk down about yourself like that!' Evelyn scolded.

'She's right,' Jake agreed. 'I'd pick someone like you a dozen times over someone like that vapid, manipulative Yvette.'

'Should you be saying things like that in front of your intended?'

'Well I certainly wouldn't say them behind her back.' He grinned. 'And Evelyn knows the only other girl in my life is Summer.'

'I do.' Evelyn shrugged. 'And I happen to agree with him. You, Angela, are worth a dozen — maybe a hundred Yvettes.'

'I don't think Rick agrees.' The words were sour in her mouth. 'If I meant all that much to him, then I can't believe he would have walked away as easily as he did. Maybe we could have stood a chance of working something out, but he barely tried. Even with this news, I don't know how we, if there even is a "we", can come back from that.'

'I'm so sorry, Ange.' Evelyn wrapped her arms around her shoulders.

'It's OK.' Angela wasn't sure if she was reassuring her friends or herself. 'And I've had enough of this conversation, if it's all right with you both.'

'Just so you know all the facts,' Jake pressed on, 'he only found out today. He's asked Yvette to leave, and he seemed pretty upset by the whole situation.'

'Thanks for telling me that.' She forced a smile for Jake. 'But I don't think it changes my answer. The very fact that it's you telling me this, and not him, just proves my point. Come on, can we just drop this now? Please?'

'Yeah.' Evelyn nodded firmly, but Angela suspected she wasn't done on the topic. 'Let's enjoy dinner. We're supposed to be cheering you up. And by the sounds of those footsteps, help is on the way.'

'Sounds good to me.' This time, her smile felt a lot less forced.

* * *

Ryan rolled over in bed and gave his pillow another good whack, trying to find some level of comfort. Not that it mattered really, as he was pretty sure there wasn't anything he could do — other than get pissed — that would help him sleep.

His mind was spinning from the events of the day. He was furious with Yvette for what she'd done — for lying to him and for taking so much away from him.

Maybe it was spending time around Sarah and Summer at Bill's, or maybe it was meeting someone who he'd actually started to envision a future with, but much to his surprise he'd found himself getting excited about the prospect of being a dad one day. And, for a little over a week, he'd been just that

— or at least an expectant father. Once he'd gotten over the shock, he'd started to feel excited about the little life that he thought he'd been part of creating. And he felt cheated now that had been stolen from him.

But far worse than that was how badly her lies had hurt Angela. It was bad enough that she'd hurt him — he would deal with it. But to hurt Angela, and physically attack Mallow? That he was never going to be able to forgive. He still couldn't forget the pain in Angela's eyes when she'd told him to go, and — like the biggest idiot on the planet — he'd walked away. He should have stayed and fought for her, for the future they'd started building, for all the feelings that he knew they shared. But instead, he'd run after Yvette, like Ruby chasing a chew toy, and by the time he'd stopped to think about it, he realised he'd crushed Angela's feelings into the floor.

He thumped his pillow again, and stared up at the ceiling. What he really wanted to do was find a way to make things up to Angela — not that he expected her forgiveness. He certainly didn't feel like he deserved it, not when he'd hurt her so badly.

And he was haunted by the image of Mallow on the floor, flopped out on one of the few areas he hadn't padded, panting and barely responding. Again, Yvette's fault, and another thing he'd struggle to forgive her for.

Not that she really seemed to want forgiveness — she certainly hadn't shown an ounce of contrition. But, then again, the more he thought about it, the more he realised she probably never would. As far as Yvette was concerned, the sun, the moon and the stars revolved around her, and nothing and no one else really mattered, except for how they could service her.

If anything, he was lucky to have broken free of that. He glowered up at the ceiling again, waiting impatiently for sleep to arrive.

* * *

'Morning, Jake.' Ryan staggered into the surgery, feeling like he was owed a bloody good night out. Usually it took a full weekend of partying to feel as bad as he currently did. He grinned in relief when a familiar volley of squawks and whistles welcomed him. 'I guess someone is feeling a lot better.'

'Oh yeah, she's given us all plenty of beak this morning.' Jake laughed. 'Not to mention trying to take a lump out of me.'

'Sorry.' He cringed.

'It's fine. I'm glad to see her attitude back. But I won't say no if you want to come through and collect her yourself.'

'Sure. I'm all ready.' He held up the travel cage he'd brought with him and followed Jake through. Mallow was on the bars, bouncing up and down and squawking as soon as he entered the room. She flung herself at his chest as soon as the door was opened. 'Hey, sweet girl, I missed you too.' He snuggled his fingers into her feathers, which were improving almost daily. 'She looks so much better. Thank you, Jake.'

'I'd love to be able to take the credit for this, but we really only offered supportive care. She's done this by herself, haven't you, Mallow?' He yanked back the finger she snapped at.

'Mallow, don't be ungrateful!' Ryan scolded. 'Sorry. She can be a bit territorial.'

'It's a good thing I don't take offence.' Jake chuckled. 'And at least she hasn't peed on me. I can't say that of all my patients.'

He followed Jake back through to reception, Mallow still snuggled against his chest. He skimmed over the bill Kiran — Jake's nurse/receptionist — handed him, then read it again more carefully. 'This doesn't seem right. I was expecting to see a charge for the overnight care at least.'

'Oh, I just ran it up as if she were a Bill's resident,' Kiran answered, and looked to Jake. 'Sorry, should I have run as a private client?'

'Yes,' Ryan answered.

'No,' Jake replied at the same time.

'Yes, you really should,' Ryan argued. 'Thank you, but I'm happy to pay whatever I owe. You shouldn't be making a loss on my bird, and I don't want Angela having to deal with any more costs either.'

'Fair enough.' He really hoped he wasn't imagining the look of approval in Jake's eyes. He didn't expect he'd get to continue the friendship they'd started to build, but at least that look meant he maybe hadn't blown everything.

Within minutes he'd paid his bill, wrapped Mallow's cage up in a blanket against the cold and headed back to his waiting lift. He'd paid the driver extra to keep the engine running so the car stayed warm, and Mallow wouldn't have to be cold for even a minute.

He bundled her back up to take her into the cottage quickly. He trusted Jake's experience, but he was still worried about the cold, and wanted to avoid her going back into shock again, so he focussed on keeping her warm, then transferred her carefully back to her own cage, where she immediately hopped around and bashed each of her toys in turn. Obviously she was glad to be home. And he was really glad to have her back — the previous night had been far too quiet, and he'd struggled to sleep with the emptiness in the cottage. Once he'd added some fresh food, he left her to settle back in and wander around as she pleased. He grinned when she climbed to the top of her cage, assuming her favourite position on the play stand he'd set up there.

'Right, you stay there with your bell. I'll be back in a minute.'

He headed into the kitchen to make a well-deserved drink, and grab a ciggy. He knew he was supposed to be quitting — and he'd done well up until recently, when Yvette had crashed back into his life, and then stomped all over it — but it helped with the stress, and stopped him opening a bottle. He'd finish up this pack, he told himself, and the last one in it would be his last. He opened a window so the smoke left the house — at least he could be responsible and look after the bird's lungs. He'd worry about his own tomorrow.

In the meantime, there were some apologies he needed to make. His agent and friends were easy enough — a few quick messages would take care of them, but Imogen was a different matter. He swallowed his pride and dialled his sister.

'You know, part of me was really tempted to send you straight to voicemail and give you a taste of your own medicine,' she griped without even saying "hello" first. 'And another part of me realises that hanging up on you will be much more satisfying if I've spoken to you first, to make sure you know damn well that I'm doing it because I'm mad at you, not that I'm too busy to answer.'

'I deserve that. I'm sorry.'

'You better believe you will be when I get my hands on you! One minute you're messaging me pictures of you and Angela, looking happier than I've seen you in years, and the next I'm finding out I'm about to be an aunt from some bloody self-styled social media journalist asking me if I'm excited to become VettyBaby's sister-in-law.'

He should have guessed Imogen would have ended up in the firing line when he ducked out of sight. 'Sorry, sis.'

'Do you have any idea how pissed I am at you?'

He winced, knowing that Imogen put quite a lot of effort into not getting caught up in his social media whirlwinds. 'I'm guessing somewhere between "very" and "I'm lucky that you're even speaking to me" angry?'

'Yeah. Somewhere in that range. Have you any idea how much cleansing this will take?'

'I did say I was sorry. And I really am.'

'I know.' She sighed heavily down the phone. 'So go on then. When's the wedding? And am I getting a niece or a nephew? Because if you know, and I have to find that out from your freaking feed, you will see me angrier than when you tried to launch my doll into space.'

'There's not going to be a wedding. Or a baby. At least, not a Finnegan one. It's not mine. Yvette cheated on me and lied about it.'

'Shit.'

247

'Yeah.'

'That, obnoxious, fake pouting, posing, bottle-job succubus!'

'Gee, don't feel like you need to hold back on my account.' He'd known Imogen hadn't liked Yvette, but hadn't realised how bad it had been.

'She messed with my brother.' Imogen's tone was fiercer than he could ever remember. 'I'll curse her all the way from here to Broclington and all the way back again.'

'You always say curses aren't worth the karma.' He wasn't sure he believed in a lot of the things his sister did, but something in her tone of voice made him think twice.

'In this case, I think I'd be willing to risk it,' Imogen muttered darkly.

'Please don't. She's really not worth it. She's already caused enough pain to people I care about.'

'What do you mean?'

'She threw keys at my bird, who needed emergency vet care — don't worry, Mallow's OK now. Then there's my embarrassment trying to sort this all out online and with our sponsors, which means my agent is probably about to break out in stress-related hives.'

'Which you'll be blamed for.'

'Obviously. But it's worse than that. I really, really hurt Angela. She told me to go, but the look on her face when I did . . . and she hasn't answered a single call or message since. I think I really, really screwed things up, Imogen.'

'Then you'd better figure out a way to unscrew things, hadn't you, Ryan?'

'I wish it were that easy.'

'If you're really not going to let me curse the bitch . . .'

'I'm not. Not worth the bad energy for yourself.'

'Well, then I have some time. Want to keep talking a bit?'

'Yeah. That'd be good. Thanks, Moggy.'

'You know you don't have to keep calling me that.' He was pretty sure he could hear her rolling her eyes. 'It's not like we're kids anymore.'

'Yeah, but it amuses me.'

'Whatever, *Ry-no.*'

He grinned at the old nickname, leaning back against the kitchen counter while his sister chattered away.

With his attention on his sister he didn't hear the flutter of wings, or the scrabble of claws on the kitchen counter. It wasn't until he'd finished, closed the window and headed into the living room that he realised anything was wrong.

'Mallow? Where are you?' He leaned down to peer under the coffee table and sofa. 'Chicken-butt?' He whistled for her and waited for a response. 'Mallow?' His heart sped up and his breath started to come faster. He checked the hall, hoping she'd wandered out to attack shoelaces again, but she wasn't there.

No! The realisation sent a shiver of cold through him. He'd had the kitchen window open. But there was no way she could have gotten out of there, could she? He'd only turned away from it for a few moments — not more than a minute or two — and she wasn't flying properly anyway. Yeah, before Yvette had knocked her off the top of her cage, she'd been fluttering a bit, trying out her wings, but she certainly couldn't fly. He didn't think.

On autopilot he strode to the kitchen and unlocked the back door. 'Mallow?' He looked around the garden, feeling like a total idiot. But there, in the conifer — was that a flash of pink?

'Chicken-butt?' A squawk and cackle of laughter answered his question. Shit. 'Come on, sweetie, come on down. Please?' She was higher than he could reach, and he didn't want to risk looking away to find something to climb on — not when she'd already proven how fast and sneaky she could be. Keeping one eye on her, he levered himself up onto the fence, the freezing wood biting through his socks and into his toes. He had to get her back indoors: her feathers were still patchy in places, and there was no way she could handle a British winter for long. 'Come on, Mallow. Please come here. Please. I'll give you your favourite biscuits . . . not just a bit either, you can have a whole one.' She bobbed up and down, cackling at him, making him nervous. 'A bowl. You can have a whole bowl full of gingerbread if you just come down now.'

He reached up to her, stretching on the icy fence to reach her. He was still too low, so he stretched even more, balancing precariously. The inevitable happened — his foot slipped and he crashed against the fence, making it rattle loudly. Mallow shot off her perch, fluttering as she squealed in alarm. The wind blew at exactly the wrong moment, lifting her up and giving her the height he really didn't want her to gain at that moment. She whistled, zooming overhead. 'Mallow, no! Come back! Please, Chicken-butt . . . come back!'

He tracked her for as long as he could as she soared in the vague direction of the village centre. When she dropped out of sight, he raced into the house, jammed his feet into the first shoes he saw and grabbed his coat and keys. When he found her, he'd need to be able to keep her warm — and he was going to find her. He couldn't even consider any other outcome.

He didn't know what he expected, but he'd hoped that he'd see another flash of pink, or that she'd realise she wasn't safe and would be glad to see him. He had to find her — he just had to.

But she wasn't there. He couldn't see her.

Panic seized him, gripping at his throat and making the icy air burn even more as he ran through the village, calling desperately. He ignored the stares of people going about their normal lives while he felt like his was falling apart. He didn't care — he'd already lost Angela, and he really, really couldn't lose Mallow. He had to find her before something terrible happened to her — there were countless awful things that could happen. Even if she didn't freeze, there were cats, electric cables, the pond, not to mention cars and probably birds of prey.

After what felt like hours of searching, but was probably only minutes, he found himself at the base of the wishing tree.

He stared at the tree and prayed, pleaded and wished for help to anyone or anything that might be listening, begging to see that flash of pink, or hear that rude cackle. Please, oh please let her be OK, and please, please help him to find her — or for her to find him. Or for someone to find her and warm her up. He already knew cockatoos' body temperatures ran higher than humans, and it was cold for him, which meant it was freezing for her — especially without her cute jumpers.

He stared up at the miserable sky that was dark and heavy with snow, and fought to keep from crying. He didn't have time for that.

Something nudged his foot, and he looked down. It was a bright red, shiny bauble the size of his fist. For a moment, he stared at the shiny sphere, thinking how much Mallow would probably like it, and regretting not getting a full-sized tree for the cottage. When he looked up, he spotted another bauble lying a few feet away. A strange clicking noise on the other side of the tree caught his attention, and he walked around to see another bright bauble — this time gold — bounce across the cobbles.

The tree rustled in the breeze, and another bauble bounced down the branches as he watched. One branch bounced a lot more than the others — rustling drew his attention halfway up the tree, as another bauble dropped and ping-ponged towards his feet.

'Mallow?' He held his breath, waiting for a response. 'Chicken-butt?' After long, painful seconds, the tree moved again and another ornament bounced down the branches. This time he was ready and listening closely, so he heard the soft 'whoop!', and spotted the pink head that peered out of the hole where the purple bauble had been.

He breathed a huge sigh of relief. This time he wasn't going to give her a chance to escape again, and he locked his eyes on the spot where he'd last seen her as he started to climb. The branches were sturdy and his trainers had enough grip so he could clamber high enough up the tree. His balance was wobbly when he finally reached the right spot, and he parted the branches to peer at a disappearing pink tail.

'Mallow.' He clucked to her gently. 'Come here, Chicken-butt. Come on. Come see what I've got for you . . . lots of treats waiting for you back at home, where it's warm and safe. Come on, baldy-butt.'

'Boo!' Mallow peeked around the trunk and cackled maniacally at him.

'Yes, yes, very funny. Now come here.' He flicked his fingers at her, wishing he'd actually brought some treats with him.

Slowly, almost suspiciously, she edged towards him, one dinosaur foot creeping over the other. Within a few seconds she was close enough that he could probably reach out and grab her — but he forced himself to wait patiently, worried that if he tried to grab her and missed he'd lose his chance. A few seconds later she rubbed her head against his fingers, and he gave her the itches she wanted. Slowly, carefully, he slid his fingers further down her back, until he could cover her wings, and then pull her towards him.

As soon as he could, he scooped her up and cradled her against his chest where she nibbled at his coat. He wedged himself more tightly against the tree to unzip his coat and shove her inside, securing her against his chest before he climbed down.

He knocked off a couple of the ornaments on his descent, and stooped to pick them up when he was back on the ground. Quickly he rehung the shiny baubles, but hesitated over the red envelope that had been knotted to the tree. He looked around, feeling guilty, even though he didn't really know why. He slid open the envelope and read the message inside. Smiling, he read it a second time: a games console for her little brother was the only thing Becky, aged seven, wanted to ask Santa for. Not what he'd expected. Thinking, he tucked the card back into the envelope and reached for the next one, curious to see what that wish would be.

CHAPTER THIRTEEN

'I'm sure Miss Whiskers will be glad to be home too.' Jake held the door open from his examination room with one hand for an older woman, holding a cat box in the other. 'Kiran will ring your bill up, and book your follow-up appointment.' He placed the cat box on the receptionist's desk before turning to Ryan, where he sat in the patient waiting area. 'Two visits in one day. Is everything all right? No ill effects?' He grinned when Mallow stuck her head above Jake's coat, whistling and blowing kisses. 'No, I'll not be fooled by you and that beak again, thank you. It's a bit too quick and sharp for my poor fingers.'

'She's fine.' Ryan smiled, still glad beyond relief to have her back. 'She's flying as well now. As of today. Bit of a surprise. I know you're probably busy, but I was hoping for a couple more minutes of your time. I can wait, or come back?'

'I'm just about to head out to Western Farm. If you can talk while I pack my bag, I've got a few minutes now.'

'That works.' Ryan nodded and followed the vet into his office. 'It won't take long. I want Angela's bill.'

'How do you mean?'

'You said this morning about adding Mallow to Angela's account for Bill's. I assume that means she's got an outstanding balance with you.'

'I'm not going to discuss another client's accounts with you. It's privileged information.'

'I don't want to see the detail. I don't need it. Just the total.' He took a deep breath. 'Listen, you probably won't be surprised to hear that I didn't sleep much last night. I started off worrying about Mallow, then thinking about everything that happened with Yvette — but mostly I thought about Angela, and all the ways I screwed up with her. And I realised that there's nothing I can do to make up for what I've done. I'm pretty sure the day I chose Yvette over her that I broke her trust and destroyed — decimated — something really special. Am I about right?'

Jake folded his arms across his chest and stared at Ryan. Even Mallow stayed quiet while he thought.

'I'm not asking you to betray her trust, Jake. I just . . . I'm really hoping that you're going to tell me I'm wrong, and that I haven't screwed up as badly as I think I have. But I am asking if it's as bad as I think.'

'Like I told you earlier, Angela will be OK. She's got good friends and family around her, and her animals. She's pretty resilient.'

'And fierce, determined, driven and passionate. And utterly wonderful in so many ways,' Ryan added. 'And she deserves way, way better than me. I can't undo what I did, Jake. I wish I could, but I can't. But I can help her, and Bill's residents, if you'll let me.'

'Is this some attempt to win her back?'

'No. I don't expect it to change anything between me and Angela, but it might help her. And I want to do that. Besides, if she hadn't been hurt by another moment of my dumb-arse selfishness, then she'd have been running more fundraising activities. So I feel like I owe her this anyway.'

'You know it's pretty high? The sanctuary's bill.'

'I figured. But I'd still like to do it.'

'OK. I'll have Kiran pull it together.'

'Thanks. And Jake? Could you maybe not tell her I've done this?'

'You know I'm going to ask why.' The vet kept his arms folded and stared.

'It's hard to explain, but . . . this isn't really about me doing something nice for Angela to get the credit for having done something nice. It's about doing something to help Angela, just to help Angela. It's about her, not me. Does that make sense?'

'Yeah.' Jake smiled properly for the first time since they'd entered his office. 'It really does. So what do you want me to tell her?'

'Anonymous benefactor?' he asked hopefully, even as Jake pulled a face. 'I know I'll probably have to tell her eventually, but I also want to make sure that when, and if, I do, it's all done. All paid for. Because I don't want her to refuse something that will help her — and Bill's — just because I've been an idiot. Please?'

'OK,' Jake nodded. 'And I'll see if I can't think of something a bit better than that.'

'Thanks. Let me know when it's ready, and give me your bank details.'

'You're sure about this?'

'Yeah.' Ryan grinned, feeling more like himself than he had all week. He was surer about this than he had been about anything in quite some time. And now he'd started thinking about it, he realised there was a lot more he needed to do. 'And, actually, there's a couple of other things I'd like to talk to you about, if you can spare me some more time later . . .'

'I reckon I can manage that.' Jake grinned at him again. 'You know, you're a lot more interesting than I first thought, Rick.'

'Thanks. I think. Oh, and by the way, my name is actually Ryan.'

* * *

'You really are my very best helpers,' Angela told Summer and Sarah, once again grateful that the lure of wild animals kept them turning up on a regular basis to volunteer. The fact that Evelyn — or in today's case, Liv — often stayed for a quick coffee when they dropped the girls off was an added bonus. Especially when black and white boxes from the café featured in their catchups.

Liv smiled as she blew on her coffee to cool it, watching as Sarah carefully measured food into a bowl for one of the hedgehogs. She checked on the list Angela had given her, and moved onto the next bowl and hedgehog. 'It's amazing how grown-up she seems some days.'

'She's really good with the animals. I wouldn't be surprised if she made a career out of it.'

'You could well be right.' Liv nodded. 'Although her plan this week is to be a superstar chocolate maker who is also a ballerina.'

'Well, I suppose she'll have plenty of energy for dancing from all the chocolate.'

'So, how are you doing?'

'Better when I don't think about it.' She pulled a face. 'How are the wedding plans coming?'

'Mine and Cal's? Or Evelyn's and Jake's?'

'Both. Either. Mostly just wanting to change the subject. Have you gotten any closer to picking a date yet?'

'To be honest, not really. We're mostly just enjoying being together as a family and working out how we fit together. Keeping my cottage for that bit longer helped things, but even then it's been a big adjustment. But it really is wonderful. And I swear every time she calls me "Mum" I melt a little bit more. It still hasn't worn off, even when she's whingeing and grizzly, and refusing to put her toys away, or demanding to wear a princess dress or fairy wings to school.'

'I really am so happy for you.'

'Angela?' Summer ran over to them. 'Please may I use your toilet?'

'Of course.'

'Thank you.' They watched as she skipped into the house, pausing carefully to wipe her feet.

'She's brilliant, isn't she?' Liv asked. 'My soon-to-be-niece.'

'Yeah. They both are.'

'Mum!' Sarah shouted. 'Do you want to come fatten up the hedgehogs?'

'I swear, every time she calls me "Mum" it still gets me right here.' Liv caught her breath and pressed her hand to her chest. 'You coming?'

'Of course. They're my hedgehogs. Well, at least until they're big enough to release in spring.'

She grabbed the heavy gloves needed to safely handle the hogs without risking their spikes. She worked alongside Sarah and Liv, who were utterly enchanted with the little critters, feeding, cleaning and checking them over. After the third cage, she realised Summer still hadn't come back.

'Do you think we should go check on her?'

'No, I'm sure she's fine.' Liv opened the next cage. 'Is this the one who got fly strike? How are they doing?'

'She's doing just fine.' Angela smiled, relieved. Fly strike wasn't as common in the winter months, and could often indicate more serious problems, but this little girl seemed to be thriving with warmth and plenty of good food.

'What's her name?' Sarah wanted to know.

'She doesn't have one yet. Did you want to give her one?'

'I think she looks like a "Cloud". What do you think, Mum?'

'I think she's the spikiest cloud I've ever seen, but it's a lovely name.'

'I think I'm going to go check on Summer.' Angela turned to head across the yard.

'No!' The urgency in Liv's voice shocked her. 'I mean, it's fine. You stay here with the hogs and Sarah, and I'll go see what's keeping Summer. OK?'

'Sure.' Angela's eyes followed her friend as she headed across the courtyard, wondering what that was all about.

257

A few minutes later, Summer came skipping back, holding Liv's hand.

'Is everything OK?'

'Yeah.' They both nodded quickly.

'Right.' Angela looked at them suspiciously. 'What's going on?'

'Nothing.' Liv grinned at her, then Summer. 'Right?'

'Right.' The girl nodded. 'Nothing.'

'Angela,' Sarah interrupted her thoughts. 'Do any other hedgehogs need to be named?'

* * *

Ryan looked down at his phone when it beeped, and grinned to himself. He hadn't initially been in favour of involving Summer in his plans, but Jake had pointed out she was the last person Angela would suspect, therefore making her the perfect accomplice. The fact that she'd been so excited to help, taking part in what she called her "Santa's Secret Mission", had surprised him, but — as she'd pointed out — Santa had been very good to her, and she should help him if she could. He hadn't expected Liv to help either, but obviously Jake and Summer had helped convince her.

He flicked through the images Summer and Liv had messaged him, scribbling notes in his pad. Some of the pictures were a bit blurred, and he got way more closeups of Summer's fingertips than he'd ever wanted to see, but the images would give him what he needed. He was pretty sure Angela was still — rightly — angry with him, and would likely reject any gift he might offer her, but he was betting she wouldn't reject something for her animals. And just in case she might, he'd do it in a way she couldn't refuse.

Once he'd gotten all the details he needed, he started making calls, flexing his plastic friend to the maximum in return for emailed receipts. It took him over an hour, but soon his inbox started filling up with the responses he needed.

Another hour after that, and a couple of calls to customer services departments, and he'd sorted out the red envelopes too. Jake had explained to him what needed to happen with that, and roped in the help he needed via Evelyn's mum and her Women's Institute friends, who had thought the whole thing a "wonderful idea" — even if they did complain about not knowing who their anonymous "Santa" was. But, despite Jake's best attempts to convince him to sign any other name, he wasn't doing it for the likes or kudos — it was about giving the gifts, nothing else.

After that, he stretched and fetched one of his new canvases, his camera and tripod, and Mallow's favourite plate. When she saw him spreading out the grubby sheet on the coffee table she started bouncing up and down, squealing with excitement.

'OK, come here, madam.' He opened her cage door and she raced up his arm to her favourite spot, snuggling against his ear while he got out the special bottles and lined them up. 'Are you ready for your spotlight moment? This one needs to be extra special. It's for Angela.' Mallow fluffed her crest and pinned her eyes at the name — she liked Angela too. 'Go on then, down you go.' He placed Mallow gently on the table, hitting record as she strutted towards the bottles to make her selections. Grinning, Ryan flicked through his phone, finding some suitably festive music for their latest — and probably most important — project, before reaching for one of Mallow's favourite new toys.

* * *

The day before Christmas Eve, Angela sat at the kitchen table, her leg kicked up to rest on a chair as she curled ribbons for tying the gifts her mum was wrapping. The system worked well for them — with Cathy being quick and neat at the actual wrapping, while Angela preferred to take her time with the pretty touches her mum was less bothered about. The kitchen smelled deliciously of the cider that had been mulling away in the slow cooker for hours — another part of their run-up-to-Christmas tradition.

She tied another sprig of holly to a parcel wrapped with purple paper — recyclable, of course — and tied it with silver ribbons. The tag, cut down from a Christmas card from last year, was carefully written and added to the parcel.

She really hoped Evelyn would like the shawl she'd crocheted for her in ombre shades of green — matching her bright eyes. She thought she would, as she'd admired Angela's ones so often. For Liv, it was a bright blue scarf, with a matching hat and gloves for when she was walking Sparks, who was definitely staying with her. Both of the women had been brilliant friends to her over the last few months, and especially since the thing she refused to think about with the person she didn't want to name had happened.

She'd decided a few nights before that she wasn't going to let a failed relationship ruin one of her favourite times of year. Instead, she'd just not think about it, or him, and would instead practice her gratitude and focus on all the things in life she had to be grateful for — like Bill's, her mum, her wonderful friends and the community around her. She'd be grateful for all the animals she'd managed to save, and all the people who'd helped her with her work. And she'd focus on finding and enjoying every bit of sparkle and light the season had to offer.

She looked up at the knock on her door.

'I'll get it.' Her mum jumped up, leaving Angela to tuck away the unwrapped gifts, in case one of them was for their unexpected visitor.

'Well, you've got a nerve, showing your face here!'

'I know, Mrs Turner.' The last person Angela wanted to hear spoke to her mum. 'But I really want to speak to Angela.'

'And what if she doesn't want to speak to you? Did you think of that, young man? Have you considered that maybe what you want isn't of any interest to me?'

Angela smothered a grin, picturing the expression on her mum's face. She hadn't been one of the village's most successful teachers — and then childminders — for nothing. And it sounded like Ryan — *no, Rick*, she corrected herself — was getting the very best of her stern teacher looks.

'Of course I have. But it's really important. I wanted to . . .'

'Yes?' Angela could picture the single, raised eyebrow perfectly. She'd seen it often enough in her youth — frequently when smuggling an animal into the house.

'I wanted to give Angela a Christmas gift.'

Sighing, she levered herself from the table.

'Thanks, I've got this, Mum.' She rested her hand on her mum's arm.

'Sure?'

'Yes, thank you.'

'I'll just be in the living room. Shout if you need me.' She shot one more disapproving look at the man in the doorway.

Angela looked him over herself, noting that he looked tired. And different . . . His hair was shorter and neater, and he was wearing the thick, padded coat he usually wore when working in her yard, rather than the smart one he usually favoured. 'Hi.' She wasn't sure what else to say.

'Hi.' The smile he gave her shot warmth through to her stomach, and her traitor knees felt weak and wobbly. Mentally, she scolded her body for still reacting to him. She also cursed the hideous Christmas jumper she was wearing — decorated with woodland creatures wearing Christmas hats — and the tinsel and holly in her hair, before reminding herself that she wasn't interested in him, and therefore didn't care what he thought.

'Did you need something?' She kept it curt, polite. That was all he was getting.

'I was hoping we could talk. Just for a few minutes. There's something I really want to tell you.'

'If it's about Yvette and the baby, then I already know. Jake and Evelyn told me. I'm sorry she hurt you so badly.'

261

'I'm more sorry that you got hurt. And that I responded so badly and hurt you. Because there's something I really need to tell you — something else — and I'd really, really like it if you would listen.'

'OK.' She nodded.

'Thank you, Angel.' He smiled when she grimaced. 'As much as you don't like it when I call you that, you really are an angel. Especially to me. I didn't know how messed up I was until I met you. I don't think there was ever really anyone whose opinion I cared about enough to want to change. There was never anyone who made me feel like I was less than worthy before. Until I came here.'

'I never meant to make you feel that way . . . And I'm sorry if I did.'

'It's OK. I needed to change, I just didn't know it. But you, and that stupid, half-naked bald chicken-butt . . . you make me feel like I want to be a better person. Because it made me feel like, if I tried hard enough, I might actually feel like I was worth the trust and affection I'd been given from you both.'

'Mallow really does love you.' She'd focus on the bird — it was easier than thinking about her own feelings.

'Yeah, but her brain is only as big as a walnut.' He grinned when Angela glared at him. 'Which, I'm aware probably means she uses more brain cells on a regular basis than I do in a week.' He watched her for a reaction.

But she only continued to glare. 'If you're waiting for me to argue with you, you'd best not hold your breath. I'm not sure I could be bothered to pick you up off the floor.'

'What you think of me matters more than anything. After I came here, for the first time in years, I took a long, hard look at myself, and I discovered that I didn't want to be what I was. I was fed up playing Maverick, and I wanted to be Ryan again, the real version of me — and it's you who made me feel like that. When I told you I was falling for you, it wasn't the whole truth.'

'I think we've had more than enough lies lately.' She looked away.

'Give me a chance, please, in the spirit of Christmas? Just hear me out.' He waited for her nod. 'It wasn't the whole truth because I'm not falling, Angela . . . I've already fallen for you — completely, totally and besottedly. There's no falling, no chance of catching myself — not that I'd want to — because I'm already completely and totally in love with you. And I'm not saying this to make you feel bad, or with any hope that you might reciprocate my feelings. I'm just telling you so you understand why I've done what I've done. And so you understand that there's no expectation or obligation on you at all.'

'What have you done?' She stared at him suspiciously.

'I got you something for Christmas.'

'There's nothing I want from you.'

'I thought you might say that.' This time his smile was sad and filled with regret. 'But it's not really for you. It's for them. And it's too late for you to say no, because it's already done.'

'Them who?'

'Them, your animals.' He handed her a large, lightweight box tied with ribbons. 'Except for this one.' The next parcel was larger and flatter, but still surprisingly light. 'But it's not really from me. It's from Mallow.'

'You expect me to believe your cockatoo bought me a gift?'

'No. She made it. I just helped a bit . . . and wrapped it.'

'Right.' Angela shook her head, not sure what to say or do.

'Merry Christmas, Angela.' He stuffed his hands into his pockets. 'And I really do mean that. I'll let you get back to your life now.' He turned slowly, then headed back down the garden path, leaving her standing in the doorway, starting to shiver while clutching two parcels she wasn't sure what to do with. She took them back into the kitchen and put them on the table, where they sat innocently, totally unaware of the turmoil they were causing. Part of her wanted to tear them to pieces and lob them in the bin. But part of her was curious too — to know what gifts were inside the bright wrappers, and what he'd meant with the cryptic comments.

'Are you going to open them, or shall I move them so we can crack on?' Her mum watched her closely. 'I don't think they're going to bite. At least, not as badly as some of your guests.'

'He said the box is for them. My residents, I mean.'

'That sounds interesting,' Cathy replied.

'What do you think that means?'

'I don't know. But I know how you can find out.'

'True. But it seems much easier to say that than actually do it.' Angela was still hesitant.

'Do you want some privacy?'

'No, it's OK.' She pulled the box towards her, slowly undid the ribbons and peeked under the lid. What she saw didn't make sense, but it did explain why the box was so light. It was just a bundle of papers.

'What is it?' Cathy leaned forward eagerly.

'I'm not really sure.' Angela unfolded the first piece of paper. She recognised the logo immediately — one of her main feed suppliers, and what looked like her account, including the large sum she still owed. She scanned the page, confused until she flipped it over. The bold black words trapped her breath in her throat for a moment: paid in full. Is this what he'd meant when he'd said it was really for her animals, and not her? With a hand that started to shake, she reached for the next piece of paper and slowly unfolded that. There it was again, those three beautiful, bold words — this time in bright, Christmas red.

'Ange, are you all right?'

She ignored her mum as she dumped the box out on the table, rapidly rifling through the papers. They were all there: her feed suppliers, the bedding, medical equipment, cleaning gear — even the bill for the special waste bins had been paid.

It looked like every bill from her blue folder of misery had been taken care of.

It was the last bit of paper that choked her the most, bringing hot tears to her eyes that she fought not to shed. At the top, Jake's badger logo smiled out at her, and the figure at the bottom made her hands shake so much that she dropped the gift.

'Can I?' Her mum picked up the bill and read it. 'Wow. Is this what I think?'

'Yeah.' Angela's voice was rough and choked by tears. 'He cleared all of Bill's accounts — and put extra in at Jake's. He's given me a vet fund, Mum. A good one.'

'Wow. I'm not sure anyone could have given you anything better. Are you going to open the other one? The one from the bird?'

'Yeah.' She laughed, still not sure what to think about all of this. 'Let's see what Mallow "made" for me.' She unwrapped the parcel to find a canvas that was covered in brightly coloured splodges and streaks. It was a bit abstract for her liking, but the colours were quite pretty.

'I don't understand.' She turned it over for her mum to see, and spotted an envelope taped to the back of the canvas. Inside was a memory stick, and she reached for her computer. There were only two files on the stick, and she opened the video labelled "play me first". She laughed when "Frosty the Snowman" filled the air, and Mallow appeared on the screen, dancing across what looked like Rick's coffee table, in front of a blank canvas leaning against a mini-easel.

She skipped along a line of brightly coloured bottles, pausing every so often to tap one. Each one she tapped disappeared from the screen, only to reappear as its coloured contents were poured onto a plate. After a few moments, Mallow appeared back on the screen, this time holding a paintbrush, and Angela clapped her hands in delight as the bird carefully dabbed the brush in the paint and splodged it onto the canvas. After a few careful splodges, the video sped up, playing back in faster-than-life speed as Mallow daubed against the canvas. After a while, she stopped and disappeared, coming back with a ball. Rick's hands appeared briefly, moving at high speed to take the canvas off its easel and lay it flat. The ball shot across the canvas, explaining the coloured streaks, and was followed by a delighted Mallow, who left bright yellow footprints.

She watched, laughing, as the painting that was sitting on her kitchen table came to life on the screen in front of her. When the video finished, she clicked open the second file — a document that was blank apart from the words "click here".

She did as she was bid, and laughed when Mallow's face appeared again. It was a website, all about Mallow and her art. There were lots of videos, but what caught her attention was the "shop" button. She clicked on the link and was taken to an auction site. She gasped when she realised that some of them were being bid on to the tune of over a hundred pounds! She scrolled to the bottom of the page and lost control of her tears. The words blurred and she grabbed for her mum's hand. 'Tell me that says what I think it says . . . please.'

'If you think it says that all the money raised by Mallow's paintings and videos is being donated to Bill's Wildlife Sanctuary, and that the donation figure is currently sitting at close to three thousand pounds, then you're right.'

'Oh wow, Mum.'

'Yeah, I know.'

'I think I need to go find him.'

'You could call him?'

'I think this conversation — whatever it is — needs to be face to face.'

'Yeah, I think so too.' She smiled as Angela started to gather things together, pulling on shoes and looking for her coat and gloves. 'Go on, go. We can finish our wrapping later.'

'Thanks, Mum.' Angela raced out of the door.

* * *

Ryan blew on his fingers through his gloves, trying to get some feeling back into them. His arse was going numb too, which was probably a good thing — the wall outside Bill's definitely wasn't comfortable. But he wanted to give Angela time to open the gifts, and he really, really hoped that once she had, she'd want to talk to him. And if she did call him, wanting to talk, he wanted to be right there for her, not make her wait.

And if she wanted to talk in person, he didn't want to waste another second. So he pulled his scarf up around his ears a bit more, shoving his hands deep into his pockets.

By the time she came out, his toes were aching from the cold and he was seriously regretting having put on trainers instead of his warmer boots, but he still wasn't moving.

'What are you doing out here?'

'I'd hoped that you might want to talk.'

'You're an arrogant so and so.' He couldn't read her expression.

'Yeah, I know that. But you're out here too.'

'Maybe I've been called out to a rescue.'

He supposed that could be true, but she wasn't carrying any of her usual equipment. 'Maybe,' he agreed, 'but I'm hoping the only person you might be minded to rescue right now is me.'

'Are you in need of rescuing?'

'No,' he told her honestly. 'I think I already got rescued.' He met her eyes, hoping she'd read what he was feeling.

She sat on the wall next to him. 'You know I can't accept your gifts. It's too much.'

'I'm not taking them back, Angel. Besides, it's yours anyway.'

'I don't understand.'

'It's your money. Bill's money.'

'I'm pretty sure I'd know if I had that amount of money stashed away somewhere.'

'It's from the videos,' he explained. 'You know how some of the videos did really well — especially the ones with Ernie and Ruby?'

'I know they got quite a lot of views.'

'They did so well that I set up a separate account for them, so I could keep track of revenue, and make sure that you got your fair share.'

'My fair share?' Angela looked confused. 'But it's your social media accounts, and you doing all the work.'

'They're your animals. Your rescues. You're the one who does all the hard work — every day. You're the one making a difference and giving them extra chances in life. I just shot some footage. The money is yours, Angela. Yours and the animals. And you can't tell me that you don't need it. That Bill's doesn't need it. I've seen your misery folder, remember?'

She slipped her hand into his, and he breathed a sigh of relief, glad to be touching her again, even if it was through thick gloves. 'I still don't know if I can accept it.'

'It's not my money. I set it up promising at least half of everything would be donated to charity. Besides, it's not really from me. It's from the animals. I just need your bank account details.'

'Funny that it's your bank account, but not your money.'

'Well, I couldn't convince Ernie or Ruby to share their bank account.' He enjoyed her laughter.

'That's because they're smart,' she teased him, and he relaxed, taking it as encouragement.

'You've spent so long caring for them, maybe it's about time you let someone look after you.' He lifted her hand up to brush his lips against her fingers. 'And if there's any chance that you're looking for volunteers for that job, I'm the first in line. Because I meant what I said, Angel. I love you.'

'Smarmy,' she complained, but didn't pull her hand away.

'I was trying for charming.'

'You're doing all right.' She smiled at him, encouraging him even more.

'I know I don't deserve another chance — you already gave me a second chance that I blew completely. But, I figured,

268

if there's anyone who really, truly understands extra chances, it's you. Is there any hope you might give me a third chance?'

She stroked his fingers through his gloves, looked up at him and smiled, and he felt his heart soar. 'I might not have completely ruled it out. But I do have a question. It might sound a bit odd, but it's something I'd really like to know.'

'Anything.' He meant it. He couldn't think of a single thing he wouldn't tell her.

'How long ago did you set it up?'

'The animal's social accounts? A few weeks after I got here. Long before you and I . . . happened, if that's what you're asking.'

'It was. So you've been working on this for a while.' It wasn't a question, but he nodded anyway. 'Can I ask you something else?'

'Like I said, anything.'

Her smile was like the sun coming up. 'Would you please kiss me? I've really missed you.'

'I thought you'd never ask.' He pushed her hair gently back, tucking it behind her ears so he could stroke her cheeks and tilt her face up. He leaned in slowly, wanting to savour the moment and make it perfect. If he got what he really wanted, this would be the last time he kissed someone for the first time ever again.

He kissed her, brushing his lips gently against hers, before she parted her lips, welcoming him into the heat of her mouth. One of her hands slipped around his neck to pull him closer, while the other tangled in his coat.

She murmured against his lips, drawing him in closer, and he lost all track of time, losing himself in her touch. When he eventually broke away to catch his breath, she was quivering in his arms.

'We should go inside, you're cold.'

'In a minute.' She ran her hands through his newly shortened hair. 'There's something I want to say first.'

'Yeah?'

'Yeah.' She smiled at him again, making his stomach clench deliciously. 'You're not the only one who fell hard, Ryan. I love you.'

'I love you too.' Her lips found his again, kissing him sweetly and warming him through.

She pulled away slowly and looked up at him. 'Tell me again.'

'If I do, will I get my extra chance?'

'Maybe. Try it and find out.' The look she gave him was full of mischief.

'I love you, Angel.'

'Yeah, you can have your second chance.' She grinned. 'Or third. Whatever.'

'I won't mess this one up, I promise.'

'I believe you.' She wove her fingers through his. 'Come on, it's getting really cold.'

'I know it's probably too late for Christmas, you're bound to have plans already . . .'

'I do.' Angela nodded as they walked towards her home.

'So do I.' He slid his arm around her shoulders. 'Family stuff. But . . . what about the thirty-first? I'd love to welcome in the New Year by kissing you.' He kissed her fingers. 'Because if it's OK with you, I plan to be doing a lot of that next year.'

Again, there was that mischievous smile he loved so much. 'I think I'd like that.'

EPILOGUE

Two days later, Becky, age seven, watched as her little brother opened the games console he'd been wanting for months, and she grinned happily, safe in the knowledge that Santa really did exist — he hadn't forgotten her either. When the WI members had delivered the parcel on behalf of Santa — because every Broclington child knew they were some of Santa's favourite helpers — there had also been a large parcel addressed to Becky, age seven, and she'd squealed in delight to discover a fairy castle in the shape of a tree, and a set of magical fairy dolls.

Across the village, many such parcels had been delivered — for young people and those who were just young at heart. There were toys that would be loved for years, a very special holiday abroad to enable grandparents and grandchildren to meet for the first time, and a new washing machine — much surprising the exhausted and broke new mother who had only hoped for a repair. Every red-envelope wish that could have been granted, was — and a few more besides, with vouchers for cream tea afternoons arriving for the hard-working WI ladies. And one by one, more stars appeared on the wishing tree.

THE END

ACKNOWLEDGEMENTS

It's been so lovely to revisit Broclington and create *Second Chances at the Little Village Sanctuary*, the third book in this series. I really hope that you, as readers, will love reading this book as much as I've enjoyed creating it. So as always, thanks go to you — who have picked up (or downloaded) and read this book. Thank you, lovely reader, without you, your support, reviews, I wouldn't be a writer — it's always a pleasure to welcome you into my fictional world!

For those of you who know me — or follow me on the socials — you'll likely have come across some of the special little critters who I've been lucky enough to rescue. Although often, I've ended up feeling like I was the one being rescued by them!

There's been a lot of research, love and support in creating this book — particularly Mallow's story. Parrots, particularly the larger ones like this cockatoo, are incredibly intelligent creatures — with many researchers saying they are as smart as a young child. Certainly they are able to talk to us human caretakers, with some even learning to use tablet computers to communicate complex feelings, thought processes, and deductive reasoning. They are also very clearly capable of great emotion, sadly including depression.

It's been a fascinating subject to study, and has greatly increased my understanding of larger parrots. So I have to give a massive shout out and thanks to the whole Special Needs Perfectly Imperfect community, and particularly Cherie, who created a safe space for people with slightly imperfect feathered ones in their lives: the pluckers, the wobblies, the ones with missing limbs and wonky beaks . . . each perfect in their own imperfect way. Thank you all for the lessons and advice.

And thank you also to the team a Parrot First Aid — especially Robyn who has offered advice, handholding and support on far too many late nights. Literally thousands of birds have been helped by you all.

A huge and heartfelt thank you to Emma GH for all the good wishes, cheers and commiserations, and for the encouragement and support that went far beyond the realms of fiction, and the role of Editor.

And a big virtual hug to Sarah who keeps me laughing through the first rounds of edits, and has been keeping up with my messy timelines for five books now — no easy task! And thanks for making sure that . . . umm . . . brother switcheroo didn't make it through. Eek!

Thanks also have to go to Becky and Kate — who I've been lucky enough to meet and work with just recently. And, of course, to the wider team at Joffe including Jasmine, Abbie, Tia, Claire, Hanna, Sasha and Lahli. Also to the tireless editors Faith Marsland and Becky Wyde, who make sure those late-night writing errors don't make it into your reading!

Also to my amazing cover designer Jarmila Takač, who captured this book — and Ernie! — so beautifully, and to the Choc Lit Tasting panel — big thank yous to bringing this one to life.

Always, thanks go to my Choc Lit sister authors — especially Kirsty Ferry whose wit, sarcasm and support has kept me smiling through so much life drama — especially the last few months.

And the biggest thanks of all go to my family: to Alex who still makes me endless rounds of tea, and is always my first reader, nagging me for chapters quicker than I can write them and spurring me on. To Dad, who has always struggled to sit still and read — but still reads my stories in record time.

And to Sammy, our own special little perfectly imperfect lovebird, who doesn't paint, or swear, but does make us laugh daily with his antics. And at least he's finally stopped stealing the buttons off my keyboard long enough to let me write this!

THE CHOC LIT STORY

Established in 2009, Choc Lit is an independent, award-winning publisher dedicated to creating a delicious selection of quality women's fiction.

We have won 18 awards, including Publisher of the Year and the Romantic Novel of the Year, and have been shortlisted for countless others. In 2023, we were shortlisted for Publisher of the Year by the Romantic Novelists' Association.

All our novels are selected by genuine readers. We are proud to publish talented first-time authors, as well as established writers whose books we love introducing to a new generation of readers.

In 2023, we became a Joffe Books company. Best known for publishing a wide range of commercial fiction, Joffe Books has its roots in women's fiction. Today it is one of the largest independent publishers in the UK.

We love to hear from you, so please email us about absolutely anything bookish at choc-lit@joffebooks.com

If you want to hear about all our bargain new releases, join our mailing list: www.choc-lit.com/contact

Milton Keynes UK
Ingram Content Group UK Ltd.
UKHW021307130924
448296UK00009B/44